B

Born and rais... graduated from Columbia University in 1969. Lustbader has had a number of fascinating careers. In addition to having written numerous bestselling novels, including *Black Heart*, *The Ninja* and *Angel Eyes*, he introduced Elton John to the American music scene. He spent fifteen years in the music industry in various capacities, including working for both Elektra and CBS Records. He is a former writer for *Cash Box* magazine where he wrote lead stories on new rock acts. In that capacity, he was the first person in the United States to predict the success of Jimi Hendrix, David Bowie and Santana, among many others.

Lustbader has taught in the All-Day Neighborhood School Division of the NYC Public School System and has also taught pre-schoolers in special Early Childhood programmes.

Eric Lustbader, who travels worldwide in researching his novels, lives in Southampton, New York, with his wife Victoria Lustbader, who works for the Nature Conservancy.

BY THE SAME AUTHOR

Nicholas Linnear novels

The Ninja
The Miko
White Ninja
The Kaisho

China Maroc novels

Jian
Shan

Black Blade
Angel Eyes
French Kiss
Black Heart
Sirens
Zero

The *Sunset Warrior* cycle

The Sunset Warrior
Shallows of Night
Dai-San

ERIC LUSTBADER

BENEATH AN OPAL MOON

HarperCollins*Publishers*

HarperCollins*Publishers*
77-85 Fulham Palace Road
Hammersmith, London W6 8JB

This paperback edition 1993
1 3 5 7 9 8 6 4 2

Previously published in paperback by Grafton 1983
Reprinted twelve times

ISBN 0 007 69715 5

Set in Plantin

Printed and bound in Great Britain by
Mackays of Chatham Ltd, Chatham, Kent

For Ralphine

Thus we struggle so that our history shall become the salvation of our children.

– From the Tablets of the Iskamen

Contents

PREFIGURE:
On Green Dolphin Street

The scarred man enters Sha'angh'sei at sunset. He pauses before the towering cinnabar escarpment of the western gate and turns in his dusty saddle. Above him, a pair of ebon carrion birds spread their grotesquely long wings, hovering, startlingly set off by the flare of the sky. Piled clouds riding like chariots of crimson fire obscure for long moments the bloated oblate of the sun as it sinks slothfully towards the heights of the city already lost within the thickening haze. It is a unique mark of the sunsets in Sha'angh'sei that the city itself and the land all around it is first engulfed by the purest crimson, sliding, as the sun disappears behind the man-made façade, into the amethyst and violet which heralds the night.

But the scarred man's deep-set eyes, slit and as opaque as dry stones, study only the winding, much-travelled highway behind him and the steady lines of jumbled traffic – ox-carts piled high with raw rice and silk, horsemen, soldiers, and travelling merchants, businessmen, farmers on foot – moving towards him and the city; the outbound flow is of no import to him.

His horse snorts, shaking its head. Gently, the scarred man strokes its neck below the short mane with a thin red hand. The stallion's coat is lustreless, matted with the mingled dust of the highway, the caked mud of narrow back roads and the grease of many a hasty meal.

The scarred man pulls at his hat, a floppy felt affair which, constructed unaesthetically, does little more than conceal his long and haggard face. Satisfied at last, he turns and, slouched in his high and dusty saddle, presses against his mount with his heels, riding through the gate. He raises his eyes as he moves, watching the perspective changing, deriving pleasure from the shifting angles as he studies the endless bas-reliefs carved into the cinnabar of the dark western gate, an epic monument to a dichotomy: the triumph and the cruelty of war.

The scarred man shivers even though he is not cold. He does not believe in omens yet he thinks it interesting that he enters Sha'angh'sei through the western gate, erected as a sinister reminder of a particularly odious aspect of man's nature. But, he asks himself, would it really make any difference if he had made his entry into the city through the green-onyx southern gate, the alabaster eastern gate or the intricate red-lacquered wood and black iron northern gate? Then he throws his head back and utters a short bitter laugh. No. No. Not at all. For at this hour of sunset, they are all stained crimson by the lowering light.

The scarred man breaks into the populous surf of the great city and his journey is slowed by the milling throngs of people as if he is passing through a moving field of poppies. He feels an end to long isolation, far from the companionship of man, a seemingly interminable time with only his stallion, the stars and the moon as his family. Yet as he rides into the explicit riot of the city, his mount walking through the clouds of jostling men and women and children, fat and thin, large and small, young and old, ugly and fair, as he passes the bursting shops, stalls, stands with striped awnings, the tangled buildings with their dense clusters of swinging signs advertising the tempting wares within, he realizes that never before has he felt such an apartness from the warmth of the family of man. And this peculiar alienness suffuses him with such completeness that his body begins to quake as if he is ill.

He digs his boot heels into the flanks of his mount and shakes the reins, abruptly anxious to reach his destination. Through this vast kinetic sea, metal jangling, dusty leather creaking, the grime of travel heavy upon him. A torrent of children, filthy, their torsos ribbed like corpses, brush against his legs like a separate eddy in this fetid surf and he is obliged to press his boots tightly against the stallion's flanks lest, howling, they pull them from his feet. He extracts a copper coin from his wide sash and flings it high into the air so that it catches the oblique light. As it disappears into the swirling mass of pedestrians on his left, the children abandon him, rushing to follow the flight of the spinning coin. They plough through the crowd, tenaciously searching on hands and knees in the slime and offal of the street.

He moves on, turning a corner at an acute angle, following the street. He inhales the rich musk of coriander and limes, the heavy incense of charring meat, the somewhat lighter scents of fresh fish and vegetables flash-cooked in hot oil and, as he passes the opening of a dark alley, the thick sweet smell of the poppy resin, so intense for an instant that it takes his breath away and he is dizzied.

The din of the city, after so long on the road, alone with himself, is claustrophobically overpowering, a constant harsh cacophony consisting of wails, shrieks, cries, shouts, laughter, whispers, chanting, a glorious babble of voices, testament to the indomitability of man.

Within the deep shadows of the felt hat, the scarred man is hollow-cheeked. A long bent nose leads inevitably to thick gnarled lips as if, in his earlier years, he had fought with his fists within the hempen circle, as is the wont of certain of the folk of the western plains of the continent of man. His hair is silver, silken, flowing long down his back, held away from his wide wrinkled forehead by a thin plaited band of copper. His face, defiantly hairless, exhibits the tracery of livid white scars puckering the flesh of his cheeks and throat like the rain on the surface of a pond. He wears a long travelling cloak of a dark though indeterminate colour, owing to the grit of his journey. Beneath it, a tunic and leggings of deepest brown. Hanging from his waist from a simple stained leather belt is a scabbarded curving sword, wide-bladed and single-edged.

He pauses beside a wine stall on Thrice Blessed Road and, dismounting, leads his mount out of the enormous crush of the thoroughfare. As he strides into the dimness beneath the patterned awning, he spies the wineseller, moon-faced and almond-eyed, arguing with two young women over the price of a leather flagon of wine. With a sweep of his deep-set eyes, the scarred man takes in the curving bodies of the women, their faces tipped high in anger. But they are restless, his eyes, and while he listens and waits somewhat impatiently, his gaze darts this way and that, alighting on a face here, the pale flash of a hand there. For a moment, he observes a man with eyes like olives and black curling hair so long that it covers his shoulders, until he is met by another man and they depart. The scarred man's head cocks at the thumping sounds of running feet; shouts echo and diminish as a body rushes past outside, elbowing through the crowd. He turns away. He asks the wineseller, now free, for a cup of spiced wine, downs it in one swallow. It is not the rice wine of the region which he finds too thin for his taste but the heartier burgundy of the northern regions. He purchases a flagon.

The sunset is fading, the sky above Sha'angh'sei turning mauve and violet as night approaches boldly from the east.

The scarred man leads his stallion left into a narrow alley, crooked and filled with refuse and excrement. There must be bones here, hidden perhaps in the high dark mounds heaped against the sides of the building walls. Human bones stripped of all flesh, all identity. The stench is appalling and he breathes shallowly as if the air itself might be poisonous. His mount whinnies and he pats its neck reassuringly.

The alley gives out at length onto Green Dolphin Street with its dense tangle of shops and dwellings. Again the air is filled with the singsong cacophony of the city and spices blot out the more noxious odours. Half a kilometre away, the scarred man finds the straw-filled sanctuary of a stable. Leading his mount to a stall, he reaches up, removing his saddlebags, slinging them over his left shoulder. He places two coins in the dark palm of a greasy attendant before venturing out onto Green Dolphin Street. He walks for a time down this wide avenue, meandering, pausing from time to time to peer into shop windows or turn over a piece of merchandise at a street stall. He turns often to peer behind him as he moves from one side of the street to the other.

At last he comes upon a swinging wooden sign carved in the shape of an animal's face: the Screaming Monkey, a dark and fumy tavern. He enters and, skirting the multitude of jammed tables and booths, speaks to the tavernmaster for a moment. Perhaps it is the din of the place which causes him to put his lips against the other man's ear. The tavernmaster nods and silver is exchanged. The scarred man crosses the room and mounts the narrow wooden staircase that folds back upon itself. On the landing, mid-way up, his gaze sweeps across the smoky room bubbling with noise and movement. Natives of the Sha'angh'sei region do not interest him: outlanders do. He studies them all most carefully and covertly before he completes his ascension.

He walks silently down the darkling corridor, meticulously counting the number of closed doors, checking to see if there is a rear egress before he opens the last door on the left.

In the room he stands for long moments just inside the closed door, perfectly still, listening intently, absorbing the background drift of sounds, setting it in his mind so that, even if he is otherwise occupied, he will automatically hear any deviation.

Then he crosses over the mean floorboards, throws his heavy saddlebags onto the high down bed with its pale green spread, moving immediately to the window, drawing the curtains. When they stop moving, he pulls one side carefully back in the crook of one forefinger, gazing out onto a heavily shadowed alley perpendicular to Green Dolphin Street. He is, he knows, within the heart of the city, far from the long wharves of the Sha'angh'sei delta. Still, if he strains, he can hear the kubaru's plaintive hypnotic work songs filtering through the hubbub. Peering sideways, he can just make out a slender section of the far side of Green Dolphin Street. A seller of herbed pork and veal is closing his shop and, immediately adjacent, the lights are extinguished in a dusty carpet shop as three brothers, pear-shaped and identical down to their embroidered saffron robes, shutter the windows. They are rich, the carpet merchants, thinks the scarred man, letting the curtains fall back into place. The more prosperous they become, the heavier they seem to weigh as if they have been magically transformed into living embodiments of the taels of silver which they hoard.

The scarred man quits the far side of the room and, satisfied that the curtains will hold in the light, fires an oil lamp atop the scarred bedside table. One corner is charred as if some former occupant had clumsily overturned the lamp. He reaches into the recesses of his saddlebags, withdraws the newly-bought flagon of wine, takes a long drink.

He washes at the nightstand until the water is black with grime and presently he hears light footfalls on the stairs. His head comes up and his right hand grips the hilt of his curving sword. He steps soundlessly to the wall adjacent to the door and waits, scarcely breathing.

A knock on the door.

A young boy, tall and dark-haired, enters carrying a tray of steaming food. He comes to a halt seeing the room empty. Then the scarred man growls low in his throat and the boy turns slowly around. He tries not to stare at the scarred man but he cannot help himself.

'Well,' says the scarred man. 'Put it down.'

The boy swallows hard and nods. He continues to stare.

The scarred man ignores this. 'Your father tells me that you are quite reliable. Is this so?' His voice is thick and husky as if he has something lodged in his throat.

Fright mingles with fascination. The scarred man sees

these often allied emotions flickering upon the young narrow face.

'Well,' says the scarred man. 'Have you no voice then?'

'Yes, sir,' stammers the boy. 'I have one.'

'Close the door.'

The boy complies.

'Have you a name?' The scarred man has gone to the night table. He lifts a bit of fowl between the long nails of his middle finger and thumb. The forefinger, in between, juts out oddly. The scarred man swirls the meat in the thick brown gravy, ignoring the long wooden eating sticks lying at the side of the plate, and pops it into his mouth. 'Excellent,' he says to no one in particular as he licks the tips of his fingers. 'Just the right amount of fresh black pepper.' He turns. 'Now –'

'Kuo.' Softly.

'Ah.' The scarred man studies him with an awesomely intense gaze, but even though he feels fear, Kuo knows that he must not show it. He stands ramrod straight, concentrating on controlling his breathing. He tries to ignore the sound of the hammering of his heart which feels as if it has lodged itself in his windpipe.

'This is for you, Kuo. If you do as I say.' A silver coin has magically appeared between the scarred man's fingers.

The boy nods, hypnotized by the shining coin. It represents more wealth than he has had in his entire life.

'Now listen to me carefully, Kuo. My horse is in the stable down Green Dolphin Street. At the first stroke of the hour of the boar you must bring it to the alley at the side of this place. This one.' He points one long forefinger towards the curtained window. 'No one must see you do this, Kuo. And once here, stay within the shadows. Wait for me. When I come, there will be another silver coin for you. Is this clear?'

Kuo nods. 'Yes, sir. Quite clear.' The secretiveness of his mission has excited him. How his friends will envy him.

'No one must know of this, Kuo.' The scarred man takes a

quick step towards him. 'Not your friends, not your brothers or sisters, not even your father. No one.'

'There is nothing for me to tell,' Kuo says, delighted with himself. 'Who would be interested in my delivering another meal upstairs?'

'Not even that!' And the boy jumps at the force of those terse words, then nods. 'No, sir.'

The scarred man flicks his thumb and, shot from the arbalest of his nail, the coin arcs into the air, shining. Kuo's fingers enclose it and he is gone, swiftly and silently.

The scarred man listens at the door. Then, as the sounds of Kuo's descent fade, he turns his attention to the food and for a time he is totally consumed in the act of eating.

Sounds drift up to him, given an eerie etherealness by the closed curtains. The cries of the night vendors, drunken laughter, the heavy creak of wooden-wheeled carts laden with tomorrow's produce and dry goods, the snort of horses, hoofs clip-clopping on the cobbles; a soft wind rustles the leaves of the plane trees lining nearby Yellow Tooth Street. Night.

Soft footfalls on the stairs and the scarred man is up, wiping his greasy hands. He bends, extinguishes the flame of the oil lamp. Silently, he skirts the bed, opens the curtains. Dim, fitful light from the thin corridor to the street seeps into the room as slowly as blood drips from a corpse.

The footfalls cease.

The scarred man has positioned himself well within the deepest shadows of the room with a good line of sight to the door. He stands immobile, one hand gripping the hilt of his sword as the door opens inwards to reveal an ebon silhouette.

'Mistral,' comes a whispered voice.

'Who is the messenger?' says the scarred man.

'The wind.'

'Enter, Omojiru,' says the scarred man and the silhouette disappears as the door is closed. There comes the sound of a lock being secured.

'Cascaras,' says Omojiru, 'have you found it?'

The scarred man hears the tremor in the voice, barely held in check as he watches the other in the inconstant light. He notes the high forehead, the flat cheekbones, the narrow thin-lipped mouth, the intelligent almond eyes and thinks, it was those eyes which took me in. But now I know that he would be nowhere without his father's influence. I regret his involvement. Not because he is ruthless and unprincipled. He would be useless to me without those traits. But because he lacks the guile he believes he has. That can be dangerous. He saw Omojiru's lips compress into the narrow line of intransigence preparatory to violent action and he recalled this man's volatile nature. How different you are from your kin, Omojiru, the scarred man thought. If your father but knew what you planned with me –

'Tell me!' Omojiru hisses, the words forced out of him as if they are under pressure and the scarred man looks away for just a moment, embarrassed for the other.

'I have found it.'

'At last!' Omojiru moves involuntarily closer and now the quavering of his voice is unstoppable.

Greed, Cascaras thinks. And power. How many would he kill to get them? 'I do not have it yet.'

'What?' The enormous disappointment shows across the young man's face, unmistakable even in the dimness.

'But I know where it is.'

'Ah. Then we will go to it.'

'Yes,' says the scarred man. 'That is the way of our bargain.' And he wonders at what point Omojiru will try to kill him.

'Where is it?' Omojiru whispers hoarsely.

The scarred man laughs silently. How transparent he is. He will do it now and take no chances. 'We will go there together, Omojiru,' he says with great patience, as if explaining a difficult and complex concept to a child.

'Yes. Yes, of course we will. I, uh, I only wished to know what to take on the journey and it would, it would depend on where we are going.'

Now the scarred man laughs out loud. 'I will tell you what to take, Omojiru.'

The door flies open, lock and hinges splintering and in that brief instant of shock, as his head turns in the direction of the violent motion and sound, the scarred man wonders why he heard nothing. Nothing at all.

The lights are gone from the hall and it is as if he looks out upon a starless night, dense with a damp and clinging fog. His hand drawing his blade but already he hears the fearful sounds of struggle, a strangled cry torn from the lips of Omojiru, conveying as much terror as pain. The sound of a whirlwind in the room and across from him a great viscous bubbling, a hideous animal grunting connoting coupling or death and with a shudder he realizes it is coming from Omojiru. Something has him and is killing him.

The scarred man's great curving blade is out, naked in the night, lifted high over his head but something is careening at him from out of the darkness. It is as if the night itself has abruptly come along, filled with vengeance and a cold implacable hatred.

His sword whispers in the air as it descends but encounters nothing. Fingers like bars of steel enwrap his right wrist, twisting. He fights, jabbing with his left fist, his feet, his legs. His knee lifts for a blow and something heavy smashes into it splintering the kneecap. The scarred man grunts as the breath shoots out of him. Pain flares. His left wrist snaps and he cries out. His blade clatters to the floor.

He is borne as if weightless onto the bed. A tightness against his chest and then more pain, lancing through him, turning his vitals to water. He soils himself and is ashamed as the stench rises about him.

Skin and flesh part. His pulse pounds like surf against his inner ear and sounds become distorted. His heart feels as if it is being squeezed in a vice; pressure in his brain. He cannot breathe. And at the brink of unconsciousness, the questions begin and repeat over and over until he must answer, the meaning behind them gone from him. The dark blood running out of his slack mouth, his heart constricted beyond all limits and his brain screaming for release, caring only about itself now. 'Yes,' hisses a voice from very near above him. 'Yes, yes, yes.' Sounding to him as if it was coming from the other side of the world. A balloon bursting against the fragile membranes of his eyes. His mind screams, filling his entire universe. Then his blood, like water from a ruptured dam, begins to fill the room, soaking the bed, wetting the floor, coursing across the room, rushing out into the hall.

ONE:

City of Wonders

Rubylegs

Moichi Annai-Nin awoke to the sound of the sea.

For what seemed quite a long time he lay with his eyes open, listening with all his senses to the sluggish crash of the waves against the ancient wood. He heard the clear sharp cries of the hungry gulls and thought for an instant that he was aboard ship. Then he heard the hoarse shouts of the stevedores and the singsong litany of the kubaru and knew he was in the port of Sha'angh'sei. This both saddened and uplifted him. He loved this city, perhaps more than any other on earth, felt a peculiar and powerful affinity towards it though it was far from his home. Yet he longed most dearly for a ship under the soles of his boots.

In one fluid motion he was on his feet and, crossing the wooden floor of the large room, threw open the accordion jalousie window-doors which ranged along the wall opening out onto the sea. The sun, barely above the horizon, turned the water to chopped gold.

He lifted one huge hand, grasping the upper lintel of the doorway leading out to the expansive veranda which ran the entire length of the building. He breathed deeply of the damp salt air, his nostrils dilated with the fecund scents, while he rubbed distractedly at his heavily-muscled chest. You eternal, he thought.

The morning light, spilling obliquely across the horizon, played over his enormous frame. His skin was the colour of rich cinnamon and when his wide, thick-lipped mouth split in a grin, which was often, his white teeth flashed. His eyes, large and set far apart on his face, were the colour of smoky topaz, though in certain low lights it was often said – quite naturally in hesitant whispers reserved for the darkest of secrets – that deep within them one could see an odd crimson spark as of a reflection from some flickering flame. His long hooked nose was further highlighted by a tiny perfect diamond set into the dusky flesh of his right nostril. His thick hair and full beard were glossily black and curling. Overall, it was a face filled with converging influences, an intriguing admixture formed from facing adversity, man-made and natural. It was a foreign face according to those in Sha'angh'sei who knew because, above all else, it held a riveting power alien to the people of this region of the continent of man.

Moichi Annai-Nin stretched and his muscles rippled. He sighed deeply, feeling the inexorable pull of the sea just as if he were a compass drawn unerringly northward. He was the finest navigator in the known world thus his present predicament was ironic indeed. Still, he did not find it in the least amusing.

He turned back into the room, moving in long lithe strides to a carved wooden table upon which sat a huge pitcher and a bowl of sea-green stone. It was the hour of the cormorant, the time had he been on a ship when he would return to the high poop deck to see all the sea before him, feeling the tides and currents and breezes, to take the first sighting of the day. He bent, pouring cold water over his head and into the bowl, scooping it up in double handfuls, splashing his face and shoulders.

He was drying himself with a thick brown towel when he heard the movement behind him and swung around. Llowan had come up the stairs from the harttin's huge working area on the ground floor. This tall, spare man with the mane of silver hair like a giant cat was bundsman of Sha'angh'sei's waterfront, in charge of all loading and unloading of cargo transported over the sea, overseer of the city's myriad harttin.

Llowan smiled. 'Hola, Moichi,' he said, deliberately using the traditional sailor's greeting. 'Glad you are awake. A messenger awaits you downstairs. He comes from the Regent Aerent.'

Moichi folded the towel and began to dress. 'What news of a ship, Llowan?'

'Are you not even the least bit curious why your friend should send for you at this early hour?'

Moichi paused, said, 'Look here, Llowan, I am a navigator and though I love your city dearly, I have had the solidity of land under my feet for too long. Even though this be Sha'angh'sei, still I long for a good ship's deck to stand upon.' He drew on copper-coloured leggings over which he strapped leather sheaths covering only the outside of his legs. He shrugged himself into a brilliant white silk shirt with wide sleeves and no collar. About his waist he wrapped a forest green cotton sash into which he inserted the twin copper-handled dirks which were his trademark. Lastly, he fastened a thin leather thong about his waist from which a silver-handled sword hung in a worn, tattooed leather scabbard. The diamond in his nostril flashed in the gathering light.

'Patience, my friend,' Llowan said. 'Since the defeat of the dark forces of the Dolman in the Kai-feng more than six seasons ago, the sea lanes to Sha'angh'sei have been clogged with merchant ships.' He shrugged, running a hand through his long hair. 'Unfortunately, one of the by-products of peace is a surfeit of people. All the navigators, called to the last battle, have returned home now. It is only just that they get first preference for the ships of native registry. You can understand that.' He turned sideways, into the oblique light and Moichi saw sharply delineated the cruel semi-circular scar at the left corner of the bundsman's mouth, arcing up to the base of the nose which had no nostril on that side. 'Why not be satisfied by the work I give you here, my friend? What awaits you out there' – his long arm extended, sweeping outwards towards the lapping yellow sea beyond the harttin's wide veranda – 'that could be so compelling?

Here you have all the silver, all the women, all the companionship you could ever wish for.'

Moichi turned from the deep voice, stood in the doorway to the veranda, staring out at the thick forest of black masts, slashes of crosstrees, the intricate spider's web of the rigging of the armada of ships temporarily at rest in the harbour or off-loading baled goods from far-off exotic shores. Too soon they would be setting sail again, leaving Sha'angh'sei's clutter behind in their wakes. Only dimly he heard Llowan saying, 'I will send up the tea. Come downstairs when you are ready; the messenger can wait, I daresay.'

Alone again, Moichi's gaze raced outwards, from the teeming foreshore, riding the white crests of the rolling sea like a storm-tossed gull, recalling those long days and nights aboard the *Kioku*, sailing south, ever south with his captain, Ronin, who had returned from Ama-no-mori transformed into the Sunset Warrior. Eyes clouded with memories of a lush jade isle, unnamed, gone now beneath the churning waves, and its lone sorcerous city of stone pyramids and gods with hearts as cold as ice; a dreamlike ride on an enormous feathered serpent high in the sky, through a land filled with sun, onto a ship sailing for Iskael, his homeland where, with his people, he returned to the continent of man to join the Kai-feng; and the lightning of that last day of battle when he scrambled across a morass of seeping dead and dying warriors, mounds of the slain and wounded, friend and foe, his clothes so heavy with blood and gore that he could barely move, to greet the victorious Dai-San.

And what occupies his days and nights now? Moichi mused. My friend. We each owe the other a life. More than either of us can repay. And even now, though he resides in fabled Ama-no-mori among the Bujun, his kin, this world's greatest warriors, though we are far from each other, still do we remain closer than if we were brothers joined in blood at birth. For we have been forged upon the same anvil, tied by the terror of imminent death. And survived. And survived.

Moichi moved out into the sunlight.

Farther south still than far-off Ama-no-mori was Iskael. So long since he had walked its blazing deserts and its orchards, heavy with luscious fruit: the long lines of stately apple trees white-blossomed in spring, ethereal clouds come to earth and, in the blistering heat of the summer, with the incandescent sun a huge disc of beaten brass, to stand within their cool penumbra, to reach up and pluck the hanging fruit, ripe and golden. He could not count his hurried arrival and even more hasty departure during the Kai-feng. He had spent all of his time aboard ship, supervising the preparations for war, plotting their course northward to the continent of man. And all the while, beyond the foreshore, alive with frantic activity, bristling with bright shards of weaponry and men saying their farewells to their families, the dusky rolling hills of Iskael beckoned, forged by Moichi and his people over centuries of struggle, from barren ground into a land of plenty. But that return, for him, did not count for the land was untouchable to him then.

He turned, watching the head of the stairwell as Yu's head appeared. She held a grey-green lacquered tray on which sat a squat ceramic pot and a matching handleless cup. She knelt before a low varnished table across from the massive wooden desk set against one corner of the room that Moichi regarded, despite his protestations, as strictly Llowan's. Its hugeness made him feel uncomfortable. Of course he was used to the much more compact and functional writing-desks built into the bulkheads in ships' cabins. But beyond that it reminded him of his father's desk in the enormous bedroom in his family's house in Iskael.

He went into the room, observing Yu. She wore a cream-coloured silk robe. She was tall and slim with a fine pale face dominated by dark expressive eyes. She had slid the tray soundlessly onto the tabletop and now sat with her hands in her lap and her head bowed, motionless. Waiting.

Moichi could scarcely tell if she were breathing as he knelt at the opposite side of the low table. Yu's hands unfolded like a flower reaching for the sun's warmth and slowly, precisely, she made the tea ceremony.

He settled himself. The quiet splash of the sea, the cormorants' and gulls' cries, a compradore's shouts, quite near, the scent of the warm sun heating the salted wood and the barnacled tar, the pale deft hands moving in their intricate orbits tying it all together, mystifying. Moichi felt a peacefulness wash over him.

Yu handed him the cup and he inhaled the spicy fragrance of the hot tea. He lifted it slowly to his lips, savouring the moment before he took the first sip. He felt the warmth sliding down his throat and into his broad chest. Energy tingled his flesh.

After a time, he finished his tea. He put down the cup and reached out his hand. Put two fingertips under the point of her chin, tilted Yu's head up. It was a face filled with broad planes, pale rolling meadows from which only the lowest of fleshy hillocks rose. What other skills lie within that body, he wondered idly. And can it matter at all? Wasn't the wondrous tea ceremony more than enough?

Yu smiled at him and her delicate hands moved to the fastening of her silk robe. Moichi stopped her, putting his calloused fingers over hers, holding them still.

He took his fingers away, kissed their tips, put them against her own. Then he stood up and bowed formally to her. She returned it. Stillness in the long room. He left her there, as quiet as sunlight.

Downstairs, it was a completely different world. Kubaru, bare-chested and sweat-soaked, trotted in and out of the wide wooden doors open onto the sprawling bund and, just beyond, the long wharves where the myriad ships waited impatiently. Wheat dust stained the air, hanging, silvered in thick bars of sunlight slanting in through the doorway and the many windows lining the harttin's seaward face.

Llowan was talking with several stevedores, perhaps discussing the disbursement of some newly off-loaded shipment. Piles of brown hempen sacks and wide wooden casks filled the harttin, separated by narrow maze-like corridors honeycombing the area.

Moichi saw the Regent's messenger at once, standing beside one of the narrow rear doorways leading out onto one of the streets of the city's port quarter. He was muscular but still with the thinness of youth. One side of his face was bruised a livid purple-blue fading to a yellow near the perimeter. The flesh was still puffy.

The messenger recognized the navigator as soon as he saw him emerge out of the bustle of activity within the harttin. He wasted no time with unnecessary formalities, merely handed Moichi a rice paper envelope. Moichi broke the blue-green wax seal of the Regent, read the note. It said: 'Moichi – Apologies for the early hour of this summons but your presence is urgently required at Seifu-ke soonest. Aerent.' Typically, Moichi thought, he had left off his new title. Old habits die hard. Moichi smiled to himself. Aerent is a rikkagin, always will be, no matter what other job he takes on; the training is ineradicable. And that, I suppose, is as it should be. He is an excellent choice for Regent of Sha'angh'sei, whether he is aware of it himself or no.

'All right,' Moichi said, looking up, 'lead on.'

He waved farewell to Llowan as he followed the messenger out.

Out along the Sha'angh'sei delta it was already sweltering even though it was yet early morning. The jumble of narrow twisting streets, which were among the city's oldest, ran with sea water and diluted fish blood. Flies buzzed blackly and the thin nervous dogs rooted in the refuse heaped against the buildings' walls hoping to find fresh fish entrails. Pairs of kubaru jogged by with loads hung between them on flexing bamboo poles bowed with the weight.

They were in a rickshaw, a two-wheeled carriage powered

by a kubaru runner. There were many halts as they bounced along but their kubaru was very good and he quickly got them away from the frustrating crowds, taking them down dark cramped alleys and bent lanes.

Moichi watched the panoply of Sha'angh'sei slide by him, thinking of the changes within the vast city and, because of those changes, how it all stayed essentially the same; its eternalness fascinated and awed him. Even though now there was no Empress to rule, just the rose and white quartz monument to her memory at Jihi Square, where the city's delta met the region's major river, the Ki-iro; even though the Greens and the Reds, or the Ching Pang and the Hung Pang as they were also known, Sha'angh'sei's hereditary enemies, united by the now-dead Empress and their tai-pan for the Kai-feng, now held a balance of a truce between them; even though the war, which had gone on for more time than anyone now living could remember and was, some said, the cause for Sha'angh'sei's creation, was at last finished forever; despite all these changes, Moichi thought, Sha'angh'sei abides, prospering, pushing ever outwards, mysterious, deadly, an entity unto itself, alive and the giver of more pleasure and pain than any one man could conceive. Still, for him, it was not enough.

'How did you get that?' he said, indicating the messenger's large bruise.

The young man touched the tender spot unconsciously with the tips of his fingers. 'Oh, combat practice with the Regent. You know, he never misses a day and he is an outstanding warrior even – even now.' He looked away from Moichi, embarrassed by his blunder.

Just then Moichi felt a shift in the kubaru's gait and he leaned out of the rickshaw. There was a disturbance in the street ahead and the runner was slowing. They were out of the port quarter now and into an area swarming with shops of a bewildering variety – a sort of permanent bazaar.

A cluster of people was blocking the street, Moichi saw,

and their kubaru was turning his head, searching for an alternative route to the Seifu-ke. But before he could turn them around, three Greens separated themselves from the pack and swaggered up to the rickshaw. They were all heavyset men with greasy black hair tied back in queues. They were dressed in black cotton tunics and wide pants. Short-hafted axes hung at their sides.

Moichi was on the point of asking them to help clear the way when he saw one of the Greens scowl and, grasping his axe, fling it, whirring, into the carriage. It crashed into the chest of the messenger with such force that, as his breastbone shattered, he was propelled part way through the rickshaw's reed back. The young man had not even had enough time to realize that they were under attack.

As blood spurted, Moichi jumped clear of the carriage, keeping the small reed structure between his rolling body and the oncoming Greens.

Time seemed to leap forward as the period of shock passed and movement began all over. People were running in every direction, screaming, and this helped somewhat. But the Greens were quartering, two, then three as the squat man who had thrown the axe leaped up into the carriage and jerked his weapon from the messenger's corpse.

Moichi had one dirk out, the point lifted slightly higher than the haft, crouched in the attacker's pose.

He ran from them and they laughed as if they had encountered a frightened child instead of a warrior and they fanned out in a wedge-shaped path. In a moment, he had whirled, one of the Greens almost upon him and, reversing the dirk, threw it, heavy hilt first directly into the onrushing man's face.

The Green screamed and reeled backwards from the enormous force of the blow. Blood gushed from his broken nose and he tried to spit out shattered teeth through his torn and ruined lips. At the same time, Moichi was whipping out his second dirk, rolling into the man. He slashed once as he went by, cutting the Green's Achilles' tendon. He picked up the Green's fallen axe and hurled it without having time for a proper aim, using his peripheral vision from whence he had seen the blurred movement heading towards him.

The airborne axe glanced off the second Green's kneecap. It hit him flat on and the man grunted as his leg buckled at the joint. But he knew how to fall, rolling and he came up – the angle had been wrong and thus the knee was merely bruised not broken as Moichi had intended. He let fly his own axe.

Moichi ducked and splinters of brick and mortar sailed at him, filling the air as the weapon crashed into a wall just beside his head.

The Green was close enough now and he lashed out with his right leg, feeling his arch make contact with the man's cheekbone at the precise angle. Bones splintered and the Green moaned, toppling over. His tongue came out, red and sticky, almost torn in two by his own teeth. But he was far from through. He bounced off the wall, hurled himself at Moichi, using his massive arms in a smashing blow against the navigator's shoulder. The dirk flew from Moichi's grasp and the Green's fingers went for the throat, the nails long and deadly.

Moichi let the hands in, looped his own around them, slamming his balled fists into the other's ears with such force that blood immediately sprayed out as the eardrums ruptured. The Green rose up, bellowing with pain and Moichi brought his massive hands together, breaking his neck.

Rolling the bloody body off him he rose, watching the third Green approach. He was the squat man and he circled Moichi with some caution. His axe blade shimmered crimson in the sunlight.

Moichi, keeping the splintered brickwork of the wall at his back, drew his silver-hilted sword. 'Why did you kill him?' he said thickly. 'We meant you no harm.'

'Meant us no harm?' spat the Green. 'He was a Red, wasn't he?'

For an instant, Moichi felt disoriented, almost as if he had somehow slipped backwards into time, into the Sha'angh'sei before the advent of the Kai-feng. 'What are you saying?' he breathed. 'The Reds and the Greens are at peace.'

The squat man hawked and a gob of phlegm spattered at Moichi's feet. 'No more, by the gods. No more! That ill-omened truce is thankfully at an end.' He brandished his axe menacingly. 'It was unnatural. We all felt ashamed. As unclean as defilers of little boys. By the great god of Sha'angh'sei, Kay-iro De, war is returned to the streets of the city!'

He rushed at Moichi then and they fought close together, breathlessly thrusting and counter-thrusting, each seeking a weakness in the other's defence.

Moichi shifted his sword to his left hand and in the same motion swung it at the squat man in a flashing flat arc. Thus occupied, the other failed to see Moichi's right hand in time, fingers extended and rigid as a board. He turned, far too late. Moichi's hand, edge-first, ploughed into the nerve cluster at the side of his neck and the Green crashed heavily to the cobbles.

The street was deserted now, save for the strewn bodies; the kubaru had long since disappeared. But Moichi could feel the eyes staring at him from the many shop windows. Taking deep breaths, ignoring the fire in his left shoulder, he hastily retrieved his dirks, shoving them into his wide sash. Returning his sword to its tattooed leather scabbard, he turned down a side street, disappearing almost immediately from view.

'What I do not understand is what set it off.'

'That is one of the reasons for your hasty summons.'

'You know?'

'Yes.'

'Tell me, then.'

'I am afraid that it is not a simple matter. Not simple at all.'

Moichi sat in a room on the second floor of the Seifu-ke. Through the large leaded-glass windows which were open now to catch any hint of a sea breeze, he saw the thick verdant trees lining Okan Road still as a painting above the nearby slanting rooftops.

Months before, after the ending of the Kai-feng, they had cleared away the old palace of the Empress, levelling its grandiose sleeping quarters and its vast work chambers, its cold marble columns and long echoing halls. Not because of any disrespect to the fallen Empress, the monument in Jihi Square was more than proof of that. The palace, like its hereditary occupant, simply belonged to another era. In its place had been constructed a three-storey dwelling – smaller and more functional – of rough oxidized brick relieved by glossy platinum fillwork at the interstices and edges. This singular combination of the grittily stark and the softly sensual gave the new Regent's home a look of having been in the centre of Sha'angh'sei's tumult for ever. This was the Seifu-ke.

Across a dark, highly polished sandalwood table, rikkagin Aerent, the first Regent of Sha'angh'sei sat in a high-backed chair of carved ebony. He was a tall, lean man with wide, powerful shoulders, thick greying hair and close-cropped beard. His face was the colour of lightly-cured leather, seamed beyond his years. It was dominated by a curving hawklike nose and dark eyes which could easily have been brooding but weren't. They were, instead, constantly full of light and life.

Just the opposite of his dead brother, Moichi thought, who had been doom-filled, tortured by his own inner nature. Looking into those eyes of Aerent's, one saw the rikkagin, the superb military leader, yes, but one saw much more. There was absolutely no opacity there; they were clear and so deep that they seemed to go on for ever. And at the core, what did one see? More than a warrior; more than a commander of men. A man. It was Aerent's deep and abiding humanity which, in the end, made him so extraordinary, Moichi thought. And Tuolin, his brother? His only family. Moichi shrugged inwardly. War. It was such utter madness. Was it luck that had allowed him and Aerent to survive while Tuolin was slain? Or was there some great force, unknowable to man, which guided the ultimate outcome of events. He shrugged again.

'It was like a return to the old days, Aerent,' Moichi said. 'The hate is there still even though none of them could say why or how it all began.'

Aerent nodded. 'Yes. Now it has begun again and it is as if the truce never happened. They have short memories for some things, the Ching Pang and the Hung Pang.'

'But how did it happen? Some skirmish between parties of the two?'

The Regent smiled ruefully. 'If only it were that simple, there might be some hope at least. But as it is –' He shrugged. 'What has happened,' he said deliberately, putting his hands flat on the table, 'is that Du-Sing's youngest son was found murdered late last night.'

'Son of the tai-pan of the Greens!' Moichi whistled low in his throat.

'And that is not all.' Aerent's heavily-muscled arms straightened as he put weight on them, onto his hands, levering himself up. He stood weaving slightly for a moment until he was quite sure of his balance. Then he walked, stiff-legged, somewhat awkwardly for the first several steps, out from behind the barrier of the table, crossing the room.

Moichi would not be so abysmally rude as to turn his gaze aside yet perhaps the sight of his friend walking compelled him to say: 'I am truly sorry, Aerent. About that young man –'

The Regent lifted a hand.

'You did more than could be expected, Moichi. He was a good lad.' He turned and smiled. 'I thank the gods you are all right. I still think I should call a physician to take a look at that shoulder –'

Now it was the navigator's turn to raise his hand.

'At least use some of this ice,' the Regent said, pushing a bowl across the table. Moichi acquiesced. The cold would stop the swelling and it damped the ache, at least for the time being.

Moichi watched his friend as he made his careful way across the room to the window. He looks more like an enormous insect, Moichi thought. A praying mantis perhaps, locked within the peculiarly articulated mode of locomotion devised for him. At length, the Regent made the window and sat down on the wide sill, his long legs stretched out before him. He put a long hand out feeling their gem hardness, saying: 'It's got so I hate to hide them now.'

'I imagine it is not something one can easily get used to.'

'Indeed, no.' Aerent smiled thinly and thought, still, luckier than some. Thank the gods I, at least, was spared the grief of soul which plagued Tuolin. Strange that only at the point of death should he find love. He was a warrior to the last. And, at the end, a true hero. Thus shall he be remembered. It is only just.

He sat straight as a ramrod, looking inwards while Moichi waited without, patiently thinking his own thoughts. Aerent felt the soft wind which sprang up, drying the sweat on his back which had caused his green silk shirt to cling clammily to his skin. The sun had dimmed behind him as the quick-forming summer thunderheads built up on the southwest quarter, racing hastily inland as if late for some important appointment. He sniffed once: the incipience of rain. It recalled to him, like the flash of a bolt from an arbalest, that sleeting morning, racing across the battlefield before the yellow stone citadel of Kamado, his sleek stallion thundering under him with such coordinated power and the fusillade he avoided by a mere hair's-breadth by rolling from his saddle. But the ground was treacherous, made slippery by the blood and gore of many so that the earth itself was hidden by the grisly mattress of the piled bodies. His mount had stumbled and panicked and, as it had swerved hysterically, his booted foot caught the edge of the metal stirrup, twisted sideways, an inescapable trap. He had been dragged across the humped ground, over bodies and fallen weapons, a hideous and lethal gauntlet. Armour had protected most of his torso and arms; at the very end, something had sheared away half his helmet so that he had mercifully passed into unconsciousness.

But there was nothing any physician could do about his legs. The nerves were gone and in any case the damage to flesh and muscle was so extensive that they had had no choice. They had left it to Tuolin's physician to tell him.

Still, he did not despair for he had no room in his bright soul for that bleak, immobilizing emotion. There is something good in everything that happens, Aerent had thought or, at the very least, something important to be learned. His body had been tested and he had come through. Now his mind was being put to the task. Here he would either survive or perish emotionally.

The physicians being useless to him once they had cut the dead flesh away, he called for the engineers, dismissing at once those who could not keep from smiling and who averted their eyes or who seemed bewildered by his summons, for those were invariably the ones who told him that nothing could be done.

Aerent did not believe this and, at length, he found a man who was both unafraid and who knew what would be required. 'They should, I feel, be more than functional,' were the first words out of his mouth and Aerent had been satisfied. 'Do it,' he had said.

Money was no problem, of course. Aerent was a hero of the Kai-feng and already a groundswell movement was forming for his appointment as first Regent of Sha'angh'sei. The city, in effect, had taken his legs from him; thus the city would restore them to him no matter the cost.

The engineer – he was the same man who had drawn up the plans for the Seifu-ke – had worked ceaselessly for a full season, abandoning all other projects and, at last, he came to Aerent with a long thin package perhaps a metre long wrapped in dark cloth.

'It is done,' he said, laying open the contents.

They were fashioned after the human skeletal leg structure, the arcing bones carved from a ruby-like substance that had all the tensile strength of the gem but also had the required flexibility. The joints were masterpieces of construction, gimbals and sockets of onyx and solid brass brushed with a dry lubricant which also protected the metal from moisture and day-to-day wear.

It took half a day to fit the legs but, then, Aerent would never have to take them off. As he worked on the last adjustments, the engineer had said, 'Of course we have many substances to mould over these "bones" so that the legs will seem almost real. But' – he tightened the last screw and stood up, admiring his handiwork – 'to be quite frank I prefer them as they are. It is what I would do if I were wearing them.'

Aerent had gazed at them for a long time, searching perhaps for some emotion deep inside himself, some guide. 'Yes,' he said at length. 'I believe you are quite correct. Let us leave them as they are.' He put his hands on the ruby bones, his fingers feeling along their lengths. Then, with the aid of a chair back, he stood up for the first time and, strangely, the immediate sensation was one of enormous freedom. It was not until much later that he realized how much lighter his new legs were compared to the ones of flesh and real bone.

The rain had begun. Aerent's spine arched involuntarily as the first drops pattered against his back. The sky above

Sha'angh'sei was dark and rippling like a great beast's underbelly. Thunder rolled distantly.

'It was all right then, after that,' the Regent said.

Moichi had to think for a moment. 'Yes. I knew which streets to avoid.'

Aerent nodded. 'Good. Those idiots!' He meant the Greens who had attacked Moichi and the messenger. 'Omojiru, Du-Sing's son, was found in a room on the second floor of a tavern on Green Dolphin Street.'

'Which one?'

'The Screaming Monkey, I am told.'

'Not the most savoury of inns. Have you been there yet?'

'No. I deemed it prudent to wait until morning. Nothing has been touched.'

'You've seen the body?'

'Yes. It was brought here. Du-Sing picked it up some time later.'

'How was he killed?'

'With great efficiency, I am afraid. It was no street brawl.'

'Hardly accidental, then.'

'No. The sword strokes were as brutal as they were efficacious. He was murdered by an expert.'

'Murdered?'

'His sword was still in his scabbard. I ascertained, subsequently, that it had not been used.'

'I see. But why does Du-Sing suspect the Reds?'

'It comes down, I think, to the places Omojiru frequented. It was rumoured that he was the black sheep of the family but the old man ignored this as much as he was able. Still, it is fairly well known that the lad used the gambling houses in the Tejira Quarter.'

'Territory of the Hung Pang.'

The Regent nodded soberly. 'And then there were the girls. It is said that Omojiru had a voracious appetite for girls. Four and five a night. None, they tell me, over the age of twelve.' His arms like corded steel and he was up again, springing lightly across the room far quicker than any normal man could manage it, the mantis afoot. 'Omojiru, it can be readily seen, was far from a source of pride to Du-Sing. Still, he was family and, of course, a Green. All other distinctions have been made irrelevant by death.'

Moichi looked into his friend's eyes. 'I do not think that it matters to Du-Sing whether or not the Reds actually killed his son.'

'In that you are wrong, Moichi,' the Regent said. 'But I see your point. The war between the Greens and the Reds is an inevitable course in Sha'angh'sei. I see that clearly now. No truce could hold for long. This city must find its own course. Not one man or one woman, nor even a group of people, can impose their ultimate will here. Even Kiri knew that, did not attempt to cross certain natural barriers, and she was a hereditary ruler, an extraordinary individual. I doubt that anyone else could have united the Greens and Reds for the Kai-feng. Well, I am here now and I am not Kiri. I do what I can, what I must to keep this city together. But Sha'angh'sei is an unstoppable entity and this is its intrinsic strength, I firmly believe. To tamper with it would be to risk the dissipating of its life-force and this I will not do.'

'You will not try to end the war?'

Aerent smiled. 'I did not say that, my friend. I merely state what is. One must learn, in this capacity, in what ways one can be most effective. In Sha'angh'sei it is often said that the direct approach is not always the most successful. I talked quite briefly with Du-Sing when he came with his escort to take the body of his son. His mind is quite made up on this matter, I am afraid. Now I must try other means to attain a reconciliation.'

'How can I be of help?' Moichi said.

The Regent nodded. 'There are two things, quite unrelated. First, come with me to the Screaming Monkey to aid in the investigation.'

'You mean you wish to prove that Omojiru was murdered by someone other than a Red.'

Aerent smiled. 'I wish to get at the truth. Omojiru may indeed have been felled by a Red assassin. There is certainly enough motivation; his gambling debts had risen alarmingly recently.' He shrugged. 'Perhaps he was expecting money from Du-Sing which was not forthcoming.' The Regent stood by the table now. It had been brought from his old barracks-house on Dawndragon Lane on his insistence. It had served him well and faithfully when he was a rikkagin, he had said, and it would do so again. He had wanted no part of the ornate silver and crystal desk which had initially been ordered by the contractors for this room. He leaned over it now, took a large-bowled pipe from a black wooden rack and made himself very busy for several moments filling it with a dark tobacco. Only after he had methodically tamped down the full bowl and got the thing going did he continue. His profile was to Moichi as he said, 'Second, I have just received a message of state from Ama-no-mori. A fast clipper out of the southern out-islands brought it in early this morning.' Moichi sat up, certain that here was news of his friend, the Dai-San. 'I am told' – he sucked at his pipe – 'that the Kunshin's daughter will arrive on tomorrow morning's tide.' He swung around to face the navigator. 'I wish you to keep her safe during her stay –'

'You mean baby-sit, by God!' Moichi cried, standing up.

Aerent smiled genially, calm as ever. 'You know Azuki-iro, my friend. Do you believe that he would send us a helpless girl?' He shook his head by way of emphasis. 'Not the Bujun. No, the Kunshin sends us a daughter whom he wants made aware of the world outside Ama-no-mori. Besides' – he grinned broadly – 'the message of state specifically requested your aid in this matter.'

Aerent paused, his pipe in his hand. A thin curl of smoke drifted up against the side of his face making him squint as if he were gazing into the sun. The Regent's dark eyes were on Moichi. Never had they seemed so clear nor filled with such compassion. He put his hand on the navigator's shoulder. 'My friend,' he said evenly, 'don't think that I don't know you. I understand your restlessness here, your desire to return to the sea. Be assured that I have talked with Llowan. But for the time being, there is nothing either of us can do. There are no ships available now and we can only exert so much pressure on the shipowners' guild. The time is not yet right for you. But soon, eh? Soon.'

Rain beat down out of a low fulminating sky as they rode through the streets of the city. They were without an escort, an encumbrance Aerent would not tolerate. The seals of state were emblazoned on the Regent's mount's harness and on his own dark swirling cape and this was all he felt was required. As for the newly-rekindled war, if Du-Sing or Lui Wu, for that matter, the tai-pan of the Reds, learned that he had been attacked, the assailants would be summarily executed by the tai-pan's own hands. An attack was hardly likely, in any event, since the Regent was well known throughout Sha'angh'sei.

There was construction on Brown Bear Road and the ground there was mired in mud so they detoured, taking Quince Street, then Park Paradise until it bisected Thrice Blessed Road, from there, carefully picking their way onto Green Dolphin Street.

They dismounted before the swinging sign of the Screaming Monkey, beaded in the rain, and Moichi called to a boy sitting just inside the doorway, handing him two copper coins, asking him to tend to their mounts.

Inside the tavern it was dark, the air thick. They shook the rain off their capes, inhaling the mingled scents of animal fat and charcoal, fermented wine and sawdust. It was quiet this early in the day; most of the chairs were still raised on the tables. Still, there were three or four figures seated, eating and drinking. A dark-haired woman with black-lacquered teeth lolled indolently in a far corner. Seeing them, she let her wrapped cloak unfurl as if by accident and Moichi caught a glimpse of a burnished calf and sleek thigh. The woman sat up, stretching so that her ample breasts arched towards him, half-spilling out of her low-cut robe.

The tavernmaster came out from behind the bar. He was a short man with a barrel chest and legs like a bird. His skull was hairless. He rubbed his hands together and assumed an obsequious attitude in the hopes of forestalling the trouble which he expected was coming.

'Yes, Regent.' His thin voice was almost a whine. 'How may I serve you? Some breakfast, perhaps? A cup of mulled wine on this terrible day?'

'Neither,' Aerent said. 'We wish to see the room where Omojiru was found.'

The other shuddered as if his worst fears had just been confirmed. 'A monstrous act, your grace. Simply monstrous. The room is up the stairs, last door on your left.' He closed his eyes for a moment. When he opened them again they seemed somewhat moist. 'Forgive me if I do not accompany you but –'

'I understand,' Aerent said.

'Nothing has been touched, let me assure you, your Grace. All has been left as – as we found it.'

'Tell me,' Moichi interjected. 'Did Omojiru pay for the room in advance?'

The tavernmaster peered at him. 'Why, he did not pay for the room at all.'

'What do you mean?' Aerent said.

'The room was paid for by another man. He arrived perhaps during the hour of the cicada. Omojiru did not arrive before the hour of the fox, I am quite sure.'

'What happened to this man?' Moichi said. 'Did you see him leave?'

The tavernmaster's face registered surprise. 'Why, no.

But – but in all the excitement it would have been easy for him to slip out.'

'Do you remember what he looked like?' asked the Regent.

The tavernmaster gave them as detailed a description as he was able.

They left him and mounted the stairs. In the large room behind them, the tavernmaster was taking down the chairs. The dark-haired woman pulled her cloak about her again, closing her eyes.

They could tell almost nothing from the room. The curtains remained drawn and what little furniture there was seemed to be in place. The bed, of course, was a mess, the sheets and coverlets torn and rumpled, stiff with dried blood and excrement. And part of the floor was stained almost black. Moichi followed this out into the hall, squatting down. He scraped at the wood, licked the tip of his finger. Blood. He stood up. Blood on the bed and the floor. A great deal of it, almost as if an entire body had been drained.

He went back into the room. Aerent was on the far side, parting the curtains. He peered out of the open window, pulled his head quickly back. 'Phew! Someone ought to tell that tavernmaster to clean up this alley. What a stink!'

'Blood all over the place, Aerent,' Moichi said. 'You saw Omojiru's body. Could this be his blood?'

The Regent shook his head. 'Not the way he was killed. The blood loss was minimal; death came far too fast.'

'Dangerous to assume now that the other man, whoever he is, is Omojiru's murderer.'

'Yes, but that leaves us with the question of what happened to him.'

Moichi looked around once more; they had searched in every conceivable nook and cranny and found nothing. Nothing but blood. 'Well, the answer is obviously not here.'

They found the boy outside, throwing pebbles at passing carts. He danced a little jig at each hit. The rain had metamorphosed into a light mist while they had been inside the Screaming Monkey.

'The horses,' Moichi said to the boy and he nodded, leading them down the street.

'Just a moment.' Moichi halted them as they were passing the dank black alley to the side of the tavern. There seemed to be a lot of movement in the denseness, small chitterings, sibilant rustlings.

Moichi went in and the others followed him into the shadows.

Refuse and garbage, excrement and – a humped shape.

Moichi bent down and hissed sharply, a quick exhalation. Squeals of the rats, scattering angrily before his looming presence.

'There is something here,' he said. 'Something new to cause such activity in these normally nocturnal creatures.' His hand reached out, fingers moving rapidly, found stiff cloth, a hard and irregular configuration beneath it. Blood-stench and a sudden geyser of fetid gas. Death. He choked.

'Gods, it is a man!'

Together, he and Aerent dragged it into the light of day.

The boy turned away and vomited, retching violently without let-up.

The eyes were gone and, of course, the nose. They had been busy through the night, those creatures; he could not have been there any longer than that.

They were both crouching over the corpse. Moichi glanced up, saw the curtains blowing in the room they had just come from. A neat drop, he thought. Tidy. Let the scavengers of the city dispose of the body.

Aerent was staring at the corpse. His eyes widened. 'By the Pole Star, Moichi, look at this!'

But Moichi had turned his head, knowing what the other had found, was watching the boy who, terrified yet unable to leave, had turned back. He noted the boy's paleness of skin under the yellow tinge, the pinched look around the corners of his mouth, the slight wildness of the eyes. Everyone in Sha'angh'sei is inured to death, Moichi thought. Even the young. Just another fact of life here. What would cause such a violent reaction in him? It was a terrible death, yes. But was that the sum of it?

'Moichi, who could have – ?' Aerent grasped the navigator's arm, appalled. 'Have you seen this – abomination? Death has been on my side for many long seasons, until I think of it now as a kind of constant companion; we have an understanding. But this – never have I seen its like. Not on the battlefield; not in the military prisons. Nowhere.'

Moichi nodded, holding onto the boy now. He looked again. The chest was a gaping maw, all white and black, crawling with tiny things. But there was nothing terrible about that; it was nature. The creatures of the world were due their right. The truly monstrous thing was that all the blood was gone. Only man could do that.

Because something had been done to this man's heart. Something perverse and evil, slowly and calculatedly, before he died and Moichi still felt the chills reverberating through him, making the short hairs at the back of his neck stand up, a vestigial reflex from the time when man still swung through the trees, walking with his knuckles scraping the earth. Someone had worked on this man with a cunning more than human and with an obvious dispassion that was quite a bit less than human. Not the quick flashing death of Omojiru for this man.

Moichi tightened his grip on the boy's arm. 'Who is he?'

The boy shook his head.

'Tell me.' Then, more sharply like the crack of a whip. 'Tell me!'

The boy flinched, closing his eyes but still he was silent. Tears stood out at the corners of his eyes.

'Tell me.' Softly.

'No. No!' he said miserably. 'I promised.' He opened his eyes, pleading with Moichi.

'Promised what?' He was relentless now. 'You must tell me.'

'I promised him I would not tell anyone!'

'Look!' Moichi barked, pushing the boy down on his knees before the corpse. 'He is dead now. Dead. Do you understand?'

The boy began to cry. Great gasping sobs shook him and Moichi pulled him close, stroking his head. 'All right,' he said softly. 'All right. It does not matter now, your promise. Do you understand? What he was afraid of has already occurred. You cannot hurt him now by telling me what happened. He is beyond that now.' He looked into the boy's tear-streaked face. 'Kuo, here. Sit here beside us.'

After a time Kuo told them what he knew of the man who had given him the silver coin and promised him another.

'Kintai.'

'How did they get it?'

'The manufacture of the saddle. It's as distinctive as a shop, you know. But they're quite clever here. Given time, they could probably come up with the exact town within the province.'

'And the horse? Anything there?'

'Do you mean species?'

Moichi nodded.

Aerent shrugged. 'That's another matter entirely. There is nothing remarkable about it. But, in any event, he could have bought it anywhere, really, even if it were a luma.'

They were sitting in the same room on the second floor of the Seifu-ke where they had talked earlier in the morning.

Kuo had talked for a long time before he had led them to the stable where he had quartered their mounts, showing them to the stall where the dead man's stallion was housed. He had brought it out at the appointed hour the night before, precisely as the dead man had ordered only to find the horror in the alley where he had expected another silver coin and a few kind words.

'I know little of Kintai,' Moichi said.

'I am not surprised.' Aerent faced the window, his hands clasped loosely in front of him. The storm had all but spent itself and, here and there, over the rooftops of the city, he could see liquid wedges of cerulean as errant clouds followed in the wake of the rain. The Regent turned from the view of Sha'angh'sei. 'It is a landlocked region far to the northwest. Not much is known of it, since its frontiers are beyond even the most northerly of the forest people with whom we have trading agreements.'

'What would an outlander from such a far-off place be doing in Sha'angh'sei with the son of the tai-pan of the Ching Pang?'

'And who was it killed them both?' Aerent tapped a long forefinger against his lips ruminatively. 'I think what we must focus on is the difference of the modes of death.'

'I agree.' Moichi nodded. 'Omojiru is killed almost instantly while the outlander suffers a most hideous and pain-filled demise.'

'Information.'

'What?'

'We can only surmise that the murderer sought information.'

'It must be of enormous importance to resort to that kind of torture.'

'My thoughts precisely.' Aerent was tapping his lips again.

'Perhaps Du-Sing should be told about this,' Moichi observed. 'It does not look now as if the Reds were involved at all.'

'Uhm. Dangerous to make that assumption at this stage, I am afraid, tempting though it may be to do so. We do not know how many men were involved. Perhaps –'

'Perhaps what?' Moichi prompted.

Aerent poured them wine, handed Moichi a crystal goblet

imprinted with the Regent's seal in silver. His brow was furrowed in worry. 'There may be a military aspect to this; that would quite logically involve both the Reds and the Greens. There are still many peoples in the world who covet this port city with its vast wealth and strategic location.'

'Surely you are not suggesting –'

'An invasion from the north?' The Regent shrugged. 'I cannot rule it out.' He sipped at his wine, barely tasting it. 'I can tell you one thing for certain, my friend. This matter is about more than just a murder. Much more.' He put his goblet down. 'Well, we have done all we can for the moment. I have sent for information on Kintai and that will take some time to compile. The newly-formed Shōbai will be most helpful.'

Moichi laughed. 'They had better, by God! Without your aid those traders would have a tough time with the Sha'angh'sei hongs.'

'The trading guild is a fine idea but who knows if it will work? There are so many divergent members from so many lands they may burst asunder with a very loud bang.' He rubbed his hands together. 'It's getting late. Will you stay for dinner?'

'Another time, Aerent. I am meeting Kossori –'

'Ach! What you see in that layabout I cannot understand.'

Moichi smiled good-humouredly. 'I think, perhaps, it is more his personality that rubs you the wrong way, Regent.'

'Huh! I set no store by useless persons, Moichi. You know that full well. How they act is of no matter to me. This friend of yours does nothing with his time, helps no one. Tell me, of what use is he to others or to himself?'

'He is a fine musician,' Moichi said, wishing now and not for the first time that he could say more.

'That is as may be, my friend, but I have little respect for those lazy enough to loll about the squares of the city all day playing music. And at night –'

'Tonight he takes me to the Sha-rida.'

The Regent turned abruptly away. 'I will forget that I heard you say that.'

Moichi was puzzled. 'Is it so terrible then? There are many slave markets within Sha'angh'sei.'

Aerent spun around, his face drained of colour. 'Do you not know?'

'What?'

The Regent touched his shoulder gently. 'My friend, you still have a great deal to learn about this city. The Sha-rida is a very special kind of slave market. One I intend to destroy one day.'

'Won't you tell me what it is?'

Aerent shook his head as if he were suddenly weary. 'I will speak no more of it. Let your good friend, Kossori, answer all your queries.' He ran a hand through his hair, walking away from the table a little way. His legs clicked quietly. 'But now, before you take your leave, we have an important matter to discuss. The Bujan ship, *Tsubasa*, is scheduled to dock tomorrow at the beginning of the hour of the cormorant. I trust that your late-night wanderings will not prevent you from meeting me promptly at Three Kegs Pier, eh?' He smiled.

Moichi rose. 'Have no fear on that score, Aerent. I will be there. And by that time I trust there will be news of the current happenings in Kintai.' He turned at the door. 'By the way, what is the name of this girl, the Kunshin's daughter?'

'Chiisai.'

Now it was Moichi's turn to smile. 'A beautiful name, at least.'

'What else did you expect?' said Aerent. 'It is Bujun.'

Koppo

Kossori lived on Silver Thread Lane, a crumbling, narrow alley that belied its name. There, it was always dark with the shadows of the surrounding, taller buildings, days of twilight, nights of perfect pitch blackness; the alleys of the city had no nightlights as did the wider streets, avenues and squares. This perpetual darkness did not seem to bother Kossori. On the contrary, it amused him. He professed to love the darkness. With all that, however, he could rarely be found at home. He preferred, as Aerent had indicated, to spend his days in the wide sun-splashed squares of Sha'angh'sei, making music. He was an exceptional musician, adept at both the fliete̅, a wind instrument and the kyōgan, an ellipsoid stringed instrument, quite thin, the tuning delicate and most difficult to master.

On any given day, Kossori could be seen in his richly-coloured tunics at Hei-dorii Square during the morning and, perhaps, Double Hogshead Square in the afternoon, playing serenely as the swarms of people swept by him at a frantic pace.

He was not a large man but he had wide shoulders and a narrow waist which, combined with his enormously powerful legs, made him a figure of no little distinction. His black hair was glossy and longer than was usual in Sha'angh'sei; the end of his queue reached down to the top of his buttocks. It was but one outward manifestation of his inner iconoclasm.

He was a man of myriad acquaintances but few friends which made his deep friendship with Moichi all the more unusual. Certainly it was his strangeness which, in part, attracted Moichi who, more often than not, found himself bored by the company of people who seemed obsessed with the pursuit of wealth and women. And no doubt it was those times more than any others that Moichi felt himself pulled towards the crashing sea, preferring the soughing of the humid salt wind through the straining lines, the comforting pitch and roll of the tarred deck, the flying spray at the cleaving bow as all canvas was let out before the following wind.

Not that either of them lacked for women. Many was the night they would set out through the vast labyrinth of the city in search of the perfect wench. They had, of course, never found such a one for then surely their sport would be through. Kossori had an enormous appetite for women. Not necessarily sex but, seemingly more important for him, companionship. And more than once Moichi had observed in his friend a serious, even a desperate drive, beneath their playful nights in the soft arms of the women of Sha'angh'sei.

This evening Kossori was in the centre of Jihi Square, in the shadow of the rose and white quartz monument to Kiri, the last Empress of Sha'angh'sei. The sculpture was of a women metamorphosing into the Kay-iro De, the patron deity of the city, said in legends to guard Sha'angh'sei from all harm. It was a sea-serpent with a woman's head and it was further said by those who claimed to have actually seen it, that this was how Kiri had died during the last day of the Kai-feng. And who could gainsay them? Moichi thought, gazing with fondness at Kiri's facial likeness. In his adventures with the Dai-San, he himself had been witness to stranger and more terrifying sights.

He approached Kossori through the milling throngs rushing home to supper with families or in the many smoke-filled taverns of the city, after which a night of carousing would begin.

Kossori was in the midst of a song. He was playing the fliete. It was one that he had made himself, eschewing the more traditional substances of bamboo and ebony for copper. The metal gave the blown notes a semi-sad plangency that were unique to this instrument.

Moichi stood on the far side of the square watching and listening. He studied the man's face, noting again the angular features: the high cheekbones, the wide firm-bridged nose and the light-grey defiant eyes. It was certainly a strong face, bold and unconventional. Yet beneath that was a deeply hidden sadness, echoed now by the music.

The song ended and Moichi moved towards him. Kossori, looking up, spied him and smiled.

'Hola!'

'Hola, Kossori. A fine tune. Is it new?'

'Completed just this morning.' He stretched out an arm. 'Come and sit down in the shade of a legend. It has been a hot day.'

Moichi, glancing up, said, 'How long ago it seems to me, the Kai-feng.'

'Uhm. Well, the human brain has a remarkable capacity for recalling pain and suffering. They dim, thank the Gods, more quickly than the memories of pleasure, which never seem to fade no matter how many years have passed.' He slipped his copper fliete̅ into its worn chamois covering, thence to its hard leather case. 'We are well clear of that time, Moichi, that I can tell you.' He shuddered. 'The world is a far better place without the interference of sorcery.'

'There is white sorcery as well as black,' Moichi said, thinking of the Dai-San.

'No, my friend. As far as I am concerned all sorcery is bad *tsuzuru.*'

Moichi knew this as a Sha'angh'sei dialect word which had a number of subtle shades of meaning. Here he was certain his friend meant 'magic spell'. But he was surprised and said as much. 'All these people' – he raised an arm, flinging it outwards towards the crowded square, taking in all the people hurrying by – 'know you as a fine musician, Kossori. Even the Regent is unaware, I think. But I know what you possess and I do not think fear is part of your make-up.'

Kossori sighed. 'There is none else in all the world to whom I would dare admit this, Moichi, but sorcery does indeed frighten me. It frightens me because it conforms to no laws I can understand. I feel impotent before it, even with these.' He made fists of his hands, put them in front of his face. 'Even *koppo* is no match for magic.'

Moichi laughed and clapped the other on the back. 'Come, my brooding friend, enough of this gloomy talk. Our world has been reborn again through the purging of the Kai-feng and the Dolman. In this new age, there is no room for sorcery in our world.' They stood up. 'I think a bit of a work-out at the doho will make us both feel a whole lot better.'

Quitting the spaciousness of the square, they plunged into the narrow swarming streets, at length turning left onto Copper Foil Street. It was the wrong end and they found themselves at once in the midst of three solid blocks of outdoor stalls so jammed with wares and milling customers that they felt like fish struggling upstream against a powerful current. Spices hung heavy in the air; cinnamon, marjoram, thyme, black pepper and heady nutmeg; flapping multi-coloured rugs and pewter lamps moulded into lewd vertical shapes; fresh vegetables and dried fruits; candies and exotic liquored sweetmeats; fresh fish on shaved ice and crawling langoustes in their saltwater-filled glass cases. The cries of the vendors filled the air like the calls of strange forest birds, carrying their strident staccato messages; customers haggled prices and sellers cried out melodramatically, pulling at their hair, turning over their goods for taels of silver and winking to each other behind the purchaser's back. Wire cages housed hissing lizards with dry wrinkled hides smelling faintly of sweet loam, and bright beaded eyes; small red and brown monkeys chittered from tiny wooden swings, unconcernedly evacuating on the dirt below them while they pointed to the passers-by; yellow dogs with matted fur crouched, tongues lolling, by the sides of the stalls or ran, loping, through the narrow aisles; children carried on their mothers' backs bawled, red-faced, tiny fists clenched, or slept peacefully, their heads at an angle, resting on one shoulder.

At last they were through the crowds, on the far side of the stalls. Here vendors had set up make-shift grills on which bits of meat and vegetables sizzled above coals glowing an incandescent white, and brown smoke hung in the air, pungent and tangy.

Kossori led the way up a creaking wooden stairway, the steps worn smooth by constant use. They passed the first landing and on the second flight were obliged to press their backs against the wall in order to let a bulky man with an enormous chest and belly pass by them. He wore only a loincloth and he was sweating heavily. They knew him casually; one of the many wrestlers who frequented the doho. He nodded to them in greeting and went on past, heading for the baths on the second floor.

They went to their lockers and changed into plain white cotton robes that covered them only to mid-thigh. But instead of heading towards the doho proper, they chose instead to climb the last flight of stairs to the roof. They often went there because it was quieter, not only more isolated but infinitely more pleasurable to be in the open, as now, beneath the lavender evening sky, streaked with haze and the black silhouettes of the circling gulls above the distant harbour.

Three sides of the rooftop were covered, at their borders, by dwarf trees, cultivated into gnarled, twisting shapes. These formed a dense tangle to screen the top of the doho from any prying eyes attempting to observe from neighbouring rooftops. The fourth side held a sharply sloping rock garden kept wet by a clever recirculating stream of water which dribbled over the rocks at their highest point. This constant moisture allowed a wide variety of moss and lichen to grow in weblike patterns in the interstices so that the rocks appeared to be one variegated whole. It was a beautiful sight, a spot meant for deep contemplation and meditation and it had been there for as long as Kossori had been coming here – which was much of his life. The floor of the rooftop was constructed of wide wood boards held down and together by hardwood pegs rather than nails. It had been lacquered many times with clear coats that, over the years turned the wood an almost bright yellow. It was perfectly flat, with excellent drainage outlets on all four sides so that there was never a problem with rain.

Over the tufted tops of the stunted trees, they could see the oddly-shaped rooftops of Sha'angh'sei stretching as far as the eye could see, seeming to roll right into the sea as they turned southwest, the buildings hiding the low sweep of the bund and its long line of harttin.

The sun's last degrees were slipping into the shimmering sea and now the reflected light became so intense that the clouds, drifting high above the cityscape, shone gold and plum even while the edges of the rooftops were darkening to black, their outlines firming up and hardening after the glaring blaze they had endured during the height of the sunset.

This evening, they were alone up here, with the wind and the encroaching darkness spreading slowly westward like a prayer shawl drawn across the heavens by an unseen hand.

As they began their warming-up exercises, Moichi said, 'Tell me, Kossori, what is it about Aerent that rubs you the wrong way?'

Kossori waited until he had completed his deep breathing sequences before he replied. 'It's what he represents, Moichi. I am afraid I'm just not very good with those in power. The Regent's not a bad sort, really. It's just what he has chosen to do.'

'But don't you think a ruler can be beneficent? Help the

state through his power?'

'No,' Kossori said simply. 'I do not.'

'But surely –'

'My friend, let me tell you something. Nothing good ever came out of power. Yes, of course, there are those whose intentions are at first good. But the taste of power is too potent a draught and they, too, gradually get caught within its web. There are no exceptions.'

'Power corrupts, in other words.'

'Corrupts, yes. The mind expands with self-importance while the soul withers into impotance. There –' His head swivelled quickly and he whispered: 'Step back.'

'What – ?'

'Quickly, man! Do as I say!'

Moichi stepped back so that the line of twisted trees brushed against him. He looked to where Kossori was gazing. South of them a shadow had materialized as if out of the night itself. It was in violent motion yet silent and smooth, running lightly then leaping across the narrow chasms between buildings as if it were but a wisp of smoke. A cool breeze off the water rustled the spiky leaves of the trees and Moichi shivered slightly, feeling his muscles tense. Still he watched the shadow approach, the fluidity of motion mesmerizing, for there seemed to be no disturbance to the continuous flow of energy: run, leap, run, leap.

Now the shadow was spurting across the adjacent building's rooftop, the image abruptly blossoming. But so swiftly did it move, that Moichi only recognized it for what it was as it landed on their own rooftop.

It was a man dressed all in matt black clothing: wide trousers, sash, open-necked shirt. His face, too, was black, hidden by a mask which left only a narrow band of flesh – just enough to give him unhindered vision – exposed. He came towards them, over the polished wood, dancing, his feet seeming to glide through the darkening air. In one hand he carried what looked like an oval box, also matt black, flat on top and bottom. It dangled by a black rawhide cord. His other hand was empty.

'Jhindo.' Kossori's breath in a hiss, close beside Moichi.

Moichi had heard of these legendary creatures. They were hired as assassins and spies and, it was said, they knew so many methods to kill and maim, to disguise themselves and to escape any trap set for them, that they never failed in their clandestine missions. This was the first time, however, Moichi had seen one in the flesh and it recalled to him the tale the Dai-San had told him of the Jhindo who infiltrated the citadel of Kamado to kill Moeru but who, instead, was slain by his intended victim. So Jhindo were not invincible after all. But, he told himself soberly, Moeru had been a Bujun and there were no greater warriors in all the world.

Now here was a Jhindo seemingly come against them.

Kossori stood very still, eyeing the figure who now approached them slowly. He raised his hands, palms outward, calm and seemingly unperturbed. 'Please continue your journey. We wish you no ill.'

The Jhindo said nothing but slowly lowered the oval box until its bottom sat on the roof's flooring. He let go the cord. He was a tall man and now, as he spoke for the first time, he seemed to somehow gain in height. 'It is your ill fortune that you happen to be here at this particular time. I cannot proceed further until all evidence of my departure has vanished.'

Kossori did not turn his head away from the Jhindo but his low words were directed at Moichi: 'Do not interfere, my friend. And, above all, do not turn your back on this one. Jhindo possess many small metal weapons which are quite lethal when hurled with precision. Face them and you have a chance.'

'I urge you to be on your way,' Kossori said to the figure facing them.

'Yes,' said the Jhindo, 'I will be on my way. Just as soon as you both are staring sightlessly up at the stars.'

He came at Kossori then, flinging out his left arm and Kossori ducked away. The movement now was almost too rapid for Moichi to see clearly but the Jhindo had feinted and from somewhere had brought out a thin twined cord, knotted in the centre. This he whipped about Kossori's neck and, stepping behind him, jerked back on the ends so that the knot jammed against the other's windpipe.

Kossori rose into the air with the force of the motion.

'Ugh!' Moichi heard Kossori's brief cry and moved to help. But as he circled the two he saw that there was nothing he could do: they were so tightly locked that any sudden movement might bring Kossori under the attack of his blow. He waited, restlessly prowling.

It was an awkward position for Kossori and he was kicking himself for letting the Jhindo get the edge on him. His breath was already labouring and the muscles in his neck were going numb from the rapid loss of blood. His head throbbed and he knew it was just a matter of time until the cord would cause him to lose consciousness. He used his legs first but the Jhindo saw this coming and danced his own legs away. Then Kossori used his elbows, ramming them hard, as if it was all he had and he heard at length the answering grunt and the cord went slack for just long enough for him to turn around so that he was facing his opponent. A small blade flew out of the Jhindo's left cuff, into the open palm of his hand and Kossori let him have it, watching the slash ballooning in towards him, anticipating the angles vectoring on the final approach. He used his right hand, knowing that, for him, it did not matter, for a blow on the inside of the Jhindo's wrist and the blade flew out into the night, skittering brightly across the wood planks, coming to rest at last, bright as a droplet of blood, shimmering. But in its place was a jitte, a double-bladed knife-like weapon, and now the Jhindo's other hand was wrapped with a row of black-metal spikes arching over the knuckles.

The jitte flashed in a blur, the Jhindo's spiked hand

following hard upon it, a lethal one-two strike. The Jhindo was appallingly quick, faster, perhaps, even than Kossori himself.

The jitte ripped aside Kossori's white robe and his flesh shone palely underneath in the wan monochromatic light of the newly-risen moon.

Then the row of spikes went home, sinking themselves into the flesh of Kossori's right shoulder.

It was the end for the Jhindo and, to his credit, his eyes registered this knowledge a split second before Kossori's rigid fingers, held at a peculiar angle, slashed down upon him. They moved more swiftly than the eye could follow, the enormous force of the blow snapping the Jhindo's right wrist as if it were made of bamboo and, in the same motion, sweeping upwards now in concert with the other hand, breaking both of the Jhindo's shoulders. And before his sagging body had time to sprawl upon the wooden rooftop, Kossori had delivered a final strike as quick and devastating as a living lightning bolt, shattering the Jhindo's vertebrae.

Moichi came up beside Kossori, feeling as if he was moving through water. He had practised with his friend many times, had even seen the killing art of *koppo* used on wood and metal. But never on another human being. He was awed by the devastation that so few short bits of motion could wreak. No wonder Kossori was never armed. What need he of conventional weaponry when he possessed the secrets of *koppo*?

'Where *did* you learn that, Kossori?'

The other was staring down at the broken body of the tall Jhindo. Blood pooled darkly, seeping through his ebon garb. 'We'll have to call someone to clean up this mess,' he said, almost distractedly.

'Kossori?' Moichi put a hand gently on one shoulder. 'Are you all right?'

'Quite good, this one.' Kossori's voice was like a ghostly spiral of smoke, dissipating on the night air. 'So fast.'

'Kossori.' Moichi stepped around in front of his friend, saw the other's eyes come slowly into focus.

He smiled and shook his head. 'It takes a little time, my friend. The mental strain is the true difficulty in mastering *koppo*. And, of course, one tends to get caught in a kind of killing vortex. Otherwise, we'd never have the strength –' He put out his hand and Moichi glanced down at the humped body as broken as a discarded marionette ripped apart by a vengeful child.

Kossori ripped off a strip of fabric from his robe and bound up the four puncture wounds made by the Jhindo's strikes. 'I was lucky,' he said. 'Those things could have been poisoned.'

Moichi went the short distance over the wood to where the oval box squatted, flat and ugly. 'I wonder what he was up to?'

Kossori joined him. 'Nothing good, of that I am certain. Open the box. No doubt a clue to his night's work will be found therein.'

Moichi stooped and opened its lacquered lid.

He saw the queue first, blue-black, gleaming with fragrant oils that must have taken hours to apply. The hair was carefully and expensively coifed. This, too, had taken much time to achieve. Below, the brown almond eyes were open as if in surprise, the thick lips parted as if in incipient protest, the yellow teeth still shining with a film of saliva. Blood had pooled about the stump of the neck, a dark and brooding pond, coagulating slowly, held inside the vessel only by the thin coat of lacquer covering the interior.

'I do not want any part of it.'

'I am asking you as a personal favour. I –'

'My friend, let me tell you, I am no good at mysteries. Never have been. That is an area of expertise over which you preside. I would be a fool to dabble in anything about which I have so little understanding or natural facility.'

'But that's just it, Kossori. If you will just listen to me, I will explain how you can help me.'

'Hmph!' Kossori eyed him suspiciously but was now silent.

They were sitting at a rough plank table in a tavern on Iron Street which was crowded and bustling with business. Set before them were huge pewter plates filled with charred fowl and vegetables seared in hot oil and sesame seeds. Between them sat a fired clay flagon of yellow wine but their handleless cups were empty.

'Last night there was a murder –'

'Uhm, yes. I imagine so. One of several hundred in Sha'angh'sei. What of it?'

'If you will stop interrupting, I mean to tell you.'

Kossori grinned and spread his plams placatingly. 'By all means, say on.' He commenced to eat while Moichi spoke.

'The strange thing is,' Moichi concluded, 'that the two were killed in disparate fashion.'

Kossori's shoulders lifted, fell. 'It only means that there were two killers. Simple.' He wiped grease from his mouth with the back of one hand.

Moichi shook his head. 'Not so simple, really. Omojiru was killed swiftly, efficiently and coldly as if by a – a machine.'

Kossori looked at him quizzically. 'Machine? What is a machine?'

Too late, Moichi realized that he had no way of explaining this concept to his friend. He himself had never seen a machine but had had it described to him by the Dai-San during their long trek through the thick jungles surrounding Xich Chih. He would have to settle for a close equivalent. 'I mean to say a nonhuman source.'

'I see. And the other? This outlander from – where did you say?'

'Kintai.'

'Yes. Well. How did he die?'

'Oddly. Very oddly. Something about it was very distrubing.' He described what had been done to the man's heart.

Kossori had put his eating sticks down beside the plate of half-eaten food. 'Extremely unpleasant, I agree. But there are more ways in this world, my friend, to get information out of a human being, than either you or I could collate in a lifetime. The Bujun, it is said, are most adept at this kind of thing. How do you suppose I can help?'

Two Greens came through the front door, glanced around the large room for a moment, then chose an empty table just to the right of the door. They sat down, one facing Moichi. They began to talk.

'I don't know, really. Just a feeling.' He shrugged. 'Perhaps there's nothing after all.'

The waitress approached them but they waved her off.

Kossori patted Moichi's stout wrist. 'Anyway, it's good that you have an interest. This city's not good for you, you know.'

Moichi smiled. The Green facing him had looked over once; he had seen it out of the corner of his eye. But when he'd taken a look, the man's eyes had already slid away. Now he was careful not to glance their way. He seemed deep in conversation with his companion. 'I find myself more and more these days thinking of home, I am afraid.'

'But that's all to the good, don't you see?' Kossori popped a last bit of vegetable into his mouth, chewed and swallowed. 'Time you went home.' He smiled. 'You don't know how lucky you are to have a family.'

Moichi had changed his angle slightly but he still could not see their hands. He reached into his sash, withdrew some coins. 'Finished?' he said and, not waiting for an answer, spilled the copper onto the table.

'You're leaving way too much,' Kossori observed. 'Wait for the change.'

'Get up,' Moichi said in an intense whisper. 'We are leaving here right now.'

He kept the Greens in sight until they had closed the

tavern door behind them. On Iron Street, with the crowds already somewhat thinned by the lateness of the hour, he took them left then left again. They moved quickly and silently. Into an alley which led out onto Green Cricket Lane. Darkness closed about them within the alley's dense shadows. At either end, the brief yellow flickering of the wider streets' night lights.

'All right,' Kossori said as they paused for a moment. 'What did you see?'

'Those Greens.' He was peering ahead, then behind. 'I think they were looking for me.'

'But why?'

'Off-hand I can think of several reasons.' He told Kossori about the early morning attack. 'Let's go.'

But they had only taken several paces when he stopped abruptly, put his arm across the other's chest. He nodded. 'In front of us.'

The sounds of boot heels rattling against the ground, scraping against refuse. The skittering of rats.

'Who goes there?' Moichi called, drawing his sword. Beside him, he felt Kossori's muscles tense as he readied himself.

For a long moment, there was absolute silence. Even the tiny scavengers were still, sensing the tension in the air. Moichi saw his shadow and Kossori's flickering along the dank walls in front of him, elongated past all human recognition, limned by the night lights along Blessant Street behind them. They seemed grotesque and monstrous in the terribly confined space.

'Moichi Annai-Nin.' Out of the darkness in front of them. 'We have come for you.' A solid voice, used to command.

'By what authority?' Moichi inquired.

'By the supreme authority of our tai-pan, Du-Sing of the Ching Pang.'

'Let's take these scum,' Kossori hissed in his ear. But Moichi ignored him.

'What is it that your tai-pan wishes of me?' he inquired.

'That is for Du-Sing to say,' the voice replied from the darkness.

Moichi saw that now there was no light coming from the exit ahead to Green Cricket Lane.

'Please do not attempt anything foolish,' the voice said. And at that moment, their shadows disappeared on the wall as bodies blocked out the light from Blessant Street behind them.

The room was lined all in bamboo, split lengthwise and lacquered clear so that it gleamed in the low light emanating from the constellation of small oil lamps scattered about on low tables and mantelpieces. Above, the skylight had been drawn back revealing the icy brilliance of the glittering stars, remote, seemingly as hard as diamonds. The moon was in another quarter, unseen.

The man who sat facing them was so enormous that he seemed to overflow the bamboo chair, despite the fact that it was so outsized that it was obvious that it had been constructed to order. He wore saffron silk pants from which, it appeared, an entire tent might have been woven and a short wrapped jacket with wide sleeves, also saffron silk, quilted and low cut in front so that much of his chest was exposed. Against the naked flesh, dangling like a second heart, was an enormous tourmaline which moved as he moved.

Yet when one looked at this man, one saw first his face which was etched with the hard cruel lines that only a lifetime of constant guerrilla warfare can cause. It was a face, flat and circular as a moon, of a power as ancient as the delta upon which the nexus of the city was built. Du-Sing, tai-pan of the Ching Pang, the Greens of Sha'angh'sei, belonged to the earth and it, it was said, to him.

'Gentlemen.' A voice like distant thunder, as tactile as it was aural. 'Tea?'

Moichi nodded silently while Kossori looked on, still as a statue.

Du-Sing's eyes moved minutely and a young man in black cotton leggings and quilted jacket sprang into motion, filling cups standing on an ornate silver tray on a table along one wall of the room. Moichi accepted his cup but Kossori ignored his. There was nothing Moichi could do about this. He sipped at the hot liquid.

Du-Sing waited until he had taken that first drink before saying, 'We worked well together, once upon a time.' He meant during the Kai-feng, when all men were joined as if from one family. 'But that was a long time ago.' The tai-pan had left just a long enough pause between the two statements to give the latter one an ominous note. 'You are remembered with great fondness from that time by the Ching Pang, Moichi Annai-Nin.' He sighed and it was like a dam about to burst, a sound of timbers cracking. 'That is why I am showing you this courtesy instead of having you executed.' He snapped his fingers and the young man in black leapt to his side, put a cup of hot tea into his hand. It was lost inside that great fist. He drained the cup in one swallow. 'And how is the Dai-San, Moichi Annai-Nin?'

'He is well, Du-Sing.'

'Good. Good.'

The tai-pan had made his point.

'Why was I attacked this morning by Ching Pang?' Moichi asked. 'As you yourself said, I am no enemy of yours.'

'Yes.' Du-Sing lifted a fat finger. 'I had thought you a friend of the Ching Pang. Yet you travelled in the company of a Hung Pang spy.'

'He was a messenger sent by the Regent to fetch me to the Seifu-ke. That is all.'

'Is it?' One eyebrow was raised interrogatively. 'We shall find out. Presently.' He peered at Moichi over the rim of the delicate porcelain teacup, etched with gilt butterflies, almost as if he were a demure girl on her first date. 'I have had a talk with the Regent. A long talk. And he has agreed to dismiss all Hung Pang from his service.'

'He has?' This did not sound at all like something Aerent would willingly accede to.

'Do you doubt the words of a tai-pan?' For a moment his eyes blazed within their folds of fat. Then the light seemed abruptly extinguished and a thin smile played about the thick lips; it did not reach any further. 'But no, of course not. You would not be so discourteous, would you, Moichi Annai-Nin? No, you have too many highly-placed friends in Sha'angh'sei not to see the supreme folly of such a course, hmm?' He signalled silently for more tea.

'Can we get on with this,' Kossori said and, alarmed, Moichi gripped his arm.

'What was that?' Du-Sing raised one eyebrow. 'What was that?' He reminded Moichi of a great stage actor; what was real and what was being put on for his benefit?

The tai-pan took his cup from his lips, swung it from in front of his face. 'Mmm, I see that your friend is somewhat more ignorant of the social graces than you are, Moichi Annai-Nin. So be it, then. I shall come to the point directly. I had been circling it only because it causes me much pain.' He put a great paw over his heart and now for the first time he rose up. 'It is my son, my youngest son, Omojiru, murdered at the hands of the Hung Pang. This is an unforgivable affront. Even your barbarian friend must be well aware of this, eh, Moichi Annai-Nin. I have no doubt that *you* are.' Now there was real fire behind his eyes and abruptly his face was transformed into the visage as awesome as that of some avenging god. He took one trembling step towards them and Moichi felt Kossori tensing again, prayed that his friend would make no move for, though he had seen no sign of guards since they entered the tai-pan's inner sanctum, he entertained no illusions that they were alone here with Du-Sing. *Koppo* or no, if Kossori made any threatening move, they would both die within instants.

'It is *my* son who is dead, Moichi Annai-Nin!' Du-Sing

bellowed. 'The seed of *my* loins. It is *I* and my family; it is the Ching Pang who grieve for him now. What right have you to interfere in a matter that does not concern you?'

'But you are inaccurate, Du-Sing. If I may point out, I am already involved through the intervention of your own family, as you put it. The Ching Pang attempted to kill me this morning. I do not take kindly to such a threat. You cannot blame me for those deaths. I have every right to defend myself. I meant them no harm.'

'Yet your companion was a known Hung Pang spy.'

'He was a messenger from the Regent.'

'Worse still!' the tai-pan cried. 'By the gods, Moichi Annai-Nin, the Ching Pang owe you no apology! The Hung Pang work against us constantly. War is war. But now they have gone too far. To coldly murder Omojiru –'

'There is good reason to believe that the Hung Pang were not involved in your son's death, Du-Sing. We have –'

'Silence!' roared the tai-pan. 'What do you, an Iskamen, know about the Hung Pang? Or the Ching Pang? Only your former friendship stands between you and execution now. Omojiru's death is our business and ours alone. Do I make myself clear?'

'Eminently clear,' Moichi said.

'We are avenging that death even as we speak. That is all you need to know.' He clapped his hands once. 'Chei will see you out.' Without another word, he swept from the room, moving with astonishing grace for one of his enormous bulk.

'I would as soon break his fat neck as look at him,' Kossori said as soon as they were out on Black Fox Street. Moichi shushed him and they turned right, walking down the wide thoroughfare. Without looking back, he knew that the eyes of the Ching Pang were following their progress. He kept their pace to a saunter even though he was anxious to quit this area of the city, a Ching Pang stronghold. One could trust no one here for they were all – shopkeepers and streetwalkers, priests and moneylenders alike – in the employ of the Greens.

'Gods,' Kossori continued. 'I can see no reason at all to have put up with that pretentious windbag's pious sermon.'

Moichi glanced at him, a smile playing along his lips. 'That pretentious windbag, as you so eloquently put it, could have dismembered us at any moment he chose. There must have been at least fifty Ching Pang waiting with weapons drawn behind the four doors to that room.'

'Huh!' was all that Kossori said but Moichi knew that he was properly impressed. 'So I take it you'll stop this investigation then.'

'What gives you that idea?' Moichi said.

'Oh, well, I don't know. Maybe the great hottentot's ominous words back there had a bit to do with it. Otherwise, I can't imagine where I could get such a far-fetched idea.' He snorted.

Moichi threw his head back and laughed, clapping his friend on his broad back. 'I should not worry overmuch about Du-Sing, Kossori.'

'Oh yes, now you'll tell me that his bark is worse than his bite, I suppose.' His voice was heavy with sarcasm.

'No, no. Not at all. I just have to be more careful in my movements, that's all. Anyway, I may not be here too much longer. Tomorrow morning, I trust, Aerent will have the information I need on this land Kintai and –'

'You mean to go there!' Kossori exploded.

'Yes, I guess I do at that. I think we have reached a dead end in Sha'angh'sei. If we are ever to find out why those two were murdered, Kintai will be the place to begin. Want to come along?'

'Me?' Kossori laughed. 'Gods, no! I have no taste for that sort of thing.'

'At least take some time to think about it. I am not apt to depart for several days yet.'

'All right. If it'll make you happy. But, I warn you, the result'll be the same.' He rubbed his hands together. 'Now what say we forget all about this mystery of yours and spend some time at Saitō-gūshi.'

Moichi laughed. 'That certainly sounds relaxing.'

Kossori guffawed leeringly. 'Gods, I hope not!'

It was an ornate, three-storey structure of glossy black and vermilion lacquered wood, reachable only across the exaggerated arc of a bridge which spanned the narrow, deep moat which completely surrounded the building. It had been constructed on a piece of land originally quite near the sea but during the time of the idai-na-nami – this great storm's wave was said to have reached so high that it blotted out the sun – who knows how long ago, the sea had broken through, sailing across the land with such titanic force that it literally gouged away the land forming two channels which became the basis for the present moat. How Saitō-gūshi had been spared from the devastation wreaked elsewhere by the idai-na-nami was still a matter of much conjecture within Sha'angh'sei. However, Onna, who owned Saitō-gūshi, was often heard to say that it was because she and her women were favourites of the Kay-iro De and had thus been spared. Many said that this must be so because, without fail, Saitō-gūshi was closed one night a week so that its inhabitants could make the pilgrimage across the city into the heart of the kubaru old quarter to attend services at the temple named after Sha'angh'sei's legendary protectress, Kay-iro-De.

Indeed, the aura of the serpentine goddess could be felt as soon as one set foot upon the bridge whose metal railings were shaped into her likeness and set within the arched wooden floor was a golden bas-relief sculpture of Kay-iro De. These manifestations of the supernatural combined with the high semi-circular structure of the bridge itself to give one the feeling that one was passing through some invisible barrier, leaving the real world behind, entering some fantastic mythological kingdom where anything was possible.

This, Moichi knew by direct experience, was far more true than any novice to these high portals could ever imagine. For within Saitō-gūshi's walls reposed the most sumptuous array of women gathered since the demise of Tenchō.

The doors were of beaten brass, bound with a rock-hard mirror-like substance. They opened inward, as did those of a heavily fortified citadel and, indeed, the thickness of these doors would do any wartime fortress proud.

Yet inside it was warm and comfortable. Off the long vestibule, all visitors were divested of their street clothes no matter how rich and elegant. They were hung with infinite care in tiny cubicles by faithful attendant children and the visitors led off to be bathed. Then they all donned the silken robes of the house. Thus did Onna make it plain to all who entered her portals that they were under her rule no matter their standing in the community outside. Here, Onna's voice was law and, in the time she had been running Saitō-gūshi, it had not once been questioned.

Once robed, Moichi and Kossori were led from the baths back into the vestibule. The floor here was bare wood, highly polished. The walls, too, were bare. But as they passed through a doorway that was almost a true circle, save for the break at the bottom where the floor intruded, they came upon the true world of Saitō-gūshi. Here all the floors were covered by deep-pile scarlet carpeting. Within the small rooms, which appeared to go on for ever, all the low tables, round trays, eating and drinking implements were of solid gold. The cool dim hallways between these rooms invariably had ebony ceilings and fragrant cedar walls. And other rooms, somewhat larger, were divided by delicate ebony railings, sculpted into scrollwork. There was even a miniature Canton temple in one far corner of the sprawling, spiralling structure so that patrons who were so inclined would not pass up a visit here for the sake of a *missa* or the spate of holy days which came in the spring and the high summer.

A woman in a pink silk robe with white carnations embroidered across it, met them just over the threshold. She was slightly plump, making her seem the fleshly embodiment of the maternal symbol. Her face was painted white, her lips a bright scarlet. Her teeth, Moichi knew, were white and sparkling – as were those of all her women – which was in direct contrast to the freelance prostitutes of the city's streets who were required to lacquer their teeth black. The woman bowed to them, smiling. Her black glossy hair swirled in an intricate pattern about her head. Stuck through it were a pair of ivory pins perhaps half a metre long. She had dark laughing eyes and her chubby pale hands never seemed to be at rest but fluttered in the air about her, semaphoring enigmatic messages. She was always gay and excited as if she were the mother of the bride on her day of matrimony.

She leaned forward, kissing them delightedly on the cheek.

'So nice to see you again, boys.' She pointed a finger at Kossori. 'But you, sweet. I see you've lost some weight. Well, we'll have you fattened up by the time you leave here.' Her voice had the tenor of a fine musical instrument played by a virtuoso, so pleasing to the ear that one had to strain to remember that it had taken her eleven years of intensive training to acquire it.

This was Onna. Or, more accurately, Onna-shojin. This was, quite literally, a title rather than a name. It meant mistress, which is precisely what Onna was. No one knew her actual name and, because she had insisted on it at first, she had become Onna to all who spoke to her or of her.

'They're ready,' Onna said. She prided herself in knowing all her patrons' wishes after they had entered Saitō-gūshi's portals once. At least as far as Moichi and Kossori were concerned, she had never been wrong.

The women were waiting for them in one of the small rooms. Golden trays with sweetmeats and a variety of exotic liqueurs from far-off lands, imported under Onna's express direction, covered a multitude of tabletops.

Two of the women were petite but well-rounded. They had pale skin and features so startlingly similar they could have been twins and perhaps they were. These were Kossori's. He never took less than two to bed. Actually, he had begun with three when he had first come here but he found that late at night other women from Saitō-gūshi's multi-tiered rooms would eventually slip into his bed after satisfying their own patrons. It seemed that gossip of this nature spread almost instantaneously throughout the building. Kossori was a superb lover with an unusually high capacity for extended sex. But even for him, four women a night was more than he could handle. So now he confined himself scrupulously to two.

The third woman was one of a number who Moichi invariably chose. She was slightly larger in frame than the other two, brown-haired and with a dusky olive-tinged skin which reminded Moichi of the Iskamen women he had left far behind. Try as he might he had never fully got used to the paleness of the Sha'angh'sei women.

'I will come to fetch you at the hour of the snake,' Kossori told Moichi as he gathered his women about him with his long arms.

'More likely it will be I who will have to come after you,' Moichi answered and the women giggled.

He was not hungry or thirsty and so the woman led him out along a passageway smelling of cedar, its ceiling as dark as a starless night and up a spiralling flight of stairs to the second storey.

She opened a door and they went in. He heard the sound of the surging sea and he went across the room, parting the fluttering curtains. The window was open, overlooking the ocean. Onna, indeed, never forgot a thing no matter how minute it might seem superficially. She was, after all, in a business which was exclusively subjective and extremely personal and to forget *anything* a patron might desire would cause a disruption of harmony. And harmony was, in the end, what Saitō-gūshi was selling.

This room was built as if it were a captain's cabin aboard ship. It might have been the only one like it in all of Saitō-gūshi or, again, it might be one among many. There was no way of telling. And did it really matter?

A low fog was rolling in, billowing across the streets just high enough to reach a man's calves. The moon was hidden by a bank of low-lying stratus, perfectly horizontal, hanging heavily in the otherwise spangled night sky.

Moichi felt a gentle touch on his shoulder and he turned round. The dark beams rose over her head obliquely, faithfully following the slant of the roof. The scent of cedar was strong even here but her musk was stronger. She came into his arms and kissed him with her open mouth. He felt the hot electric flick of her tongue. Her hands fluttered along his body and his robe slid, sighing, to the floor.

There was something tremendously erotic about being totally naked while she was still clothed and this reversal somehow reminded him of Elena. Had he chosen this woman because of that?

Her busy fingers reached for him and she gasped as she found him tumescent.

Abruptly, her robe was open, hanging from her like the wings of a bird, and she was using her thighs to climb his thick, muscular body, panting into the hollow of his neck.

Outside, in the spreading branches of an ancient pine tree, battered by the idai-na-nami but unbowed, a great owl blinked twice into the lamplight streaming through the window, called out, hooting into the night.

In the dead of night, he found himself standing in the centre of a familiar street. He was in Sha'angh'sei but as he looked around he wondered how this could possibly be for the street was totally deserted.

It was Green Dolphin Street, he was certain. For wasn't that the sign of the Screaming Monkey swaying in the wind almost directly in front of him? Yes, of course. And there was the alley where –

His head felt tight, as if someone were squeezing it in a giant vice. And now his nostrils dilated. What was that stench?

He looked down. In his hand was clutched a handwritten note. He squinted but the uncertain light made it impossible to read. Nevertheless, he knew what it said: *Meet me in the alley on Green Dolphin Street.*

And he had come, it seemed. But why to this alley out of all of those on this long winding street?

The stench seemed fiercer and somehow he knew that it was emanating from the alley on the other side of Green Dolphin Street. He should go there. It was why he had come, after all. But he seemed frozen in his tracks as if split apart, one half not obeying the other.

Fear rooted him to the spot.

He did not want to venture into that dank dark alleyway.

And now he saw himself as if from a height, an ethereal presence watching, helpless, as his body walked towards the alley. *No!*, he wanted to cry out. *No, stop! Don't go in there!* But he seemed voiceless, too, unable to quell the feeling of mounting dread which filled him as he saw himself enter the ebon portal.

Yet now, instead of disappearing into the shadows, he found that he could follow himself and as he did, the swinging sign of the Screaming Monkey, Green Dolphin Street, then all of Sha'angh'sei disappeared as if it had never existed.

He saw, hovering, his body bending over a lumped shape, saw the corpse of the man from Kintai, destroyed, blasted, a hideous work of art, an abomination.

And then he knew that it was not this pathetic remnant of a human being which had terrified him but rather that thing which had perpetrated this evil.

He forced himself to again look upon that horror so that he should never forget and in that instant an idea began to occur to him. Perhaps it was the angle in which he found the body or, again, the kind of wreckage made of its appendages. Something. Something . . .

'– chi, wake up.'

Someone was shaking him, gently. But he almost had it now and he turned away, mumbling.

'Better let me do this.' Another voice and a firm grip, pulling him up, up, off the bed, out of sleep.

Annoyed, he used the side of his hand in a sword-strike, felt it caught in mid-air, halted by a grip of iron.

'Take it easy, my friend. Wake up.'

It was Kossori's voice. Moichi opened his eyes.

He left the bed without a word and dressed quickly. Looking back, he saw her sleek skin dappled in moonlight and he leaned over, kissed her lips.

Then they were away.

It was the dead of night. The moon had already long passed the zenith of its nocturnal path. Too low now even for the line of thick stratus, it hung huge and swollen and pale as bone just over the black rooftops, slipping, slipping away towards the horizon. The stars glittered coldly, seeming as close as the moon.

'We shall have to walk,' Kossori said. 'I dare not summon a rickshaw.' He glanced at Moichi. 'Are you all right?'

Moichi forced a laugh but his face was sober. 'Oh, yes. Just – I had a most peculiar dream, that's all.'

There were few people about now, one or two drunks staggering along buildings' walls, a family asleep, huddled in a sheltering doorway, a pair of fragile old men rolling dice. Shadows flitted, larger than life, skittering along the brickwork like a magic lantern show as they drew near night lights, then passed them.

After a time, Kossori said quietly, 'Will you tell me then – about the dream?'

Moichi sighed heavily, still feeling mored in wisps of the nightmare. 'I saw myself on Green Dolphin Street, opposite the alley where Aerent and I found the body of the man from Kintai.' A dog barked and then was still, padding hungrily through the rubbish strewn helter-skelter across an alley somewhere ahead of them. 'I found myself examining that body again but now it seemed – I do not know, it seemed as if I was seeing it in a new light.' A light female voice came to them, wafting from a darkened second-storey window in a building of brick to their left, singing a plaintive Sha'angh'sei folksong in the kubaru dialect.

'What was different this time?' Kossori asked.

'That's just it, I cannot remember.'

He could make out the words now. A tale of lost love.

'Ah, well. Perhaps it is not so important,' Kossori said.

In the village of my birth –
There is a fountain in a square –
Dappled, such a tiny square in among the beech –
It was there I met a man from the sea –
Smelling of rich brine, sea-lace twined about his feet –

'Dreams are often important,' continued Kossori. He shrugged philosophically. 'At other times – who knows?'

I never saw him again, my great mer-man –
Perhaps he slipped away beneath the rolling waves –
But now I am in Sha'angh'sei –
And the sea is always with me –
My mer-man, ah!

They came abreast of a house recently gutted by fire and through the gap could see all the way to the upper reaches of the city. High on the hill, lights still shone brightly in the large mansions of the walled city where the rich hongs lived guarded by the paid protection of the Ching Pang. Here and there, sculptured trees defined themselves in the illumination, taking on an almost celestial corona. Closer to hand, a whippoorwill flitted from tree to tree, calling. Now they had left the human voice far behind.

They turned a corner. A light flared momentarily in an alley; the smell of sweet poppy smoke pungent in the air.

'How did it begin for you,' Moichi asked. 'The *koppo*.' Because he wanted to take his mind off the dream.

Kossori whistled tunelessly for a moment, imitating the whippoorwill, trying to get it to answer him but either it could tell the difference between man and bird or it was gone. Moichi heard the clap-clap cadence of their boots against the gleaming cobbles of the street clear in the night. The moonlight cast shadows as sharp as a sword-edge.

'It was self-defence, in the beginning.' Kossori's voice carried eerily in the stillness; only the cicadas giving concert, even the night birds had disappeared. 'I could never successfully handle a dirk or a sword.' He shrugged. 'After I got beaten into the dirt twice, I had had about enough.' The flames of Sha'angh'sei's night lights were narrow boundaries between which they passed like shades. Beyond, there seemed to be nought but empty space, echoing vertiginously.

'I had no home then,' Kossori continued, 'and I went to the only place I knew well: the bund. When I was younger, I would be there before dawn, watching as the great three- and four-masted schooners manoeuvred into port or weighed anchor, their bellies full of produce, bound for distant shores. And' – here he chuckled – 'I used to imagine myself stowing away far below decks, wedged between the huge sacks of rice where no one would find me, coming out only when we were far out to sea – too far to turn back – and presenting myself to the captain, some tall strong man with a face as tanned as leather, offering to work as a sailor or even a cabin boy to pay for my passage. No matter where we were bound. What difference to me?' He laughed softly. 'But I lacked the guts, then – or, more likely, I had too much common sense even at that age to attempt such a foolhardy adventure. They would have made mincemeat of me.'

He shook his head and began to whistle again, this time the notes heavier, darker, seeming to come at random as if this meandering melody would help summon his past back to him. 'Still, I suppose some things are best left to the imagination, eh?' He pursed his lips, preparatory to whistling, then paused. 'But you asked about the *koppo*. Ah, well. By that time I had already taken a piece of bamboo I had found in the market and was working out the placement of the air holes. It was a crude fliete̅, I admit but I was quite the crude musician, then.' Laughter in a doorway, startlingly close by, abruptly cut off.

'I lived for a time on the ground floor of harttins along the bund, staying just long enough in each one to avoid discovery.' He smiled. 'Once I fell asleep atop enormous sacks of poppy resin and dreamed the dream of emperors.

'The tasstans took me for a while but, of course, there was never enough to go around – of *anything*, food, clothing, you name it. It was heartbreaking and after several times filching half-rotten apples and mouldy mushrooms, I gave it up and never went back to the boats. It was far too depressing a way of life.

'There was nothing for me then. Nothing at all. I wandered about the wharves through the nights, working with the bamboo fliete̅, learning to play it slowly, wonderingly, ecstatically as one learns the body of a cherished lover. Sometimes the night cooks along the bund would hear me and call me in for a meal. But when I tell you that music was my only solace, I am not being melodramatic. And it was only my music which stopped me from tying a stone to my legs and dropping into the harbour.

'During these spells of depression, I would spend long hours trying to reason things out, morbidly returning to that heavy weight which I would certainly need for I knew that I lacked the determination of spirit to voluntarily allow myself to go under and stay there until the water flooded my lungs.' He snorted, an almost derisive sound. 'That, however, was not all idle cerebration. I had actually gone into the water one dark bleak night when I could no longer bear to be alone, when even the stars and the moon ceased to be my friends and it seemed as if I was the only person in all the world; everyone was a million kilometres away, on those cold stars.'

He glanced at Moichi. 'It sounds mad, I know, but the more I thought of it, the more convinced I became that it was real. I began to shiver and before I really knew it, I was stepping off the pier and was going down like lead. Down and down.' He shook his head convulsively. 'That's when I knew it. Down there. It was a hell terrifyingly real. I wanted life – to breathe, to see the moon and stars, the sun, to feel the rain and the wind, to live, to live.

'I struggled to the surface and dug my nails into the slimy wood of the wharf just below the waterline, gaining my breath back. After that, I never truly contemplated suicide; what was waiting for me down there in the deep was far worse than whatever little life held.

'But that was a fortuitous night in my life – No, much more than that. It was a kind of sign, a symbolic turning-point because it was just after that that I met Tsuki.

'I had just come from one of the bund taverns looking for a free meal. Without luck. The one cook who liked me was off that night. I walked back out, strolling along the bund, playing the fliete if only to distract myself from the complaints of my stomach. The moon was full, I remember. A harvest moon, they sometimes call it out in the countryside: flat as a rice-paper disc and as glowing and golden as the sun itself. In retrospect, that was really the strangest part because that's what her name means: the moon.'

Down the street, an ox-cart was approaching, making its slow and creaking way.

'She was red-haired and green-eyed with flecks of a soft brown swimming inside the irises. Her skin was full of freckles, filled with the sun and she was wrapped in a sea-cloak of the deepest blue.' Kossori's eyes had taken on a far-away look and he ignored the rumbling cart as it drew near. 'She smiled when she saw me and stopped, listening to the melody. I still remember it. Want to hear it?' And without waiting for Moichi to reply, he pursed his lips, whistling a meandering tune, as rough and mournful as a barren moor on a chill winter's morn. While it was a far cry from the accomplished complex melodies Kossori composed these days, Moichi nevertheless found within it a haunting quality prefiguring the artist's development.

'Beautiful,' Moichi murmured.

Atop the oncoming cart, a sleepy kubaru sat on the rough wooden bench. Next to him was a hunched figure, asleep perhaps, his hood pulled over his head. The reins were slack in the kubaru's hands as the ox mooched along. A dog, annoyed by the noise, ran out from a doorway, barking at the ox's heels until the kubaru lifted his head and shouted down at the yapping animal. The cart trundled past them, moving as slowly as if it carried within its wooden framework all the world's worries.

'It has a quality, yes,' Kossori said softly as if addressing the wind. He had been silent for a time after the ending of the tune. 'But still the awkward music of a boy.'

'"You play very well," she said to me. And, although I didn't, I was pleased at the compliment. "Who taught you?" she said. I taught myself, I replied. "Really?" she raised one eyebrow. "You have real talent." Now I really didn't believe her and, wondering what she could possibly want from me, said: Now how would you know that, lady? I think perhaps I expected anger but instead she threw back her head and laughed. Then she pulled out the most beautiful fliete̅ I had ever seen. It was wrapped in tar-cloth to protect it from salt air. It was of ebony and all the holes were rimmed with silver. She began to play. I could not in ten thousand years describe to you what she played or how but suffice it to say that she was a virtuoso. "I suppose that now you would like to learn how to play this way." The laughter was still on her face. Yes, I said. Yes I would. "Then come with me and I shall teach you." She lifted up one arm, the sea-cape spreading like a great wave and I was enfolded.'

They had come to the end of the street, a singular occurrence in Sha'angh'sei, where all thoroughfares seemed without real beginning or end. It debouched upon a wide square – one with which Moichi was unfamiliar – surrounded by two-storey dwellings, all with delicate wrought-iron balconies strung in an unending line like some grotesque confection. The square was deserted and, though these buildings were obviously entirely residential in nature, they nevertheless had the appearance of being deserted, an unthinkable actuality in crowded Sha'angh'sei.

'The townhouses of the rich,' Kossori said, as if reading Moichi's mind. 'Many of those who live within the walled city find it convenient to maintain residences in the city's lower reaches – when they want to descend into the mud with the common folk.' He laughed, a harsh, discomforting sound.

How he hates authority in any form, Moichi thought. And how he covets the wealth of the fat hongs who, in truth, rule this city.

Kossori led the way, taking them obliquely across the deserted square from right to left and presently they had plunged back into the twisting labyrinth of the city's streets, taking Purple Peacock Way into Frostlight Lane and thence to Pearling Fast Road. They were very far indeed from the Nanking, Moichi knew, Sha'angh'sei's main thoroughfare. In point of fact, they were a good distance from any well-known landmark.

'She took me to that inn,' Kossori continued, as if there had been no interruption in the flow of his narrative. He was taking his time, Moichi knew. But he was also aware that he was hearing a tale that was both extremely important to Kossori and which, he was quite certain, no other had ever heard. Kossori was an individual of few friends and great reticence. Moichi was being accorded a singular honour and he was careful not to take it too lightly. 'It was the same one where I had been thrown out earlier that evening. Now they were ever so solicitous for, it seemed, Tsuki was well-known here. If she was not from Sha'angh'sei, then she was obviously a frequent visitor –'

'You did not ask her where she was from?'

Kossori glared at him as if he had been asking the other to get ahead of himself. 'No,' he said slowly. 'It never occurred to me to ask.'

Moichi shrugged and remained silent, listening.

'She had them bring food for me. In all my life, I never ate so much nor has food ever tasted so delicious to me. In time, I was sated and we went up a winding rickety staircase, along a dark hall and thence into a warm room with an enormous high down bed against the far wall. Above its covers, a double, leaded-glass window was open onto the now-quiet bund and the ships at anchor just beyond. The scent of the sea was very strong.'

'I can see where this is leading.'

Kossori turned to him. 'No, my friend,' he said quietly. 'I don't believe you do.' He pointed left and they turned off Four Forbidden Road into a tiny crooked lane, seemingly without a name. 'I went to sleep, exhausted.'

The lane had begun to run on a slight incline and Moichi became abruptly aware that they were ascending its winding way up a hill. It was darker here, the narrow houses piled one against the other without surcease. Too, the city's night lights were fading, left behind in the tangle of wider streets and the starlight, where it touched them, gave their faces and hands a slightly bluish cast.

'I awoke late in the night,' Kossori continued, 'when the moon had already gone down. I heard the cry of a gull quite close and that put me in mind of being on a ship far out to sea. I think I even imagined I could feel the pitch and roll of the vessel beneath me. I was still half-asleep and, turning over, I came in contact with her curled body. Her warmth and the scent of her rich musk suffused me. Quite without thinking, I put my arm around her. She stirred and, in her sleep, put her hand against my cheek and neck with such tenderness and a kind of specialness that I cannot adequately describe save to say it was as if I was the first and only person she had ever touched in that manner; I began to weep silent tears. There was an inexplicable tightness in my chest and crying seemed the only way to ease it. She awoke then, by what stroke of magic I still cannot imagine. Her eyes, so close to mine, seemed like the sighting of a far shore through some mysterious telescope. Her kiss was the most beautiful in the world.'

The lane, in its myriad turnings and switchbacks, at length crested, giving out into a rather wide street totally devoid of residential life. Large shops lined both sides without the usual second-storey apartment windows in evidence. Rather, here, the upper levels stared blackly at them, windowless, apparently used for storage only. They paused for a moment.

Moichi was moved by Kossori's story but, beyond that, he found himself shaken by the intensity of emotions he felt being recreated. It had obviously been an enormously powerful union. 'And she taught you to play the fliete̅,' he said.

Kossori nodded. 'That. And the *koppo*.' He pointed to a narrow alleyway running between two shops. 'It is just behind there tonight, the Sha-rida.'

But Moichi grabbed his arm, held him back. 'The black death take the Sha-rida, Kossori! Finish your story.'

Kossori smiled, spread his hands. 'But I have, my friend. I have told you all there is to tell.'

'But what happened to her? Where is she now, this woman of yours?'

Kossori's face darkened. 'Gone, Moichi. Away, very far

away. She disappeared one day as if into the very air. I made inquiries all along the bund but no one had seen her. If she had departed in some ship bound outward into the world, no one knew of it.'

'And she never returned?'

'No,' Kossori said. 'Never.' One hand went to his sash. 'But she left me this.' He lifted out an oilskin case from which he slipped a fliete̅ of ebony and silver.

'Her fliete̅!'

'Yes. And, of course, there's the *koppo*. She was an adept and, as such, well capable of teaching. So now I know how to use my hands to break bones, a feat which, some believe, is sorcerous in nature. Naturally, that's not so. Well, you know that. I've taught you all the basic responses. Those, as you well know, are much easier to learn than the attacks. But here is something I'm quite certain you *don't* know because we have never spoken of it. *Koppo* is nearly three-quarters mental. A gathering of internal energy, a focusing, an application derived through physical means.' He lifted his open hands up.

'Have you ever been in a battle with another *koppo* adept?' Moichi asked. 'I mean a real enemy, not working with a teacher.'

Kossori smiled. 'No. And I doubt I ever will be. There are extremely few *koppo* adepts in the world. Its tradition is ancient yet so shrouded in mystery that it is rare even to find an individual who knows of it, let alone one who practises it.'

'But what would happen,' Moichi persisted, 'if you did come up against one – hypothetically, that is?' And as he asked the question, he wondered what it was that was making him pursue this line of thought.

Kossori shrugged, concentrating. 'I'm not sure, really. I doubt, however, that its outcome would be determined by force. Cunning is the key to victory against a *koppo* adept. And quickness, of course. Such battles, I would imagine, are quite brief, even among adepts. Shock is one of *koppo*'s most potent traits; it's over almost before it begins. But by cunning I mean that one would have to find a way of breaking one's opponent's concentration. A split-instant would be sufficient. Unless one can manage that, there is little hope of surviving such an encounter. You see, the *koppo*'s power is often called mizo-no-tsuki, or, the moon on water. The surface of a river gathers up the moonlight as long as the sky is clear. But should a passing cloud slide across the moon's face, then the light is gone and darkness prevails.' He laughed and clapped Moichi on his back. 'But why be so serious, my friend? You need have no fear. The only *koppo* adept you will meet could never harm you.'

But Moichi did not return the smile for his thoughts were elsewhere. Something Kossori had said, a word, or a phrase, he was not certain which, had triggered off a remembrance, up until now forgotten, from his recent dream.

Light and shadows. It had something to do with – Then he had it and he exclaimed excitedly, gripping Kossori's arms.

'I have it!' he cried. 'I have it! Kossori, the dream I had tonight. It *was* trying to tell me something. In it, I recreated the scene of the real-life discovery of that body. Never mind that one was during the day and the other, night. The *light pattern* was the same. That dappled was deep, disrupting perspective just enough so that I did not know what I was seeing.' He saw Kossori looking at him uncomprehendingly. 'Don't you see? My eyes and therefore my brain picked up all the detail, storing it away. It was only my conscious mind which was fooled. That's why it came out in the dream!'

'What came out in the dream?'

'That man from Kintai,' Moichi said excitedly. 'I think he was killed by *koppo*.'

Circus of Souls

It was a configuration of shabby tents; a five-pointed star. Once, no doubt, they had been gaily coloured but over the years sun and sand and rain and snow had faded the patterns until now they were barely distinguishable.

Circling the tents at irregular intervals were reed torches set into holes carved into the tops of wooden pilasters. These were quite old, their paint and lacquer worn away so that the natural wood grain showed through and this had been smoothed and polished until it shone. The pilasters depicted fierce warriors with great curling beards with glowering expressions and rings through their noses; mermaids with fish-scaled tails wrapped around their bodies, their upper torsos naked and very human, bits of sea shells and periwinkles peeping through their long winding hair; or, again, maidens of war, replete with ornate breastplates and greaves, their calloused hands gripping long spears.

In all, the place had the air of a rather disreputable carnival struggling to survive, an anachronism in the midst of changing time.

They had at last quit Blue Illusion Way, the street of fancy shops and, as they plunged into the utter blackness of the alleyway, Kossori had said to him, 'You must be mistaken, my friend. What you have described to me, what was done to this unfortunate man's heart, is certainly not *koppo*, but a rather extreme, perverse form of torture whose origins are totally unknown to me.'

'I do not mean his heart, Kossori, but rather what was done to the rest of the body. Will you at least take a look at the corpse?'

'Yes, of course. But I doubt I'll confirm your suspicions.'

He shook his head. 'Can't I interest you in something else? Let your friend the Regent pursue this matter of the man from Kintai.'

'No.' Moichi's tone was firm. 'I want to see it through now and, in any event, I promised Aerent.' There was a pinpoint of light now in front of them where the alley apparently ended and he put a hand on his companion's arm, stopping him. 'That reminds me. Aerent would not discuss the Sha-rida with me. What exactly is it? I had assumed it to be merely another of the slave markets which proliferate throughout the city.'

'If that were so, there would be no need to keep its constantly moving location a secret or to hold it only when the moon is down, during that time some call the shallows of night.'

'It is illicit.'

'Illicit, yes.' Kossori laughed. 'As illicit as anything can get in Sha'angh'sei.'

'Aerent said that he meant to eradicate the Sha-rida.'

'Ah, good luck to him, say I.' Kossori breathed deeply of the night. 'Others have tried before him. Even the Greens. It is impossible. Best to forget its existence rather than attempt to destroy it.'

'But why is it so difficult? You knew its location this night. Surely there must be others.'

'Absolutely. And that is what, in the end, assures the Sha-rida's existence.'

'That sounds like a contradictory –'

'Look, my friend, it is not a matter of *how many* people know of the Sha-rida but rather *who* those people are.' He pointed ahead and they began walking again. 'Come. I will show you what I mean.'

Thus they had come upon Ebb Tide Square, a curious name considering how far inland they were. Once, perhaps, it had been the site of fancy apartment dwellings. But these had been abandoned over the years as the structures decayed and rotted until now they were totally unsalvageable as proper houses. Like the ruined stumps of an old man's once strong teeth, shards of brick- and woodwork still stood amongst the mortared and dust-covered detritus.

And in the centre, the flapping tents of the Sha-rida.

If the make-shift structures appeared grubby and filled with patchwork, it was a perfectly practical solution to the clandestine existence of the place, for, as Moichi saw clearly now that they were upon the flapping tents, they were made so that they could be struck in a moment's notice. It would certainly be to the Sha-rida's advantage to be able to pack up and disappear as quickly as possible.

Too, the shabbiness was in sharp contrast to the denizens of the Sha-rida. These were almost to a person swathed in dark anonymous robes or cloaks. But once within the warmth of the tents, they were obliged to let them fall open somewhat and Moichi was startled to see that all of them, men and women alike, were of the wealthiest segment of the city's population.

'They are the only ones who can afford to patronize the Sha-rida,' Kossori told him. 'Now you begin to see why the Sha-rida is virtually invulnerable to any law. It is these selfsame patrons who see to that.'

Moichi glanced discreetly around this largest of the tents, the centre one. There was enough gold, platinum and jewels here, he surmised, to keep the entire kubaru population of Sha'angh'sei, including the vast numbers who lived on the tasstans in the harbour, in food, clothing and shelter for many seasons.

'But what is it,' he asked, 'that they can get here that they cannot obtain at any of the legitimate slave markets?'

'The Sha-rida is a flesh bazaar like no other in the world.' The brazen torchlight illuminated Kossori's dark gleaming skin, highlighting his brooding eyes. 'Here only the most beautiful men and women, young and in perfect health, are sold. And there is but one reason they are bought.'

'Sex?'

'Death.'

For a time, Moichi said nothing, his eyes wandering about the tent which was rapidly filling up now so that they were obliged to move closer together, people now close enough to brush shoulders.

'Why do you come here then?' Moichi said. He felt overcome by shame and he was angry, too, for it was Kossori who had brought him here without telling him what was going to happen.

'I come here every so often to absorb by proximity some of the intense perversity which is its reason for existence.'

'But you brought me here without –'

'My dear friend, I do not remember you taking the time to ask me about the Sha-rida until we were already upon it. And this after the rather explicit warning given you by the Regent.'

Moichi was silent. He is right, he thought gloomily. I cannot blame Kossori for my own lack of responsibility. But was it really that, so simple an answer? He thought not, now. Life, he had found, rarely provides easy answers to anything. That was for plays and such. The real world was far too complex to distil down. Eliminate complexities and you invariably lose meaning. It was, after all, that he had *wanted* to come to the Sha-rida, despite what Aerent had hinted, he concluded.

'Watch, now, Moichi,' he heard Kossori murmur at his side. 'Now it begins.'

Upon a stage at what had been arbitrarily designated the front of the tent, a stage that Moichi had not noticed before now, stood a giant of a man. He was shirtless and the titanic muscles of his arms and chest bulged, glistening in the flickering torchlight as if they had recently been rubbed with oil. This man had no neck. His head, as large and round as a great pumpkin, seemed attached directly to his massive shoulders.

'This night the Sha-rida comes to Sha'angh'sei,' he announced in a voice like a thawed river. 'It is close to morning and before the dawn we will be gone. It is a little time. Yet, too, it is a time for celebration. I am Mao-Mao-shan, master of the Sha-rida, hunter of a flesh beyond the meat of food, beyond the penetration of sex. I, Mao-Mao-shan, am the purveyor of a flesh designed for the ultimate sensations.' He reached out an arm as thick as a treetrunk, sweeping it back theatrically. 'Thus do I direct your attention to the exquisite fruits of my nocturnal labours. For my work is your gain and your only enemy now is the rising of the sun. Please, then behold the coming of the supplicants of the dominion of death!'

It was an effective speech; Moichi felt a slight shiver run through him, though he knew this was but hocus-pocus – extremely artful, he had to admit, but hocus-pocus none the less.

A section of the tent's wall to the left of Mao-Mao-shan ballooned outwards and a man stepped on stage. He was tall, with a finely-muscled body of chocolate brown. His startlingly pale blue eyes stared straight ahead, oblivious to the intense stares of the throng. He wore not a stitch of clothing. Naturally not, Moichi thought. What need had these people to see their potential possessions with clothes on? The thought might have been amusing had not the situation been so hideous.

'Twenty years old,' said Mao-Mao-shan. 'The bidding begins at 400 taels.'

Moichi turned to Kossori, whispered, '400 taels of *silver*?' And when the other nodded, thought, My God, that is a city's ransom.

Movement in the crowd.

Mao-Mao-shan nodded. '400 taels, yes sir. And?' He looked around. Out of the corner of his eye, Moichi saw a thin sandy-haired man in a dark cloak, nod. 'And 450 to you, sir. Very good! We are on our way. But surely, this magnificent soul is worth far more. Why for 450, I could – Ah, yes, madam, thank you. The bid is now 500 –'

Moichi turned around, saw a fiery-eyed woman of indeterminate middle age. She glared at him and he quickly turned back to the spectacle on stage.

So the bidding went on, until it reached a ceiling of 750 taels and the fiery-eyed woman came rustling forward to claim her soul, as Mao-Mao-shan called the chocolate-skinned man. As soon as she had taken possession of the man, the tent wall at Mao-Mao-shan's side ballooned once more and a slender young woman stepped onto centre stage. She was blonde and blue-eyed.

As the bidding began, Moichi turned his head towards his friend, whispered fiercely, 'How can you condone this? It is monstrous!'

'I don't condone it, my friend. I accept it as a part of life. There's a world of difference there.'

The bidding was sluggish and Mao-Mao-shan began to exhort the crowd, regaling them with tales of the woman's fiery nature, fanciful yet effective – the bidding took off in a flurry. He was quite a showman.

'You yourself,' Kossori continued, 'do not believe in slavery, yes? Yet you tolerate it here in Sha'angh'sei. Why?'

'Because – well, I suppose because it's part of the way things are here. I –'

'You see!'

'But the analogy – Kossori, what they do here –'

'Take a look on stage, my friend. No, I mean a good long look. Have you see anyone there who seems to object?'

Now that Kossori mentioned it, it seemed quite a curious thing. None of the souls appeared in the least upset at what was transpiring. Perhaps they did not know. But a quick query of Kossori dispelled that notion.

'No, my friend, all are quite aware of what is to happen to them. It is not the *finding* of the souls which occupies Mao-

Mao-shan's time so much as the *weeding out* of the undesirables.'

The slender woman was sold for 500 taels.

'You mean people queue up to – to die?' Moichi was incredulous.

'That is precisely what I mean.'

'But why? I cannot possibly –'

'Perhaps,' he said quietly, 'it's that they desire release.'

'Now a very special acquisition,' Mao-Mao-shan was saying from his lofty position. There was a soft stirring within the throng as the wall parted and a man appeared. He was not naked but rather was garbed similarly to Mao-Mao-shan. He was barechested, though not nearly so big as the master of the Sha-rida. He wore dark pantaloons and high dusty boots. Around his waist was wrapped a wide sash into which was negligently pushed a curving dirk. This man paused at the edge of the stage and reached backwards, as it were, through the tent, jerking viciously. A woman stumbled after him, out onto the stage.

Immediately, Mao-Mao-shan was into his spiel but Moichi paid him no heed. His eyes were riveted on the female. She was naked as the others had been.

She was tall and a narrow waist accentuated her wide shoulders and flaring hips. Her legs were very long.

'Don't you see?' Kossori said. 'The Sha-rida is part of the embodiment of the liberation of the spirit of mankind –'

She had high cheekbones, a thin-bridged nose with delicate flaring nostrils like some animal at bay. Her defiant eyes were pure cobalt, the deepest blue Moichi had ever seen. Her hair was long, flowing loose over her shoulders, wild and tousled now as if she had been in a struggle. It was the colour of flame.

' – Here the darkest part of the human soul is loosed and assuaged, turned outwards instead of inwards to fester. We all have it inside ourselves, in differing degrees –'

Her legs were the most beautiful Moichi had ever seen. Firmly thighed and lightly muscled, seeming to run on for ever. He lifted his eyes.

' – Here lust and death commingle.'

And his eyes locked with hers for just a moment. A kind of shock travelled through his body until he was certain that his very flesh vibrated. Then the contact was broken. The bidding began, running briskly from almost every quarter of the crowd with but the minimum of intervention from Mao-Mao-shan. He knew a prize when he had one.

What had happened? Moichi asked himself dazedly. Some message had been conveyed across the physical space separating them, across the wider gulf of their different cultures.

The bidding stood at 850 taels, hovering there for some moments. 'Come, come,' Mao-Mao-shan proclaimed. '850 taels of silver is a paltry price to pay for this soul. I can tell you honestly that a soul of this magnitude has not crossed my path in many a season. Now what – Yes sir, my compliments. The bid is now 1,000 taels!'

There was a concerted gasp as the throng reacted to the enormous price and heads craned to catch a glimpse of the bidder. But Moichi was staring straight ahead at the women on the stage. There was something peculiar – her wrists! She had moved slightly as if she too were interested in the person from the crowd who had offered that much silver for her and he could see now that her wrists were tied behind her back. Not only that, but as she shifted further, he observed that she had been working on the hempen bonds, attempting to free herself. He nudged Kossori.

'Eh?'

'I thought you said that all who came here were willing.'

Kossori nodded. 'That's so.'

'Observe yonder,' Moichi said, indicating the woman on stage.

'By the gods! I don't understand –'

The bidding resumed. A rather elderly woman with a desiccated face upped the price to 1,200 and a voice boomed out within the tent, shouting angrily, '1,500!'

Now Moichi turned to look for it was the same individual who had caused such a stir with his 1,000 tael bid. He saw, within the crush of bodies, a tall man in a black cloak which covered him from head to boot-top. Moichi could not make out any features for the light was poor in that direction and the man had kept his hood pulled up. Yet he was readily distinguishable from those about him for he stood at least a quarter of a metre taller than any of them.

'1,800,' called the desiccated woman.

The tall man shouldered his way forward, brushing protesting people from his path. He lifted his head to call out, '2,000 taels, by the god of iron!' And Moichi thought he saw a cold glitter emanating from within the hood as if the light had caught the lens of an eye.

Moichi turned back to the stage and found the woman staring at him. And now he knew the content of her message.

'2,500 taels!' he bawled, to make certain all could hear him

'What!' Kossori caught his arm. 'What are you about? Are you mad? You don't have that kind of –'

'2,700!'

Moichi did not have to turn around to know the voice of the hooded man. He was closer now, edging towards where they stood, hard by the stage.

'3,000!' Moichi called.

'3,100!' Then, in a lower tone, 'You disgusting slime, if you make another bid, I'll –'

'Hey, you – !' Kossori had turned around to confront the tall man.

While Moichi called out, '3,500 taels!'

There was movement behind him, as the hooded man fought the throng to get to him, hissing, 'I warned you – now

– Out of my way, scum!'

But now it did not matter because Moichi had given the woman on stage enough time. She had slipped her bonds and, in a flash, had torn the dirk from her captor's sash, having used the scuffle in the crowd as a distraction.

Without a moment's hesitation, she plunged the full length of the curving blade into the man's flesh, slipping it deftly between the third and fourth ribs on his right side.

There was so much noise now that Moichi could not hear his cry but he was already moving. 'Come on!' he called to Kossori and, aware that the other was following him, he leaped upwards, found a shoulder in the now densely-packed crowd to launch him onto the stage.

So stunned was Mao-Mao-shan at this unseemly and singular conduct that he failed to react to Moichi's presence until it was far too late. Moichi hooked a boot behind the huge man's ankle and pulled. Mao-Mao-shan went down like the side of a house.

Moichi put his arm protectively around the woman's bare waist, feeling her warmth. Kossori was with him and as they made for the opening in the tent's wall, he glanced out into the crowd. There his gaze alighted on the tall man who was flinging people from him as he made his way towards the stage. He was bellowing something that Moichi could not make out for the din. He had expected to see a sword in the man's hand by now or, at the least, some other weapon but the hooded man's hands were empty.

Then they were throught the wall and into one of the smaller, dimly-lit satellite tents. This one, obviously, was where they held the souls to be bought because it was filled with young men and women, all handsome, all perfect, ready to be possessed, as Mao-Mao-shan would say.

The trio ran through this milling bunch, who stared at them blankly, murmuring to each other. Outside, the night was cool. Some of the torches surmounting the ring of carved pilasters had guttered and gone out and Moichi led them across the ruins of Ebb Tide Square, towards a darkened section of the perimeter.

He found the alley and they fled down this ebony path, the sounds of their boot-soles beating back for the moment the clatter of the pursuit. Moichi was certain who would be leading that pursuit and it was not Mao-Mao-shan.

'This is madness!' Kossori panted as they ran. 'How could you have –'

'Save your breath, my friend,' Moichi said. 'What is done is done.' They were coming up on Blue Illusion Way and Moichi knew that they were going to need some of that in order to escape the man in the black hood. Sounds echoed back at them in the narrow alley as the men from the Sharida entered the alley. 'Anyway, I doubt you would have allowed her to be sold to death, knowing she was being held prisoner.'

'All right, all right.' Kossori brought them up sharply as they entered the wide streets of shops. 'There's little time so a debate is inappropriate now.' Echoes behind them, gaining rapidly. 'Take the girl right. A block then take a sharp left. You'll know how to get home from there.'

'But what about you?' Breath hot in his lungs; shouts from behind them in the blackness of the alley. At least they had stopped out of the line of sight of their pursuers.

'Never mind me.' Kossori waggled a hand in the air. 'I will decoy them. Now go. Quickly. For this to succeed, they must believe you and the girl are in front of me.'

'But –'

'Go on now. Go on. In a moment it will be too late and we shall all be caught like fish in a net. Off with you now.'

Moichi grasped the woman's hand, hurling them both down Blue Illusion Way, aptly named, he hoped. At the corner, he resisted the temptation to look back, rushed them both into the concealing shadows of the cross-street. Looking up, as they ran on, he found he indeed did know which way to go and, orienting, he pushed them onwards down black back alleys with the squealing rats leaping from their path, along brightly-lit streets and across tree-shadowed squares. Until, at length, they broke out onto the Nanking and Moichi hailed a passing rickshaw. He was obliged to shout twice for the sleepy kubaru woman appeared not to hear him at first. He launched the woman unceremoniously into the covered section, leapt in beside her and gave the street address of his harttin. As they began to move, he slipped off his cloak, covering the shivering woman and her magnificent nakedness.

They jounced along into the night.

'Aufeya.'

He watched the play of muscles beneath the silk: the strength of her thighs, the tautness of her buttocks.

'A pretty name.'

She turned to face him, watchful yet totally unafraid. Like some great mythical feline she was filled with a dynamic animalism.

'What are you looking at?' she demanded. 'Have you never seen a woman before?'

Moichi went across the long room to the desk, poured them both wine. He turned, holding one cup out to her. Her eyes never left his; she made no move. He shrugged, put the cup down, sipped at his.

'Have you –'

'I will answer no question,' she cut him off. 'Do not be so foolish as to think that because of what happened back there, I owe you anything.'

He went back, near her, sweeping aside the closed jalousies so that the bund, quiet at this early hour, and the peaceful harbour beyond, were exposed. It was still quite dark, dawn some time away yet, but small lit lanterns swung from spars like indecisive fireflies, dispersing the blackness here and there.

'If you had waited until I had finished,' he told her, 'you

would have known that I asked no question. I was about to say, have you ever seen anything more beautiful?'

Slowly, almost reluctantly, as if she half-expected it to be some kind of ruse, she turned her head away from him, gazing out at the harttin's view.

Moichi passed her, stepping out onto the veranda and, a moment later, Aufeya followed.

The air was very clear and even the minute sounds of the night carried, the faces of the long line of harttin acting as a sounding board. He could hear the click-click of dice being thrown; the creaking of ships' fittings and, a long way off, the vague singsong of a kubaru's worksong. Closer at hand he could discern the patter of liquid as someone, undoubtedly too full of liquor, urinated against the side of the building.

'What is a – harttin?' Aufeya asked.

'It is the Sha'angh'sei term for a trading warehouse. All the wealthy hongs have harttins in which to store their produce as it is off-loaded from incoming ships or awaiting exportation.'

'And this is your harttin?'

'No. It belongs to Llowan, the bundsman of Sha'angh'sei.'

'Then what are you doing here?'

'Waiting.' He went to the outer railing, leaned his forearms upon it. Masts rose blackly before him, combining with crosstrees and furled shrouds, taut ratlines and rigging, to give the scene a surreal geometric overlay.

Aufeya took two steps towards him, paused, like a doe scenting water but unsure of what might lurk within the foliage lining its bank. 'Waiting for what?'

'For a ship, *querhida*.' He saw her stiffen, staring at him, but she was silent. 'A ship to sail home to Iskael.'

'Are you – You are a captain, or what?'

'A captain?' He smiled. 'No, I am a navigator.' He turned away, his thoughts seemingly far away over the breast of the sea.

She regarded him for a time, her cobalt eyes as black as coal. He did not see it, but she trembled ever so slightly, her head shaking and she slipped her hands into the crooks of her arms, folding them just below her high firm breasts as if trying to hold herself together. The terror had come upon her again just after the storm had driven her small lorcha off-course and into port. It was a rugged craft but built expressly for sailing along the coast; it was not an ocean-going vessel and thus could not withstand a fierce gale without the protection of a harbour in which to ride it out.

She was dismayed to find that they had come upon Sha'angh'sei. A horrendous mistake but unavoidable now. Beyond the port's limits the storm still raged; they had no choice but to stay until the gale moved on or spent itself here.

The storm had divested them of some sorely-needed supplies and she had gone ashore to restock. That was when the man in the black cloak had found her. Terrified, she had run from him – and straight into the arms of Mao-Mao-shan. Thus she had been taken for the Sha-rida. It was but a clever ploy, she knew. In Sha'angh'sei, the open place where nothing could be hidden, the man in the black cloak could not seize her directly without incurring repercussions he could ill afford. Thus he had made a deal with Mao-Mao-shan. She had seen them talking, knowing that the man in the black cloak was paying for her in advance. Her auction at the Sha-rida that night would be a sham for she had already been sold. Then had come the intervention of this man and his friend. Fortuitous to say the least. But was it? She knew the deviousness of the man in the black cloak all too well. Was this but another ruse of his? She would, of course, be more inclined to talk to a friendly face. How could she be certain? She shivered again, involuntarily, as she thought of the man in the black cloak and his vengeance. Dihos, what a fool she had been! But now the end had come. No, she told herself sternly, not the end. *An* end. What that would be was still in doubt and she was going to do her best to see that she had, at least, some say in its formation.

'You said you are from a land called Iskael,' she said so abruptly that he turned his head towards her. 'Tell me about it. Where is it, for instance?'

'Far to the south,' Moichi said. 'Farther even than Ama-no-mori.'

She snorted derisively. 'Ama-no-mori is but legend.'

He shook his head. 'Have you never heard of the Dai-San?'

'Of course, everyone has.'

'He is my friend and he lives there now.' He raised a hand as if brushing an insect out of the air. 'But that is of no matter. Iskael is a land of a hot sun filled with rolling deserts and rich orchards and the highest mountains in the world, dominated by one peak, taller than all the others. It is said, in the sacred tablets of my people that this mountain was made by the hand of God.'

'Your people believe in one God?'

'Yes, *querhida*.'

She stiffened and backed away. 'You said it again.' Her voice was a tightly-coiled whisper. 'You are playing with me. You knew all along.' She was backed against the far railing, her hands gripping the wooden rim with such force that her knuckles were blue-white. 'You work for him.'

He heard the near-hysteria in her voice now, knew she was on the edge, stupidly took a step towards her. 'No, I promise I –'

'I will die first,' she cried and, whirling, launched herself over the railing.

Moichi leapt, wrapping his arms about her legs while she was in mid-air. Her forward momentum carried him into the railing, the top bar slamming into his stomach so that he bent over, the air rushing out of him. He almost lost her then but he gathered his strength and hauled her in, back onto the safety of the veranda. But he was off-balance and still somewhat out of breath and her planted heel on the back of his instep caught him by surprise. He lurched backwards with her on top of him, felt her slim elbow drive powerfully into his side.

She fell on him, twisting, trying to get leverage and now he knew that words were useless. The heel of her hand smashed against his shoulder but it opened her up and his right hand shot upwards, straight as a lance, the blow to her cheek stunning her so that she fell limply at his side, mouth hanging open, eyes glazed and by the time she recovered he had made certain she was a captive audience.

'Listen to me, Aufeya,' he said calmly as she began to struggle. 'Listen to me and I will let you up.'

'I make no bargains with my enemies.' Her eyes were on fire and if looks could kill, he would be a charred corpse.

He slapped her across the face. 'Will you stop for a moment!'

She stuck her neck out, tried to bite him. 'Get away from me!' she screamed. 'Get away! I will listen to none of your lies! Your tongue is like honey but I know who pays you – !'

Exasperated, without thinking, he leaned forward, putting his mouth over hers. But what had begun as a means of shutting her up soon changed. He felt her lips, cool and moist, under his and there was a slight taste like cinnamon, tart and sweet at the same time, as if she had just eaten a ripe apple. And he felt the same kind of current pass through him that he had experienced when her gaze had first struck him in the Sha-rida.

Perhaps she felt it too, for her eyes flew open watching him, several expressions darting across her features. 'What – What are you doing?' she whispered in a husky voice when he pulled his lips away.

Moichi cleared his throat, unconsciously relaxed his grip. 'I meant only to silence y –' He began to move but she already held one of his own dirks at his throat. He lay perfectly still, feeling intensely her body lying half-atop his, her heat in proximity, the heavy heaving of her breasts so close beneath the thin layer of silk. There had not been sufficient exertion and, looking into her eyes, catching a hint of the struggle there, he knew that she too had felt the certain magnetism.

'Now tell me the truth.' Her voice was still low and thick with suppressed emotion.

'Or you will slit my throat?' he inquired.

She said nothing, merely moved the blade of the dirk a fraction closer to the tendons of his throat.

'You have already heard the truth from me, Aufeya.'

'I warn you, do not fool with me!' Now the razor-sharp edge of the blade commenced to crease the skin. 'You knew I am a Daluz'. How could that be if you do not work for *him*?'

'I do not even know who "him" is.' He felt the trickle of blood even though the blade itself was out of his line of sight and he had not actually felt the thing moving. 'I am a navigator, remember? I have been to many parts of the world. I have been to Dalucia twice. Daluzan names are unforgettable. I knew the moment you told me yours.'

She seemed to ignore this last and he became concerned that her hysteria had narrowed her perception to such an extent that she now would hear only what she wanted to hear.

'Where in Dalucia?' Voice as tight as a strung bow, pulled back, waiting for release. He had the uncomfortable impression that the arrow was pointed directly at him.

'The port of Corruña. We were bringing cedar and silks.'

'*Describame la puerta della Corruña*,' she snapped in idomatic Daluzan. '*Jao de Corruña*.'

So she came from that city; it was the capital of Dalucia, he knew. He told her everything he could remember about the harbour.

She tossed her head, hair like a burnished metal crown, even in this darkness. 'This means nothing. If you are in his pay, you are sure to be well coached.'

'My God, Aufeya, what do you want of me?'

'The truth, only.'

'Who is this man you speak of –'

'*I* ask the questions!' she snapped.

'As you wish.'

'Yes, as I wish.' She paused as if considering. 'Why should I waste my time explaining to you what you already know?'

'Perhaps I do not know it.'

She came to a decision, let him sit up against a section of closed jalousies; the point of the dirk hovered close, ready to strike should he attempt to attack her.

Behind her silhouette, he could see a thin line of pink begin to spread itself along the far horizon, broken in myriad places by the hulls of the ships at anchor. Grey was in the sky now, bleaching back the darkness and he could feel rather than see the wheel of the gulls. Soon they would be calling, calling to the ascendant sun. 'This is my favourite time of day, the dawn,' Moichi said. 'Hour of the cormorant, we call it at sea.' He thought of his appointment with Aerent and the visiting Bujun girl. He would have to be going soon.

She watched him carefully. 'If you had a ship, you would go home to Iskael. That is what you said.'

'Did I?' He was surprised. 'How odd. No. First I would go to Kintai.'

It was as if he had delivered a physical blow, so shaken was she. But she recovered enough to say, 'What do you know of Kintai?'

'Nothing,' he said, spreading his hands. 'In truth, I only learned of its existence this morning. If you know something of the place I would be obliged –'

'How did you hear of it?' The tension had returned abruptly and he was wary again.

'There was a murder here last night. One of many, I have no doubt. But this matter is altogether out of the ordinary. Two disparate men were killed by disparate methods. One, the son of the tai-pan of the Ching Pang was slain by a professional and highly proficient swordsman. The other was tortured horribly. He was killed, I believe, by an arcane and ancient art known as *koppo*.' He paused here to observe what effect, if any, his words were having on her. Her eyes had gone dead, seemed now as flat and opaque as stones drying in the sun. 'This man was an outlander. He came, we believe, from Kintai.' She was on her haunches, her gaze turned inwards. He could now have disarmed her with the minimum of personal risk. Yet, curiously, he decided to remain motionless. 'I think we can help each other, Aufeya. It seems more than coincidence that has thrown us together.'

Her eyes focused on him but she said nothing.

'Will you tell me about the man now? I truly know nothing of him.'

'His name is Hellsturm,' she said finally, her voice containing a strange metallic edge, 'and he has pursued me for ten thousand leagues. Now, if I believe what you have just told me, only I am left now to stand against him. He has murdered Cascaras.'

'You mean the man from Kintai?'

She nodded. 'Kintai was where he had just come from, where he had been searching for – He is – Daluzan, like me. A trader.'

'But what – ?'

'It is the man in the black cloak. The one you bid against. He is Hellsturm.'

'And he killed the man from – He killed Cascaras?'

She nodded again. 'It could only be him.' Her free hand curled into a tight fist, pounded her knee. 'Oh, how he must have gloated to see me here! It was that cursed storm! I should never have been near Sha'angh'sei. Cascaras and I had split up, he to come here to hide and I – Well, it does not matter now.'

'It matters a great deal, Aufeya.' He stretched out a hand, palm upwards. 'Won't you give me the dirk now?'

'No,' she said. 'No, I believe – I believe I can trust you

now but I don't know this place. I will feel safer if I keep it for a while.'

'All right,' he said. 'Keep it as long as you like.'

She put it away within the silk pants he had given her. They were a spare pair of Llowan's work pants which he had liberated on their way upstairs as they came into the harttin. His would have been far too big on her.

The sea was awash in pink and pale yellow as, abruptly, the sun heaved its top over the horizon. True to form, the gulls began their crying as they dipped towards the sea's flat face, searching out their breakfast. Their melancholy calling filled the air.

'You said Cascaras was tortured,' Aufeya said. 'How bad was it, do you think?'

'As bad as it could possibly be, I'm afraid.' He described to her what they had discovered.

She shuddered and some of the life seemed to go out of her for a moment. 'Then I must assume that Hellsturm has broken Cascaras, that he is now in possession of Cascaras's half of the information.'

'Information about what? Is there some form of attack being planned against Sha'angh'sei?' he asked, echoing Aerent's fear.

Aufeya laughed harshly. 'Oh, no!' she said. 'Nothing so mundane, I assure you.'

Below them, along the bund, sounds were starting up at such a rapid pace that they quickly began to overlap one another, the commencement of another day's city serenade. An armada of fishing boats was already out at sea, having successfully avoided the clogged shipping lanes through which laden clippers and schooners from the world of man were now manoeuvring in order to take the spaces dockside vacated by ships which had spent the night in the harbour, and now, fully loaded, had raised canvas and weighed anchor just before first light. These passed each other in a stately quotidian dance, making up much of the morning's routine.

He had so many questions to ask her and so little time in which to ascertain the answers. In fact, he realized guiltily, he had no time at all. The hour of the cormorant was here and he must be off. No matter how much he wished to stay with Aufeya, he had his duty to think of, not only to the Regent but to the Dai-San himself.

'I want you to stay here,' he said, standing up. He could hear the movement downstairs, of the kubaru and the stevedores. He thought briefly about asking Llowan for help but almost immediately realized that would be an unfair request. The bundsman already had more to do than he had time in which to work each day. And anyway, Kossori would be better able to handle Aufeya's protection until he could return. And return he would, as quickly as possible, with Aerent in tow.

Aufeya rose also, her beautiful face troubled. 'Where are you going?' Her hand instinctively reached into her pants for the hilt of the dirk.

'I have an appointment. An official one, I am afraid, and it is one I dare not miss.'

'Then let me go with you.'

'No, I am sorry, Aufeya, that is impossible. This is an affair of state.'

'I won't stay here alone.' The fire had come back into her eyes and he was thankful for that. She was quite a capable individual when aroused. He smiled to himself at the double meaning.

'I do not mean you to stay alone, although I am quite certain that this is the safest place in all of Sha'angh'sei for you now. Kossori will guard you until I return. He was with me last night at the Sha-rida.'

'The man who decoyed Hellsturm and the others.' She nodded. 'Yes, quite clever. But what has taken him so long?'

'He would not risk coming here until dawn brought out the city's crowds. There was a chance they might try to follow him once they realized we were not with him.'

There was a clatter on the stairs, as if on cue. Aufeya drew the dirk with lightning speed and even Moichi, who was certain he knew who was climbing the stairs, felt his hand close about the hilt of his sword.

But it was indeed Kossori and he relaxed visibly, making the obligatory introductions. There was no time for more than that. As his friend went to the desk, downing the wine Moichi had poured for Aufeya, he told him he would be back as soon as he could and not to let Aufeya out of his sight until then.

'You had no trouble slipping away?' he asked.

'I led them a merry chase, my friend, you can be sure,' Kossori replied, pouring himself another cup of wine, downing this too. 'All the way to the Tejira Quarter then down to the Serpentine.' He sighed, turning to face them. 'I have had a most tiring night, my friend.' He grinned wolfishly as he eyed Aufeya. 'And I see, as a hero, I am about to get my just reward.'

Moichi laughed shortly. 'I would not be so anxious to try this one out, Kossori. She is as deadly as a snow wolf.'

'Is that so?' Kossori eyed her even more keenly. 'The more arduous the chase, the keener one enjoys the spoils, eh?'

Aufeya was still brandishing the dirk and Moichi went over to her. 'Pay him no mind. He is in rare good humour over this night's sport.'

'Sport?' she cried. 'We are most deadly serious here. You cannot imagine the import of what has transpired.'

'No, not yet,' Moichi agreed with her. 'But we shall soon enough, I promise you. Just as soon as I return from Three Kegs Pier. Nothing will happen while Kossori is here. A better protector in Sha'angh'sei you could not find.' He changed rapidly into a fine honey-coloured silk shirt with open neck and wide sleeves, tight rust-coloured calfskin breeches. In the midst of this elegant garb, his old tattooed scabbard seemed out of place indeed.

He put his arm around Aufeya's shoulders, took her back out onto the veranda. They stood by the far railing. In the harbour, an enormous four-masted schooner, known as a globe-spanner in sailor's vernacular, was manoeuvring slowly towards one of the long wharves reserved for just such behemoths. Even with fully half its canvas furled, it was a magnificent sight, guided as it was by a trio of Sha'angh'sei's harbour boats, dwarfed like toys beside its grandeur.

'Aufeya,' he said softly. 'I will not be gone long.' Looking into her eyes was a task now and he wrenched his gaze away with an effort. 'I want to ask you something before I leave. Did you – Did you feel it also? Last night at the Sha-rida? And then – when our lips touched just before?'

He was still conscious of his dirk in her left hand; it hung down loosely, its point towards the wooden boards of the floor.

She lifted her right arm and her fingers touched the contour of his cheek, tracing it. 'We are unique in this land, you and I, Moichi.' It was the first time she had used his name and he felt a shiver pass through him. 'We are both children of the one God. These heathens of Sha'angh'sei worship many gods – as do most of the people of the world of man. Many gods must dissipate power, don't you think? Some others believe in no God at all. Surely this is not good.' Her hand was at her side again but his skin still tingled where she had brushed it with her fingertips. No one had ever conveyed so much in such a simple common gesture. 'I had thought the Daluzan were the only people left who believed in the one God. Now I find you. Surely this cannot be coincidence.'

'I do not believe in coincidence.'

'What do you think it is then?'

'Sei,' he said and noted her uncomprehending look. 'The Bujun call it karma. There are many words for it, I imagine.

Part of the life-force which brings people together at a certain time and place. For some reason.'

'What is the reason with us?'

He traced the features of her face with his eyes, resting for a moment on the half-open lips, rose-coloured and shiny. Impulsively, he leaned towards her and kissed her. Then, surprised, he found her arms reaching up around his neck, the kiss prolonged, intensified, her body warm all along the length of his own.

'Go now,' she said, standing primly back. She shook her hair, copper where the sunlight struck it. *'Vejira con Dihos.'* And he saw her eyes glowing with the enormous fear she felt for the man Hellsturm. She struggled hard to suppress it and only because he was so close –

She went with him, back into the room. Kossori watched them silently, as they parted and Moichi went quickly down the stairs.

He looked back just before the floor cut off his line of sight, saw her standing in the centre of the room with the new morning's light spilling all around her, seeming to him, a physical manifestation of the invisible aura she possessed. Her eyes met his just before he disappeared down the stairwell but the confluence of emotions he saw there confounded him all the way to his assignation.

Snatch

Three Kegs Pier was quite a distance down the bund from Llowan's harttin but, once outside, Moichi resigned himself to walking. A rickshaw was out of the question though he passed several vacant ones. These were cruising in search of those new to Sha'angh'sei, just off the docking ships, who would not know any better. Not only was walking far faster in the early morning crush of sweating kubaru, hustling sailors, stevedores, knots of passengers, fat hongs and their representatives and bodyguards, and the inevitable giōmu, the sidewalk merchants who moved from pier to pier as passengers disembarked, but it was definitely cheaper since the hiring of a rickshaw was based on time, not distance. Time was, quite literally, money for the kubaru.

It was the beginning of a fine day. The air was clear, completely devoid of the haze which enveloped the city, to a greater or lesser extent, each evening. The sky was white where the lemon sun burned, still fairly low on the horizon but, aloft, the curving vault of the heavens was a deep endless blue; traces of white puffy clouds trailed like unfurled sails here and there.

As he shouldered his way along the bund, Moichi became engrossed in the seemingly endless riddle into which he had quite unsuspectingly plunged. What had begun as an apparently simple act of reprisal now had become something more complex and, it was being made clear to him, sinister.

If Aufeya was right, he had discovered the identity of the murderer. But knowing who he was and running him to ground were two different matters, he knew. The man, Hellsturm, had all of Sha'angh'sei within which to secrete himself. But as long as Aufeya was also hidden here, he would not leave. Apparently, Cascaras had but one half of the information Hellsturm wanted. He would stay in Sha'angh'sei until he got it, or until Moichi captured him. In this, he knew, Aufeya could be most helpful. In fact without her, he would have no clue to where to find the man in the black cloak for, he realized now, he had no idea what Hellsturm looked like; he knew only that he was tall, hardly enough information to set about finding him in this awesome labyrinth. But Moichi possessed the real trump – Aufeya. For Hellsturm wanted her – desperately, if one could judge by the distance he had pursued her.

He had still been filled with Aufeya's aura as he had come down the stairs into the harttin's busy commercial area. Briefly, he filled Llowan in on who was upstairs and why. Then telling the bundsman where he was headed, he stepped outside.

He was almost within sight of Three Kegs Pier now and he was close enough to see that the Bujun ship had not yet docked. He breathed a sigh of relief. If he hurried, he might have time to give Aerent some of the more important details of what had transpired this past evening.

Briefly, his thoughts turned back to Aufeya. He would have preferred not to leave her but he knew that even had he been able to take her with him, she would be in more danger out here. Hellsturm, he was quite certain, had not come to Sha'angh'sei on his own. Over and above the fact that the murders in the Screaming Monkey indicated that there had been two attackers, he was sure he had seen others moving to Hellsturm's command just before he had ducked out of the main tent in the Sha-rida. In this respect, Aufeya had been correct. Sha'angh'sei was too much of an open place – despite the intricate webs of secrecy which inundated it – for outlanders. But this could work both ways. While Hellsturm was obliged to work circumspectly to capture Aufeya he could, by the same token, take advantage of the city's enormously effective spy network to aid him in finding out where she was hiding. No, all things considered, the harttin was the safest place for her. And there was Kossori. Moichi would rather have him guarding Aufeya than a score of Ching Pang.

With that, he cleared his mind of the matter and prepared himself to meet the daughter of the Kunshin.

The Regent was awaiting him, three-quarters of the way out on Three Kegs Pier. The pier itself was clogged with kubaru runners and stevedores preparing for the Bujun ship's arrival. Because the vessel was not a merchantman, there were no hongs or shipping agents about. Which was lucky, Moichi saw now, as he went carefully along the wooden planks. Their space and more had been taken up by a military guard of honour fully three pilings in length.

As he passed their glistening, fastidiously-pruned ranks, he came upon Aerent who was gazing out to sea, presumably in the direction of the coming ship. He held his hands behind his back and this pose, combined with the brilliantly shining dress breastplate with its plumed shoulder-guards, caused him to appear once again as the commanding rikkagin of the forces of mankind.

'Hola, Aerent!' Moichi called.

The Regent spun around on his ruby legs. The sunlight, lancing through them, made them seem eerily translucent, causing him to cast a crimson shadow.

Aerent smiled. 'Ah, good morn. Good morn.' He unclasped his hands from behind his back, rubbed at the side of his nose. 'And how did you find the Sha-rida? To your taste, perhaps?'

Moichi laughed. 'No, Regent, I think not when all is said. Still' – he cocked his head – 'there are some good elements to it.'

Aerent's face darkened as he said, 'Tell me one then.'

'It was at the Sha-rida that I found out who murdered Omojiru and the man from Kintai.' This was not, strictly speaking, quite true for he had found out about Hellsturm *after* leaving the Sha-rida. But he could not pass up the opportunity to consternate Aerent.

The Regent's surprise was evident and Moichi began to outline what little Aufeya had told him. At that moment, they heard a sharp cry from the far end of the pier and both turned. A lookout had his hands cupped to his mouth. 'Here she comes!' he cried and, turning, pointed into the sunrise. Sure enough, as they squinted against the light dazzle, the sails and masts and then, only moments later, the bow of the *Tsubasa* could be made out as the Bujun ship appeared over the horizon.

Moichi, staring longer at the vessel than the Regent, drew in his breath involuntarily. 'Look at that, Aerent!' he said excitedly. 'She fairly flies over the water as if she were a winged creature.' And Aerent, looking again, saw that this was true. The *Tsubasa* which had, just before, been at the limit of their vision now had leapt into prominence.

'Where is this Daluzan woman now, Moichi?' the Regent inquired.

'She is quite safe at the harttin.' He was about to add that Kossori was with her when he remembered that his friend did not know of the musician's martial prowess.

'Clearly we must interview her as quickly as possible.' He rubbed at his beard. 'This Bujun arrival has come at an accursedly inconvenient time in light of what you have just told me. Well, there's nothing for it but to make the best of it. We cannot afford to offend the Kunshin's daughter, can we? I have been informed that she is carrying a communiqué from the Dai-San. I daresay you will be interested in that, my friend.'

There was a contained rustling behind them from the military contingent on loan from several of the city's ranking rikkagin as the *Tsubasa* hove to just outside the harbour's limits. She had cut sail drastically and now seemed to float majestically upon the water, patiently awaiting a sea lane opening into port.

She was a most beautiful vessel, Moichi thought. Sleek, somewhat slimmer than the oceangoing schooners common to the Sha'angh'sei area. Her upper hull was painted a glossy black from the sheer-strake to just above the waterline where a thin gold band separated it from the vermilion of the lower hull. Its bow was high and curving with the figurehead of a cock. This was, he knew, the Bujun symbol for growth and exploration.

'This woman is Daluzan and the man in the alley was, too,' Aerent mused. 'Moichi, did you know that Kintai is on the northwest borders of Dalucia?'

Moichi turned from the Bujun ship, making its painstaking way into the harbour with the aid of a small Sha'angh'sei escort boat, to look at the Regent. 'Interesting. It appears as if I should take my leave of this place after all, Aerent.'

'With the Kunshin's daughter just about to arrive? Impossible.'

'Why? You can take care of her, surely.'

'In any case, it is a moot point, don't you think? You have no ship.'

'I do now,' Moichi said. 'Aufeya's lorcha. I mean to sail it north to Dalucia.'

'And what of this man, Hellsturm? I want him.'

'As do I, Aerent. And Aufeya is my means to trap him.'

'Uhm. Risky, that. The woman –'

'The quicker we get him, the easier it will be for her.'

The *Tsubasa* was nosing into Three Kegs Pier now and kubaru and stevedore alike rushed to and fro along the length of the wharf, handling the thick hempen ropes thrown down to them by the Bujun crew. They hauled on these ropes, lifting their voices in singsong litany, working in concert, in time to the music, at length securing them to the thick metal stanchions along the wharf. This was one of the many incalculable benefits which made Sha'angh'sei the most important as well as the wealthiest port on the continent of man. Its waters were deep enough quite close in so that large vessels – even the four-masted behemoths – need not stand off at a safe distance from shore and ferry their cargo to the mainland. Ships were loaded and off-loaded directly at the piers thus saving time and money. At Khiyan, for instance, where Moichi and the Dai-San had embarked aboard the *Kioku* for their voyage south, this had not been possible; the ship, standing off, had had to send a longboat in to pick them up.

The shuddering of the pier brought him out of his thoughts. Timbers creaked and wavelets lashed at the wooden pilings beneath them. The *Tsubasa* had docked.

Chiisai was an apt name for her.

She was the only daughter of the Kunshin and she looked like a flower. Moichi had no idea what her name meant but what he thought of the moment he saw her appear on the high poop deck above him was a plum blossom. Dark and vibrant.

She was small, he saw, as she approached them, coming slowly down the ornamental gangplank, stepping onto the pier to meet them. But that, he soon found, was deceiving for she was no girl but a full-blown woman.

She had a delicate flower-petal face with long, dark almond-shaped eyes and the high cheekbones of the Bujun. Her mouth was wide and sensual, which was unusual. She wore the wooden clogs used for ceremonies and she was garbed in a silk robe reaching down to the tops of her feet. It was pure white, perfectly dazzling in the strong sunlight. Embroidered upon it were a series of leaping flying fish in a pale blue-green.

This was all as it should be. But as she came to a halt before them and bowed, they bowing back in turn, Moichi became aware of something odd about her appearance. For a moment, he was quite at a loss to define it. Then, abruptly and with somewhat of a shock, he saw that her hair was bound in the traditional Bujun queue usually reserved for the male warriors.

Two tall Bujun stood still as statues at either side of the upper end of the gangplank, still on the ship. No one had accompanied her down. This, too, seemed odd for this was the Kunshin's daughter.

She smiled. 'Aerent, Regent of Sha'angh'sei, I bring greetings from my father, the Kunshin, from all the peoples of Ama-no-mori and from the Dai-San. We wish you well in your new post and offer our congratulations.' She lifted out a small wooden box sealed all around its edges with pitch to keep out the moist salt air. Upon its top was imprinted in platinum the seal of the Kunshin of the Bujun, three plovers in full flight within the circle of the world. 'With all our good wishes.' She extended the box towards him.

Aerent, Moichi saw, had been taken somewhat by surprise. Now, as he took the gift from her, he seemed very moved.

'Thank you, Chiisai. It is an honour to receive such a token.'

'Oh, it is no token, Regent, I assure you.' Chiisai said. Her eyes were still laughing. 'Will you not open it?'

Aerent complied, using the edge of his dirk to slit through the congealed pitch. He prised open the lid of the box and stared inside. He was quite still for several moments. Then he carefully lifted out the platinum ring. It was a setting of exquisite manufacture, the set-piece of Ama-no-mori's finest metalsmith. Within the setting sat a perfect pearl.

Into the stunned silence, Chiisai said innocently, 'My father felt that this was a fitting gift for the ruler of the greatest seaport in all the known world.'

Slipping the ring upon the fourth finger of his left hand – his heart finger – Aerent lifted his gaze to her face. 'I am most delighted, Chiisai. And overwhelmed.' He gave her the present he had selected for her – a Sha'angh'sei quilted jacket of the finest silk and artistry upon which had been embroidered both a blue heron, the Sha'angh'sei symbol of grace and a rampant tigress, Bujun symbol of the mastery of the land. Now he felt it to be totally inadequate in light of his own gift but she seemed genuinely delighted with it, donning it immediately.

Aerent stepped back a pace about to introduce Moichi but Chiisai, looking up out of the corner of her eye, said: 'And this must be Moichi Annai-Nin. Ten thousand pardons for my bad manners but I required some little time to acclimate myself.'

'That is quite all right, lady.'

She laughed. 'Please call me Chiisai. It would be most unforgivable of me to continue this formality with you, so great a friend of the Dai-San.' She gazed up at him without a trace of awe but with a respect and affection he found surprising in its intimacy. 'He wished for me to give you this when I saw you.'

Moichi expected her to hand over the communiqué Aerent said was to be forthcoming but instead she embraced him, her grip firm and warm, as one warrior would another. A link stronger than blood, Moichi thought. My brother.

'The Dai-San misses you greatly, Moichi.'

'And I him.'

She stepped up beside him, put her arm through his, as carefree as a little girl. 'Well, I see you have turned out the guard of honour, Aerent.'

'It is to your liking, Chiisai?' the Regent asked.

'As to its grandeur and display, most certainly.' She ducked her head. 'Yet I must tell you in all candour that it was quite unnecessary. This is a visit of an unofficial nature. My father wishes, and I wish, to make it quite clear that there should be no official tours, no dinners in my honour, no escort, in short, absolutely no affairs of state.'

'I see,' Aerent said as they began to walk past the precise gleaming rows of the guard of honour though he most assuredly did not. 'May I ask then the nature of your visit to Sha'angh'sei?'

'You may,' she said, laughing. 'Regent, you must learn to treat me as a woman and not the daughter of the Kunshin.'

'Indeed, lady. I shall endeavour to do so.'

'Good. Now as to my being here. My father feels strongly that I should not spend my entire life on Ama-no-mori; the Dai-San agreed with him. I am here to learn. That is why, you see, official parties and such will do me no good. In fact, I prefer not to have it widely known who I am.'

Moichi laughed. 'You set us quite a formidable task, Chiisai. In Sha'angh'sei, secrets of that nature are difficult indeed to keep from spreading.'

'How is the Dai-San?' Aerent said.

'Well and happy. My father is delighted to have him by his side. They are quite inseparable these days. They often ride out from the castle, spending many days in the wilds with only the plovers for company.'

'I am happy to hear it.'

'The Dai-San wished me to inquire after your injuries but I see that there is no need.' She had no more than glanced at his articulated ruby legs once since stepping ashore.

They were at the foot of Three Kegs Pier now and about to enter the maelstrom of the bund's frantic activities. Behind them, stevedores were off-loading Chiisai's baggage, directed by the Bujun sailors. There was no sign of either captain or navigator and this Moichi found strange indeed.

But there was little time to contemplate such matters for Chiisai was already leading him into the hive of the bund. Her skin, he observed as she reached back to pull him forward and the wide sleeve of her robe slid back for a moment, was lightly tanned. This, too, was out of the ordinary. Bujun women prided themselves on soft white skin and wide bamboo parasols, he had been told by the Dai-San, were plentiful in the streets of the cities, rain or shine.

The jostling of the kubaru, the smell of the spices, the

grain dust clouding the air, the shouts, half-songs, all like stepping out into the surf of an unquiet sea.

Chiisai seemed to know where she was going for she took them into the throng, heading towards the far side of the bund. There, almost directly across from Three Kegs Pier, was a small blue and white striped tent set up just in front of a harttin's windowless wall.

They stopped in front of the tent's opening and she said: 'What is this place?'

'It is the tent of a shindai, lady,' Aerent said.

'A shindai.' She said it as if tasting a new flavour, testing its sound out on her tongue.

'Yes, as the local diviners are called.'

'A fortune-teller. How delightful! May we?'

Aerent frowned. Personally he did not like the shindai, certainly set no store by their divinations. But, save for their systematically fleecing the visitors, they were completely harmless. 'By all means.'

Moichi, for his part, as he allowed himself to be dragged inside the tent, wanted no part of this. He was frankly anxious to return to the harttin and Aufeya.

It was dim inside the tent and already hot but he could make out the figure of a woman with a vaguely porcine face. For all that, she was quite pretty as she stood up and met them, smiling. 'Welcome,' she said. 'You have come to see your future.' She spoke to them all but Moichi had the uncomfortable sensation that she was directing her remarks to him alone.

'Lovely lady,' the shindai said. 'Please take this deck of cards and arrange it in any manner you desire.'

Chiisai took the pack, turned the bottom one over, then one after the other she looked at their faces. They were all blank. 'I do not see how it can matter,' she said, but complied with the shindai's request. Then she handed the cards back.

The shindai held the cards in her right hand face

downward. With her left hand, she picked up the top card, turning it face up. On it was imprinted the figure of a bird.

'Ah,' the shindai said. 'You are about to embark upon a long and arduous journey.'

Aerent laughed. 'You are a little late, shindai. This lady has just come from such travel.'

'Nevertheless,' the shindai said firmly, 'travel is indicated. And in the future not the immediate past.'

She slid the card, face up to the bottom of the deck, turned over the second, now the top, card. It depicted a statue of a half-clothed human, placed quite oddly, in the midst of a forest.

'This is what aids you.'

'What?' Chiisai exclaimed. 'A statue?'

'The statue is the symbol of artistry and beauty.'

Again the shindai's hand moved and the third card was displayed. The figure was difficult to discern for it seemed a black pictograph against a black background. But now, as the shindai's hands moved, the light hit the card in such a way that the black disappeared, leaving behind, like spindrift at low tide, a spare shape etched in black. It appeared to be a human skull.

'Death!' Chiisai breathed.

'Now, really –' the Regent began, thinking this had gone on far enough and that he was a fool to allow his guest to be frightened by this shindai witch.

'Not death, lady,' the shindai interrupted him in a voice that brooked no further interference with her work. 'Most assuredly not death. This is what crosses you. A man. A man will *desire* your death.' Everyone in the tent heard her added emphasis.

'Will?'

'Yes,' the shindai nodded. 'He does not appear to know that you even exist now.'

'Then why will he want to kill me?'

'That I surely cannot tell you, lady.'

The shindai's hands were quiescent now.

'Is that it?' Chiisai asked.

'Yes. The Three Servitors have been exposed. They are the governors of the immediate future.'

Chiisai turned to Moichi. 'Have yours done now.'

He was about to protest when Aerent caught his eye, gave him a discreet but distinct negative shake of his head. Without a word, Moichi took the deck and shuffled the cards quickly and negligently. He wanted only to end this bit of nonsense. He handed the pack to the shindai.

She displayed the first card. It was the sun.

The shindai cleared her throat. She seemed somewhat startled. 'This is the symbol of Goal. I must say that I have never before encountered it in the guise of the First Servitor. Most unusual. Here it would be the significator of great change.'

Second card: this had an entirely black background like Chiisai's third card before it had metamorphosed to white, the more common colour. In its centre was what appeared to be a bier, etched in white and upon that reposed a female figure, also outlined in white.

'This is what aids you.'

'A corpse?' Moichi almost laughed in her face.

'The past,' the shindai said evenly even as her hands were bringing up the third card.

This time they could all hear the tiny gasp of her indrawn breath.

The third card was blank.

'No one,' said Chiisai. 'Isn't that marvellous!'

'Not no one,' the shindai said gravely. 'Everyone.'

'Everyone,' Moichi scoffed. 'But that is impossible.'

'Perhaps so,' the shindai said. 'Yet it is what the Third Servitor reveals.'

Aerent dipped into his sash and placed a silver coin in the shindai's hand but she shook her head. 'Oh no, sir, I cannot take any payment for this reading. It is my gift to this couple.' She looked at Moichi and Chiisai.

'You are mistaken, shindai,' Moichi replied. 'We are no couple.'

'If I'm in error, sir, then I do apologize most humbly. But either way I will accept no payment.' She placed the silver coin back into the Regent's sash as deftly as if she had been a pickpocket. 'Good day to you all,' she said, bowing. 'Good day.'

After the stifling interior of the tent, the colours, odours, sounds of the port quarter of Sha'angh'sei swept over them like an invigorating tide.

'I hope,' Aerent said, 'that you take these divinations in the spirit in which –'

Moichi stopped listening. He was watching a kubaru runner hurtling along the bund pell-mell. He knocked over a stevedore, leapt a chestnut merchant's impromptu stall. He seemed to be heading directly towards them and Three Kegs Pier. Moichi thought he looked vaguely familiar and, at that moment, he caught the kubaru's eye. The man obviously recognized him for he veered away from the dockside and sped hurriedly towards them. He shouted, bowled over a pair of kubaru. Sacks of rice flew into the crowd, opening and spilling out. Cries of anger trailed him.

The kubaru paid no attention, completing his run. He reached Moichi.

'You must come now!' he said. The combination of the dialect and the cutting of the words caused by the man's panting, made it difficult to understand him completely. Still, the gist was readily apparent. 'Come now. Right away!'

Now Moichi recognized the kubaru and felt a knife twisting in his vitals. The man was already pulling at him and he needed no further urging. Without a word he set off with the kubaru at his side, hurtling down the bund.

'What has happened?' Chiisai asked, turning to the Regent.

Aerent's face was ashen for he too had recognized the kubaru. 'I am afraid to speculate, Chiisai. Please come with me.' Taking her elbow with his left hand, he guided her towards the bund's landward fringe. There he hailed a passing rickshaw and, lifting her into it and quickly following her, he gave the runner an address. 'Take the streets,' he told the kubaru. 'We are in a hurry.'

Llowan was the first to meet Moichi at the doorway to the harttin. He seemed to have aged and his hands were shaking.

'I cannot imagine how this happened, Moichi,' he said, his voice unsteady. 'There was so much business this morning. Such confusion.' He shook his head sadly. 'But there is no excuse. This is my fault.'

Moichi put a hand on his shoulder. 'Whatever has happened, it has nothing to do with you. *I* brought them here.' Then he was mounting the stairs, three at a time, emerging to find . . .

The room looked as if a fierce storm had hit it. The bed was askew, chairs were broken, Llowan's enormous hardwood desk was demolished, a pile of broken firewood in the far corner.

The jalousies had been smashed in at least three places and, fearing the worst, he went out onto the wide veranda.

Shards of the jalousies, furniture littered the floor and – He knelt, staring at the droplets of blood strewn about. He picked through the debris not knowing what he was searching for until he found it. His dirk lay just under his fingers, both blade and handle smeared with blood, still wet.

He picked it up, stood, looking around, wiping it off. They were not here. He went back into the room, started towards the far end. Aufeya was gone which meant that she was not dead but had been taken by force; there was no time here to get the information from her. Where would they have taken her? Surely not somewhere within Sha'angh'sei, a foreign city where they would be at a disadvantage. But would they have also taken Kossori?

At that moment his eye caught a dark spot in amongst the desk's debris. He leapt forward, hurling the cracked wood and hanging brass fittings from his path.

Within a crude tent made by the splintered desk, he found the body. The face, curiously, had been untouched and it appeared as calm as if it had been sleeping. But the body. Arms and legs were broken in too many places for him to count but it was the hands which magnetized his attention. They were bloody pulps, the knuckles looking as if they had been crushed one by one with precise and sadistic care. Moichi felt cold sweat break out along his face.

This broken corpse was all that was left of Kossori, the man who could defeat half a dozen Ching Pang without breathing hard.

What devil, Moichi thought numbly, had done this?

But he already knew the answer.

TWO:

Pursuing the Devil

The Lorca

'It is good to have a rolling deck beneath my feet again.'

He breathed deeply of the salt spray and turned, briefly, gazing over the stern's sheer-strake. Sha'angh'sei was but a memory, floating somewhere beyond the low-lying haze to the south.

'Can you really speak their tongue?' she asked. He nodded affirmatively and she continued: 'It is most strange, is it not, to think that all the peoples of the world devised one tongue long ago that amply fits them all.'

'The Bujun have their own tongue.'

She nodded. 'True. But we all speak the common tongue, also. Odd that these people do not.'

She meant the Daluzan.

He went slightly for'ard, putting his hands on the rail separating the elevated aft deck from the rest of the sleek lorcha and, cupping his hands at the sides of his mouth, called to the men in the shrouds: '*Ganarse las velas! A la babór!*' Immediately, he saw with some satisfaction, they altered the sails so that they picked up more of the following wind and the vessel began to sweep to port. '*Navegas viento en popa!*' There came an answering shout from the sailors in the shrouds. The lorcha now sailed before the stiff wind with every centimetre of canvas full out, racing up the coast of the continent of man, northeast to Dalucia.

They had come, eventually, and taken the ruined body away, silently and without disturbing him as he had stood in the centre of the room, exactly where Aufeya had stood, staring at him as he had left. Aerent had seen to that. But he had not come upstairs and Moichi had been grateful for that because he thought that he could not bear to see another living human being then without lashing out with his dirk.

He blamed himself, deeply and without quarter. It did no good for the pragmatic part of himself to point out that he had done what he had thought best; that he had had no way of knowing. How *had* Hellsturm found out about the harttin? For he had no doubt that Hellsturm was behind the death of his friend and the snatch. What a pejorative word: *snatch*. But it was proper and fitting for the most heinous of crimes. Just as it did no good for him to ask himself, What else could I have done? It was just too ironic that his meeting at Three Kegs Pier had not been a high affair of state as he and Aerent had believed it would be. He could have taken Aufeya after all.

God, what a monstrous death! And Aufeya? Perhaps she already lay in her own lost fluids in some dank back alley, like her friend Cascaras, a gaping hole in her chest over her heart. Oh God, he cried inwardly, let it not be so! Then where had Hellsturm taken her? It could be anywhere.

He heard a sound on the stairs as someone came up. Who would dare? He felt rage burning within him and whirled. He found that he was still holding the dirk he had given to Aufeya.

It was Chiisai.

What did she want? he thought savagely, feeling an unreasoning resentment. It was her fault. If she had not arrived –

'I thought you might like to talk,' she said, 'to someone who is a foreigner also.'

And with that, his anger dissipated and he felt ashamed. No one was at fault. Sei, he thought. Karma. Is that not what he had told Aufeya? That seemed so long ago, now. Another lifetime.

'He was a good friend,' Moichi said, his eyes wandering around the room.

'He put up a valiant fight. But perhaps the odds were too high.'

'He could take on six men at a time.'

She came towards him through the rubble. 'Interesting. He must have been up against a most formidable foe.'

Moichi was abruptly sick of the room and he went out through the ragged gap in the ruined jalousies, onto the veranda. The day was still fine, the weather bright and placid. The air was the most pellucid he had ever seen it here, reminding him of the air far out at sea.

Chiisai stepped through after him.

He looked for the spot where he had found the dirk lying abandoned. Then he looked closer. Where the dirk had been was no piece of wood. Neither was it the floor of the veranda. He knelt, reached out.

'What have you found?' Chiisai asked.

'I'm not certain.' He stood up with it. Surely he could not be mistaken. It was a strip of silk ripped from the shirt he had given Aufeya. There seemed to be blood on it. He turned it over. For a moment nothing registered. Then he saw it for what it was: a symbol or, more accurately, a pictogram. He knew it was kubaru but he did not recognize it.

'Quickly,' he told her. 'Ask Llowan to send up that kubaru. The one he sent to Three Kegs Pier to fetch me.'

In a moment, she had returned with the man. He stood hesitantly inside the room even after Chiisai had indicated to him to go through; he would not move without a sign from Moichi.

When at last he came out and stood next to the navigator, Moichi could see the real concern on his face. 'I am most sorry, san,' the kubaru said. 'Most grieved.'

'Thank you,' Moichi inclined his head. 'I am most indebted to you.' He indicated the blood-soaked strip of silk. 'Perhaps you may help me again.'

'Whatever you ask.'

'Tell me,' Moichi held out the silk, 'what this means.'

The kubaru took the strip as gingerly as if it were a priceless piece of hand-blown glass.

'That is a kubaru symbol, is it not?'

'Yes,' the kubaru nodded. 'It means "home".'

After he had gone, Moichi said to Chiisai. 'Home. Aufeya left that for me, clever woman. Hellsturm takes her back to Corruña. That is where I must go now.'

'But you shall not go alone,' Chiisai said.

'I must,' he told her. 'Aerent cannot go with me.'

'I was not speaking of the Regent.'

'Oh, no,' he said. 'You will stay here with him. Here in Sha'angh'sei, as your father ordered.'

'Did not Aerent tell you I brought a communiqué from the Dai-San?' There seemed to be the ghost of a smile playing at the corners of her mouth as she lifted out a small metal cylinder from beneath her robe, handed it to him.

He opened it suspiciously. It was written in the Dai-San's own hand. *'Moichi, my friend,'* he read, *'Chiisai can be the only one to deliver this to you. She will do so directly by hand and only when the two of you are alone and unobserved. What she told Aerent is only a half-truth. This was done to protect him as well as herself. Chiisai is with you now under my orders. Of course, the Kunshin, had no objections. She is to stay with you now no matter what is to happen until such time as she deems it appropriate to do otherwise. I am leaving this to her discretion. You know me well enough that I need say no more. Our trust is our bond as brothers.'* Moichi looked up at her but she only shook her head.

'I know less of this than you do.'

He was certain she was lying but knew that she had good reason to do so. This was hardly his concern, in any event. If she meant to come, that was all right with him, as long as she kept her place and did not get in his way.

She smiled at him. 'I know what you are thinking.'

'Oh, really? What?'

With a deft gesture, merely a flick of her wrists, her silk robe had parted and now slid off her shoulders, puddling the floor at her feet.

'You see,' she said. 'I *can* be of help.'

Moichi stared.

Underneath the fallen robe she wore an intricately carved breastplate of black metal inlaid with gold filaments, tight black leggings of the supplest leather. Around her waist was buckled a thin belt studded with pink-and-white swirled jade from which hung the two traditional Bujun swords, the *katana* and the longer *dai-katana*.

She laughed when she saw his expression, a kind and gentle sound.

I should have realized, Moichi thought. All the signs were right in front of me.

The shrouds cracked in the wind and the yards creaked as the Daluzan lorcha sped through the water. They were professionals, the men who manned this craft and it had not taken them long to accept Moichi. He spoke their language and he knew what had happened to Aufeya. Since she had been missing they had been terrified at the prospect of her death.

'So we return home,' Armazón said. He was the bosun, a burly man with a thick shock of white hair and a seamed, leathery face, beaten into a proud configuration by the wind, sun and salt sea. His eyes were bright bits of lapis, liquid and knowing but withholding depths from the casual observer. He shook his head now. 'I had no good feeling about this voyage from its inception. I begged Aufeya to find some way to reach a bargain with that man.'

'Hellsturm?' Moichi said.

Armazón nodded. Spray flew into his face as the lorcha bucked down then up through an oncoming wave.

'*A babór*!' Moichi cried to the helmsman and the vessel immediately swung to port. This was a well-designed craft,

Moichi saw, and he appreciated this. It was tremendously responsive, much less ponderous than the larger three-masted schooners. But because of its smaller size, it was much more prone to the subjugation of the whims of the sea. If Aufeya had set sail in a three-master, she never would have run afoul of that storm.

To his left, the coastline was a green and brown ripple, distancing itself as the lorcha moved out to sea. '*Basta!*' he cried and the lorcha returned to its northeasterly course.

'What did she say?' Moichi had returned to his conversation with the Daluzan bosun.

'Say?' The man snorted. 'Why, she laughed at me and said, "You poor fool. No one can make a bargain with Hellsturm. Once he is given a task to perform, there is no one who can stop him." '

'*Given* a task?' Repeated it because it had been some time since he had heard so much Daluzan. The language had so many nuances, spoken inflections changing the meaning of words which, if written, were constant, he needed to be certain of what he had heard.

Armazón nodded.

'Hellsturm is working for someone? Who?'

The bosun shrugged. 'I do not know. I am not family. It is a matter strictly for the Seguillas y Oriwara.'

'You mean the sea-merchant family?'

He squinted up at Moichi. 'Yes, Aufeya's family. You did not know?'

Moichi shook his head. In any other land, it might have been a strange name. But, he knew, the Daluzan custom was for two people to combine their names when they were wed. He had, of course, heard of the Seguillas y Oriwara when he was in Corruña. It would have been surprising if he had not. The family was quite wealthy and owned a sizeable fleet of merchant ships.

'You have heard of Milhos Seguillas, *piloto*?'

'Yes.'

'One of the finest men in Corruña, in all of Dalucia for that matter. Then he had to go and marry the foreigner.' He spat sideways into the creaming sea. 'That was his downfall, mark my words well.' He looked at the backs of his hands, strong and blunt and capable, as dark as tanned leather; the sea had made them that way. 'Dead now, the senhor is. Dihos make peaceful his soul.'

There was something peculiar in the inflection that made Moichi ask: 'How did he die, the Senhor Seguillas?'

'Violently, *piloto*. He died abominably, if the truth be known.'

'How did it happen?'

Armazón spat again over the side. 'Just passing the time, eh, *piloto*? Something to do to wait out the journey.'

'I think you misunderstand, Armazón,' he said seriously. 'I wish only to get Aufeya back and to destroy Hellsturm. Anything you can tell me –'

He broke off at the other's grating guffaw. 'Pardon me, *piloto*, but you are a foreigner, unused to our ways. You wish to destroy this man, Hellsturm. Very admirable, I admit. He is an evil man. But you do not know him. We have a saying in Dalucia, *piloto*. Easy to say, hard to accomplish. You know it, eh? No? Well, now you do.'

'I have seen what Hellsturm can do. He murdered my friend.'

'Ah.'

'I will destroy him.'

'Bravo, bravo!' Armazón clapped his hands derisively. 'You will pardon me, *piloto*, if I do not join in the celebration just yet, eh? I have a somewhat more pragmatic turn of mind than do you, apparently.'

'You were about to tell me about the Senhor's death.'

'Ah, yes. So I was. He was murdered in a duel.' He squinted up at Moichi once again, gauging the response to what he had just said. 'Oh, yes, I know what you must be thinking. One enters a Daluzan duel as a matter of honour and one accepts, honourably, what Didos decrees as the outcome. That is part of Daluzan law. It is fixed. A constant. No one may interfere in a Daluzan duel.' His face was a sea of seething emotion, as if the words, like individual bricks, falling free from his lips, anticipated the crumbling of some strong wall. His voice became a hiss of suppressed hate. 'I tell you this, *piloto*, as certain as I am standing on this desk now speaking to you, someone violated that sacred law. Someone interfered.'

Moichi stared at him silently. The man was working himself up into a state of great agitation.

'This is how I know, *piloto*. I knew Milhos Seguillas well, very well I might even say. We sailed together on many a prosperous voyage, not all the time as master and bosun, if you catch my meaning. Aboard ship, well, *piloto*, who am I to tell you? The tenants of the sea are much different from those held on land, eh? Restrictions are lifted, prohibitions vanish like so much mist, eh? Eh? Here one is free to be oneself. The chains of class and wealth ne'er apply. That was the kind of man Milhos Seguillas was. He was a high lord who cared more for the sea and those loyal to it than all the silver in the world.' He squinted up at Moichi. 'She is a cruel mistress, the sea, eh, *piloto*? We both know that. She is harsh and unforgiving but like a lover she cradles those who are faithful to her. Think that's superstitious nonsense?' He hawked and spat, clearing his throat, as if from the clotted emotion spilling out. 'Listen to me well, *piloto*. Milhos Seguillas was an expert swordsman. Expert! He would not have been killed so quickly in a duel unless –' He paused, his mouth hanging open, as if he felt himself on a precipice and, in voicing this hidden knowledge, he had begun to fear his own words. 'He was poisoned, *piloto*. Poisoned just before the duel began. I saw the body. I know. A substance few know of, derived from a plant indigenous to a region far to the northwest. But Daluzans, they have little contact with poison.'

'But for Senhor Seguillas to be poisoned in such a manner – This could not possibly be accomplished by his opponent,' Moichi pointed out.

'Precisely, *piloto*. You have cut directly to the heart of the matter. Senhor Seguillas's foe had a cunning accomplice. One so fantastically clever that the Senhor never even suspected.'

'What are you saying, Armazón?'

'Just this, *piloto*. Senhor Seguillas was poisoned by his wife!'

'My God, man, do you have any proof of this?'

'Proof? Aye. Proof enough. Not such that would prick the interest of a magistrate. But, I'll warrant, enough to satisfy me. I knew Senhor Seguillas. And I know his wife.'

'Does Aufeya know anything of this matter?'

'Not a bit, *piloto*. Leastwise, not from these lips. I've breathed nought to a soul save yourself.'

'Then why have you told me?'

'You said you wished to save Aufeya. Well and good. You are not Daluzan. You are not blood. You can go where others, constrained perhaps by the conventions of the land, cannot. You must help Aufeya and Senhor Seguillas. You must avenge his death. Kill Aufeya's mother!'

Moichi looked away from those blue eyes, burning with a manic passion. Thick cumulus were building themselves low on the horizon ahead of them to the northeast. Their tops were pure white but as they continued to mount, he caught a glimpse of their dark undersides. Storm clouds. A squall was forming. It was far off, too distant to be an immediate threat for the wind had not yet changed. But the gulls to port were already beginning to wheel, crying, towards the high shore.

He stared into those blue eyes. 'I can promise you no such thing, Armazón. Aufeya is my concern, not her mother or her dead father.'

The bosun's eyes blazed and he trembled with rage. '*Cobardé!*' Spittle flew from his glistening lips. 'You meddle in matters over which you have no understanding. You are an outlander! What is Dalucia to you? Less than nothing.' He laughed grimly. 'Ah, for you! Save yourself the misery, *piloto*. Throw yourself overboard before you reach Corruña. Let the sea take care of you for you look death in the face and you do not even know it!' He went away from Moichi in a rush, leaping for'ard, swinging around the mainmast, almost colliding with Chiisai as she came aft, before disappearing into the for'ard hatch.

Chiisai came up from the position she had taken up near the bow soon after they had set sail. All the day, she had stayed there, studying the configuration of the shoreline, constantly checking it against the detailed maps aboard the lorcha.

'We are making exceptional time, Moichi,' she said, making no mention of the altercation with Armazón. She pointed to port. 'See there, already we are near the coast city of Singtao.'

There, where she pointed, he could see the cinnabar smudge of the urban sprawl, far smaller than mighty Sha'angh'sei but important in its own right. The city's colour was no illusion of the light for it was here that the famed red clay was exported to the world of man. It was the finest in all the world, and artisans, no matter where they resided, insisted upon using it.

The light was peculiar now because the vast bank of squall cumulus had not lowered entirely and the sun, caught behind it, nevertheless managed to fight through the underside so that the sea was illuminated by what sailors called the trail of the Oroborus, brilliant as molten metal where the rays hit it, as deep and brooding as iron everywhere else. Above the storm, the sky was a peculiar canary yellow fading to a cold dense grey.

His nostrils dilated and he scented. 'It is coming now,' he told her. 'And quickly.' As if to underscore his words, there came a deep but distant rumble of thunder, echoing across the sea. He looked to port. All the gulls were gone now, having sought the safety of the shore. For us, too, Moichi thought.

'Un buque!' The piercing call of the lookout vibrated in the air. A ship.

'Dónhe?' he called.

'Adelanté!'

He gazed straight ahead. For a moment he saw nothing but the heaving sea, made dark and dull by the confluence of the flying thunderheads. They were very close now. Then he oriented and saw the triangular sail emerging from out of the cloudbank which now seemed to dip right into the heaving water. Whitecaps were appearing with alarming rapidity.

'Qual' clasé de buque?' He called to the lookout. These were unfamiliar waters to him. Better to rely on the Daluzans here.

'Momente, piloto!'

The wind, gusting erratically, was plucking at the canvas with intensity as the storm approached; the rigging sang its mournful tune. Normally, he would have called for them to strike canvas. But some sixth sense, borne to him upon the sea, caused him to delay. He wanted a positive identification first. He swung abruptly around as a particularly strong gust threatened to turn them. *'Firme! Firme, hijho!'* This to the helmsman who he knew was young but trustworthy in a crisis.

'Do you not think we should make for shore?' Chiisai said.

'Not yet.' Moichi had turned back, was listening for the lookout's identification. 'Hellsturm already has a sizeable headstart on us. We cannot afford to let them build on that advantage. They have outrun the storm, I have little doubt. We must weather it.'

'I have felt the force of the storms here in the northwest.' She was, of course, speaking in relation to her home,

Ama-no-mori. Moichi thought of Sha'angh'sei being in the south, which it was in relation to the rest of the continent of man. 'And that was in a solid three-master. Do you think –'

But Moichi had signalled her to silence. He was concentrating.

'*Una lorcha!*' The lookout's cry came. '*Daluzan!*'

'One of theirs,' Chiisai said.

'*Vigilarse cuidadosamente!*' he cried to the lookout. Watch it closely. Because there was something not quite right. He turned to the helmsman. '*A la babór! Aprisa!*' Quickly now! The lorcha swung to port, heading in towards the shoreline. Moichi, after a brief glance into the shrouds, kept his gaze fixed on the other vessel.

'What's the matter?' Chiisai asked.

He ignored her, calling: '*Rohja! Don' está?*'

A young sailor working at midships called for a man to replace him, scrambled aft. '*Piloto.*' He was tall with a broad chest and muscular arms. His face was long and thin, dominated by the dark brooding eyes of a predator. He was dressed in a white cotton shirt, dark trousers and a purple headband. An exceptionally functional outfit.

'What do you make of that?' Moichi said, pointing to the oncoming ship.

The sailor peered ahead. 'A lorcha.'

'Daluzan?'

'The design is Daluzan. That is not the same thing.' He continued to peer ahead but the low light was making sightings difficult. 'Strange sail,' he said.

'What do you mean?'

'Just that I have never seen a Daluzan vessel with black canvas before. Perhaps you should ask Armazón.'

'I am asking you, Rohja.' Gaze flicking from the oncoming craft to the cumulus behind it. Flash of lightning, blue-white upon the mirror of the sea. The other lorcha had altered course but it could be heading in to shore as was Moichi's vessel. He kept their course, heading in but his head was full of the calculations of vectors; he needed no instrumentation for this.

'I think they mean to intercept us, *piloto*.'

'They may just be heading in to shore, as we are,' he pointed out.

'The angle isn't right.'

'Tell me, Rohja, would Senhora Seguillas y Oriwara send a ship after her daughter?'

'Not likely, *piloto*. No one knew where we were bound or even that we had gone until after we had set sail.'

Rohja was increasingly agitated but Moichi remained calm.

'The lorcha is primarily a merchant vessel, is it not? Correct me if I am wrong.' It appeared now as if the other lorcha would reach them before the storm did.

'That is true, *piloto*. But I must point out that this is so only on short voyages around Daluzan waters. For a trip along the coast' – he shook his head – 'it is far too small a vessel to be in the least practical. You would not be able to load enough cargo to make the voyage worthwhile.'

That, of course, was the point; the anomaly of the other lorcha, it was coming on far too fast to be carrying any kind of load. He called sharply to the helmsman: '*Recobrarse la cuarsa!*'

The man spun the wheel as sailors leapt to the rigging as the lorcha swept to starboard, then righted itself. They were now moving out at a tangent, away from the shore, into the full face of the storm. The wind howled, just below gale level and the sky was a grey mass, low and rolling like steam from a kettle. The horizon to the northeast had disappeared into a kind of continuous blur as rain slanted violently down.

'You have been of much help, Rohja,' Moichi said. 'Now go and fetch Armazón from belowdecks. We shall surely need him.'

The man left the aft deck immediately. In a moment, the bosun appeared with Rohja just behind him. Both were armed with straight narrow-bladed swords.

'Not Daluzan, then,' Chiisai said.

'If they are not, we shall see very soon now.' He moved back along the deck until he was standing next to the helmsman. 'Listen to me closely now, *hijho*, and move this vessel as I speak. Immediately, do you understand? Each moment is vital and any delay may undo us.'

'I understand, *piloto*.'

'Good.'

The other lorcha had altered its course away from shore. It was close now, tacking away from the wind so that it could cut across their bow and intercept them.

'*Hijho*,' Moichi said. 'Steer us directly for them.'

'*Piloto?*' The man was startled.

'Do as I say, Oroburos take you!' Moichi barked. 'Head for him now!'

Armazón rushed aft with Rohja in his wake as he discerned their course. The lorcha swung in an arc, directly for the other vessel.

'Are you mad?' Armazón cried. 'With all sail and in this gale we shall surely destroy each other. Sheer off!'

Moichi ignored him, addressing Rohja instead. 'Will the canvas take the strain?'

Rohja glanced upwards. 'Yes, *piloto*. There is no problem from rips –'

Moichi heard his tentative tone. 'But – ?'

'But there may be some danger of capsizing. With all sail if the storm caught us dead on, we would go over and down like a stone.'

'He is right, *piloto!*' Armazón brandished the sword. 'Either way, it is suicide! Sheer off, devilfish take your eyes!'

The helmsman was sweating and Moichi murmured reassuringly to him, '*Firme, hijho. Firme.*'

They were heading directly at the oncoming lorcha, the fierce wind propelling them dizzyingly across the waves. They were coming up on it with appalling swiftness, the storm front just behind. It was gaining on the other ship.

Fittings creaked as the canvas strained in the bucking wind and men scrambled constantly to keep the sheets at their proper angle. They were making all speed.

But Moichi's gaze had swung away from the other lorcha. He watched the rising of the squall, calculating distances and speeds, the vectors coming together. It was going to be very close.

Dimly he heard Chiisai call his name. He turned, saw Armazón, sword gleaming, mounting the short companionway to the raised aft deck.

'Get away from there, *piloto*! Leave the helm. You will kill us all in your madness!'

'Chiisai,' Moichi said softly so that only she could hear. 'Stand just here, on the other side of the helmsman. See that we stay bow on to the other ship no matter which way he twists.'

'Stand off this deck, bosun,' he said, moving forward as he unsheathed his own sword. 'You have a job to do. I want the men armed in the event we are boarded. See to it!'

'I shall see to your death first, *piloto*!' He swung wildly at Moichi, who slid his upper torso away from the blow and, at the same time, sent a vicious two-handed slash obliquely across the other's blade. It sheared through like a stalk of ripe wheat. Moichi stepped up, sheathing his sword, and let fly a balled fist into the bosun's face. His arms flung out wide, Armazón plummeted backwards onto the main deck. There he lay, stunned.

'Rohja,' Moichi called, 'see that he is all right. Then make certain the men are armed. I want no surprises. Quickly, now. There is little time!'

He returned to the helm, saw that they were still dead on.

'Good,' he murmured. 'Very good.'

The other lorcha was now quite close. So close, in fact, that he could see the individual men manning it. What –?

'Rohja!' He saw the man. He had just returned from

belowdecks. 'Look to the other ship! Are those Daluzan?'

'No, *piloto*, they are not!'

Moichi had thought not. Those men were larger than the Daluzans, broad-shouldered and heavily-muscled in a narrow-waisted athletic way. They had hair as yellow as the sun and their skin was so fair it appeared almost white.

'What folk mans that lorcha?'

'Tudescans,' came the reply.

'Who are they?' Chiisai said. 'I have never heard of them.'

'Nor I,' Moichi replied. 'But we are about to find out.' Rohja scrambled aft in answer to Moichi's summons.

'The Tudescans are from the north, from a land above Dalucia.'

'What could they want from us? Are they pirates?'

'No, *piloto*, not to my knowledge, though they are most certainly a villainous lot.'

Moichi considered this for a moment. There were six different words for villainous in Daluzan that he was aware of – perhaps there were more – and all had their own various shades of meaning. The one Rohja had used had many ramifications. Too many to contemplate now but he filed the information away for later study.

'*Ahora*!'

The two lorchas were bearing down upon each other now and he could see the frantic activity on the other ship as it tried to manoeuvre away so that it could close alongside.

As it had worked out, he was obliged to cut it very fine and if it did not work, their vessel would be beam on into the ravaging squall with all sails full and that would be the end, as Armazón feared. Nothing in the world could save them from going down.

'Steady,' he urged the helmsman. 'Steady. They are trying to shake us off.'

Sheets of rain, so heavy they were almost solid, were closing in rapidly, cutting light drastically, and judging distances accurately was now a major problem, mainly because the blurring effect tended to foreshorten the distances. So it took a fraction of a moment longer for him to guide the lorcha as his brain interpreted the images of his vision and made the necessary readjustments.

Howling, gusts of wind buffeted the sails giving the men great difficulty. But they were good and their course held true. Still he shouted encouragement and they redoubled their efforts.

Beside him, the helmsman had begun trembling. In just a few short moments, the two bow waves would be mingling. It was going to be that close.

'Steady,' he crooned into the wind. 'Steady as she goes.'

Masts bending in the gale. A sharp cry along the main deck. Ignore it.

'Keep her bow on!' Moichi cried. He pulled the shaking helmsman from his post; he had done as much as could be expected.

The yards creaking. Howling like the hounds of hell.

'Steady now!' he told himself, his fingers gripping the helm, guiding it. He felt the thrill of the ship wash over him then, knew she had recognized his competence, acknowledged his leadership. She acquiesced, truly his now to command.

The men sweating, hauling on the lines, heels trying to find a no-slip purchase on the tarred deck.

'Right there.'

Felt Chiisai close beside him, welcoming her warmth and support.

'Right here.'

The rain rushing towards them like a vast funereal shroud, a waterfall of black liquid metal, thick and blinding.

'Yes, right here!'

The other lorcha, big and dark, looming over them like a gargantuan tombstone, blotting out even the oncoming storm with its bulk, with the ebon of its spread sail, taut and leathery as a bat wing.

Abrupt wetness beginning and the helmsman crying out in fear because he thought it was the first onrush of the other ship's bow wave washing over them and Moichi crying: '*Ahora!* Now! Now! Hard to starboard!' He spun at the wheel, but the seas were already so heavy that there was enormous resistance. Chiisai leaned into it with him and then the trembling helmsman, his teeth chattering and his eyes rolling wildly so that the whites showed all the way around. 'Heave! Heave!' the helm began to turn. 'By the Oroburos, put your weight into it! Heave!'

The lorcha bucked, swung to starboard.

A solid wall of water rose up and the helmsman screaming again because he could already feel the titanic death shudder of his vessel as the other lorcha hit it.

'Don't let up! Heave!'

And they were into the squall, another world, crossing the threshold. The downpour obscured everything and they hung onto the wheel, all three of them, lest they be washed overboard. But Moichi was already turning his head towards the portside, watching, watching through the clouds of hissing water, seeing, as if through some magic viewer, the smudge of the other lorcha, made dark and bulky by its angle and proximity turned broadside into the storm in its attempt to turn away from their charge. It was breaking up. He heard the splintering even above the crash of the storm, thought he could even discern cries in a strange language, guttural, cuneiform writing come to life in speech, dying now amidst the torn spars and splintered hull.

He heaved with them, bringing them out of their starboard arc, back onto a straight course.

He relinquished the helm to the helmsman and turned to find Chiisai staring at him. She put one small hand, fingers outspread, on his chest. His shirt had blown open and she touched his bare skin. Rain drove at them relentlessly, filming their faces, running down their necks. They were drenched to the skin.

Mer-Man's Tales

During the long night he dreams of home. Of waiting Iskael, baking in the swollen summer's sun. It is the season when nothing moves along the vast tracts of the desert; not caravans which, in the fall, will journey forth, laden with spices and cedar; not pilgrims making the arduous trek to the holy sites at the foot of the mountain built, so it is said, by the hand of God. It is the time when the desert is ruled by the scorpions and sandsnakes during the day and the fleet packrats at night.

It is the time when he is a boy, already tall and muscular, when he rides his father's land on horseback, supervising much of the work. He is accompanied by Al'eph, his tutor, a man of indeterminate age who is present in order to assure Moichi's father that the boy's secular and religious studies do not suffer because of his work.

'My boy,' Al'eph calls to him, as they rein up, atop a low bluff, 'it is time for your midday lesson.'

'Not today, Al'eph,' he says. 'Please.'

'Moichi, I cannot force you but I am constrained to point out that your father is already most anxious about the slow progress of your studies. This will do nothing to assuage his anxiety.'

'It is my life, Al'eph,' Moichi says. 'I know you understand this even if he does not.'

The other nods. 'This is quite correct, my boy. But neither am I the one with the ferocious temper. You are not the only one brought on the carpet if matters are not to his complete satisfaction.'

'I know what you put up with,' he says, 'and I appreciate

it. But today the sun is hot and the shaded waters of the brook in the northwest quadrant seem irresistible.'

Al'eph sighs. 'All right. Go take your swim. But in return you must promise to rendezvous with me here just after sunset. We shall return home together as your father would wish it.'

Moichi lifts a hand in assent, digs his boot heels into his mount's flanks and he is off, galloping down the far side of the bluff, over the rolling fields of wheat.

In the manner of dream movement, he finds himself at the brook, dismounted, staring through a gap in the dense greenery. He sees the frothy water, so inviting. But this day the brook is not deserted, despite its distance from any major or minor roads.

Within the stream stands a girl with short auburn hair. He moves slightly to get a better view and sees that she is in the process of disrobing. Already she is without her blouse and her skin, clouded with freckles, is tanned almost to the colour of teak. Lithe muscles ripple as she bends, placing the blouse on the far bank and he catches an all too brief glimpse of one breast, firm as a ripe apple, the nipple hard. Then she turns her back and he sees the deep groove of her spine, shadowed all the way down to the tops of her buttocks, so unutterably erotic that he feels his legs begin to tremble with the force of his longing.

The water rushes onward, hiding her feet and ankles, the bottoms of her calves. She wears only a pair of cut-off pants now and her bare legs, like the bifurcated stalks of some exotic flower, hold his attention. They are beautifully formed, so full of a hidden excitement that, for a moment, he imagines himself to be a desert explorer who, after seasons of searching, at last comes upon a previously undiscovered mine of precious gems.

His breath comes as hard as a bellows and he is terrified that she will hear his stentorian wheezing. The blood, pounding through his veins, sounds like hammerblows upon his inner ear and his head seems to jerk with every pulse.

As if in terrible confirmation of his thoughts, the girl turns, stares directly at him. He freezes, not even daring to breathe. He stares, mesmerized, as if seeing an ethereal faerie creature come to life. Her eyes are enormous and as green and bright as polished jade, long sooty lashes giving them a highly mysterious aspect. A broad forehead, small nose and generous lips. Her face is captivating.

Then she turns away, miraculously without having noticed him and he feels a kind of chill after that hot stare, as if a cloud had passed before the face of the sun.

Her hands are working now in front of her, hidden from him and this, too, increases the eroticism of the moment. Then, incredibly, she sways slightly back and forth as she works her pants down her hips. And she is completely naked.

She begins to turn again but he can stand no more. Moving back into the deep shadows of the foliage, he feverishly tears at his clothes. He is sweating. Buttons catch at the material of his shirt, cloth sticks to his back and arms as he tries to pull it off.

At length, he is ready and, moving to the gap, he thrusts himself through and, without pause, hurls himself into the water of the brook.

It is like ice and his flesh is raised in goosepimples. He lifts his head from the water, shaking the droplets from his brow and eyelashes but he is alone in the brook for as far as the eye can see.

They sailed into the port of Corruña on the wings of fair weather and a stiff fresh wind out of the southwest quarter.

Far from the sprawling splendour of the Sha'angh'sei that tended to awe the initiate, Corruña was nevertheless a beautiful sight. The Daluzan port was comparatively small and perfectly compact. Stone jetties, mostly man-made, thrust out into the blue water, amply accommodating the many swift lorchas that, as Rohja had indicated, plied Daluzan waters on short-range trade.

Immediately to the northeast, a deep lagoon was sheltered by a narrow curving peninsula, like a welcoming cape to weary travellers in larger craft. Near the bow, Moichi could make out seven three-masters at anchor there.

The city itself was laid out in a wide crescent, the arms of its extremities encircling the port. Corruña was a swath of white cubicular buildings built around spectacular circular plazas whose centres were invariably filled with beautifully sculpted fountains or small arboreal sanctuaries. Bells seemed to peal almost constantly, emanating from the blunt towers of the myriad iglesias.

The Daluzan culture did not use brick in their constructions, perhaps for aesthetic reasons, using only wood panelling and stippled stucco in their interiors. Almost without exception, the buildings of the city were made of a kind of fired adobe that was meticulously sealed against the cold of their winters then thickly whitewashed to a matt finish.

If the houses of Corruña seemed at first colourless, the citizens were just the opposite, for their clothing, in which they took inordinate pride, was of the most brilliant colours; every shade and its harmonic was represented amid the tight formalism of the men and the swirling ruffles of the women.

The lorcha nosed slowly alongside a jetty and fore and aft lines were thrown to the waiting hands. Moichi, awaiting their docking, was watching Armazón. He had made an enemy there, he knew, when he had knocked the bosun down in front of his crew. He shrugged mentally. There had been no help for it. But he knew that, while he was here, he would have to keep a weather eye on the man. He had told Chiisai the gist of his talk with Armazón but nothing further was said of the matter.

They bumped against the wharf and Moichi, moving back to midships, stepped off the lorcha, followed by Chiisai. As they stood there, breathing deeply, adjusting to being on land once more, Rohja came up.

'You will, no doubt, wish to go to the house of the Seguillas y Oriwara,' he said. 'Allow me to be your guide.'

'If you give us the directions, I am quite certain we will find our way,' Moichi said. 'If you would be amenable, I would ask you to do something for me.'

'If I am able, I will be most glad to help.'

'Good. I want you to hang around here. Do whatever you normally do. I want to know if any ship coming in on the same line as we did, docked here. It would be, oh, either early this morning or late last night. Do you think you can do that?'

Rohja grinned, adjusted the purple headband. His eyes were bright. 'Aye, *piloto*. It will be easy.'

'Do not make the mistake of taking this lightly, Rohja,' Moichi cautioned. 'This man we follow is most dangerous and he is certain to have confederates here. I do not want to place you in jeopardy –'

'Please do not trouble yourself on that score,' Rohja said. 'I can take care of myself. No one will know what I am about.'

'That includes Armazón,' Moichi said pointedly.

Rohja snorted. 'I need no reminder on that score, *piloto*. There was no love lost 'tween the two of us long before I sided with you back there.'

'Just be careful.'

'Armazón is an old man. He will cause me no trouble.'

Rohja was about to go but, on impulse, Moichi held him back by asking, 'Do you know anything about the duel in which the Senhor was killed?'

The sailor thought a moment, then shrugged. 'Not much, *piloto*. I did not myself see it – I was not in the employ of the Seguillas y Oriwara, then – but I was told that the Senhor was overmatched from the outset.'

'Was the Senhor an expert swordsman?'

'By all accounts he was. But there is an ancient Daluzan

proverb: "Excellence is fleeting for perfection does not exist; there is always someone better."'

'A most sobering thought,' Chiisai said. Rohja was one of the few Daluzans Moichi had encountered who had a true grasp of the common tongue. They had used it now not only for her benefit but to ensure privacy in this public place.

'Indeed,' Rohja agreed. 'Most melancholy. But we Daluzans believe that it teaches one humility.'

'Do you know, Rohja,' Moichi said, 'whether it was a fair duel?'

'All Daluzan duels are fair, *piloto*, by definition.'

'Armazón seems to think otherwise.'

'Ah, Armazón. Well I cannot say that I am at all surprised.'

'Why is that?'

'Well, he loved the Senhor, *piloto*, yes, as if they were brothers. But something transpired during the last year of the Senhor's life. I do not know what – none of the men, I suspect, do – but perhaps four seasons before the Senhor was killed in the duel, he ceased to use Armazón's lorcha –' he turned and pointed – 'this one, in point of fact. The Senhor's fleet is vast, you no doubt know, but he steadfastly sailed with Armazón until –' he shrugged – 'It happened very abruptly, you know. Very strange after so long a time.'

'Did they have a fight?'

'If there was one, it did not occur in public. And, of course, Armazón would never speak of it.'

'But what has this to do with what Armazón suspects happened in the duel?'

'Just this. Ever since the Senhor's death, he has changed.'

'That is understandable, given –'

'No, no. I mean over and above his feelings of grief. He has become, I don't know, someone else – unrecognizable to any who knew him in the old time when the Senhor was alive. He is driven by an emotion I detest. Guilt.' He shrugged. 'Over what, I do not know.'

Moichi looked over the other's shoulder at the gently rocking lorcha. 'Perhaps we will never know now. Listen, Rohja, we should meet tonight. Can you suggest a place?'

The sailor thought for a moment. 'Aye. There is a fisherman's taverna near here, along the docks. It is called El Cambiro. It lies at the foot of Calle Córdel, where the street ends at the sea.' He squinted up at the sun. 'Give me until midnight, *piloto*. These matters, you know, cannot be rushed. Sailors are a stony lot on land' – he grinned broadly – 'until the liquor loosens their tongues, eh?'

It took them some time but, at length, they were directed to the Plaza dell' Pesquisa.

It was constructed of shimmering white cobbles which flashed in the sunlight like diamonds. In its heart was a thick copse of green olive trees half-hidden within which was a tiny bubbling fountain. This last was of a grey stone, rough-grained, almost like coastal granite, carved into the shape of a man with brawny shoulders, a full curling beard and the tail of a fish. He had deep-set eyes and arching eyebrows. His hair was composed of ringlets of tiny crustaceans. The stone swept up behind him, apparently left in its natural state so that it looked like a miniature cliff from whose lip the water spewed out and over him. His entire surface gleamed under the liquid lens of the font.

'The Daluzan are a religious people,' Moichi said to Chiisai when she commented on the statue, 'much given to superstition, folklore and myths.'

'I heard about the Kay-iro De of Sha'angh'sei from the Dai-San,' she said, still staring at the miniature figure.

'Yes, well I think that the time of her physical manifestation is gone now though, no doubt, her spirit will never leave Sha'angh'sei.'

'But time is cyclic, don't you think? These creatures' – she indicated the fountain's figure – 'or others very like them will return again in some other age.'

'No doubt,' Moichi said with a wry twist of his lips. 'But not, I trust, in ours.'

The buildings around the Plaza dell' Pesquisa were a good deal larger and more ornate than most they had seen on their way through the city and this oversize effect gave to the plaza a rather austere grandeur that was singular in Corruña.

There were benches of scrolled wrought iron scattered at different points around the copse. On one, two old men, small with sun-dried skin like leather, sat smoking pipes and chatting idly in the shade. They were both dressed in pure white linen suits, as elegant and neat as if they were on parade. This colour, Moichi knew, was reserved here for the elderly.

'Perdóname, senhores. Don' está la casa della Senhora Seguillas y Oriwara?'

They both looked up, ceasing their low chatter, staring at him from head to foot. They gazed at Chiisai for a time before returning their attention to him. One of the men pointed a bony finger at Moichi, said something to his companion in Dalluzan dialect so rapidly that Moichi failed to understand it. The other man laughed shortly, not unkindly, cocked his head, his sea-blue eyes on Moichi.

The old man who still pointed at Moichi said, 'You are not Daluzan. Not of the blood.' He tapped the side of his nose with a finger. 'I can tell.' He smiled enigmatically. There were gaps between his square teeth, stained yellow by smoke. 'But you could pass, I warrant, in a pinch. I'll just bet you could, yes.' He stretched backwards, pointed over his shoulder. 'There lies the house you seek. On the far side of the plaza.' He smiled again. 'Is it not always so, in life?' His companion nodded sagely at his side, though he had been addressing Moichi. 'Good day to you, senhor. Senhora. Good luck.'

Moichi nodded, murmuring his farewells and, with Chiisai, went out from the edge of the copse, across the sun-splashed plaza, past the rustling olive trees, the buzzing cicadas, the small black-winged birds flitting from tree to tree, leaving the figure of the fountain behind.

He wore a sea-green silk shirt with wide sleeves and tight cobalt blue trousers into which his high brown seaboots had been carefully tucked. His sword hung, scabbarded, at his side and the twin copper-hilted dirks were thrust casually into his wide leather belt.

Chiisai still wore her armour breastplate but had changed into tight pants the colour of palest sea-foam, also tucked into her high boots. Over her armour she wore her Sha'angh'sei quilted jacket. Her twin scabbarded swords were clearly visible.

The Seguillas y Oriwara house was an enormous white-façaded two-storey structure on the north side of the plaza. Its left side abutted another building but, on its right, a street led off the plaza. Lush trees lined this thoroughfare and what portions of the house Moichi could make out behind this verdant screen, were covered in ivy, reaching around along the upper storey on the front of the house.

A copper and hardwood staircase curved out and around as gracefully as a swan's neck as it ascended towards the high double doors at the front of the dwelling. These were wood-panelled, banded with bronze strips which, Moichi was certain had, at one time, found service on an oceangoing schooner for a time and the minerals of the sea had combined to give them a greenish patina.

They went up the staircase and Moichi knocked on the doors. The small wrought-iron balconies projecting from the upper floor windows in front contrived to put them in an obliquely-banded light.

The doors swung ponderously inward.

Two short, dark-haired Daluzans in black cotton one-piece suits held the doors but the man who confronted them was not Daluzan at all. He was tall, towering even over Moichi, dwarfing Chiisai, but seemed too thin for his height.

His gaunt face was hairless except for a thin black moustache which drooped forlornly on either side of his mouth. His dark eyes were almond-shaped and his skin had a yellow cast. The vault of his domed head soared upward above his narrow-bridged nose.

This man is from Sha'angh'sei, Moichi thought.

'Yes?' the man said in perfect Dalluzan. 'What is it you wish?'

Not the most cordial of welcomes, Moichi thought. The man wore a Daluzan suit in light yellow which consisted of high-waisted trousers and loose-fitting shirt tied about the waist with a narrow braided cord sash. If he was armed, he concealed it well.

'We wish to speak to the Senhora Seguillas y Oriwara,' Moichi said.

'I am afraid that will be quite impossible, senhor. The Senhora is entertaining no visitors.'

'Nevertheless, I believe the Senhora will wish to see us. We have come to Corruña aboard one of her own lorchas and bring news of her daughter.'

Something glittered far back in the man's eyes and he inclined his head. 'Follow me, please. I will inform the Senhora.'

The doors were closed behind them as they went down a short vestibule and, passing through an arch of stained glass, entered into the main hall of the house. This was two-storeys high and was domed, almost cathedral-like, panelled in pecan-wood and hung at regular intervals with small tapestries depicting scenes of the sea and its denizens: sea-lions, porpoises, whales sounding. At the end of the hallway a most singular stairway wound upward. It appeared at this distance to be carved out of an enormous ship's figurehead, a maiden of the sea, long tangled hair blown back by the wind.

On either side of the hallway, rolling doors stood closed. As they passed the first one on the right, he saw it slide open for just a moment and glimpsed within the shadows beyond dark flashing eyes in a young female face.

The man with the drooping moustache led them through a rolling door further along on the left and into a drawing room. Then, bidding them wait, he left them.

Here the plaster walls were painted green, as dark as the depths of the ocean and were hung with paintings whose subject matter was invariably religious in nature.

'The Daluzans must have a very different feeling about religion,' Chiisai said, pacing from painting to painting. 'How depressing. Is there no happiness associated with their gods?'

'They believe in the one God, Chiisai,' Moichi said. 'As do my folk.'

'Ah yes, the kami is unknown to these people.'

'Kami.'

'Um hum. The minor gods whose task it is to guide the souls of the dead back into their new lives.'

Moichi realized he knew very little of Bujun religious thought.

'We see existence as an enormous wheel; life is merely one part of it.' She was at the last painting now and she paused. 'Death, we believe, brings an end to the corporeal only. The spirit lives on and is returned to life guided by the kami and the individual's karma. That is most important.'

She was interrupted by the sound of the door sliding back. They both turned. Framed in the doorway was the figure of a statuesque woman. Her hair was long, framing her oval face and it was, startlingly, the colour and lustre of silver. She had the kind of face which would shine through all around her no matter the circumstances. Moichi could feel her intense aura all the way across the room and was reminded piercingly of Aufeya. She wore a silk suit of deep green which perfectly matched her large inquisitive eyes.

'I am the Senhora Seguillas y Oriwara,' she said in a voice like an ice floe. 'May I know why you have come here?'

Somehow Moichi was not surprised by this abrupt and

decidedly inhospitable greeting. The Daluzans were quite schizophrenic in this regard. They were fiercely polite, even to the point of exasperation. But on the other hand they could as easily be disconcertingly blunt when they so chose.

'My apologies for disturbing you, Senhora,' Moichi said, inclining his head slightly. He used the polite grammatic construction. 'I am Moichi Annai-Nin of Iskael and my companion is Chiisai of Ama-no-mori.' He paused, hoping for a reaction. He got one.

The Senhora's eyes widened a fraction and she stepped into the room. The moustachioed man stood just outside the room's threshold as still as a statue.

'An Iskamen and a Bujun,' the Senhora said. With some of the chill gone from her voice, he could hear its true melodiousness. 'An odd pair, to say the least.' She indicated the man behind her. 'Chimmoku tells me you claim to have sailed here aboard one of my lorchas. Which one?'

'The *Chocante*,' Moichi said. 'Armazón is the bosun.'

'I see.' The Senhora glanced back at Chimmoku for a moment, her hands clasped against her long thighs. 'I did not even know that particular craft had left Corruña.'

'Senhora, your daughter commandeered the *Chocante*.'

'Indeed.' The eyes flashed briefly. 'And where was she headed, Moichi Annai-Nin?'

'That I do not know. I came across her in Sha'angh'sei.' No point in telling her about the Sha-rida. 'She told me she had been blown off course by a storm. That she had not meant to come to Sha'angh'sei.' He took a deep breath. Now for the difficult part. 'She also told me that she was being pursued by a man.' He paused again, expecting an outburst. But the Senhora stood calmly before him, her expression unchanged.

'Tell me, Moichi Annai-Nin,' the Senhora said slowly, 'why have you come here?'

'Your daughter has been abducted,' Moichi said.

The Senhora turned and glanced at Chimmoku again

before addressing him. 'I am afraid there has been some mistake.'

'Pardon me for saying so, Senhora, but no mistake has been made. A man named Hellsturm –'

'Hellsturm –'

'Yes, you know him then?'

'What? No. No, I know no such person. The name – seemed odd to me, that is all.'

'This man Hellsturm snatched Aufeya –'

The Senhora drew herself up, her eyes imperiously cold. 'What is it you want from me, senhor. Money? Ships? You have made a grave error. You will get nothing from me. Now if you will –'

'Senhora!' He felt as if reality were slipping through his fingers, dreamlike. 'Perhaps my knowledge of Daluzan is inadequate. Shall I repeat myself? Your –'

'Yes, I know. My daughter has been abducted by a man with an odd name. Quite a fanciful story – a mer-man's tale, in Daluzan idiom.'

'My friend was murdered by this man Hellsturm. He gave his life to protect Aufeya.'

'I am sorry about your friend, Moichi Annai-Nin. Truly I am. But, you see, this has no interest for me.' The Senhora nodded in dismissal. 'I have no daughter.' At last her hands unclasped. 'Now, good day to you both. Chimmoku will see you out.' With that, she turned and left them there.

Outside, they stood at the edge of the plaza for a moment. The Seguillas y Oriwara house towered over them, mute and mysterious.

They went towards the copse of olive trees, sat down on a bench near the fountain. The old men were gone but the blackbirds had not abandoned their arboreal world. Oblique light found its way into the plaza between the gaps of the surrounding buildings and the tops of the trees were aflame with the light of sunset.

'Were you able to understand what was said in there?' Moichi said.

Chiisai nodded. 'Pretty much. I'm excellent in linguistics.' She changed into Daluzan to illustrate. 'Why do you think the Senhora was lying to us?'

Moichi raised his eyebrows and smiled. 'Well, I see you *are* a fast learner.'

She laughed. 'I had Rohja teach me in the evenings when he was off-watch.'

'Very clever of you.' His smile faded as he recalled the recent scene inside the Seguillas y Oriwara house. 'Something is very amiss.'

'I'll say. The Senhora's daughter leaves Corruña secretly, is threatened by a strange man, is finally captured by him and the Senhora's only reaction is to deny Aufeya's existence. It makes no sense.'

'Not yet it doesn't. But at least we have a starting point.'

'You mean the Senhora?'

'That is exactly what I mean.'

'But she will tell us nothing.'

'Then we shall just have to find a way of making her talk, won't we?'

'On the other hand, if Rohja successfully finds out about where that other ship docked, we might not need the Senhora's help at all,' Chiisai pointed out.

Moichi was about to tell her that life never seemed to be that simple when he heard a hissing sound from within the shadows of the dense foliage and he turned, one hand on the hilt of his sword. Just above and to one side of the fountain, he saw the vague outline of a human head. He and Chiisai rose and went closer, standing beside the fountain. He saw the face clearly then and recognized those eyes as the ones regarding him from behind the sliding door in the Seguillas y Oriwara house.

'Senhor,' she breathed and he nodded. 'I could not help

but overhear what you told Chimmoku. Do you know what has happened to Aufeya?'

'As I told the Senhora,' Moichi said. 'She has been abducted.'

'Oh, Dihos!' The young woman's cry was choked off as she brought her hands across her mouth.

'What do you know of this?' Moichi demanded. The woman seemed to shrink back into the shadows, murmuring.

'Let me try,' Chiisai whispered to him and then, to the woman, 'What is your name, senhora?'

'Tola, senhora. I am Aufeya's *doncella.*'

Chiiasi turned her head. 'Maid,' Moichi whispered.

'I am Chiisai,' she said. 'And this is Moichi. We are friends of Aufeya.' She pointed for emphasis. 'Moichi saved her life in Sha'angh'sei.'

Tola stared from Chiisai to Moichi, 'Is this so?'

Moichi nodded.

'How – How does she look?' Tola asked.

Both Chiisai and Moichi looked bewildered. 'She was fine,' Moichi said. 'But you must have seen her before she left.'

'Yes.' Now it was Tola's turn to look puzzled. 'But that was many seasons ago. No one here has seen her since she – she left with the Tudescan.'

'Who was that?' Chiisai asked. 'What was his name?'

'Why, Hellsturm, of course.' She wrung her hands. 'Oh I knew that was an ill-omened day.'

Chiisai leaned forward, touched the *doncella.* 'Are you certain, Tola? Aufeya *left* Corruña with this man Hellsturm.'

'Ay, yes, senhora. How could I forget? That day the Senhora told all of us, "As far as this house is concerned, my daughter is dead."'

'What do you mean?' Chiisai asked.

'Dihos! I have been gone too long. *Perdóname*, I must go.'

'Wait!' Chiisai cried but Tola was gone, darting into the trees and out the other side, using the shadows of the building to reach the far side of the plaza.

They found a smoky taverna of white adobe and blackened wood in between a barber's shop and a building that was obviously a communal medical clinic; there was a long queue passing through the wide open doors and out into the street. Inside, they could make out the shapes of several prone figures and the smell of various herbal-based medicaments.

The taverna was not as crowded as those in Sha'angh'sei. It was painted a brilliant white, its low ceiling banded by thick beams. One wall was taken up by an enormous stone hearth whose function was obviously ornamental for the kitchen could be seen behind a wooden copper-topped counter.

They found an empty table. The only people near them were a pair of curas – Daluzan priests – garbed in the traditional black dresses and stiff square hats. One was quite young with rosy cheeks and a thick bulbous nose. The other, obviously older, with salt-and-pepper hair and a spade-shaped beard, was a cura of no little rank, Moichi observed, for around his neck swung the gold chain and heavy double-cross pendant, symbol of the Daluzan church.

As they sat down, a beautiful waitress brought them a pot of compaña, the very fine local wine, golden in colour. Moichi ordered for them while the woman poured the wine.

'Is it not interesting,' Chiisai said, after she had sipped at the cup, 'that now the matter of Aufeya has been somewhat clarified but also made more complex?'

'Yes. We now know why the Senhora disavowed her to us.'

'At least it was not a lie.'

'In that sense, no. But, on the other hand, she made no attempt to aid us and I find that curious. After all, Aufeya is her daughter. Would she really prefer to see her dead rather than lift a hand to aid her?'

Chiisai shrugged. 'We could debate that point all night and not reach a satisfactory conclusion.'

Moichi grinned at her as the food arrived. 'You have a way of cutting right to the heart of the matter, Chiisai. I like that. Now this is what I propose. When we leave here, I will return to the Seguillas y Oriwara to find out what I can. As for you, there is yet another avenue that needs exploration. Cascaras, the Daluzan Hellsturm tortured, is from here also. Aufeya told me that he was once a trader of sorts. I would like you to follow that up.'

'But where shall I begin? I hardly know enough of Corruña yet.'

'There is a place in the centre of the city, the mercado. It is a meeting place for the merchants and traders, not only of Corruña but of all Dalucia. I would suggest you start there. Perhaps someone knows where in Kintai he journeyed.'

'Humph,' Chiisai exclaimed with mock-hurt. 'You just don't want me around when you interview the Senhora.'

'Whatever gave you such an extraordinary idea?'

'I saw the way you looked at her.'

'I didn't look at her in any special way,' he lied.

'I was joking, actually.' She smiled archly. 'But now I wonder, you've protested so vehemently.'

'On another subject,' Moichi said pointedly. 'I want both of us there when we rendezvous with Rohja. So meet me at the top of Calle Córdel just before midnight.'

She nodded and began to eat.

As their conversation sputtered to a halt, Moichi was able to pick up some of what transpired between the two curas at the next table.

'– the money goes, Don Gode?' said the cura with the spade-shaped beard. 'The entire western façade of the iglesia must be dismantled so that it can be enlarged. Do you suppose we can count on the Palliate for all the funds for this?' His tone was disdainful.

'But all that stained glass is so frightfully expensive,' said Don Gode, the young cura. 'Surely, Don Hispete, we can devise a less expensive style in enlarging the iglesia. And the money saved could be used to help feed and clothe –'

'My dear Don Gode,' the other interrupted, heaving a great sigh as if the cares of the world were crouched upon his shoulders, 'have you any conception of the areas of Corruña our iglesia encompasses? These are monied *partitioners*, men and women of great prestige and honour. And our new iglesia must reflect this granduer.'

'But we are taught –'

'Yes, yes. I know all that,' Don Hispete said irritably. 'I was once in the Palliate seminario myself. Although, Dihos knows, it seems far away to me now. But when you have been with us here a sufficient amount of time, you will begin to understand the complexities of running an iglesia in the Palliate.' He reached into a serving dish, plucking out a tiny boiled potato dripping with cream. He popped it into his mouth, said around it as he chewed. 'What you must remember, Don Gode, out here in the field, as it were, is to forget everything you learned at the seminario.' He laughed uproariously, swallowing. He plucked up another potato. 'Come, come, my boy, surely you know I speak figuratively. But the hard truth is that life out here is much different. Books, after all, are no substitute for life, eh?' He lifted one fat forefinger. A thick gold ring gleamed, embedded in the pink flesh near its base. 'Do you understand? No?' He brought a sliver of meat to his mouth, chewed on it. 'I agree. It would be so very nice to use the money we have so laboriously raised to aid those who are neediest. But reality dictates otherwise.'

Grease glinted along his half-open lips. A bit of meat sat on his rounded chin, atop the curling black hairs of his thick beard. 'However much our hearts tell us to do otherwise, we have a duty to the Palliate that must override such personal preferences.' He took a quick gulp of wine and belched. 'We get our money from our *partitioners*, Don Gode. Let me tell you it's quite a task making ends meet in these times. Oh, seasons ago it was much easier but we have grown since then and times have changed, quite naturally. It is now a most complex business. Money makes the Palliate flourish, Don Gode, never forget that. Faith is all well and good. We serve that up and it has its place, surely. But faith will not cause the Palliate to survive and prosper. Only money can accomplish that feat.'

'But, begging your pardon, Don Hispete, our first duty is to bring solace to those in need; to show them the way towards salvation in this life. That is the miracle of the Palliate.'

'Uhmm, yes.' Don Hispete broke off a haunch of seared meat at its white-and-pink socket. 'But, it too is a miracle, Don Gode, what money can do for the Palliate. And without that, well,' he shrugged – 'the Palliate would be able to reach no one.' He tore into the flesh with his white teeth. 'Be of calm spirit, my boy,' he said. 'It is all for the glory of Dihos.'

Fugue

The Plaza dell' Pesquisa was deserted.

He stood deep within the shadows of the olive trees, having chosen a spot with excellent visibility to the east and west as well as to the north where he could observe the Seguillas y Oriwara house undetected.

He had been in this spot for some time now. No one had come in or out of the front door during that time. Four people had passed by without stopping.

He checked his other views, drew a blank, and returned his attention to the big house. Doors were only one method of entrance.

He moved now with extraordinary quickness and silence, flitting from shadow to shadow, out of the plaza. An old man went slowly past and, some time later, a young couple arm in arm, coming from the opposite direction. No one saw him.

At length, he gained the darkness of the small side street to the right of the house. The second tree in had the right configuration and he climbed it, moving out from the trunk onto a thick limb which arced inward towards the vine-covered side of the building.

He put the toe of one boot into a vee notch where one vine became two and, ascertaining that it would indeed support his weight, launched himself upwards. Hand over hand, his fingers grasping, tugging experimentally, he ascended.

High above the street, he became aware of the soft cries, as of thin wire whistling through the air and, once, he felt the tentative brush of a leathery wingtip. He was not fond of bats and these seemed unusually large but, though they continued to dip near him, calling in their peculiar high-pitched speech, they posed little threat to his progress once he had acclimated himself to their swooping presence.

Along the wall he went, clinging like some nocturnal animal on a hunt and soon he was at the corner of the house. There was some illumination here, mostly from the flickering lights around the plaza – he looked skyward; banks of stratus cloud obscured the rising moon – but he was reasonably certain he could navigate this last stretch of wall without being observed from below.

The immediate problem now, however, rose from another quarter. For the first hand- and foot-hold he was totally blind and would have to rely on touch.

Cautiously, he reached around the corner, extending his torso as far as he dared to give himself as wide a search area as possible. He felt his fingers close around a thick vine on the front of the house. He tugged. It held. He tightened his grip and let go with his feet.

Afterwards, he would remember how absurdly lucky he was to have held on with his right hand because the new vine ripped under his weight and he slammed against the side of the building, his face scraping against the ivy as he slid downwards. He let go with his left hand and swung for a moment, supported by just one hand-hold. Gravity dragged at him, beckoning him down to the street below.

He used the toes of his boots to stop his swinging and, pressing his chest against the side of the house, searched for another vine along the front. Found it and used it. This time it held and, within breathless moments, he was swinging onto the right-hand balcony which framed the shuttered second-storey window.

He crouched on the strips of wrought-iron for a moment, feeling vulnerable in the light. In addition, he noted from this vantage point that the balcony was more decorative than functional. If it was not meant to hold this heavy a weight –

He reached out a dirk and insinuated its point into the corner seam of the wooden shutter. Found the simple metal latch and flipped it upward.

Slipped into the room beyond, pulling the shutters to behind him.

He found himself in a smallish room with a high down bed and an ornately carved wooden dresser above which hung an outsize oval mirror framed in lacquered bamboo. A bamboo rocking-chair stood immobile in one corner as if awaiting its master's return. The room was scented faintly and a lamp was lit on a small table at the bedside. This, in itself was peculiar, for the room had a deserted air, despite the obvious attempts to make it seem otherwise.

In three strides he had crossed the room and put his ear against the door. Too thick to hear anything. Cautiously, he opened it a centimetre at a time. A passage with a curving balustrade overlooked what he took to be the first-floor hallway.

He went out, standing quite still. He could hear the murmur of voices, echoing slightly and he knelt, peering through the wooden bars. The Senhora Seguillas y Oriwara was standing at the front door, talking to Chimmoku. Apparently he was about to depart for he was wrapped in a dark cloak.

'– as quickly as possible.' He heard her voice drift up to him. 'And for the sake of Dihos, make certain he does not follow you back.'

Chimmoku nodded silently and slipped out the door. Moichi now had to make an immediate decision, to stay here with the Senhora or to follow Chimmoku on his nocturnal errand. He chose the former not only because it had been his original plan but because circumstances had proved to be his ally, leaving him alone with the Senhora. To go against that now would be to court disaster.

The Senhora had bolted the door behind Chimmoku and was now coming towards him. She began to ascend the stairs.

Moichi went quickly and silently back to the room from

which he had gained entrance to the house and closed the door to a slit. Despite the lamp burning, he was quite certain this was not the Senhora's bedroom. In a moment, he heard her passing him and ventured a look. He saw her go through a door at the far end of the passage. Over it, attached to the wall, was a polished brass ship's bell.

There was no help for it now, he thought. And any procrastination allowed that much more chance that he would still be here when Chimmoku returned. He wanted to avoid that.

Taking a deep breath, he opened the door, went out into the passage and, without a sound, went into her room.

Chiisai had little difficulty in finding the mercado. It was an enormous one-storey structure in the heart of Corruña divided into myriad stalls, each rented to a different merchant or trader. The proprietorship of these spaces could be permanent or quite fluid, changing hands many times within the space of several days as traders came and went with their seasonal wares.

At times, as now – that is, at night or during inclement weather – the entire mercado was covered. However, during the dazzling sun-drenched Daluzan days, the separate stall roofs were taken away, giving the vast place a brilliantly dappled, endless feel.

Even now, after the day's selling had ceased, there continued to be much activity within the mercado albeit of a different nature from that which went on during the daylight hours. The mercado of Corruña, it was said, never slept.

Here, throughout the night, shifts of workers unloaded fresh produce, craftsmen toiled at their work in leather, silver, gold, precious and semi-precious stones, pearls, paintings, tapestries and sculpture in stone and clay; far in the back, the sweating metalsmiths worked their red-hot forges, creating their weaponry. For the day was for selling only and, at night, the artisans populated the mercado like a mythic flock of nocturnal tribesmen who disappeared with the coming of the dawn, replaced by the hard-bargaining merchants.

This was the real mercado, one which few people in Corruña ever saw, for this was not an all-night city as was Sha'angh'sei.

Chiisai stood on the mercado's threshold, entranced, as if she stood on the brink of the promised land. She was used to seeing artisans at work, for every Bujun was also an artisan of some sort – *What good is a Bujun*, her father had told her often, *with just the knowledge to kill?* – but never had she seen so many at once and the sight was dizzying.

Slowly, she strolled down the long aisles between the stalls, watching a man split an uncut diamond here, a woman spinning a cape of silver thread there and, further on, a man etching a delicate design onto a huge leather scabbard by dropping acid onto it.

She paused, fascinated, to observe a woman carving what appeared to be an enormous ruby into the likeness of a human head. She waited until the woman put down her tools to rest to ask, 'Will it be a man or a woman?'

The woman turned to look at her, wiping at her forehead with her arm. She was dark-haired and long-eyed with thick lips and a long exquisite neck that Chiisai immediately envied. Her face had been moulded by years of determination or so it seemed to Chiisai.

'A woman,' she said. 'Eventually.'

'Is it very difficult?'

'Darling,' the woman laughed, 'it is very nearly impossible.'

'Then why do you do it?'

'Because it's there, for a start, and no one else around here would dare to attempt it, man or woman. This is my second attempt; the first one I consider a failure.' She put a hand out, her fingers long and delicate, questing like the feelers of some complex insect, stroking the coolness of the ruby's irregular side. 'Here, come here, darling and feel what I feel.' Chiisai put out her hand. 'But I love the ruby for itself, you see,' the woman continued, 'because it withholds from me its very essence.' She smiled. 'Until the very end.'

'And that is important,' Chiisai said, not knowing whether she was asking a question.

'As important as drawing breath,' the woman said, 'for me. For without mystery, life would be nothing and I should wish, when I put my head down on the pillow at night, never again to awake.'

Chiisai took her hand reluctantly from the ruby. 'Do you have a finished piece of yours here? I'd like to see one.'

'I don't think –' the woman searched below the counter of the stall. 'Wait, I've found one.' She lifted up a warrior carved out of tiger-eye. 'It is not so fine, I'm afraid. It's a very early piece. Still –' she set the figure down on the counter top and Chiisai picked it up. Something about it struck her.

'This warrior's face looks familiar to me.'

'It's a Tudescan,' the woman said. 'Have you been to Rhein Tudesca? That is where I am from.'

Chiisai looked up. 'You are Tudescan?'

The woman nodded. 'My name is Martyne.' She offered her hand. 'And you?'

'My name is Chiisai. I am Bujun.' She took the hand, found it cool and firm. 'I hope you'll pardon my ignorance, Martyne, but I thought all Tudescans had light hair.'

'Most do but only my mother was Tudescan, you see. I have her light eyes but my father's hair, I imagine.'

Chiisai returned her gaze to the figurine. It was marvellously carved. She could clearly see the cruelty of the man's visage. 'We were attacked by Tudescans yesterday,' she said. 'On the sea.' She waited a moment, then said, 'You do not seem surprised.'

'Why should I be? They are evil people. That's why I am in Dalucia now.'

'But you made this,' Chiisai pointed out, indicating the warrior.

'Yes. I made that as a reminder.'

'Of what?'

'My father came from the sea. He was a freebooter who sailed into Rhein Tudesca one day. And there he met my mother. And now they are both dead.'

'I am sorry.'

'So am I. They were exceptional people, my parents. But my mother disobeyed the law and they were both slain for that transgression.'

'What could she have done that was so terrible to have warranted execution?'

'She married my father,' Martyne said simply.

She whirled as he closed the door behind him. It made a sound not unlike a sigh of resignation.

Her eyes flashed and he saw the earth-brown motes swimming in their jade depths. She wore a loose cream-coloured silk blouse with a drawstring front below which was an oval opening displaying the swell of the tops of her breasts, and a long skirt of a green so deep it appeared to be black.

'You!' she hissed. 'How did you get in here?'

Not '*What do you want?*'

Her hands hung loosely at her sides.

'I came in through a second-storey window.'

'Get out of here this instant!'

It was worrisome because there was no fear and even now her fingers were fully extended, not balled into fists of outrage.

'Not until I get some answers, Senhora.'

Had to drag his eyes away from the sight of her heaving bosom. Not the way. He advanced. 'Senhora –'

She stood her ground. 'Get out!'

Felt his muscles tensing of their own volition and he began to worry in earnest because there was information trying to get through.

'Senhora, please. You must listen to me. Your daughter's life –'

'I will not debate with you.' Her voice was like ice.

Image of Cascaras, dead in the alley.

'I will not leave.'

She moved then and, just before he was borne backwards by the full weight of her lightning attack, he knew what it was. As she leapt, he caught a glimpse of her fingers, together, fully extended. They tumbled to the floor, rolling over and over, for he knew now that any cessation of movement on his part and he was finished. The one word reverberated through his brain as the back of his head slammed against the wooden boards and he saw a shadow looming over him.

Koppo.

'The folk of Rhein Tudesca live solely by laws,' Martyne said, as they sipped compaña. 'It is how they are born and brought up. A network of laws. And that is how the country runs. Efficiently, effortlessly. Bloodlessly.' Her face was drained of all colour in the telling of this. 'A Tudescan may marry another Tudescan and no one else.'

Chiisai said nothing, staring into the depths of the golden liquid.

'The Tudescans hate outlanders,' Martyne continued. 'Oh, they tolerate those with whom trade is vital but visitors to Rhein Tudesca are strictly limited and the crews of the merchantmen bringing imports are never allowed shore leave. And any outlander in the country is escorted at all times.'

'You have not been back.'

'No,' Martyne said. 'I would never return.'

'Do you know a Tudescan named Hellsturm?' Chiisai said abruptly.

'No. Should I?'

Chiisai shook her head. 'Not really. There's no connection other than that you're both Tudescan.'

'I have no interest in others from Rhein Tudesca, Chiisai.'

'Perhaps, then, you know of a Daluzan merchant named Cascaras.'

'Oh, yes. Certainly.' Martyne poured them both more wine. 'But it has been many seasons since I have seen him. He was about to leave the city. He used to have a stall over there' – she waved a hand towards the vastness of the mercado – 'but that was some time ago. We became friendly because he specialized in archaeological artefacts.'

'You knew him well, then?'

She shook her head, her dark hair a nimbus like the night. 'Not really. He would have liked to – get to know me better. But I found out that a number of artefacts he had were stolen.'

'From collections?'

'Oh, no. He was a grave robber. He looted digs at night. Mostly to the northwest. He knew that region so well I often told him he ought to give up the thieving and become a cartographer.' She gave Chiisai a small smile. 'He wouldn't hear of it, of course. He loved the excitement far too much – as well as the enormous profits.'

'Did Cascaras say anything to you when you last saw him? Anything at all?'

'Why are you so interested in him?'

'He was murdered, Martyne. In Sha'angh'sei.'

'Sha'angh'sei?' Her eyes opened wide. 'Why would he go so far south?'

'He was being pursued by this man Hellsturm. He was tortured. We believe by Hellsturm.'

'If Hellsturm is Tudescan there is a sure way of finding out.'

'There is? What?'

Martyne turned away from Chiisai and her hands reached out, stroking the faceted ruby again, a touchstone, a talisman against bad memories. 'The Tudescans are a remarkably savage people, in many ways, despite the veneer of civilization they have cloaked themselves in.' She paused, taking a deep breath, let it out as a shudder. 'The day my parents died, it was my birthday. I saw them coming down the block because I was sitting in the open window, waiting for them. They were bringing home my presents. They were struck down as they were crossing the street. Two men had obviously been waiting for them. It took such little time, so little effort and they were sliced open, lying there in their own blood, already dead. One moment there, the next, not. I don't really remember much of what happened after that. I must've hid because they were certain to search the house. Then I was out on the streets. How much time had passed I have no idea. I only knew that they would be looking for me and that I had to get to the border. I tried not to sleep but, of course, that was impossible after a while. I was in the back of an alley one night when a combination of sounds and movement woke me. I should have run then but something held me, a kind of odd paralysis. Lucky it was, too, because I would have run right into the three warriors; it was a cul de sac, you see.'

She paused, her slender fingers exploring the ruby's contours as if reading the past, divining the future. 'They were dragging a woman in from the streets. Perhaps she was a prostitute, perhaps not; there's no way of knowing. They raped her there in front of me, a kind of bloodless ritual without even the semblance of passion. And then, when they were finished with that, they sliced open her chest. There was something more they wanted from her; information, I imagine. They got it in the end.'

Chiisai felt a cold constriction fluttering around her own heart. 'What did they do to her?'

Martyne's eyes were bright with the memory. 'You really wish to know – all of it?'

Chiisai nodded her assent.

'In Rhein Tudesca torture is a high art. In a society of secrets, you see, it is believed imperative that those in power possess the means to obtain those secrets. You understand?'

Chiisai thought of what Moichi had told her about how Sha'angh'sei society operated, so full of secrecy yet open, too. 'No,' she admitted, 'I'm afraid I don't.'

Martyne shrugged. 'Well, no matter. I suppose you'd have to actually go to Rhein Tudesca to understand fully. The Tudescans have perfected a way to expose the living heart and massage it artificially so that the victim's life processes are slowed or speeded up from there. They can cause great pain in this fashion without the coming of death. No one can withstand this form of torture but it is only one of a great many.'

'This was Cascaras's fate, I'm afraid.'

'Then I shall pray for the peace of his soul.'

Chiisai touched her. 'Please, Martyne. It is important that you try to remember if he said anything to you before he left.'

Martyne sat back, passed a hand across her forehead. 'Let me see. It was quite a while ago, the beginning of summer. He was off – now where did he say? I can't really remember. Well, the northwest, anyway –'

Yes, Chiisai thought. Kintai is to the northwest of Corruña.

'He was quite excited, I recall. "When I return, Martyne," he said, "I will be so wealthy, so powerful that you will have to give me your hand in marriage." But I paid him little mind. He always had a scheme or two which, he was certain, would make him as wealthy as an emperor. This I told him, for wealthy or no, powerful or no, it made no difference to me. I did not love him, therefore I would not marry him. Of course, this had little effect on him for, as a man who believed that money could buy him anything, he felt I was just leading him on. However what he said to me was this. "You do not understand, Martyne. This time I have truly found it, the key. With it I will have mastery of the whole world. But this, too, you will comprehend when I return from the land of the opal moon."'

For a moment Chiisai stood perfectly still. She felt as if she had lost all breath and the rhythmic thudding of her heart was like a series of concussions against her rib cage. She cleared her throat. 'Martyne, did I hear you aright? Did Cascaras say he was journeying to the land of the opal moon?'

'Yes. I did not recall it before. Why? Surely, it's merely a figure of speech?'

'Merely a figure –' Chiisai stared at her. 'You do not know?'

'Know what? Cascaras often talked in such flowery language. It was a kind of verbal code he made up for himself to protect his destinations from those who might overhear.'

'Not this time.' She put down her empty cup and rose. 'Martyne, you have been of enormous help. More than you realize. At last I know the cause of all of this.'

Martyne was staring at her curiously for this last was said to herself.

'I'm glad I could help but –'

'Never mind. Perhaps I'll be able to explain it to you one day. Goodbye, Martyne.' And on light feet she left the mercado.

Behind her, a shadow detached itself from a darkened corner and slipped out after her into the night.

The room was painted a very dark blue, deeper even than the evening sky. The hue was enhanced by the domed ceiling crisscrossed by narrow arching gilt beams. Around the walls, too, the blue plaster panels were surrounded by gilt edging. Paintings of ships were hung at intervals.

The room was dominated by an enormous down bed, very high, with a brass headboard and a coverlet of exquisite manufacture of various shades of green. Great leaded-glass windows opened out onto a lush garden at the back.

In all, it was an unusual chamber bespeaking iconoclastic tastes. Yet by far the most remarkable feature was the painting. It hung as huge as a harvest moon directly over the bed in a heavy ornate gilt frame. It was so arresting, so chilling that one was compelled to wonder how she could sleep at night beneath its visage.

It depicted a Daluzan farmer, muscles bulging, skin shining with sweat, in an open field which was painted in such perspective that it appeared to go on for ever, flat and changeless. One great arm was around his wife's waist who cowered into the protection of his massive chest and shoulder as she desperately held onto a small child. In his other hand, the farmer held a great wooden-handled scythe which he had obviously been using to harvest his field. Now, however, it was raised into the darkening night sky, for swooping down upon him and his terrified family was an enormous creature, half-man, half-bat. The wide wings seemed to beat at the heavy air. Long curving talons extended from animal hands and human feet, darting at the farmer's throat.

Just as the Senhora Seguillas y Oriwara's extended fingers were slashing at Moichi's neck. Yet, oddly, he was able to take in the whole room as he struggled across the floor.

Moichi knew the basic blocks but this could only be termed a holding action for he had no offensive training in *koppo*. Too, if she were an adept, it would not take her long to circumvent his knowledge of the basics.

His flesh stung and his bones began to ache. He blocked another vicious strike aimed at his collarbone. Were it to land, he would be immediately disabled.

He rolled her over, using the force of her own momentum to bring them both around fully and, as he rode on top for just a instant, used his superior weight to drive his elbow and forearm into her stomach. Still she came on with a nose strike which would surely render him unconscious if it struck and, in utter desperation, he jammed his elbow home again, crouched and using the full bulk of his shoulder, driving downward, thinking of her as a male opponent.

'Oh!' The breath whooshed out of her and she tried to double up. She tried to gasp but he held her down and no air was coming in. She gagged, about to choke on her own vomit and he let her up, pinioning her arms behind her in a grip like iron. She rocked against his shoulder, gaining her wind. Astonishingly rapidly, he felt the strength returning to her arms. He tightened his grip on her wrists.

'Now, Senhora,' he said. 'Like it or no you will listen to what I have to tell you.'

He stared coldly down at her. Her eyes flew open, the pain fast diminishing and, as he watched the tiny brown flecks in the jade, he began to realize how extraordinarily beautiful she was.

With an effort, he began to speak. 'Cascaras is dead, Senhora. Tortured and then butchered in a Sha'angh'sei taverna.'

'What is that to me?' she said savagely. 'I know no one by that name.' She twisted violently, attempting to free herself from his savage grip.

'Perhaps not,' he said calmly. 'But I think you do know of him. For he was a friend of your daughter's. When I met her, Senhora, Aufeya was in Sha'angh'sei, about to be sold at auction in the Sha-rida.'

A swift intake of breath and, for the first time, he saw true emotion swimming within the jade seas of her eyes. Fear.

'Yes, the Sha-rida, Senhora, where a hideous death awaits all who are sold. This would certainly have been her fate had not I and a friend intervened. Later, she told me she was being pursued by a man, the same man who, I believe murdered Cascaras. It was but ill-fortune which took them both to the same city for they had planned it otherwise.' He watched her face closely and it seemed to him that it was constantly changing now but perhaps it was only the dim light combining with his own fancy. 'Aufeya was terrified of this man, Senhora, and I made the mistake of leaving her for a time. He came and took her, this man, and in the process, slew my friend. And I tell you now, Senhora, I mean to find Aufeya and bring her back just as I mean to destroy this man, Hellsturm.'

Her arms pinioned behind her caused her firm breasts to thrust out at him as if awaiting his caress. In their battle, the tied top of her blouse had come undone and now he could see all of the tops down almost to the nipples. These were most apparent as they pushed against the thin material. He tore his gaze away and said, 'Now I want you to answer my questions.'

She stared up at his face and under her acute gaze he felt himself suffused with a peculiar feeling.

'Let go of me,' she whispered. 'Please.' Her eyes closed for an instant, then opened. She was very close to him. He shifted his grip on her wrists to aid circulation and this brought her torso forward so that the hardened tips of her breasts grazed his chest.

'Release me,' she murmured against the hollow of his neck. 'Release me and I'll tell you all you wish to know.' She moaned as if in pain. 'All I know.' Then, as if she were reading his mind, 'I will not use the *koppo*.'

Slowly, his hands came away from her wrists. But he did not take his eyes from hers for it was there that he would know if she meant to betray him.

She flexed her fingers, bringing them upwards. She stared into his eyes. Her fingers came against him. This time softly, with no malice.

'What do you wish to know?' Voice like the sigh of the wind at night.

Her arms reaching, her fingers climbing his chest, past his shoulders until they went behind his head, twined in his hair. She pulled his head down to hers.

'I shall tell you,' she whispered, 'everything.'

But her lips opened under his, her tongue licking at his teeth. Her torso pressed against him and then she moved in some subtle way he was unable to fathom and her legs were apart, scissoring about his hips. He felt the frantic pressure of her as his arms surrounded her, pressing at the base of her spine.

A rustling; and then a soft moaning, echoing on and on and on.

There was time now before she met Moichi at the top of Calle Córdel and, striding along Corruña's nightdark streets, she began to look for an open taverna, hoping that it was not too late. She needed some time alone, to think.

She had taken the first corner on her side of the street as soon as she had left the mercado even though her mind had been filled by what Martyne had unknowingly told her.

It was a matter of routine. Bujun training. It was, in fact, part instinct which was, perhaps, one of the reasons why it was so monstrously effective.

Turning the corner was the first basic, used whenever one was in a foreign city, and she had automatically begun to listen to the sound of her own footsteps, then sorting, one by one, through the other sounds of the night around her, trees rustling in the wind, the cicadas' whine, an explosion of distant laughter, echoing, a door slamming and, further away, a dog barking angrily. Then she picked up the footfalls.

And she had known she was being followed almost as soon as she had made the turn.

She did not vary her pace but continued to walk down the street as if nothing was amiss. She required two things now from her surroundings. Another corner and a deep doorway, although a dark alley would do, too, in a pinch.

A corner came up and she went round it to the left, her eyes alert for the deep shadows. Time became critical now because there was little of it. She had to have disappeared before –

Found it. Slipped in on the left.

Waited, listening intently.

She remained quite still as she heard the sound of the footfalls approaching. She tensed her muscles, ready to – She frowned. Something wrong in the sound.

'Chiisai?'

Gods! she thought. It's Martyne.

'Chiisai!'

She began to sweat because she knew what was wrong now. The sounds of the footfalls had changed. There were two now to look out for and she was remembering what had been done to Kossori.

Could see a figure now. Martyne. A silhouette turning chiaroscuro as she passed a lantern. Then a return to darkness. And it had to be now before she passed once more into light. It was a chance and Chiisai briefly debated whether to let her pass by. But this, too, was dangerous, especially if Marityne was on the other side.

Darted out, one hand reaching for Martyne's arm, the other cupped over her opening mouth. Back into the doorway.

'What are you doing here?' she whispered fiercely.

'Chii –' The hand came over her mouth again.

'Whisper!'

'I came to warn you,' Martyne whispered breathlessly. 'Someone is following you.'

'I know.'

'Oh.' And then. 'Oh, I'm sorry. Now I've ruined it.'

Chiisai gazed out along the street. 'Perhaps not.' She strained to hear the footfalls. The heavier ones. And now she heard them, knew it was too late to get the other woman safely away from here. Well, she would just have to push her back into the shadows and hope no one saw her.

'Don't worry,' Martyne whispered. 'I'm armed.' She reached silently down to her waist, withdrew something.

Chiisai stared at it. It was fully half a metre in length, longer than any knife she had ever seen before. Its blade was of an unusual construction, triangular. Chiisai had seen one like it in a village in the countryside of Ama-no-mori. It was a hunter's knife, it was explained to her, the blade giving it exceptional force when it pierced the animal's flesh. 'One must reach a vital organ quickly and without destroying the flesh for one hunts only for food.' This knife of Martyne's, she knew, was a potent weapon, perfect for close combat.

'It's a miss'ra,' Martyne whispered. 'A Tudescan military weapon.'

Chiisai saw by the way she held the miss'ra that she knew how to use it. And abruptly she was happy to have this strange woman at her side for she could pick out at least three distinct sets of footsteps. Closing now.

She drew her dai-katana, the Bujun longsword. It was named, as was the custom with all such weapons, at the moment it had first tasted blood. Chiisai's was known as *kishsu-shi*, the Deathrider.

She could see the glint of metal now as they passed through the penumbra of the lantern and then returned to darkness. She turned to Martyne, whispered, 'If we should get separated somehow, meet me at the top of Calle Córdel at midnight. No one must follow you there. Do you understand?'

Martyne nodded. 'You can count on me.'

Chiisai fervently hoped so.

With a chill battle cry, Chiisai leapt into the street, the dai-katana held high above her in a two-handed grip, already beginning its lethal downwards sweep as soon as she had planted her feet firmly on the cobbles.

They were massive, their shadows, looming, larger by far even than Moichi. But she was a Bujun, a warrior from birth.

Kishsu-shi split the night air, humming, then slammed into the collarbone of one of the men on the left, opening him up to his navel. The corpse danced drunkenly, spewing blood and organs into the street. The man had not even had time to cry out.

Their swords were straight, perhaps heavier than her own, double-bladed. But they had not been forged by the Bujun, the supreme masters in such things.

Her blade wove a deadly web of silver in the air as pink and gold sparks flew at the points where the weapons intersected, clashing deafeningly one against the other.

Her opponents, she saw now, were sturdy Tudescans, immensely powerful and disciplined. These two before her worked in perfect unison, timing their blows and movements as if both sword arms belonged to one body.

Chiisai was aware, after only a few moments, that Martyne had neither been lying nor exaggerating about the savagery of the Tudescans. These were animals in the guise of men, murderous fanatics, appallingly dangerous.

She began to feel the fatigue for it was as if she battled an ungiving brick wall. Yes, she supposed she was quicker in her reflexes but these warriors had but to move their huge weapons fractionally in order to block her thrusts. This, of course, was what they were counting on. Once she slowed down, even slightly, they would move in for the kill.

There was a strategy open to her. She could feign more fatigue than she actually felt, thus forcing them to commit themselves prematurely. But this, she felt certain, would fool but one of them. Still –

She slowed down her defences and, immediately, the Tudescan on the right attacked her with ferocious acumen. Chiisai cried out and, ducking beneath the murderous blow, swept her sword in on a horizontal strike, leaning into it with all her might. The man went down as if pole-axed.

Now she stepped back, hearing for the first time the sounds of battle behind her. Martyne.

She withdrew her shorter blade and now she stood, feet wide apart, doubly-weaponed. She attacked, slashing high against the next warrior, using *kishsu-shi* in a horizontal strike across his chest. This he blocked effortlessly by bringing his own sword up obliquely. But Chiisai had already begun the inward movement of the shorter sword. He saw it at the last instant and all he could do was move his body. It was not nearly enough to save him. The blade's point punctured him on the left side but, as Chiisai compensated for his defensive motion, the sword slashed in towards his spine. His knees buckled and he knelt on the cobbles as if praying to his gods. Then he toppled over and lay still.

The third Tudescan moved in more cautiously. But she had made a mistake in watching his face and thus missed the blur of his sword point. It had not been aimed directly at her so there was no reflex action on her part. But the warrior had contrived to slap her short sword a glancing blow. Still, the blade was so huge and the force behind it so awesome that the strike sent her short sword whirling out of her grasp, clattering across the cobbles.

She went low then high and he blocked them both. And all the while he was forcing her back, slashing at her again and again. She realized that she was expending energy more rapidly than she would want. She saw too that she was coming to an alley which meant a more confined space. She would be at a distinct disadvantage wielding the long dai-katana. The only thing to do was to get rid of it.

Thus, in the entranceway to the alley, she allowed him to disarm her. Then she fell, rolling into him with enough force to bowl him over. As he went down, she withdrew her dirk and slashed out, stabbing.

He was now constrained to release his own sword for, at these close quarters it was more of a hindrance than a help. But he got one hand up quickly enough to ward off her first blow, deflect the second, and then he was into a counter-attack which almost undid her.

She panted and fought while he endeavoured to get on top of her in order to use his superior weight to full advantage. She knew, however, that if she allowed this to happen, it would be the end for her and so she switched hands, driving the dirk's blade from the opposite side. He saw it only at the last moment and he tried to deflect it again. But this time he was unprepared for the angle and missed it coming in.

Nevertheless, it was not a killing blow, the blade passing through the fleshy area just above the pelvis on the right side. He gritted his teeth and tried once more for supremacy but Chiisai held on, twisting the blade, with a tenaciousness that balked him.

Then he threw her off and, gaining his feet, stumbled off down the alley, thinking only now of returning from whence he had come.

Chiisai, aware of his intent, was obliged to make another split instant decision. To stay and help Martyne or to follow the Tudescan. In the end, it was not much of a decision because, realistically, the odds were piled on one side. And the odds said that if she were able to successfully follow this warrior without being detected, he would lead her to Hellsturm. Once his base was known, she would hopefully still have time to make the rendezvous with Moichi.

Sheathing her dai-katana and retrieving her short sword, she went carefully down the alley, following the Tudescan home.

'You know, you look Daluzan.'

Her fine face was softened now by the loss of tension, streaked with a combination of saliva and sweat.

'That is why I did not believe your story.'

And Moichi thought, She looks almost as young as Aufeya now. Younger, in some sense. She possessed a kind of little girl quality that was hard to describe. Soft and vulnerable yet without a trace of weakness he despised in people.

'I am quite wealthy,' Senhora Seguillas y Oriwara said softly, 'as you no doubt know. This makes me a target.' She was completely naked, lying beside him atop the coverlet of greens, her body magnificent in its dusky sensuality. Shadows pooling in the sweeping concavities lent her flesh a mysteriousness of aspect matching her spirit. 'There are very few days that go by when someone or other is not seeking money.' She sighed softly, turning against him in the enormous bed. The darkness of the painting rising above their heads was subtly oppressive. 'I rarely go out now because often – far too often – these people no longer ask but demand.' Her eyes stared into his. 'Can you understand that position, being a man?'

He laughed, attempting to leach away some of her returned anxiety. It had leapt from her to him at first contact and had pursued him doggedly throughout their time of loving. 'But with the *koppo* –'

She shook her head. 'You see, you *don't* understand. Whether I am a warrior, whether I can defend myself in whatever manner I choose, has absolutely no bearing on this.' She put a hand on his chest, spread her fingers, caressing his skin. 'Tell me, would a man, whether skilled or no as a warrior, *ever* find himself in such a position?'

He saw her point and shook his head. 'No.' She relaxed somewhat.

'You mean that, don't you?'

'Yes, of course. I would not say it otherwise.'

'Not even to please me?'

'Do I not please you in ways that are more honest?'

For the first time since he had met her earlier that day he saw her smile. 'Yes. Yes. As I have pleased you?'

'As you have pleased me, yes.' He took her hand from his flesh, kissed it. 'Do you not care about your daughter?'

She came onto her back, staring up at the domed vault of the cathedral ceiling. 'A very long time ago,' she said in a quiet voice, wrapped in the veils of the past, 'I was an independent woman. I sailed the seas on my own ship, battled, taking what I wanted, commanding a crew of thirty-seven, all fiercely loyal to me and me alone. Does that surprise you?' She looked over at him for a moment, just the flick of a glance.

'Not particularly. There is a storm inside of you. I felt it all the time we made love, a tidal wave of emotion. You are far too strong to be known as someone else's wife, no matter how influential or wealthy he might be.'

She made no comment to this, merely returned her gaze heavenwards and continued. 'I was happy yet, at the same time, filled with an inexplicable sadness which would overwhelm me when I lay down to sleep. It got so that I began to dread, then hate, the night. I could not remain in my cabin, oppressed as I was by that nameless terror so I would walk the decks, avoiding those on watch, save for the bosun who, the first night he saw me up and pacing, brought me a mug of hot grog. And every night after that.

'It helped somewhat, being alone in the night as if I could cleanse myself in the starlight and the moonlight. But all that ran through my head was the thought, It's not enough

'But what was it I wanted?'

A nightingale, perched upon the branches of the spreading pine in the garden outside the opened windows, began to sing. Over its shoulder, he could see the thinnest slice of the new moon like a sliver of delicate melon served up at the end of a banquet. Above the tree top, the sluice of the stars, part of the river of heaven, as sailors throughout the known world called it.

'Soon I became convinced that it was more money I craved. Thus I assuaged my sadness and fear by falling in with someone I met in a far-off port by the shore of a river that has no name. We made a pact. I was given many – implements which would aid me – and within the space of a single season I had gathered in more money than I had in the previous eight or nine. I began to sleep at nights and I was certain that I had found my cure.

'My partner, of course, got half of all I took in but that bothered me not at all for the ship was always riding low on the sea with the amounts of gold and silver and precious stones I had acquired.

'So it went for many seasons, the ease of it at first astounding and then, in the course of time, taken for granted. But all too soon I found myself again not able to sleep at night as I lay awake, crying in my cabin. I had not, after all, found my cure.'

He watched the rhythmic rise and fall of her breasts as she spoke, the play of soft light and shadow over the features of her face.

'Now my partner requested certain things of me – assignments, you might call them. Some I had no compunction against doing, others did not sit well with me. But when I balked, my partner insisted and I found myself, abruptly, in an untenable position. Thus I began to be manipulated as I was coerced. Now this peculiar unformed terror seized me always until at last I could bear the pain in my mind no longer. I went to my partner and said that I had no stomach for the work. I was laughed at. She spat in my face and told me that, didn't I know? All who worked for her did so for the length of their own lives.

'I told her that I could not bear to work for her a moment longer and threw at her feet all the arcane implements she had given me. She was enraged. She shook her fist at me, saying that she could slay me now but would not, that one day I would remember that moment and wish she had destroyed me then.'

She turned her head and looked at him, the light turning her jade eyes black for a moment.

'But I had to leave, you see, for I had at last found out what it was that distressed me so. In the course of my travels I had met someone. I had left him, you see. Well, I had to; my work dictated that. Now I realized that he was what I missed so terribly that it was a scar upon my heart, throbbing every night. I never saw him again, of course. One never does in situations like that; the world is far too vast. And, in any event, too much time had passed to make such a search practicable.

'Thus, when I took leave of my partner, I went ashore in search of a man who would make me happy. In due time, I met Milhos Seguillas and never again have I been to sea.' She was silent for a moment and Moichi found himself wondering, despite his fascination with her story, just what all this had to do with Aufeya. 'I do not want my daughter to repeat my mistakes,' she said at last.

'I am afraid there is not much one can do about such things. Life, it seems, is sometimes the only valid teacher.'

'Yes, I have learned that. The hard way.'

'What do you mean?'

She sat up, as if some inner turmoil would not now let her rest.

'We have not been – on the best of terms, Aufeya and I. Not for a long time. And before she left – before she left what little we did speak to each other was awful. We argued constantly.'

'About what?'

She turned her head away from him for a moment, her thick hair sliding across her shoulders. 'Oh, well, the usual things between mother and daughter. Everything – everything was blown out of all proportion.'

'Why did she run away then?'

She was silent, still turned away from him.

He reached out and touched her neck. 'She *did* run away, didn't she?'

'I don't want to talk about it.'

He could feel the tension singing in every muscle of her body. 'Yes, you do,' he told her gently. 'I think you want to talk about it very much.'

She moved back against him, a minute shift but it conveyed so much. He felt the vibrations, realized belatedly that she was crying silently, perhaps ashamed that he should see her thus, more naked than ever she could be in purely physical terms.

Slowly he put his arms around her, holding her to him.

He rocked her gently, waiting for her to continue.

At length, she did. 'I had only been in Corruña a very short time when I met Milhos, you see. Before that – directly before that – I had been in Rhein Tudesca on the last of my business assignments for my partner. I had met a man there, a strange, magnetic, beautiful man and for the time I had been in port – well, I stayed with him. It was Hellsturm.'

Outside, the nightingale had ceased its song and now even the darkness itself seemed to be holding its breath. But the night seemed a million miles away to him, part of another universe where people loved and laughed, did mundane things such as have dinner, go out to a play or perhaps just stroll quietly down near the sea. Here, a kind of chilling numbness had entered the room at some time when he had been looking elsewhere. Now it seemed to enwrap them both even as the leathery wings of the gigantic man-bat sought to enfold the Daluzan family above their heads.

'Many seasons later, he came to Corruña for he had heard that was where I was bound when I left him. By that time, I was already married to Milhos and deeply in love. But none of that seemed to matter to him. He wanted me. He was persistent but, at last, I prevailed upon him to leave me alone. I spent a night with him. Milhos knew none of this, then. I knew how he would take it. He was a man of great honour.'

'Then, for many seasons, life went on and I forgot all about Hellsturm. I became pregnant and I had Aufeya. Both Milhos and I were delighted. She grew up. Time seems to accelerate when you have a child. Then, inexplicably, Hellsturm returned as if from the mists beyond time itself and it all began again. Except this time there was Aufeya.' She put her hands against her face, her fingers slender and lovely, her long nails gleaming. When she took them away, her eyes seemed haunted, the green dulled. 'She was at an age when – everything seems difficult. She is an extraordinarily beautiful girl, my Aufeya, and at that time she was just ripening. She is wild and never more so than at that age.

She longed to be a woman and thus delighted in keeping around as many men as she could manage. It was a goodly number. I objected to this most strenuously, sending them away. And she was furious. But I did not think it right. I, too, was wild when I was her age and I begrudged her no wildness of her own. But I had had no benefit of parents in my youth and had got into so much trouble that at times later I would wonder how I lived to become a woman. This danger I could not allow to touch Aufeya. Yet my restrictions only served to make her more contrary and we argued ceaselessly.'

She shook her head and he watched her eyes. 'Into this came Hellsturm, wanting the same thing. This time I refused him utterly; it was out of the question, I told him. I had thought, I suppose foolishly, that that one night would get rid of him for ever.' She ran her fingers through her hair, her head lifted, and now he saw the motes in her eyes, as bright as flecks of gold. 'He got to Aufeya. At school, at the mercado, at a taverna; there were any number of places. He told her many things, some, I imagine, based on the truth. But he has a way of twisting everything, even the truth, so that it serves his purpose. He has a tongue of gold, that one.' She took his hand, palm upward, traced the lines of his thumb and fingers. 'Easy enough to guess what happened next. He seduced her as he had seduced me so many seasons before. But in the process he poisoned her mind against me. She went off with him, Dihos only knows where. And that was the last I saw of her.'

'What about the Senhor?' Said it very softly.

He felt her shudder. 'I had to tell him, then, naturally. His temper was, at times, uncontrollable and, as I said, he was a terribly proud man. He challenged Hellsturm to a duel.'

Now Moichi recalled Armazón's words and wondered. Could he be right? Could the Senhora have been in league with Hellsturm against Milhos Seguillas? But for what reason? There was one possible answer. The Senhora had loved her husband but perhaps she loved her daughter more.

'Dihos, I was terrified! I knew from experience what Hellsturm was like and I knew that despite his prowess Milhos had little chance of surviving against him. So I pleaded with him. I cried, I screamed, I threatened. But it was no good. I am not Daluzan, you see. I am not of the blood. I had no clear idea then just how sacred was the Daluzan duel. Once the challenge had been given, there was no way to rescind it, even if Milhos had wanted to, which he certainly did not. There was no turning him away.' She stopped abruptly, as if she had come to the end of her tale.

'Go on,' he prompted.

'There is nothing much left to tell, really. Milhos met Hellsturm and died.'

There was a silence for a time and he listened to the quietude of the night interrupted, only briefly, by a soft clatter of wings. He wondered if a storm was on the way. Inside this room, he had no way of telling if the wind had shifted.

'I had heard about the duel before, I must confess.'

Her hand moved back and forth over the turned-back coverlet, smoothing non-existent wrinkles.

'Aboard the lorcha,' he continued, trying to get her attention. 'But then it had a somewhat different ending.'

'Oh?' She did not even turn around.

'It was said – that the duel had not been fair.'

She laughed without humour. 'Would that it were so, Moichi. For then Hellsturm would be fair game for me to hunt down and kill. I hate him with all my heart and soul.'

'But he's taken your daughter.'

'She went with him willingly.'

'Then tell me why, when I met her, she was terrified of him. "He has pursued me for ten thousand leagues," she said to me.'

'People change. Perhaps she has grown up. She knows

now just how evil people can be.'

He felt the need to return to the other question. 'There was talk of you poisoning your husband in order to let Hellsturm win the duel.'

Her head turned. 'What? Who told you such a lie?'

'Armazón.'

'Ah. I might have known.'

'It makes no sense.'

'Oh, yes, Moichi. It makes perfect sense to me.'

'He was devoted to the Senhor.'

She nodded. 'Yes. And hopelessly in love with me.'

Chameleon. That was the basis of it.

The Bujun were masters at observing nature and learning from it. The chameleon was a harmless creature. It was non-aggressive and it could be outrun by many predators. What nature had given it was the remarkable ability of camouflage so that it could blend in with any surrounding.

The Bujun had taken this and adapted it for the basis of their surveillance techniques.

Now she knew that it was not going to work.

Because there was something missing.

In order to be able to blend in with one's surroundings, one first needs those surroundings. In Sha'angh'sei or in her own native Eido, there would be no problem. But this was Corruña.

She needed people and there just weren't any.

So it was not going to work.

Because the only way the wounded Tudescan would lead her to his base was if he believed that no one was following him. If he even suspected her presence, he would lead her on a false trail.

Naturally, the density of people during the daylight hours is much higher than at night. But cities such as Sha'angh'sei or Eido never sleep and even in the dead of night there is a sufficient amount of people about.

Not in Corruña.

By sound alone she was liable to be given away and the moment he suspected she would have to call it off. Now each moment she delayed increased the chances of his spotting her.

She did the only thing she could do.

She went off the streets.

He rolled off the bed, went across the room to the windows, stuck his head outside and sniffed. A red-winged blackbird, disturbed by the intrusion, clattered away in alarm. A storm was indeed coming; from the west. Back inside the room he kept his back to the huge painting; it still gave him the creeps.

'Perhaps they had a fight,' he said. 'A falling out.' He meant Aufeya and Hellsturm.

'I hope so. Knowing them both, it seems likely.'

He turned on her. 'You are certainly taking this calmly.'

Her dark eyes watched him intently for a moment. 'You do not know my daughter at all well, Moichi. She precipitates fights like clouds release rain.'

'Fights are one thing,' he said patiently. 'But she was obviously terrified of the man. He tortured Cascaras, then murdered him. He was a friend of Aufeya's.'

'Ah, well, there you have it then. Hellsturm is a jealous man, when it comes to his women.'

'She said to me, "Now I am the only one." I know what I heard. In any case, Cascaras was old enough to be her father.'

'That would certainly not deter her.'

'By God, Senhora, I do not understand you!' he thundered.

'Quite right, my darling, you don't.' She reached up for him. 'Now come here.'

'What do you want?'

'What do you think?'

He knelt atop the bed and she drew him towards her. He kissed her opened lips, his mouth sliding down the smooth column of her neck. She was quite irresistible. Apart from the lushness of her body, Moichi had been with women who were as finely formed. But she had an aura that was palpable; a kind of sexual intensity which spoke directly to the very core of his being. Downwards to her hanging, shivering breasts.

'Mmmm,' she moaned.

Afterwards, the first thing she said was: 'You are in love with Aufeya.'

His head snapped up and he stared into her eyes.

'What makes you say that?'

'A mother knows.' She laughed, not unkindly.

He pulled away from her embrace. 'This is fun for you.'

She smiled. 'And why not? I haven't had much fun lately.' Her fingers reached for him. 'Can you tell me honestly that you did not enjoy it yourself.'

'No. But you know very well what I mean.'

'Yes,' she said, her eyes flashing, 'I know only too well. But you must take my word for it. Aufeya is in no danger. Hellsturm will not harm her.'

'How can you be so certain?'

'Because,' she said softly, 'I have promised to return to him.'

The major problem now was the inconstant moon.

Clouds had begun moving in from the northwest, riding past the face of the horned moon; its silver light played in and out.

Because of the night's monochrome illumination, perspectives and distances were difficult enough to judge under normal circumstances.

These were far from normal circumstances. Distances were, of course, increased and motion was a constant. But cerebration was continuing all the time.

The only real danger was at the edges.

Chiisai raced across a flat rooftop, slowing only just before the low tile parapet. Now the moon had gone in once more and the dense shadows leapt upwards, distoring the space between the buildings. Corrections had to be made on the run.

She sprang across the narrow abyss, hit a small stone on landing and tumbled, immediately drawing herself up into a compact ball. Rolling dissipated much of the momentum and she was on her feet again, silently flitting amid the flock of bats hovering about the rooftop.

The Tudescan had never left her sight and now, though he checked behind him at odd intervals and was quite thorough in other ways, using shadows and doorways where he could, he was totally unaware of her.

Across the maze of Corruña they fled, the hunter and the hunted.

'It's part of the bargain we made,' she said. 'He cannot touch her now.'

'But I tell you that he already has.'

'That is quite impossible.'

'Then something has changed. Perhaps there is an element you know nothing about.'

'He would not put in jeopardy what he desires above all else.'

Restless, he went back to the window, searching for the moon. It was only a wan glow now, behind small and puffy cumulus driving in from the northwest.

A storm for certain, he thought.

It was nearing midnight.

'I have to go,' he said.

'Will you come back?' Her voice seemed suddenly small in the huge room with the cathedral ceiling and the terrible painting.

'Yes,' he answered. 'How could I not? But perhaps not again tonight.'

'In the morning then.'

'All right.'

She turned on him abruptly and he saw a fear shining in her jade eyes. He started slightly, seeing Aufeya there.

'Promise me you'll come, Moichi.' Her fingers gripped him with a fierce pressure. 'There is only you now in all the world.'

'I –'

'Are you not my friend, Moichi?' she asked desperately. 'Has this evening meant so little to you?'

'It has meant a great deal to me,' he said, thinking that perhaps he did understand her now. He had been given a gift, something quite precious, something she withheld from almost everyone. Save Hellsturm, now. It was ironic. Almost amusing, if it had not been so utterly, desolately tragic. This woman's love for her daughter transcended everything else. Now it was his turn. He could accept or refuse. 'It means a great deal to me. It always will.'

'We are friends.'

'You do me a great honour.' It was formal, even seeming somewhat stilted after their previous intimacy. Yet, he knew full well, one was of the flesh and the other – well, it was quite easy to make the body perform. Drawing the spirit in was quite another. There was no coercion for that; only corruption.

As if on cue, they came together, kissing each other chastely on the lips. Inside, he felt her spirit swirling towards him, felt his emerging. They danced.

The room was quite still.

Presently, they drew apart, she to draw on her robe, he to dress for the street.

Before he left, he asked her one question, 'Why do you have that painting in this room?'

'It is of the diablura. Do you know of it? No? In the

Daluzan religion the diablura is the ancient of night, the emperor of evil.'

'The devil.'

'The devil, yes.'

'Why is it here?'

'To remind me, always.'

'Come and sit next to me, little one,' the Dai-San had said. This was what her name Chiisai meant.

They were in the palace of the Kunshin, just outside Eido, the capital of Ama-no-mori.

'Have you any idea what you wish to do with your life?'

She looked at him. He had been in Ama-no-mori for some time now but she never tired of searching the seemingly endless configurations of his strange visage. Every time she thought she had committed it to memory she would look again and find it different from how she had remembered it, though she might have seen him just the day before. Sometimes there was only some subtle change, at other times the differences were great.

He might appear frightening to others, like a god embodied and come to earth for, more than anything else, this was perhaps just what he was. Yet to her, he was much more. He was a brother. A brother she never had, but had always yearned for.

'Are you playing my father's role now?' she asked him, only half-serious.

He smiled his peculiar smile, a devastating gesture and she realized abruptly how she cherished his friendship and his love. He stood up, towering over her. He took her hand in his, her skin feeling the harsh abrasive hide of the gauntlet.

'Shall we go outside.' The construction was of a question but the inflection was not.

It was just past midday. The heat of the lemon-coloured sun struck them, enveloping them in its warmth. Cicadas shrilled and grey plovers shot up from their hiding places in the tall grass.

The horizon was laced with the domed configurations of the cryptomeria and the high sword-edged pines. Far in the distance loomed the purple slopes of Fujiwara, wreathed now in a gentle haze. And, before it, she knew was the newly-completed shrine at the site of Haneda Castle, birthplace of the Dai-San, destroyed in the titanic death-struggle between dor-Sefrith and the Dolman during the time of his birth.

'Are you happy here?' Though the Dai-San spoke perfect Bujun, the ancient of languages, which only a few Bujun still learned, the configurations of his mouth lent his speech peculiar inflections which took some time to decipher.

Chiisai wondered at his using the old tongue. She, of course, being the Kunshin's daughter, was also fluent. She longed to know what he wanted or, at the very least, what it was she was expected to say.

As if divining her thought, he said, 'Tell me the truth, little one. Nothing else is important.'

'All right,' she said, gratefully, feeling as if a great weight had been taken off her. Under his intense gaze, she felt a melting within herself and, with it, a subtle tension which had been holding her, ebbing. 'No, I'm not.'

He nodded. 'I understand.'

'You do?' She had not believed that anyone would, which was why she had, until this moment, held this knowledge secret even, in some ways, from herself.

'Oh, yes,' he said, his voice like the rolling of thunder over a vast plain. 'I, too, have known the restlessness which now haunts you. There was no reason to hide it, little one.'

'But my father –'

'My darling, your father understands these things. He asked me to speak to you because he knows well the power of Bujun tradition.'

'I could not tell him these things directly.'

'He surmised this.'

'I want to go away,' she said, for the first time truly realizing it herself. 'But I don't want him to think that I am abandoning him.'

'I am quite certain that whatever sadness he feels will be dispelled by his thoughts of your happiness.' He looked away from her. 'Now that that's settled, where would you like to go?'

'I – why I don't really know.'

'Would you care to sail to Sha'angh'sei?'

Even recalling it now, hearing his echoey voice again in her mind, she knew he had said it with complete innocence, totally devoid of overtones or hidden meanings.

She had been delighted and had accepted immediately.

He said, 'When you arrive, I want you to see a friend of mine, little one. You have heard me speak his name often. My bond-brother.'

'Moichi –'

'Yes. Moichi Annai-Nin. This is very important, little one. I want you to see Moichi Annai-Nin. I want you to give him the gifts I have for him.'

'How long shall I stay in Sha'angh'sei?' she asked.

He turned to her, the sunlight striking the odd planes of his face. Never had he looked more startling nor more beautiful to her. 'That is entirely up to you but I imagine that you may wish to stay there quite some time.'

Now, as she flitted like some human bat across the sloping rooftops of Corruña, Chiisai wondered at that long-ago meeting. She thought that, for once, the Dai-San had been proved wrong for she had surely not stayed in Sha'angh'sei for any length of time. Yet though she might well have felt alone and afraid in this strange city, she felt only a kind of excited warmth stealing over her. Was this truly why she had come to the continent of man? And was it merely a coincidence that she had arrived at Sha'angh'sei? It was, after all, the continent of man's largest port and, not so coincidentally, the closest one to Ama-no-mori.

Still, she could not put out of her mind the fact that the Dai-San had suggested it as her destination. She had never questioned that nor second-guessed herself. Surely it had been she and she alone who had been master of her fate. She had always been free to choose whatever destination she had desired. She had chosen Sha'angh'sei.

Or had she?

Echoes of the Dai-San's last words to her rebounded in her mind now. *I imagine that you may wish to stay there quite some time.* Did he know something that she did not?

She shrugged mentally, putting the puzzle aside for the moment. She had more pressing matters to occupy her attention.

They were now in the far western quarter of Corruña and the Tudescan, despite his twists and turns, was still heading almost due west. At this rate, they would soon leave the city far behind them.

She glanced upwards for a moment, checking the position of the moon to gauge the time. It was but a diffuse glow now, sifting through the scudding clouds which had begun to move in more strongly from the northwest. Perhaps a storm, she thought, and fervently hoped that it would hold off until the Tudescan reached his destination.

He was still moving west and she knew that unless she broke off now she would never make the rendezvous with Moichi. Sweat broke out along the line of her forehead and along her upper lip but, wiping it away, she remembered Martyne and silently prayed to her gods that the woman had been victorious and would make the rendezvous in her stead. For the moment, she ignored the other problem.

For now the Tudescan was at last slowing, carefully making a final check in all directions. This was it and, waiting until he had completed his survey of the surrounding area, she swung down from the rooftop into the street behind him, grateful, because the diminished light was making long-range surveillance hazardous.

They were in a section of the city densely-packed with two-storey buildings – only Corruña's iglesias seemed to be taller – windowless, with flat, undecorated roofs. Warehouses, she surmised, for it was here that the major overland trade routes to other Daluzan cities, and to the lands beyond Daluzan's borders, converged at Corruña's western outskirts.

Here, for the first time, she saw families of people asleep in the streets, against building walls, in darkened doorways. These were workers who awakened each day just as dawn was about to break in the eastern sky to meet the vast silent caravans arriving from far-off lands, paid a few coppers to off-load the myriad dry-goods, ferrying them on their backs to the nearby warehouses of the merchants.

She went carefully between them as had the wounded Tudescan and, at length, in a huge courtyard, she spied a small caravan of perhaps six camels waiting to depart. They were within the shadows of the high western gate of the city.

It was to this group of men, squatting around a small fire, that the Tudescan went. Chiisai dared not get close enough, in the quiet, desolate night, to hear what they were saying but she crept up until she had a decent view. One put a blanket onto the ground for the wounded man, working on him, while another, squatting near the prone man's head, questioned him about what had transpired. There came a quick movement from the squatting man. He shouted something that was quite incoherent to her and hauled the wounded man up onto his feet. He seemed enormously powerful. There came more shouting and, abruptly, she felt movement behind her and whirled, saw two huge eyes staring past her out of a small face. It was a young cambujo girl, one of the many children of the workers' families who lived here without proper housing. She had been awakened by the noise and now craned her neck to see what all the commotion was about.

Chiisai returned her attention to the scene of the argument just in time to see the brief flash of metal as the angered man thrust a knife into the stomach of the wounded man. He threw the corpse from him with the tip of his boot as if it was just so much fetid garbage. Could this be Hellsturm? If so, he had not taken kindly to his henchman's failure.

Now Chiisai could feel the presence of the young girl closer behind her, so near, in fact, that she could discern the other's shivers. She turned her body slightly and opened out her right arm. The girl crawled into the warm space and Chiisai wrapped her in her cloak.

Then, as she regarded the caravan camp, she knew that she had run out of time. All the men were standing. One of them kicked desultorily at the fire. Another swung a canvas saddlebag onto the neck of one of the camels. She saw now that the animals had been feeding. They were nearly finished. When that happened, she knew, the caravan would be off.

She looked at the shivering girl crouched beside her, head on her shoulder, then back to the readying caravan. From her sash, she drew out three copper coins, held them out so that the girl could see what they were. Then she pressed them into the small hand, closing the fingers around them.

The girl lifted her head, staring at her wonderingly and Chiisai put her lips to the girl's ear for long moments. The girl's eyes were wide, black as obsidian.

'Do you know where to go?' Chiisai whispered in Daluzan.

The girl nodded emphatically.

'You must start now,' Chiisai said. 'What is my name?'

'Chiisai,' the girl said. She smiled up at the strange face. 'Chiisai goes northwest.'

Water's Edge

Calle Córdel was deserted when he arrived.

It was just before midnight, he judged, squinting up at the smudge of moonlight. This, too, was fast disappearing as the cloud cover thickened. He sniffed, could smell it now.

The storm.

He pulled his Daluzan cloak tight about him but the rising wind plucked at its edges, exposing the silken lining.

Had this been one of Milhos Seguillas's? If so, he knew it was a singular honour that the Senhora had given it to him. She was so much a lady –

He looked around him. Shuttered doorways and darkened windows. Only a few flickering night lanterns for company.

Where was Chiisai?

He glanced upwards reflexively again but now all traces of moonlight had left the sky. In the distance, he thought he could hear a rolling boom of thunder.

A thin grey dog with a matted coat padded down a side street, stopped, regarded him for a moment, then lifted its leg and urinated against the side of a building. It turned and sniffed it before mooching slowly onwards, nose to the ground for any trace of something to eat.

The trees whispered their enigmatic sighing song; they bowed slightly.

Past midnight now.

Where was she?

He turned abruptly at a sharp sound. Boots against cobbles. For a moment, they stopped and he turned away. Then they resumed. He turned back.

A woman came into view, tall and long-necked. Her face was in shadow.

She stopped when she saw his bulk, tentative now but unafraid.

He saw that she carried a weapon in her left hand, at the ready.

'Who are you?' he said.

She said nothing but continued to stand in the centre of the street. There was no one else around.

He moved a step closer. The shadows made it impossible for him to tell anything about her. This he did not like.

The knife with the triangular blade was lifted so that he could see its explicit threat.

'Come no closer,' she warned. Her voice floated to him eerily on the night.

He felt the change in atmospheric pressure and the rolling crack of thunder was now unmistakeable. He stared from the black pool of her face to the knife-blade. With a start, he saw that it was dark and shiny. Blood. This woman had but recently been in some kind of fight.

'Do you need any help?' he asked.

She stood as immobile and silent as a statue.

'Are you hurt?'

'I am unharmed,' she said after a time. 'Will you leave willingly now or –' the blade moved a fraction higher.

'I am here to meet someone,' he said. 'A friend. I will not move.'

Now she took a step forward, partially into the aureole of light from a nearby lantern, swinging now in its cage as the rising wind tossed it. 'You are not Daluzan.'

'No.' He saw her face for the first time. Long and narrow and attractive. A strong face, full of character. He wondered who she was. Then it occurred to him that she would be asking herself the same questions. 'I am Moichi Annai-Nin of Iskael.'

This statement seemed to quell some of her suspicion and he saw her relax somewhat. He saw her peering at him closely.

'You are not Tudescan.'

He stiffened. 'What know you of Tudescans here?'

'Too much,' she said. 'My friend and I were attacked by four Tudescans some little time ago. They followed her from the mercado and –'

'Chiisai!'

She stepped up to him, placed the knife-point just under his breastbone.

He made no move, merely stared into her eyes. They were large and glossy and intelligent.

'Quickly now. Tell me,' she snapped. 'Are you friend or foe?'

'Chiisai is my friend,' he said evenly, taking no offence at her brusque manner. 'She is the only daughter of the Kunshin of the Bujun.'

'She is royalty?' said the other. 'She did not tell me.'

'She would hardly wish it known,' he said. He noticed that the knife-point still touched his shirt front. 'I set a rendezvous with her earlier to meet me here just before midnight.'

Now the knife disappeared inside the other's cloak. 'I am Martyne,' she said. 'Chiisai told me to meet her here at midnight if we were separated in the mêlée. We were.'

'What has happened to her?'

'She is all right. She killed two of the Tudescan warriors and wounded a third. Perhaps she did this deliberately for she allowed him to escape and then went after him.'

Clever girl, Moichi thought. But now they were out of touch with each other. He shrugged mentally. There was nothing he could do now but carry on with what he had planned to do. He had no idea where she was. He would just have to wait to see if she contacted him.

'Come on,' he said turning. 'I have to meet a Daluzan in a taverna at the foot of Calle Córdel. You might as well come along. I want to hear the whole story.'

* * *

El Cambiro was at the foot of Calle Córdel, hard by the wooden wharves of Corruña.

The smell of the sea was thick in the air, rich and heady and robust and Moichi, breathing deeply, felt instantly invigorated.

The creaking of the ship's fittings as they rested some distance out at anchor came as clearly to him as if they had been alongside. That was the water, he knew, an excellent conductor of sound both above and below.

Fishermen were already taking down their nets from where they had hung drying in the hot sun all the long afternoon. Now they spread them out along the quiet quays, before the dew got to them, rotting the hemp, picking out the last bits of seagrape and flotsam that had caught there the day before, then rolling them carefully up into long lines, taking them, two to a net, on board their fishing lorchas, stowing them on deck, then covering them with a tarpaulin.

A bit of canvas fluttered in the wind, thumping; the slap-slap of the tide against the piling, increasing as the coming storm whipped up the surface of the sea.

Beyond the sanctuary of the port, he could see that the sea was already heavy. Visibility was unusually clear and the horizon, restlessly shifting with the sea swells, stretched blackly away.

The taverna was a low, squat structure of whitewashed plaster with a swinging wooden door, through which lemon light poured beckoningly, and a creaking sign over its frontage, depicting a giant crab, so elaborately carapaced it seemed prehistoric.

They went inside.

The place was as wide as it was deep, its rough-hewn walls echoed in the plain wooden tables and chairs, stained with a combination of drink and sea water. The ceiling was low with thick wooden beams striping its length. An enormous fire crackled in a stone hearth set into the far wall. A dark wood bar curved along the left-hand wall. Behind it, shelves lined with bottles. It was smoky inside and smelled of liquor and fat and tallow.

Moichi led Martyne to an empty table in a corner opposite the bar where he could see the door without having to turn around. They ordered a local brew as thick and dark and almost as sweet as mead.

The place was not quite half-full. A seaman sat slumped over near the hearth, his head cradled in his burly arms, a line of empty glasses at one elbow. No one bothered to take them away, not even when he twitched in his sleep and sent one of them crashing to the earthen floor.

A pair of weathered sailors, their faces lined and scarred, played dice, the rattle rhythmic and soothing like the slap of the sea against a ship's hull.

The fat man with the greasy jowls and the three-day-old beard behind the bar hummed a tuneless sea-shanty, wiping at the already gleaming bartop.

It was well past midnight.

A tall Daluzan sailor came in and, taking off his knit cap, smacked it against his thigh several times. He went to the bar and the fat man drew him a drink then went back to his wiping. The sailor took the glass to an unoccupied table and slumped down. He took a long swallow, smacked his lips noisily.

Moichi sipped at his drink not liking it much. Martyne had told him as much as she knew but he wished that she knew more. She had obviously provided Chiisai with a crucial clue to the key to this entire affair. This she had repeated to him but he still had no idea what it meant. He was abruptly angry at Chiisai for running off. Unfortunately, he had to agree with what she did. To allow such a chance to slip past would have been inexcusable. But, of a sudden, he felt in the dark and it was a truly uncomfortable sensation. He felt as though he were battling shadows.

The door opened, pulling him away from his gloomy

thoughts. A cambujo boy, thin and small, came in and looked around. He had a package under his arm.

He spotted Moichi and trotted over to where he sat with Martyne. He handed Moichi the package and started to leave.

'What is this?' Moichi asked.

The boy turned around, shrugged. 'Only what it seems, Senhor. A package for you.'

'How do you know me?'

The boy shrugged again as if this was his only gesture. 'The man on the pier gave me the package. He told me what you look like.'

'What man? What did he look like?'

'It was dark, Senhor. Very little light. I did not notice.' He turned away and ran out the door.

Moichi stared down at the package for a moment. It was fairly small, wrapped in oiled paper with fisherman's twine. Carefully, he unwrapped it.

Martyne gasped.

It was a man's heart, covered in blood. It was wrapped with a sweat- and blood-soaked purple headband. Rohja's.

Moichi covered the thing up with the oiled paper and very quietly said, 'I want you to get up and walk out of here as if nothing has happened. Go back to the mercado and forget all about this. Do you understand?'

'I want to help,' Martyne whispered. 'Anything I can do –'

'I have just told you what you can do. Please do it. Now. I will have Chiisai contact you when it is safe; when all this is over. I'm sorry I brought you here, Martyne. It was foolish on my part. Please go now.'

She stared at him for a minute then nodded briefly. She slid out of the chair and went to the door, went through it without looking back.

When she had gone he stood up. He left Rohja's heart

where it sat, covered, on the table and left the taverna.

Now he burned with a cold fury.

There was nothing but the sea and the sky.

The racing clouds had erased even the shadows.

He thought that it would be fruitless but he did it anyway. Nothing could have stopped him. He prowled the jetties and wharves, the tavernas and fish markets, the homes of the waterside cambujo and the two or three gigantic warehouses dockside. He searched for Hellsturm for surely it had been he who had barbarously plucked the heart from the young seaman. He recalled Martyne's description of the Tudescans. *They are like beasts.* But she was wrong for no beast would ever do such a thing for sport. Beasts hunted to eat; killed so that they might continue to live. There was a terrible calculatedness in this that went far beyond bestiality. It was demonic.

Just the splashing sea and the lowering sky and Moichi Annai-Nin betwixt, striding the creaking timbers of the docks, his eyes alight with a ferocity as the anger shook him. And along with it, he felt a kind of seeping despair. For the world would never change. Men and women and, yes, children too would die as others were being born: and new cities would be built upon the rubble of the old; and ever, ever would there be those who worshipped evil, who practised its dark secret rites, seeping from them like coagulating blood.

He was alone in the dark for now even the fishermen who had earlier been abroad, were belowdecks in their lorchas, asleep before the coming of dawn, the last guardians gone, it seemed to him, and now Corruña was alight with the myriad dreams of its inhabitants and he, alone in all the city, awake.

He thought, unbidden, of Kossori, of the man's youth when he was utterly alone along the Sha'angh'sei bund and he felt tears welling up behind his eyes. Now he knew what it was like. So desolate, not like the real world at all. Even animals had somewhere to go.

At length, having exhausted his search and perceiving that it was near daylight, he turned his mind to more practical matters. Chiisai. She was his only possible link now to Hellsturm. She would, if she could, he knew, send him a message. But to where? She knew of three places he might be in Corruña. The tavern, El Cambiro, where she knew they were to meet Rohja; the house of Senhora Seguillas y Oriwara; and Aufeya's lorcha. He rejected the first immediately. Even if he had met Rohja, Chiisai knew that they would be there for only a short time; much too risky. Another kind of risk held true for the house; Chiisai would have no way of knowing how his 'interview' with the Senhora turned out, whether he was now considered friend or foe there; that was out. Only the lorcha remained.

The sailor on watch saluted him as he came up the gangplank.

'Has anyone come on board tonight?' Moichi asked him. 'Other than members of the crew.'

The man shook his head. 'Not on my watch, *piloto*. But I have only just come on.'

'Who had the watch before you?'

'Armazón, *piloto*. He is below now.'

'All right. I am going to see him. If anyone comes – anyone at all – call me immediately.'

'Aye, *piloto*.'

Moichi went for'ard, easing himself down the companionway belowdecks. He went past the tiny but superbly efficient galley, for'ard into the crew's quarters. Most of the berths were, of course, empty as many of the men had chosen to spend the night in the city with their families or girlfriends. Armazón was not in his berth.

He turned and went aft to the captain's quarters. This was where Aufeya had slept and even on the return voyage, Moichi had not stayed there, preferring to give it to Chiisai. Now he found Armazón asleep on the captain's wide bed, one arm flung across his face.

Moichi woke him.

'Oh, it's you,' Armazón said. 'Thought we'd all seen the last of you.' He rolled back onto the bed.

'Has anyone come aboard tonight?'

'Huh. No. Nobody.'

He went up the companionway and off the lorcha. He had just stepped onto the timbers of the pier when he thought he caught a movement deep in the shadows near a pile of wooden casks. They were empty, rotting husks now.

He saw a small face appear and took his hand from the hilt of his sword. He moved towards the face but it darted away from his and he was obliged to leap over the barrels. He grabbed hold of the small body.

'Come here, little one,' he said. 'Who is it you seek?' He saw her clearly now, a small girl.

'Begging your pardon, Senhor, but would you tell me your name before I answer?'

Moichi laughed. 'Yes, of course. I am Moichi Annai-Nin.' He gazed at her. 'And who might you be?' He put her on his lap.

'Alma, senhor. I have a message for Moichi Annai-Nin.'

'Tell me it then,' he said, on edge.

She lifted one small hand up to his face. 'Please, senhor, let me see your nose.'

'My nose? Why in –' Then he perceived that she was looking for the diamond set into the dusky flesh of his nostril. 'Have you found it then?'

'Yes, senhor. The message is from Chiisai. She told me to come to this lorcha but to speak only to you. I have been here for some time. I went aboard earlier but the man blocked my way and said he had never heard of you and to go away. When I didn't, he said you would be away all night but had told him to take any message that might come. I did not believe him, Senhor.'

'And you did well not to,' Moichi said, tousling her hair.

'Tell me, Alma, what did this man look like?' She described Armazón.

'Chiisai found me near the western gate, senhor. There a small caravan was about to depart. Not a trade caravan for we knew nothing about it. She said to tell you that she is well and that she travels northwest.'

'She follows the caravan.'

'Yes, senhor.'

'Did you see any of the men in the caravan?'

'Not well enough to describe them to you.'

Was Hellsturm among them, he wondered.

'I did right to wait, senhor.'

'Yes, Alma, you did.'

'It's scary here, at night.'

'Is it.'

She nodded. 'Yes, it is. That man from the lorcha came around once or twice, looking for me. But I hid behind the barrels and he didn't find me.'

Moichi hugged her affectionately. 'You are very brave.' He dug into his sash and gave her a silver piece. 'This will buy much food and clothing, Alma. But if you take it you must promise me you'll do something.'

'What, Senhor?'

'Buy yourself a warm cloak.' He stood up, putting her on the timbers. Her arms reached up and he lifted her. She kissed him on the mouth. A decidedly un-childlike kiss.

'Go on now,' he said softly. 'See that you go straight home.' He watched her silently as she ran down the length of the quay, as unobtrusive as a shadow and disappeared amidst the streets of the city.

He went aboard the lorcha again, coming silently into the captain's cabin. He hauled Armazón out of the berth.

'What – What are you doing?' the other spluttered.

'No one came aboard asking for me, eh?'

'Why, no,' he said, righteously. 'I told you that. Anyone who says different is a blasted liar.' His fingers prised desperately at Moichi's grip but it was like iron.

'It's you who lie, Armazón.' He jerked the bosun towards him. 'About the Senhora. Now about the cambujo girl.' He dragged the man off the bed; his pants were half off. 'What a twisted mean soul you have. You disgust me!'

'Listen, listen,' Armazón cried. 'It was probably Rohja who has filled your head with all these stories about me. They are totally untrue, believe me! He wishes only to become this ship's new bosun. He'll say anything to get that –!'

Moichi slapped him across the face and he whimpered. 'Shut up, you insect! Rohja is dead but while he lived he said not one word against you to me.' He began to drag the man down the ship to the companionway. 'The little cambujo girl found me on the dock.'

'But she lies!' Armazón pleaded. 'I wouldn't give the little beggar food, that's all. And who could blame me? If I gave some to her, I'd have to give to all of them.'

'Do you think I'm an idiot to believe such a tale?

He hauled the bosun topside. He found a suitable length of hemp and tied Armazón's wrists above his head, then he slung the man up over his shoulder and began to ascend the mast.

Terrified, Armazón screamed. 'I'll see you pay for this! Gods, what are you going to do to me? I'll see that the Senhora Seguillas y Oriwara hears about this!'

'You do that,' Moichi said grimly as he tied a knot to the crosstree. He let Armazón go so that he hung there by his wrists.

Back on the deck, Moichi turned to the man on watch, saying: 'Tell the men. Whosoever cuts this man down will answer to me.'

The sailor, switching his gaze from Moichi to the strung bosun, swallowed convulsively, said, 'Aye, *piloto*. I will tell them.'

Dawn was just breaking and the gulls had begun their echoing cries as they skimmed the sea in search of food. Apparently, the storm had changed course during the night and brushed by the city; there had been no rain.

He went away from the rising pink sun, from the coming warmth, from Armazón's cries.

After a while, there was only the sound of the hungry gulls.

'It is the day of descansan,' he said. 'She is at the iglesia.'

'I have come to see her.'

'Yes, I know.' His eyes were hooded in the shadows of the doorway, his long drooping moustache giving him the aspect of a lean and hungry animal. 'She asked me to give you the directions.'

'I do not have much time.'

'She anticipated this also.'

'She did? Or you?'

Chimmoku's thin eyebrows lifted but his gaze remained impassive. 'I? I had nought to do with it.'

'Do you miss Sha'angh'sei?' Moichi asked abruptly.

The man stirred uneasily. 'Perhaps,' he said, 'sometimes. But the Senhora lives here in Corruña. Here, too, am I.'

'Did you meet her there?'

'In Sha'angh'sei? Yes.'

'Along the bund.'

'Along the bund, yes. Is this important?'

'I thought you might be the man –'

'Here are the directions.'

The bells were tolling from its tall spire, shining gold in the newly wakened sunlight. Bronze turned bright and brittle as they swung in the belfry. The sound was echoing and somehow melancholy.

It was a towering structure, brilliant white now at the top, still in shadows lower down near its arched open doorway; the last pools of the night. To left and right, flanking plane trees, large, ancient, whispered in the wind.

The doors were of oak on their lower half, thin strips of hardwoods, one light, the other dark above so that a kind of natural toning was achieved without the use of paints or lacquers.

A wide white-stone stairway led up to the doorway.

Daluzans drifted in, wrapped in cloaks of muted colours. The women, who dominated this early in the morning, all wore lace shawls about their heads.

Inside it was cool and echoey. Incense drifted in the still air and there seemed to be the distant drone of muted chanting. Low backless benches of highly polished wood ran the length of the interior from back to front, separated by three aisles. Where the seats ended in the front, there was a flight of low steps leading up to a platform. On the right was a carved wooden pulpit and on the left was what looked like a miniature balcony. Stone figures lined the walls on either side.

He went to the centre aisle and found her near the front. He slid in beside her.

'I'm glad you came,' she said without turning her head.

'Senhora, I have little time –'

But she merely smiled and put a long forefinger against her lips.

There was movement at the front of the iglesia and the congregation rose. A priest appeared behind the pulpit and Moichi was astonished to see Don Hispete, the cura with the spade beard on whose conversation he had eavesdropped at dinner the night before.

Don Hispete lifted his arms, said, *'Todos y cada unos, sea ustedhes bienvenhido alla'iglesia del' Dihos Sanhos.'*

The congregation knelt, bowing their heads. Moichi found himself again surprised. The cura's voice – his public voice – was totally different from the one he had previously heard. This was persuasive and charismatic.

'Bien.'

The congregation returned to their seats.

'This is the day of descansan,' Don Hispete said. 'A most important and, indeed, significant day on our calendar. For it recalls to us the sufferings of our forefathers. This is a day for sorrow; for us to feel deeply the loss of those departed and those far from home and, by this day, remembering, free our daily lives.

'Yet descansan has another purpose. For it is this day that we devote ourselves to the acknowledgement of evil so that we may know its many shapes and therefore rise up against it and protect ourselves from its wickedness.

'Thus, my children, should we feel the diablura's great wings flutter in the air about us for without him we could not understand the eternal goodness of Dihos. Thus we reflect on the deeper meaning of the descansan and its difficult revelation of the darker side of ourselves and, in recognition, better define our own goodness . . .'

Afterwards, she ascended the stairs with him and took him behind the pulpit, through a plain but quite solid wooden door. They went down a short stone corridor at the end of which was another door. She knocked and immediately opened it.

They were in Don Hispete's rectory. It was small and cosy and cluttered in a quite homely way. There were several overstuffed chairs, a functional wooden desk and high-backed chair, and shelves upon shelves of books all the way up to the ceiling. Half of the left-hand wall was a leaded-glass window beyond which he could see a leafy garden. A small door, half-open led out to it.

Don Hispete had apparently just sat down behind his desk but, when he saw them enter, he rose and came round the side to greet them.

'Senhora,' he said, smiling almost reverentially and, bowing, put his lips against the back of her proffered hand.

'Don Hispete,' the Senhora murmured. 'We loved your sermon.' She turned as if startled to find someone standing next to her. 'Oh by the way, this is Moichi Annai-Nin, a friend of mine.'

'*Bienvenhido, senhor.*' The priest inclined his head but

did not extend his hand. The social amenities, it seemed, were reserved for those he knew well. 'May I offer you a drink?' He was looking directly at the Senhora.

'Please.'

He reached out a tall crystal decanter three-quarters filled with deep red wine. He poured them all drinks and then, lifting his own goblet, said *'Salhud!'* He drank deeply and they followed suit.

Don Hispete put his goblet down on the desk beside him and returned to his high-backed chair. He folded his hands across his stomach. 'How may I be of assistance to you, Senhora?'

'Has Hellsturm returned to Corruña?' she said abruptly.

The priest stroked his spade-shaped beard with one forefinger before spreading his hands. 'Senhora, I cannot –'

But she had already risen, had gone across the small room. Now she stood before the windows, apparently regarding the foliage of the garden.

'Such beautiful trees,' she said. 'You know, Don Hispete, those olive trees, there, are old, very old indeed. Grandfathers of their line.'

'Yes, Senhora. Indeed they are.'

'It's such a pity to destroy them.'

Once more, the priest spread his hands. They reminded Moichi of a sea anemone about to ensnare an unwary fish. 'One hates to see the destruction of nature, Senhora, wherever it might be. But in this case it serves the purpose of Dihos because it will further his glory.'

'Oh, yes.' Her voice was as sweet as honey. 'The glory of Dihos must indeed be served for that is the primary function of the Palliate. But Don Hispete' – she turned away from the window to face the cura – 'the Palliate cannot function without the support of the congregation, is that not so? I cannot imagine that the Palliate would pay for – well, *everything*.'

Two thin vertical lines had appeared in the centre of the priest's brow.

'Is that not so?' she repeated.

Reluctantly, Don Hispete said, 'It is so, Senhora. But I fail to see what –'

'And this expansion that the iglesia is contemplating is expensive, is it not? Almost exorbitantly so, one might say.'

'Now really, Senhora, I must –'

'And it requires the support – the *complete* support – of every *partitioner*, does it not, Don Hispete?'

'Yes, Senhora, it does. But everyone must know he is expected to –'

'But those with, oh, shall we say, above-average wealth are being called upon with somewhat more, er, zeal than the others.'

Don Hispete sat as still as a statue now.

'I am one of those so I know first-hand, as it were.'

The priest tried to speak, had to clear his throat before beginning again. 'The Senhora is not contemplating withdrawing her pledge.' His voice seemed thin and strangled now.

'Why, I *contemplate* nothing of the sort.' Her voice was still sweet but it was now obvious that she was mocking him. 'Wherever did you get that idea. How absurd!'

She sat down beside Moichi. 'Now,' she continued, 'shall we return to my first query?'

'Senhora, you put me in quite a difficult position.' His face held a pained expression. 'You know well that I cannot break my sacred trust to the Palliate.' A thin line of sweat was rolling slowly down one side of his face.

'I do so love those olive trees, Don Hispete. I had not realized until I came here just how much I would miss them if they were cut down. And, you know, now that I think of it, there are others who feel just the same way as I do. Now –'

'Senhora, please –' His voice was a whine now. But her eyes had locked onto his and, at length, his gaze lowered to the hands clasped in his lap.

'He has been in the city,' he said softly. 'Here and gone. He left at dawn.'

'What was he doing here?' Her voice was as sharp as a whiplash and Don Hispete winced under its dominance.

'That I do not know, Senhora. This I swear.'

'It was not on business of the Palliate?'

The priest looked up, ashen-faced. He made a quick sign across his chest, 'Dihos, no, Senhora! We – We dismissed him after that last – uh – incident.'

'Incident.' Her voice was filled with loathing and contempt, 'Is that what you call it now? Well, you were always quick with the euphemisms.'

Don Hispete shuddered, 'Please, Senhora.' His voice had been reduced to a whisper.

'Who does he work for now?'

'I – I am not certain. I –'

She stood up and somehow it became one of the most threatening gestures Moichi had ever seen.

'I cannot tell you, Senhora,' the priest babbled, clutching the gold chain about his neck as if he feared she might lose control altogether and strangle him.

'Don Hispete, this interview is terminated.' It had the finality of a door slam. She turned and, on cue, Moichi stood up.

'Wa– wait, Senhora.' He rose, still fingering his chain. 'Please.' She turned back, waiting calmly now that her victory was assured. He blew air in and out of his mouth in rapid gusts; the skin of his face was gleaming. 'I have heard that he works now for *La Saqueador*. Sardonyx.'

The Senhora cried out as if she had been run through with a blade.

Don Hispete came around the desk, his face filled with fear. 'Senhora! What –?'

Moichi grabbed her, felt her trembling uncontrollably as if gripped by some terrible force.

'Get me out of here!' she gasped at him.

'What is it?'

'Quickly. For the love of Dihos!' she cried. '*Quickly!*'

He picked her up and took her out, down the corridor, through the now empty iglesia proper.

On the wide stone steps, dazzling in the sunlight, he set her down.

'Senhora,' he said. 'What happened?'

She kept her arms around him for support as she said, 'You were right. Dihos, you were right. I understand it all now.'

'For God's sake, Senhora, tell me!' he cried.

'Moichi, Sardonyx is the freebooter who was my partner so long ago.' Tears welled up in her eyes. 'She vowed a terrible vengeance upon me and now it has come. Hellstürm will not honour his pact with me now, that was but part of the deceit. Dihos, he has taken her to Sardonyx! I am undone!' She sobbed against his shoulder.

'Senhora,' he said softly. 'Senhora.' He stroked her hair, felt her soft-strong body quaking against him. He only partially understood her grief, he knew. But a tightening knot in his stomach made him realize his concern for Aufeya. The danger to her was not only real it was now dire. It was the northwest for him now upon the fleetest of steeds. 'Senhora,' he said, 'I must go after Hellsturm. Now. And you can help me.'

She looked at him, tears still rimming her eyes. He tried to smile. 'How ridiculous,' she said, 'to continue to call me that. I cannot continue to be so formal with you, Moichi. Not now and not ever again.' He saw the dancing motes in her large jade eyes. 'Call me Tsuki.'

He felt that all his breath had left him and, for a moment, he thought he might stumble. Kossori, he thought. Oh my God, Kossori! She is your love.

THREE:
The Firemask

Intimations

Normally the rain would have worked against him but now he blessed its delayed arrival. The storm had stalled off the coast and now had turned around, heading inland with much of its initial force dissipated out at sea.

It did not matter to him that the hoofprints of the caravan were all but obliterated by the dust turned to mud because he knew where they were bound.

He had Tsuki to thank for that as well as for the luma he now rode and the one whose reins were attached to the back of his saddle.

Tsuki. *The moon*, it meant.

Where are you now, Kossori, my true friend?

I hope you approve. I think you do.

The rain slanted down, hissing, a grey-green blanket limiting visibility, soaking everything; it obscured his pursuit from prying eyes.

He was already half-a-day's ride from Corruña's western gate, heading northwest for Kintai. His luma's slick coat was a tawny topaz, fitted with a black leather saddle, silver pommel and red leather harness. The somewhat smaller mare was a deep blue in colour. He was grateful for these luma, for their high intelligence combined with their great speed and endurance, made them more desirable than mere horses. But, he knew, they were wild and difficult and expensive to train, thus there were few of them about.

He plunged off the far side of a ridge of brown fertile land into a long softly undulating valley. He wiped the rain from his eyes. Trees were sparse here and, for as far as he could see, low bush and scrawny brown plants dominated. He dug his heels into his luma's flanks and rattled the reins. The stallion leapt ahead, lifted his head and snorted into the wind.

How strange life is, he thought. Stranger than any tale ever spun at night in a warm tavern or around a leaping fireside. How it returns in a circle; the end is the beginning. If Kossori had but known he defended Tsuki's daughter with his very last breath.

A death, Moichi thought, should not be useless. Sad, yes, that life should come to an end but inevitable, too. And, being so, should there not be meaning in the final act? In this the Iskamen and the Bujun were somewhat alike. Perhaps in other ways, also.

It was a hero's death for Kossori. More heroic now than he would ever know. Or again perhaps not if, as the Bujun believed, the soul is spun out, interweaving a long procession of lives until perfection is achieved and it leaves the endless wheel of life and death.

So for the Iskamen. God is history, his father never tired of telling him, and in history lies man's only salvation.

Now, at this moment, as he pounded across this plain, so desolate in the rain, flying after evil, Moichi knew that his faith had survived. The blood of his forefathers pulsed through him, too strong to be long discarded or ignored. Tears came to his eyes, mingling with the rain, as he thought of his father and the man's enormous faith in God. Perhaps you were not so very wrong, after all, Moichi thought, recalling their bitter arguments of faith, the long silences suffered by the rest of the family, the long days and nights of anger and frustration. All the time lost because they were both so strong-willed. But he knew now that they had not fought over faith. No, that had been a convenient but spurious battleground both of them had chosen rather spitefully. You were so intolerant of me, Father. How you resented my growing up so independent of your will. I was so unlike Jesah who, perhaps because he was the second, you were able to mould into your own likeness. He did whatever you told him while I resisted. Why would you not let me be, Father? What was it you were so frightened of? It couldn't be, as you professed so many times, that I would turn away from God because you did that to me yourself.

He rattled the reins again, sounding the litany of his long journey over the land. I will never know, now, because you took that answer with you when you died. Like God, there was not a forgiving moment in your life. The end was, indeed, like the beginning.

All life is so personal, he thought, wonderingly.

There was death in the air.

He sniffed again and though he was far from his beloved sea, he knew it still. He believed in auguries. Not in any superstitious way but in the manner of the Iskamen, whose turbulent history was filled with such messages from God, guiding His people.

The rain lessened somewhat and, as the mistiness lifted, he could discern the fulminating sky, low, fantastic shapes alight in the darkness of the billowing clouds. Far to the northwest, lightning forked, blue-white and ghostly and, a moment later, came the crack and after-tremor of the thunder, rolling against his ears.

Onward the luma fled.

No cultivated field, no house, no sign of man at all could he see. Just the pattering of the rain. Then, as the rain further abated, a line of weathered mountains appeared, marching like battered veterans along the horizon towards yet another war.

'I have no hope now,' she had said into his chest as he had held her. 'It is Sardonyx and I am vulnerable.'

'Vengeance is mine, sayeth the God of my people,' he said, recognizing his father there.

'You do not undertand, Moichi. This is Sardonyx we speak of and you must know before you leave. She is a sorceress.'

He laughed. 'Sorcery is gone from our world, Tsuki.'

But she shook her head. 'No. She can do the impossible.'

'Then she is but a conjuror, a clever one. I have met some

of those. It is all illusion.'

'No, Moichi. No. Please do not make that mistake. I know, believe me. That which she creates is real, terribly real. Beware her power. Beware it.'

It was nearing sundown and the high mountains loomed over him; he was on the last stretch of the vast plain.

Trees were more plentiful now and grass grew, long and wild so that his luma was obliged to slow its pace, wary of rodent burrows hidden from view.

Almost directly before him he saw the slopes of two mountains meeting in a narrow defile which seemed the only way through. It was a question of light now. It would perhaps be safer to camp here for the night, then proceed through the narrow pass at first light. But far too much time would be lost that way and the caravan already had a large headstart on him.

There was no choice, really.

He made full speed towards the defile.

To the east, the sky was still dark and unsettled but above and to the west, ahead of him, the sky was clear, lavender and plum as if bruised by the storm's passage. The plunging sun was too low for him to see directly but the world was filled with its reflected illumination.

The moon was already out, a thick crescent and as crimson as a drop of blood.

The way became immediately rocky and the grassland sparser as he neared the foothills guarding the mountain range. Great boulders of granite and sparkling schist built themselves on all sides.

Soon he was engulfed in the defile itself. Thick jutting shelves of rock shot up high into the air, oblique, the evening's light spilling down them like a cataract, turning the entire defile mauve. Natural rock terraces stretched themselves above his head, rising in tiers until they were lost in the haze.

As the sky darkened into night, the rock walls seemed to close in on him, the terraces expanding until but the merest sliver of sky remained.

Signs of the caravan's passage were more in evidence here. At first he believed this to be a result of the floor's more sheltered position in the defile, but as he looked closer, he discerned that the signs were fresher. He was closer to his quarry than he had realized.

This place seemed devoid of life. No avians flew overhead, not even the scavengers, no lizard, no insect. He began to experience an acute sense of isolation now, so strong that it was almost tangible.

The nature of the rocks had changed, also. He was obliged to pause and light a brand made of tightly-woven hemp treated with pitch. By this flickering light he saw that the rocks were now streaked with orange and sulphurous yellow and their configurations became contorted, almost tortured, as if they had been formed during some painful upheaval of the earth.

He reined in and drew his sword.

Around a bend ahead of him, he saw the glow of another torch. He waited, uncertain even what to expect.

It was a solitary figure on horseback and now, as it approached, he saw that it was a woman. She was impossibly tall, narrow-skulled and sunken-eyed. She was dressed in a simple farmer's tunic of dun-coloured cotton. She was unarmed.

'Greetings,' she said, her voice floating towards him, ghostly in the confines of the defile.

'Greetings,' Moichi answered.

'I heard your approach,' she said. 'I get so few visitors these days – I was curious to see. I hope you don't mind.'

'Not at all,' he said. 'But I'm afraid that I have little time for small talk or pleasantries at the moment.'

'You are in a hurry. Yes,' she nodded, 'it's plain to see. Your mission is urgent. Is it all right if I ride along with you to the end of the defile? Then we may talk without my hindering you.'

Moichi nodded and spurred his luma forward. The woman turned her mount, fell in beside him. There was just enough room for them both. The jiggling of their harnesses echoed eerily off the rock faces.

'Whither are you bound?' she asked. 'I know this land well. Perhaps I can help direct you to your destination. It's plain you've never been here before.'

The mist was returning, although the rain seemed to have departed. 'I already have directions, thank you,' he said as politely as he could muster. He frankly did not like having anyone distracting him in such a perfect place for an ambush. If she had heard his approach, could not others?

'They might be incorrect, you know,' the woman said thoughtfully. 'That often happens these days. People are not so conscientious as they used to be, somehow. Not very fashionable, I expect, though I know little enough of the world. Who was it gave you these directions?'

Moichi glanced at her briefly. What was wrong with her face? The inconstant light of the torches made it impossible to see clearly. 'A friend,' he said noncommittally.

'A friend,' echoed the woman. 'Yes, of course. It would be. Well, even friends are liable to make a mistake – when much time has passed.'

Moichi was about to ask her to amplify that statement when she said. 'I fear I have tarried too long already at your side.' She spurred her mount into an awkward gallop and, in but a moment, had disappeared into the deepening mist ahead. He wanted to call her back for he had been puzzled by their rather one-sided conversation, but there was nothing he could do to deter her save shout and that he could not risk.

He rode on, keeping to his former pace and presently he felt rather than saw the sides of the defile widen. Raising his torch, he could just barely discern that the rock faces had begun to lose a bit of their steepness. This effect increased rapidly and he picked up his pace. Soon he had emerged.

On this end, the defile debouched onto a long valley. Above, the sky was streamered with stars. Below, the land seemed as flat and featureless as newly-ploughed fields.

Over the rolling grasslands he flew, the wind whipping against his face, cool and invigorating. He revelled in the open space around him, feeling as if he had newly awakened from some nightmare where he had been trapped in a coffin.

Not long after, he spied a pinpoint of light on the near horizon. Cautiously, he made for it; the signs of the caravan's passage were fresher still, at the last site the camels' dung had been warm. As he neared, he saw that it was a small cottage set on the near bank of a wide sluggish river which, he saw, straggled west for a short distance before turning south perhaps half a kilometre past the house.

He drew in and sat atop his luma for a time, looking about and listening to the chirruping of the cicadas and the quiet croakings of the river frogs. Above him, the moon seemed greatly magnified, as if seen through a lens. It was as red as blood.

At length, he dismounted and led the luma forward. He peered into a window, saw only an old woman, her back towards him. Suddenly, he realized he was famished and, striding to the door, he opened it and stepped inside.

The old woman was bent over a circular stone hearth set in the centre of the floor on a sort of stone plinth. 'Close the door,' she said without turning around. 'The night air is cold and it disturbs me.' Her voice had the quality of chalk streaking along a slate board.

She had a thin face, he saw as she at last turned round, a patchwork of skin, it seemed, crisscrossed and sealed by the seams of time. And the skin seemed glossy, as if it were not skin at all. She had a wide, loose-lipped mouth upon which red paint had been carelessly smeared and shiny button eyes that were all pupil like a bird's.

'Are you hungry?' she said. But she was already setting the table with rough-hewn bowls and crude utensils. 'I have a stew all ready.'

Now that she mentioned it, he did smell the rich aroma of food and his mouth began to water. He looked beyond her, saw a black metal pot hanging over the flames of the hearth.

'Have you seen a small caravan pass this way?' he asked.

'Come,' she said. 'Sit and eat.' She was ladling the stew, thick and hot into the bowls. There was a large loaf of black bread on a wooden board, a knife lying beside it.

He sat down.

'Haven't been outside all day,' she said. 'Don't do that so much any more.'

'Did you not see the rider then?'

'The rider?'

'A woman. Odd-looking. Very tall. Surely she came this way.'

'I believe you met my daughter.'

'She's not here.'

'Obviously. She is hunting.'

'At night?'

'It's the only way here. All our game is nocturnal.' The old woman pointed to his bowl. 'Is my cooking so poor?'

He took a bite of the stew. It seemed to have no taste. He sniffed. It smelled delicious.

'Do you follow the caravan?' the old woman asked. She reminded him of someone. 'It's plain to see you're a traveller.'

Something caught his eye.

'Aren't you hungry? Of course you are. Eat up, now.'

What was it? Time seemed to have slowed down. He began to hear his own breathing, as stentorian as that of a dragon's. He seemed to have trouble moving, also, as if the air had turned to jelly.

'Go on with you. Eat. Eat.'

Corner of his eye, a million miles a-w-a-y . . . Took some time to register. Firelight dancing, pretty patterns. Hauled himself together mentally. Slipping, slipping a-w-a-y . . . Firelight. Not the firelight. Below that, glinting like the sea on a moonlit night remember the time for God's sake wake up will you what's happening colours r-u-n-n-i-n-g together something important there moonlight chopping the surface of the sea into ten thousand f-r-a-g-m-e-n-t-s-s-s-s pull yourself together man and con-cen-trate. *Concentrate.* No circle. That was it don't let it slip away now a-w-a-y-No, stop it! *Stop it!* The hearth was not round. It was a pentangle. *Pentangle*, you nit-wit, don't you understand?

He did.

Lunged across the table at the old woman, caught her wrist fast sliding away from him, colours streaming all around him like a flight of bubbles feathers fanning the hot humid air sticky and sweaty after working all day in the sun tremendous thirst tongue sticking to the roof of his mouth bloated and so dry that all he could think of was . . . *Get her!* he screamed at himself. Twisted his arm, felt her wrist snapping like an old dry twig.

The old woman reeling backwards the house tremored she stumbled the house shimmered she fell the house dissolved about him.

Dazed, Moichi sat in the grass, hands flat on the earth. He felt as if he wanted to vomit. Unperturbed, the night chirruped and croaked on around him as if nothing untoward had happened. Some paces away, the luma, heads to the earth, munched grass contentedly. What did they know.

Abruptly, he did vomit. It was over as quickly as it began. He felt weak and he turned over, lay back, staring up at the infinite river of stars, glittering and close by as if he could gather strength from their illumination. The moonlight hurt his eyes so he closed them. He found that his chest was heaving as if he had run a long distance. But he'd run longer than that, he knew. He had run for his life.

Tsuki's words had saved him.

He had met Sardonyx and almost been defeated. Almost. What information had she desired from him? And what had he given her? Not much, he was certain.

He walked back to the luma, feeling somewhat better and swung up. Beneath the river of starlight, he headed north-west, after the caravan.

When he saw her, his heart lightened.

She crouched in the lee of a great glittering granite boulder perhaps a thousand metres from the encampment. Just another shadow.

Immediately, he saw her, he dismounted and, leading the luma behind him, crept towards her. The animals were perfectly silent and would remain so now; they knew the enemy was close.

Chiisai whirled, her short blade out but he passed into a patch of starlight and she recognized him. They embraced joyfully.

'Thank the Gods you have come at last,' she whispered, her beautiful oval face sobering. 'My horse gave out yesterday and I have been on foot ever since.'

Quickly, he brought her up to date.

'I'm so relieved that Martyne was unhurt. I was worried about her since I left. But as for Aufeya, I think perhaps we are already too late.'

'What do you mean?' he hissed. 'Has Hellsturm already killed her? Then why didn't you stop him?'

'Calm yourself,' she said. 'I understand your concern. But the fact is, she is not within the caravan.'

'Not here? But how is that possible?'

'I cannot say for certain, Moichi. But I believe that Sardonyx already has her.'

'She's at Mistral with Sardonyx.'

'Mistral?'

'A strange castle. Tsuki informed me. On the northwest shore of an ever stranger lake known as the Deathsea.'

'I see.' Chiisai's brow was furrowed in thought. 'There seem to be plans within plans here.'

'What do you know? Martyne told me –'

'Yes. The land of the opal moon. I could scarcely believe it when I heard.' She put her back against the rock and, after taking a quick glance at the caravan's encampment, continued. 'There is a legend that I have heard, although I do not think it has Bujun origins. Perhaps it had its genesis during the time that Ama-no-mori was part of the continent of man.'

'You mean during the sorcerous wars.'

'Yes. It is said that there came into being at that time, a place where all time ceased to exist, where all time coalesced, an opening in the fabric of our universe, like the incision of a surgeon's scalpel. Perhaps it had been inadvertently created as a byproduct of the continuing pernicious spells being conjured, or perhaps through a means totally unknown to our world. In any event, this eye of time, once it was discovered, opened up terrifying possibilities. If one could slip through, for instance, all the secrets of the future could be had and brought back; victory for the first sorcerer through would be assured. Yet it was not to be so simple a task, for, this eye of time was inimical to humans and even sorcerous spells proved no protection from the deadly vortex. Thus the site was abandoned and its location forgotten; and thus it passed into the realm of legend.'

'Are you saying that Sardonyx has learned of this – eye of time's location?' Chiisai nodded. 'But what good would it do her? *This* is the future those sorcerers would have come to; they would have found nothing.'

'You miss the point, Moichi. If Sardonyx manages to gain entry there, she can *go back* to the time of the Kai-feng or beyond; to a time when sorcery was potent. She could bring back –'

He raised a hand. 'Enough! I see what you mean. But –

are you saying that the location of the eye of time is here in Kintai?'

Chiisai nodded. 'The legend tells us that the eye is located in a land where the moon is always full and when you look at it it appears round as a ball, not flat as in other lands. Its colour is not the silver of the north nor the gold of the east nor the blue of the west nor the orange of the south. No, it is of all these colours and more. An opal moon.'

Almost involuntarily, Moichi looked skyward. 'But look there, Chiisai. The moon is horned and is as red as a rose.'

'Yes,' she whispered, 'so it is. But the legend states that the one entrance to the land of the opal moon is across a plain lit by ninsō-waru, the Demoneye.'

'So here we are.'

'Yes.'

'Then, if Sardonyx's castle is near here, she has been in possession of that bit of information for quite some time. This is not what Cascaras and Aufeya possessed.'

'No. There is, unfortunately, more.' She sighed. 'After the end of the sorcerous wars, there came into being a story about an artefact. It cropped up in a number of disparate places giving that much more credence to its veracity. Somewhere, it was postulated, was the key to the puzzle of the eye of time. Some, even, claimed that they had seen it but since each gave a different location and none, it seemed, proved to be correct, its actual existence was discounted by most. Still, others dreamed and hoped, keeping its name alive. The Firemask.'

There was a brief hissing along the narrow ledge of shale.

He remained motionless, staring into the tiny ruby eyes of the scaled lizard, its horned ridged crest making it seem like an apparition out of pre-history. Its forked tongue flicked out, questing along the rock as it regarded him incuriously. A slow pulse beat in the hanging flesh at the juncture of its neck and lower jaw. Then it had scuttled past him into a crack in the rock face. It stared stonily at him.

He squinted upwards. Streaky clouds, faintly luminescent, drifted overhead but never coming near the bloody moon.

He ignored the pain in his chest, straining his ears, listening for the tiniest sound out of place. There was loose shale down there below him and a totally silent approach, he knew, was next to impossible. It could be a lot worse, he reflected. Hellsturm could be a Jhindo and then he would be for it because the night was the Jhindo's world. But Hellsturm was only a *koppo* adept. He laughed inwardly but there was little humour in it; he was not, after all, the Dai-San and this man had destroyed Kossori.

While he waited, crouched high on the narrow ledge, alone in the night, he had time for thought. It had all begun well enough. He and Chiisai had both decided that they could not let the caravan reach its destination which they knew now to be Mistral. Hellsturm and presumably now Sardonyx already knew half of the vital information; Aufeya possessed the other half. They knew just how explosive that information was. Pieced together from what Martyne had told them about Cascaras and what Aufeya had told Moichi about Hellsturm, it became the only possible conclusion. Together, Cascaras and Aufeya had discovered the location of the fabled Firemask.

Whatever Hellsturm now brought to Mistral would have to be intercepted. There was no alternative.

The caravan encampment was centred in a shallow dell bordered on the left by a dense copse of oak trees and on the right and to the rear by sheltering rock.

There were four Tudescan warriors. Hellsturm was shadowed by another man, short and squat but as muscular as a bull. This man was not Tudescan but Moichi recognized him as Tülc, a member of an obscure tribe of folk to the north. They lived on the vast snow-covered steppes and wore the skins of predatory animals such as the wolf and the bear. Their headmen wore the skulls of these animals, covering the top halves of their faces. Moichi had come across a Tülc aboard the second ship he had signed on with. What this man was doing so far from home Moichi never learned but it had not even occurred to him to ask for Moichi, too, was far from his native land and had no desire to talk about his own reasons for leaving. But he had learned other things from the man. The Tülc were a fierce people and, in many ways, only semi-civilized. What one was doing with Hellsturm was impossible to ascertain.

In all, there were six.

'A fair match-up,' Chiisai had whispered, grinning. But he had not shared her optimism.

The Tudescans were up and battle-ready in an instant, even though he and Chiisai had come upon them as silently as they were able. They had another advantage, however, for the Tudescans seemed contemptuous of a woman warrior. Until, that is, Chiisai dispatched the first man they sent against her with one swipe of her dai-katana. She ducked under the attack of the Tudescan and skewered him from front to back just below the breastbone.

Cursing, Hellsturm immediately sent two men against her.

For her part, Chiisai was as calm as the water in a lake as she faced this dual charge. She stood her ground, unmoving, hands placed one above the other on the long hilt of her weapon, holding it vertically so that the tip touched the earth.

The Tudescans split, coming at her from both sides. The one on her right drew fractionally first, beginning an oblique strike but so massive were both the warriors, they appeared to be giants rumbling towards her.

Left to right the strike came and, two-handed, Chiisai brought the dai-katana up to block precisely as if she were holding a wooden staff that had neither cutting edge nor swordpoint. In the same motion she continued the sweep horizontally and down so that, as the point dropped below the second warrior's incoming blow, it lanced inward with a blur, slicing the Tudescan open from right side through to his spine. His weapon flew from his hands as he went down.

Now she ducked under the first warrior's cut and, leaning forward, tried a reverse blow. This he parried and, in counter-attacking, used such force that she was almost struck from her fighting position. She recovered in time to deflect a strike aimed at her neck but the flat of the heavy sword smashed into her shoulder. She winced and twisted her blade upwards so that the point pierced the warrior just above his Adam's apple, slashing into the brain.

Moichi was now fully engaged in combat with the remaining Tudescan warrior. The man struck twice and on the third blow succeeded in separating Moichi from his sword. Moichi cursed himself silently for not having been a better student. But he had never been sufficiently interested in swordsmanship. Pity he had not known about this moment then.

The Tudescan's face split in a feral grin as he moved in for the kill. That expression stayed permanently in place. He had not even seen the motion of Moichi's left hand. Foolishly, the grin still in place, he stared down at the thick copper handle protruding from his chest. He coughed once and pitched backwards.

There was only Hellsturm now. And the Tülc. That one moved towards Chiisai as Moichi turned to confront Hellsturm.

The hood of his cape had been pushed back and for the first time Moichi saw his face.

He was stunningly handsome. This came not so much from the individual features of his face – his nose was too straight, his mouth just a touch too wide, the lips thick and sensual – but by an intermix which made the whole something unusual. There was about him the distinct air of an animal, dangerous, cunning, and amoral, all part of the undeniable masculine magnetism which had drawn both Tsuki and Aufeya.

His deep-set eyes were black and this, too, seemed to be the only colour he wore. His leather helm was ebon as were his chain metal corselet, leggings and high boots. The only touches of colour were at the front of his helm and the buckle of his wide weapons belt. Here had been painted a small blood-red cross surrounded by a circle of the same hue.

Moichi picked up his dirk, wiping the blade clean on the dead man's cloak, then retrieved his sword. During this time, his eyes never left the figure in front of him. He put away the dirk, held his sword, point slightly higher than hilt, in front of him.

Hellsturm smiled at him and came forward, his white teeth gleaming in the moonlight, sharp and moist and pink-tinged. He did not touch the sword which swung slightly, scabbarded at his side.

'You know what I am.' It was the first time he had heard Hellsturm speak. It sounded like the sibilant whisper of a summer's breeze and the dissimilarity between visual and aural was so enormous that he was shocked. Hellsturm might have been talking to his lover. Moichi winced inside when he thought of that: Tsuki and Aufeya.

He had a chance if he could get Hellsturm to draw his sword. If he couldn't – he lunged forward in a feint but the other danced nimbly away and shook his head, his tongue clicking against the roof of his mouth so that now he sounded like an old lady.

'Oh no,' he said. 'No, no, no.'

And raised his hands like blades.

Moichi sheathed the useless weapon, manoeuvred so that his side was presented, giving a narrower target but Hellsturm was too swift and he came on and it was all Moichi could do to deflect the three, four, five strikes in rapid succession.

He backed off but Hellsturm followed. He blocked an eye-strike but only partially deflected the next. Pain like a hot lance shot through his chest and he did the only thing he could do to stave off death. He ran.

He had the face of a weasel, Chiisai thought, set into a head that seemed far too big for the torso even though that was itself quite massive. He looked like a freak. He had tiny eyes and almost no nose but the large gaping nostrils gave him the animal-like countenance. His ears, too, were small but the lobes were distended, possibly by the stones set into them. He was dressed in wolf-pelts and he stank.

She allowed the Tülc the first strike.

Its tremendous force shook her down to her ankles and had her blade been forged anywhere other than Ama-no-mori, it would certainly have been shattered.

He allowed her not a moment's let-up but swung at her over and over without discernible rhythm so that she found it increasingly difficult to defend herself. Each time he appeared to fall into some pattern of attack, he would shift out of it and she would find herself slightly off-balance and thus vulnerable.

Her arms began to ache, the pain becoming fierce in no time at all until it became a chore to lift her own sword over her head.

The Tülc came on, a feral grin lighting his face; she had seen that kind of look before, knew what this man would do to her before he killed her.

In that instant of inward-looking, she missed it. The movement had to have been minute but ordinarily she would have picked it up. Too late. The blur shot towards her and she felt as if her right shoulder had been dipped in flame. She cried out as the force reeled her backwards. She stumbled and the dai-katana flew from her grasp.

She landed, clutching her shoulder where the spike was embedded. It had come from the hilt of the Tülc's sword, some hidden spring releasing it.

Now he stood over her, staring stonily down and threw his blade from him. He withdrew something from beneath his furs and when Chiisai saw it gleaming in the moonlight, she knew that she was finished.

The lizard, its skin dry and cool, had gone but a small sound had taken its place and he tensed, knowing that Hellsturm was on his way.

Still, he had no clear plan. He had known only that he had to get away from the machine of death, find some sort of cover. Now he racked his brain, trying to recall everything Kossori had ever told him or showed him about *koppo*. He did not give way to despair though he knew that this man who now pursued him had killed Kossori and he had thought his friend all but invincible.

The sound came again, no more than the scrape of leather against rock but now he could see the beginnings of an outline, already closer than he had imagined. Not much time left.

He resisted the impulse to move. Right now he was fairly certain that Hellsturm had not spotted him despite the fact that he was moving in the right direction. No sense in giving the Tudescan any more of an advantage than he already had. The trouble was his own mind was a blank. He still had no idea what – he lost the silhouette. One moment it was there, the next, gone.

Where was Hellsturm? He thought desperately.

There was total silence now. But a kind of deafening noise pounded against his eardrums and he realized he was listening to the sound of his own pulse. He scanned the darkness before him.

He sensed rather than heard anything and was in the process of turning when the blow hit him, glancing off his forehead and then he was rolling, half-dazed, knowing that if he had been motionless when the blow had caught him, it would have split his head open like a ripe melon.

He struggled to his knees but Hellsturm kicked him hard in the side and he went down. Hellsturm was on him, not giving him time to recover and he was having to block a series of vicious sword-strikes to his sternum without the benefit of a clear head or proper leverage. Sweat was in his eyes and he shook his head back and forth very quickly to clear his vision but this only intensified the pain. Sharp points digging into his back and dust rising, clogging his nostrils and he was almost pinned now and that would be it because he knew that once he became immobile for even the briefest time, he was dead meat.

They were at the verge of the shale ledge and as another sword-strike blurred towards his face, he felt them going over, tumbling, weightless for just an instant as if they were hung suspended in mid-air. Then, abruptly, gravity took hold once more and the earth rushed up towards them with terrifying swiftness.

He willed his body to relax but Hellsturm was still on top of him and he hit with his right shoulder first, the full weight of both bodies combined with the momentum; he felt as if he were caught in a vice. He cried out, feeling something inside tear and then a popping that was, surprisingly, without pain and he knew that his right arm was dislocated. Knew, too, that there was no hope now. None at all.

She had seen this weapon before. It had a long wooden haft ending in a sickle-shaped metal blade. From the end of the haft swung a long link chain with a studded metal ball. The sight of it terrified her. With good reason.

Chiisai was a shujin, that is, a grand master in martial arts. Only shujin were allowed to wear the dai-katana. And she was one of only a very few women in Bujun history to be so skilled.

Yet Chiisai had known defeat in Ama-no-mori. Once.

Her opponent had wielded this weapon.

She was paralysed with fear; she had never beaten this

weapon and would not do so now.

The chain whirled in the air, circling and, as it lashed out with blinding speed, the Tülc grinned. She screamed as the chain whipped about her neck, driven by the force of his throw and the weight of the ball. The sound was not unlike the snapping of a hungry wolf.

Her breath was cut off and she was being strangled, her continued screams but a soft sussurrant rattle deep in her throat, as in a nightmare when one opens one's mouth to call out and no sound is heard. Panic welled up inside her, clutching at her stomach. She choked, watching the grinning gap-toothed face looming sweatily over her as his thick filthy hands drew tighter by small degrees the chain around her throat.

He threw the weapon casually into the air, caught it by its haft, chopped downwards in a tight arc, the sickle blade carving a swath closer and closer to her heaving breasts.

She struggled feebly with her legs and he hauled back on the chain as if she were a fish on a line. Her lungs felt as if at any moment they would burst.

A pearly blackness invaded her, mistily seeping into the edges of consciousness and she knew that death was near. She was hypnotized into immobility, staring up at him, impaled, certain that this was indeed happening but to someone else, not her, not her.

Then, keeping one hand wrapped around the chain, he let go of the haft with the other hand, and, carefully, not taking his eyes off her, undid his belt. Then the blade came down, slicing through the leather ties holding her breastplate together. He used the blade again to turn it over, away from her. Now there was only a thin layer of clothing and he stared, mouth half-open, at what lay beneath the silk. He unbuttoned his pants and they slid down the hairy trunks of his legs.

Her gaze slid down to the juncture and the outrage of what he was going to do somehow galvanized her out of her immobility. She no longer thought about her one defeat or this strange weapon which had caused it.

It was life now, and life only.

She went back to basics. For all she had left now was the iai, a movement she had had to learn before the cut, the parry, or the strike. She heard again her instructor, Henjō saying to her, *If you cannot get it out in time, there will be no need of any of the rest. Do you understand?* She hadn't, really, then. But she had learned it anyway, learned it well, for Hanjō was the finest iaijustsu of all the Bujun. Now she understood and blessed him.

Thus there seemed to the Tülc that there was no movement at all. One moment she was exposed, at his mercy and he straddled her, rampant, the next, he felt a sharp searing pain lancing through his groin and lower abdomen.

His eyes bulged and spittle drooled from one corner of his hanging mouth. He dropped the weapon. All sensation was gone from his legs and they would not support him. He tumbled to his knees, straddling her outstretched legs. His trembling hands clasped his oozing vitals, holding them inside his rent flesh. In front of him, awesomely close, was the juncture of her thighs and he stared longingly there as a chill swept through him, a frost colder than any he had ever experienced before and he thought of the huge snow-wolves of his frost-rimed steppes and the intense joy of the hunt like an orgasm, the hot red blood spilling upon the virgin white earth, so stark and, in its way, holy and now with every pump of his labouring heart, his own blood was pouring through his impotent fingers into the dust before him. The last thing he saw was another part of him lying on the ground near him. He reached for it as if, with it, he could hold onto the life that was fast slipping away from him. He toppled over, dead before he hit the earth.

Chiisai was clawing desperately at the chain strangling her. The weapon itself was caught beneath the Tülc's heavy corpse and she had to roll him over in order to extricate it and thus ease the pressure. Her nails were gone and her fingers bloody as she, at last, freed herself from the chain.

Tears welled in her eyes as her lungs heaved involuntarily. Vertigo set in and she knew she dared not get up. She lay on the wet earth, gasping, feeling that she would never get enough oxygen, felt the pins and needles, the numbness beginning along her nose and cheeks and lips, knew that the carbon dioxide was building too rapidly and deliberately slowed her breathing. Slow and deep. Deep and slow.

For what seemed to her an endless time, she was content to just breathe, such a simple, ordinary function, staring sightlessly up at the slow wheel of the sparkling icy stars and the blood-red moon, crying, crying but knowing now that it would be all right.

It came in on his blind side and he lost all hearing there. He was moving away but it was not enough and the *koppo* blow caught him just above the right ear. My God, he thought, this is no man but a monster.

He reeled drunkenly away, bouncing off a boulder but Hellsturm followed relentlessly. Once he felt the granite at his back, he knew what he must do and, gritting his teeth against the pain and the shock, he slammed his right arm against the curved face at what he estimated to be the proper angle.

Light flashed behind his eyes and he groaned, his stomach heaving. Felt the pop, though, as the bone returned to its socket. Pain flared as shock dissipated its effect on the nerves; thunder following on the heels of lightning. Sweat broke out all over his body and he shivered, taking a deep breath. He wiped his eyes with his good arm as he lurched away from the rock.

Felt Hellsturm close behind him and he ran into the night, climbing as if this alone could save him.

God is my saviour, he found himself thinking. He watches over me always. It was what his father used to say to him as a child just before he went to bed. He discovered, too, that he no longer found it a saying to scoff at. It had its own meaning for him now. It was a kind of inner strength that stopped him from giving in to despair.

Sounds close behind him told him that Hellsturm was gaining. The blocks, the constant movement would be useless now as he felt the energy draining from him with each step he took. But, he knew now, it had been useless from the beginning, nothing more than a holding action that had only prolonged the inevitable. What had made him think that he would be any match for this devil? He had fought beside the world's greatest hero but what made him think that he was one himself.

Still, he sped upwards, his soul unable to admit defeat even as he was haunted by its spectre. He ascended towards the stars and the bloody Demoneye which hung over him like the gloating greedy face of Sardonyx.

The ledge upon which he ran described a sharp turn to the left and he followed it up, the stone crumbling under his boot soles, using hands along the inner face to guide him, help propel him along, running, stumbling, catching himself, breathless, running once more. His lungs were straining and his throat felt as if it was covered with dust. Excessive sweat pouring from his body from the exertion only further depleted his last fading strength.

Water. He needed water. Suddenly this seemed an even more powerful imperative than outrunning Hellsturm.

Abruptly, he quit the ledge, swinging up onto the true face of the rocky hillside. Tore two fingernails in the process but now he was heading inwards, still climbing, away from the plain below, scrambling over rocks and scrub brush, hunting, buying time, the only thing left that was of any use to him.

He crested the hill, panting, willing his breathing to slow, moving downwards now, on the far side and he found himself amid lush foliage. He felt the first faint surge of distant hope because he could scent it now. Water.

His toe struck a projection, a rock or a root, he could not tell which and he tumbled down the last bit of the incline and then he was on his knees on the narrow bank, scooping the cold water of the stream into his mouth in great gulps until he remembered and stopped, though his body cried out for more and his mouth was still dry. He took a last mouthful but, instead of swallowing, let it stay in his mouth. Then he ducked his head and splashed his head and shoulders. It soothed the ache somewhat. He spat out the last of the water, knowing that if he took too much, he would vomit it all up at the first hard sprint.

He picked himself up and carefully forded the stream which was wide but quite shallow, the gurgling water not even cresting his boot-tops. But the stones at its bottom were sharp-angled and slippery and he did not want to risk a fall.

He gained the far bank without incident and moved into a thick copse of pine. He climbed a ridge, turned and followed it until he found a spot that suited his needs. Here, he had an excellent view of the stream without himself being exposed. He crouched and waited. And with each moment, he grew stronger. Yet he knew full well that mere physical strength would not be enough.

He put his back against the bole of a tree, smelling the heady scent of the bed of brown pine needles carpeting the rich earth all about him, hearing the sad call of a whippoorwill high up in the branches overhead. He looked upwards, saw a brown-and-white speckled owl close by. But there was something strange about it. He looked again. Its eyes were closed. The owl was nocturnal so it should be wide awake at this time. Why wasn't it?

Then he had the answer and with it came the knowledge of victory. He had a chance now, he knew. One chance in ten thousand. But it was better than no chance at all. But he had to have time to think it through.

It was the moon. Even though it was not full, it was yet

magnified in this strange land and its bloody illumination was of such a magnitude that it had caused the owl to shut its eyes.

Moonlight on the water of the rushing stream.

Like a key jarring open a lock in his mind, a memory had surfaced. 'One of the reasons,' Kossori had once told him, 'that *koppo* takes so long to master is that it is more than half mental. One must learn to attain a spirit "as calm as moonlight". That is, an attitude of dispassion, being at once aware of the landscape in general as well as the specifics of detail. While this attitude is maintained, the *koppo* adept may be considered invincible. But should some element be inserted which is distracting, which interferes with this attitude then, as a cloud passing before the face of the moon turns all the world dark and shadowy, he can be undone.'

Demoneye exploded into a thousand shards as Hellsturm plunged into the stream and gained the far bank. He paused there, his senses questing for his prey.

Without moving the rest of his body, Moichi felt around on the pine carpet with his hands until he found what he wanted. He hefted it in his left hand, judging its weight, then tucked it into his belt round the back so that it was out of sight.

But in so doing, his elbow had passed through a small patch of moonlight and, like a hound to the scent, Hellsturm's handsome head swivelled around, orienting on him.

Hellsturm launched himself up the incline more swiftly than Moichi had thought possible. His long, lean legs pumped in seeming defiance of gravity.

The lethal hands were raised and Moichi moved back. He stumbled and he was obliged to block a blow as he was falling backwards.

The man's strength was appalling, even at this stage and Moichi almost felt his nerve break as he was borne under the demonic assault.

The blows were getting through now and there was no

more time. In a moment, he would be beaten to a pulp. Gritting his teeth, he used his right arm, the one that had been dislocated to block the blows raining down on him. The pain was like a living thing, eating at his flesh but it could not be helped because he needed his left hand. It darted behind him, the fingers closing around the cool, hard surface, pulled it out.

Now.

Head was on fire from an only partially-deflected tiger-strike.

Now, now, now.

'Tsuki!' he called. 'Over here! Quickly!'

It was a desperate thing, a ploy once used so often that now no one used it.

Hellsturm's head jerked, eyes opened a fraction. His hands hesitated an instant, a cloud passing before the face of the moon.

Out of the shadows and the darkness Moichi swung upwards with all his might, trapping Hellsturm's right hand between the trunk of the pine and the saw-edged rock in his fist.

There came a sharp, cracking sound as if a tree had been felled. The skin shredded and Moichi bore down, grinding the rock into the bone. Blood spurted as the knuckles splintered one by one.

Hellsturm's head snapped back and his sensual lips drew away from his teeth. The whites shone all around his eyes and Moichi could smell the stench of his sweat.

But Hellsturm still had his left hand and he used it now, driving the rock from Moichi's grasp, oblivious to the pain, using it as if it were a mace to bludgeon his opponent.

Moichi drove upwards with the toe of one boot, caught Hellsturm in the stomach. But his chain mail absorbed most of the impact and, seemingly oblivious, he bore down. He had hold of Moichi's right shoulder now and he dug his fingers into the already wounded socket.

Pain was a blanket that completely covered Moichi. His eyes teared and he cried out, his arm hanging numb and useless with the agony.

But now his left hand was scrabbling at his belt and he grasped the hilt of one of his dirks. He tried to withdraw it but in the battle it had somehow become twisted up in the fabric of his shirt.

Hellsturm, his handsome face twisted into a mask of hate and bloodlust, continued to dig into the flesh of his shoulder, pulling at his arm. In another moment, the bone would be pulled from its socket again and the pain would be overwhelming. If he passed out now –

He had it! The dirk came free and, without further thought, he slashed upwards, not really aiming because there was no time. He felt the bone slipping, grinding against the socket and he yelled. The blade of the dirk shot through the night, the edge opening Hellsturm's face from right eye across the bridge of the nose, through to the left eye.

Hellsturm let out a howl like an animal and his body jerked upwards. He stumbled backwards, his ruined hand to his ruined face. He tripped and almost righted himself but the incline was too steep and there was too much blood on him: he was blind, blood filled his ears and mouth and he had no balance. He crashed backwards obliquely and his spine cracked against the trunk of a pine. His momentum was such that he spun off drunkenly, careening down the embankment, spinning, until he hurtled into the rushing stream, entangled in the rocks, the bloody illumination of Demoneye dappling the body as if it were no harsh intruder upon the harmonious landscape.

The Anvil

Beyond the ending of the plain was the forest and beyond that the bright shore of the Deathsea.

It was midday before they breached the far verge of the forest. It seemed a dismal place, heavily overgrown with dense tangled foliage, ropy vines and thorned creepers; the earth in between littered with great malevolent-looking mushrooms as lividly white as snow. But there seemed little in the way of fauna. What birds inhabited its upper reaches were strictly nocturnal, disappearing before the sun heaved its bulk above the torn horizon.

They were both relieved to quit its dark and intense interior.

But what they saw now surprised them, for the Deathsea was a deep and waterless scar upon the face of the land, a rotting skeleton divested of all skin and flesh.

The Deathsea was dust and swirling ash, glittering unrelievedly in the sunlight, undulating sharply, its sloping sides turning into a baking oven.

They paused at the edge of it, staring directly across its length and there, upon the far shore, just visible, were the shadowy towers and fenestrations of Mistral, the home of Sardonyx.

They decided almost immediately to take the shortest route, through the Deathsea. The thing was perhaps twice again as wide as it was long and they estimated that it would take them the better part of four days to skirt it.

The temperature climbed alarmingly as they descended and, once, Moichi considered turning back but he could not bring himself to voice his thoughts. His thoughts ever strayed to Aufeya and what she might be suffering at the hands of Sardonyx and his resolve deepened.

All about them was dust and decay. Not the kind of oozing rot one might find in the depths of some leafy jungle or in a fetid swamp but rather a peculiar kind of desiccation that bordered on fossilization as if all moisture had been sucked from the sea.

The deeper they descended, the fiercer the heat became, a dry baking heat which mounted until they felt as if they were roasting on a spit. Yet the absolute lack of humidity made it bearable and kept them going.

The sun was white and hung, swollen, seemingly motionless above them. Moichi, who had much experience with terrible heat in the doldrums of the southern latitudes, wrapped an extra shirt over the top of his head and around his forehead, bidding Chiisai do the same. He did not want either of them passing out with sunstroke.

They spoke infrequently and then only in monosyllables. Much of this had to do with the heat, the expenditure of energy was debilitating. Yet there were other reasons, also.

Just past noon they ate desultorily, without appetite. Chiisai would have forgone the meagre meal entirely if he had not insisted that she eat something; the sunlight sapped the body's energy all too quickly.

The floor of the Deathsea levelled off now but they seemed still to be in the shallows. Presently, as if dropping from a shelf, they found themselves descending on a steep incline to the true bed of the Deathsea.

They paused once in the afternoon to water the luma who, like camels, tended to store up much of their needed liquids. Chiisai took two sips of the tepid fluid but Moichi declined. Limiting strenuous exercise, he knew how to conserve his body's own water and keep drinking to a minimum.

In the depths, they passed a skeletal carcass, rearing up higher than a house, the rigid dry bones casting thin escarpments of shadow, bars of dark and light, rippling across the seabed. The immense skull, which lay half-buried in the dust, was long and narrow, almost all jutting jaw. It had double rows of teeth and a minimal cranial cavity.

Further on, they came across the desiccated carcass of another kind of creature. This one seemed to have had wings, the bones spread out on either side of the carcass delicate and perfectly round and, he saw where there was a break, hollow. The lack of water vapour, of course, made the Deathsea perfect for the preservation of once-living things.

The sky above them was cloudless, white where the sun hung, fading to a pale blue; but now he saw before them a kind of haze hanging between them and the far shore. He shook his head and shaded his eyes, fearful that the heat was playing visual tricks. He nudged Chiisai and she followed his pointing finger and nodded.

What they saw was a cloud, so low down that it seemed to brush the floor of the Deathsea. Its top did not rise higher than the shoreline.

It seemed to be moving, fuzzy and continually in motion and definitely heading towards them.

Then it was upon them and they were abruptly engulfed in a swarm of giant flying insects. There was a droning buzz in their ears but the creatures themselves moved too fast for them to get a good look at them. They were merely blurs, whizzing and darting. Yet not once did any of the creatures came close enough to touch either of them and they seemed harmless enough.

They urged their luma onward and were soon past the horde. They glanced back, watched the insect cloud make its slow steady way across the Deathsea. Moichi wondered what they fed off since there was nothing to eat in this desolate place.

Dusk came early since, as soon as the sun dropped below the sea's high bank to the west, their evening began even while the rest of the world was still bathed in sunlight. It was a blessing for the temperature began to drop almost as soon as the shadows began to creep over the bed of the sea. Apparently whatever the ground was composed of it did not retain the day's accumulated heat for long.

Soon they were engulfed in shadow.

They stopped early and made camp, exhausted not only from the day's journey but from their toils of the night before. All the day, Moichi had kept his damaged right arm close to his side, forearm across his thigh; the heat felt good on it.

They settled into a space with the gigantic ribs of some creature arching over their heads like a cathedral shell. Its skull was wide and thick, a long straight horn protruding from its forehead.

The temperature plummeted but there was nothing with which to make a fire. It seemed inconceivable that just a short time ago this dust and air had been shimmering with heat. The luma stood close together, snorting, their blown breath making tiny clouds of mist and Moichi and Chiisai took their cue from their steeds, huddling together for the warmth their own bodies provided.

There was time for talk after they ate but both seemed reluctant to do so. Moichi had seen what she had done to the Tülc but he still had no idea what had been done to her. He knew Chiisai well enough to understand that she was a naturally talkative person and this silence was disturbing. Yet still he held back from speech. He felt, instinctively, the importance of her initiating this talk. That she had something on her mind he took as given.

'How is your shoulder?' Her voice was soft and muted. 'Is the pain bad?'

'Not so much now. The heat helped a great deal.'

'You should put it in a sling.'

'Considering where we are bound, that's not a very good idea.'

'It's going to be of little use to you in any event.'

'Tomorrow, I'll see if I can get it over my head.'

'You're mad.'

'Yes. Perhaps.'

She laughed but it seemed to choke in her throat and she was crying against his shoulder, silent tears rolling down her high-boned cheeks.

'It's all over now, Chiisai,' he said, the words sounding foolish to his own ears.

'"What is terror,"' she whispered, '"but the face of one's own fears."' This is a saying among the Bujun. One which I had heard many times yet never really understood until last night. I stared death in the face, Moichi, and I was not afraid. But the Tülc –' She hesitated and he knew that this was what had been eating at her, the source of her brooding silence. Bars of red and black striped them – moonlight and shadow caused by the giant curved ribcage within which they huddled. His luma stamped once and was still. 'The Tülc would have taken me. Dead or alive, I don't think he cared. Perhaps, even, he wished to see me die while he was still –' She stopped, unable to go on for long moments. Yet, otherwise, she seemed in control; her body was calm. Her arms clutched him more strongly and he knew that she had not yet come to the difficult part – for her. 'I have never – been with a man. And when I saw him standing over me – standing there and – I could not allow that to happen. I – I was afraid and I am ashamed.' The last was said in a rush as if, once having made up her mind to tell him, she was making certain she would not back off at the last instant. 'I lost my nerve.'

'No,' he said. They were so close that his deeper voice had a kind of sonic overtone. 'It saved your life. Nothing to be ashamed of in that.'

'I'm not fit to be a warrior, let alone a shujin.'

'Listen to me, Chiisai,' he said, cupping her chin so that she looked directly into his eyes. 'One thing I learned very early in life is that good healthy fear is, at times, the only thing that keeps you alive. Just think. You're here now. If you hadn't been afraid –' He shrugged. Still she was silent. Perhaps time was all she needed; then again perhaps not. He shrugged mentally. His own battle had been quite an ordeal. Through it, some ghosts had been exorcized. But, he knew, others still remained.

That night he dreamed of coming home, not in bright searing flashes or odd disconnected scenes; not, to put a fine point on it, in the timeless image-laden language of dreams, but rather as if he were awake, recalling the incidents of his past.

The wind had told him. At least that was how he would always recall it.

He awoke come cormorant and went up on deck. It was the *Biy'hee*, his first ship. The sea was as calm as a sheet of slate and the sun was a glow as it hung just below the eastern horizon where its pale light had already pushed back the night.

But everything was not the same as when he had gone to bed. The difference was the wind. Sometime during the short southern night, it had changed, backing up until now it was coming out of the south.

He took a deep breath and scented it there, hanging like the pall of a haze. He crossed to the starboard taffrail, his eyes scanning the horizon. But there was nothing to see save sea and sky. Sky and sea. Still, it was there.

He turned and called out the change in course to the helmsman then, cupping his hand beside his mouth, he cried into the rigging and within moments all canvas had been broken out. Moments later, the first mate came on deck and Moichi informed him of the change.

He had been away, it seemed to him, for a very long time, but perhaps this was merely subjective. Certainly Alara'at seemed unchanged. The Iskamen port city from whence he had first set sail so long ago teemed with life. Yet, as he manoeuvred the *Biy'hee* in towards the wharves, he could detect, here and there, a new edifice or some reclaimed ground he remembered as wilderness now transformed into a square or a tiled plaza. But this was natural, for all healthy cultures must expand over time. The tall shady palms were still there, however, lining the shore on the near side of the first buildings.

His father had been the last person he had seen when he left as a boy, turning his face up for the brusque farewell kiss that he thought was more tradition than emotion.

And now it was his father who brought him home again. For that was the message the wind had brought him, that his father was dying.

And so it was. The main hall of his family's house was ablaze with the myriad white candles of death.

It was just past mid-morning and there seemed little activity. No one paid him any heed until his brother, Jesah, opened the cedar door to what he knew was his father's room and stepped into the hallway.

They stood staring at each other, while servants hurried by them, these two brothers who were so dissimilar both physically and psychologically. Where Moichi normally seemed massive he was dwarfed in the presence of his younger brother who was a veritable giant of a man. And, of course, Jesah followed their father in all things. He had always been contemptuous of his older brother's interests, considering them unworthy of one who might have been – nay, *should* have been – shouldering his responsibility as future leader of the family.

Jesah cleared his throat. 'Well,' he said. 'You've come home, Moichi. You picked a perfect time to show up.'

'I came because he's dying, Jesah.'

'Ah, yes.' He clasped his hands in front of him, a gesture which he affected, believing it gave him a rather solemn liturgical air. Moichi rather thought it made him look like a prissy school instructor. 'From what far-off land did you come?'

'I was on the high seas, seventeen days out from Bylante'an.'

'A long way away. I'm surprised you made it.'

'He's my father.'

'Yes, *I* know that.'

'Just what does that mean?'

'You've been away a long time but I see you haven't changed.'

'I did the only thing I could. It was you or me. You could never defend yourself decently. That boy was killed. One of us had to take the blame and leave Iskael.'

'You *wanted* to leave!' The resentment in Jesah's voice was tangible. 'You dreamed of shedding your responsibility to father – and to me and the girls. The family never mattered to you. Let Jesah take care of that, you thought, it is what he loves anyway.'

Moichi stared at him. It was the first time that he had got an inkling that, perhaps, Jesah did not relish his position. 'Jesah, I –' he began.

His brother cut him off. 'Father has been calling for you,' he said curtly.

'I would see him.'

'All right.' As if he were giving permission to an outsider. He stepped aside to allow Moichi entrance.

He had been in his father's room many times as he was growing up. When he was a child, it had been his parents' room. Until his mother had died of a disease no physician could diagnose. Quite naturally, his father felt that it was a sign from God and there followed a year of prayer and stringent discipline as if the entire family had been guilty of some sin for which each member now had to atone.

It was a place unlike any other in the house. The stone and brick kitchen, for instance, was light and airy with many windows overlooking the rolling grazing land; the sitting room was dark and cavernous, dominated by the immense flagstone fireplace, whose hearth had seemed like the very mouth of God when he was small, the great flat stones rising through the roof and breaching, he had once believed, to the very heart of heaven. His father may or may not have instilled this grotesque and absurd image but surely he did nothing to dispel the notion; the bedroom he shared with Jesah he always found cosy and comforting (the girls' rooms were in the opposite wing and he had never seen those). But his father's room was enormous, easily the largest in the house, bigger even than the sitting room or the kitchen which included the long cedar dining table around which the entire family sat without fail three times a day. And, of all the rooms in the house, it alone had a sloping roof, this owing to the fact that it was part of the original dwelling which, over time and the furtherance of a large family, his father had found necessary to add to considerably. It felt old, too. Not the oldness associated with must and death and – well . . . ageing, but rather a peculiar kind of stolid antiquity which Moichi found secretly delightful, like a warm down comforter thrown over the shoulders on a chill winter's night. When he was quite small he used to love to creep clandestinely into that room and just sit, not moving, not touching anything, not even looking anywhere in particular. Just sitting in his father's great scarred wooden chair by the desk which might have contained all the secrets of the ages, and let the aura of the room seep slowly into him. And he found that as he grew older and thus more subject to the daily aggravations of life, that this room's silent breathing atmosphere had the power to calm him, as if it were, somehow, alive.

Now there was a different feeling about the room. As he stepped over the threshold and pushed the door to behind him, he felt again the ancient quietude hovering but held at bay, perhaps, by the new sadness here.

He crossed the bare polished floor and stood beside the

high brass bed. He seemed suddenly very tall, the slanting roof almost brushing the top of his head so that he unconsciously stooped a little.

The figure in the bed seemed frail indeed and he realized with a start that he had been thinking of him for quite a while as he had been when he was young. He had deliberately disregarded the encroachment of time and, like a child still, refused to believe in age advancing at all. Not for him. Not for his father.

He could never bring himself to think of his father as an old man, not even now, ravaged as he was by time and disease. The man had always been far too vital. That he was immobile now on the bed attested to the gravity of his condition. Like a horse, his fiercely defiant will would not allow him to go down save under dire circumstances. And, perhaps for him, death was the only one.

Now Moichi leaned over the bed, listening to the unquiet sussurrus of his father's laboured breathing, sounding as if there was fluid in his lungs, and he was unaccountably reminded of the nights he would lie awake as a child, watching the painfully slow progress of the moon in its arc as it rode, like a schooner, the vast sea of stars, listening to Jesah's gentle, shallow breathing from the bunk below, as he dreamt of the unknown sea lapping at the shores of Ala'arat far away.

His father's eyes were closed but the veined lids seemed as thin and translucent as tissue. There were blue circles around his eyes, as if the flesh was somehow being eaten away from within so that now the lethargically pumping blood was closer to the surface, bubbling, threatening to break through, to breach, at last, the portals of mortality which had kept it safely in check for a lifetime.

A lifetime.

As he stood silently over his father he thought that here is someone I don't know. This person with the old and tired face might as well be a stranger.

His father died at sunset, peacefully, without saying a word or opening his eyes, the shallow breathing ceasing, it seemed to him, just as the distant sun slid behind the high peaks far to the west, their tops so high it was said that even the rock had capitulated and turned to solid ice.

Darkness came for them both, the shadows stealing through the window and into the room as if sent as a messenger and he realized that the transition had been so swift or, again, so subtle that he had missed the actual moment of his father's passing.

He turned and went out of the room.

Jesah and his three sisters and their husbands – two of them were married – filed past him into the room and he left them to it. No one said a word to him.

He went through the long wide hallway and into the kitchen, still smouldering, since it faced south and west, with the last of the reflected light of dusk and, though the sun was gone from the sky, still it was gloriously illuminated.

He opened the back door and went out, hearing at once the cicadas' shrill singing and the infrequent throaty calls of grey plovers. He became aware of a brown-and-white jack-rabbit sitting up on its powerful hind legs half within the tangled shadow of a thorn bush, staring at him. For a long while they were both immobile. Then the rabbit's nose twitched as if he were a character out of a children's story-book his mother used to read to him and he saw the long rodent's teeth underneath. In a flash, the creature was away, bounding into the tall grass.

He heard a sound behind him, knew someone had slipped through the door. He did not turn around and, for a moment, was strangely angry that anyone would have the temerity to see what he saw, hear what he heard, to intrude upon his private world.

Someone took his arm, slim strong fingers wrapping themselves around his right elbow.

It was Sanda, the youngest of his sisters. He watched the

sweep of her long dark hair as the wind took it and her enormous black eyes set wide apart and deep within her face. She was strikingly beautiful; fine-boned yet strong of countenance. With a start, he realized that she looked more like him than any other member of the family.

'It's so good to have you home again,' she said, her voice rich and musical. 'You'll not go away again, will you?' Her head rested against his arm; though she was tall, he was taller still. She required no answer but said, 'Remember when you used to put me on your shoulders and take me riding?'

'Yes, I remember.'

'And father would be so cross with you.'

'You were much younger then.'

But she had already turned her face into his chest, her body racked with sobs. He put his arms around her, filled with a great sadness, not for his father, that dead stranger lying in his parents' room inside the house, but for Sanda, this young woman, for all the time away from his land and from a little girl whom he loved and whom he had missed terribly.

'You know, I always loved you for that,' she said. 'I was so proud that you thought enough of me to stand up to him and to Jesah.' She held him tightly. 'You were the only one who treated me as an individual, not as someone who was always the last in line, who got the clothes when everyone was finished with them, who was always belittled because everyone else already knew the things she was trying to find out.' She wiped at her eyes. 'Do you know you never teased me. That's what I loved about you most.'

Moichi laughed softly. 'I could never deny you anything. Remember the time I took you with me into Ala'arat without anyone knowing and you saw that bit of jewellery in a shop window as we passed. You wanted it so desperately and I laughed at you and told you you could have it when you became a woman.'

'I remember,' she said, her eyes as soft as mist. 'When I started to cry, you went back and bought it for me.'

'I couldn't bear to hurt you. You know how children are. They want everything they see and then, a day later, it's lying somewhere, forgotten. But I knew I'd hurt you and I couldn't bear that. I remember you wore it every day and when father asked you where you got it, you told him one of the boys at school had given it to you.'

Her eyes flashed. 'I still wear it.' And her slim fingers plucked at the small star hanging around her neck on a thin chain.

'Do you not have a man who gives you jewellery now?' he said, mock-severely.

'Not yet.' She put her arms around him and squeezed. 'And anyway I'll never take this off no matter what anyone else gives me. It's a reminder of too many happy days.'

He would never remember the funeral with any degree of clarity. It was as if his conscious mind had pulled a misty curtain across that time so that now, even in dream, it had a vagueness, as if he had never been present at all at the actual ceremony.

Afterwards, as was the Iskamen custom, there was an elaborate if solemn banquet for the family and friends of his father which would precipitate the seven days of fasting.

Moichi sat beside Sanda. To his left was a tall, rather elegant woman. At a point when Sanda was gone, he became aware that the woman was staring at him. He turned and looked at her for the first time. She had black eyes and dark hair wound round and round her head. She wore a shimmering bottle-green gown which covered one shoulder while leaving the other one bare. The neckline swooped to the tops of her firm breasts.

'Please excuse me for staring,' she said in a slightly husky voice. 'But are you the other son. The one who sails the seas.'

Their eyes locked for a brief moment.

'I am Elena.' And when the blank look remained on his face, she added, 'Justee's wife.'

Moichi was astonished. The death of Justee's son in a brawl had been the cause of Moichi's swift departure from Iskamen a long time ago. Justee's son had picked a fight with Jesah and pulled a knife. Jesah, being unfamiliar with fighting, would surely have died if Moichi had not taken the other boy on. Justee, whose land bordered Moichi's father's own was only slightly younger.

'Unfortunately, he is ill,' Elena was saying. 'Else he would be here with me to honour his closest neighbour and friend. When he recovers, he will come to the grave of your father and say his prayers for his safe journey and his eternal peace.'

'Did you know my father well?'

'Alas, no. I am only recently married to Justee. After his last wife died – he took me.' Moichi thought this a peculiar way to put it. 'I'm so sorry about your father. Please accept my heartfelt –'

'Excuse me,' Moichi interrupted her, standing. He felt suddenly claustrophobic and he went out of the room. He went into the kitchen but this time it was crowded with cooks and servers. He saw Sanda in one corner going through the reserves of wine with a server and thought, They still have her doing the chores.

He went out into the quiet night, searching for his stars, the Southern Cross and the Lion constellation but it was overcast and not even the first-magnitude stars could be seen. The moon was but a pale haloed smear etched upon the cloud cover. There was a wind from the southeast, bringing with it the heat and spiced aridity of the Great Desert. He thought again of his father but no emotion surfaced; he felt nothing.

'Do you not miss this land?' a voice said behind him.

He turned to see Elena standing behind him, framed by the lemon light of the open back door. She seemed at that moment both coolly aristocratic and terribly vulnerable.

'I'm – sorry if I caused you to leave. I wanted to tell you –' She stopped, as if bewildered by him. 'Would you mind if I stood beside you for a while?' There was nothing in her voice, save, perhaps, sadness.

He nodded mutely and turned back not knowing why he had given his consent. He should have sent her back inside the house. He heard the movement as her thighs brushed against the fabric of her gown then smelled the light musk, felt the heat of her body close by.

'I always miss Iskael,' he said after a time.

'Then why do you leave it?'

There was a rustling in the tall grass to their left and he imagined that the brown-and-white jack-rabbit was back.

'My first love is the sea,' he said, surprised by the softness of his voice. 'But one can have more than a single love.'

'Yes. I see.' She lifted a hand, wiped back a stray strand of hair behind one ear. Out of the small silence that built itself, she said. 'No doubt you wonder why I married Justee.'

He said nothing, knowing that any answer he gave would be superfluous and that, in any event, she would tell him now because that was what she had come out here for.

'He was so very kind to me. I came here from the south, where the border skirmishes are ceaseless even to this day.' She meant between the Iskamen and their neighbours of Aden. It was an ancient and bitter dispute for the Iskamen, it was said, had been born in Aden. 'That was how my family died. My parents, my sisters.' She paused to lick her lips. 'I arrived here with nothing and Justee took me in. I was not a beggar but, in truth, I had nowhere else to go. My father had once spoken of him but that had been such a long time ago, when I was but a little girl.

'Justee never asked how long I would stay or even if I would go at all.' The strain of the moon waxed for a moment and then the running clouds passed thickly before it, blotting out its light. 'His wife was already ill, then, had been for some time and he would become easily vexed by her constant requests, the attention she required. There was a need for me and I stayed with her constantly until she died. Afterwards, he came and asked me if I would marry him.'

'Did you do it out of convenience?'

'Convenience? What do you mean?'

'For his money.'

She seemed surprised. 'Not at all.' But did not take offence. She shrugged. 'Perhaps I needed a father then.'

He heard all of the pent-up frustration in her voice. 'But not now.'

'I don't want to hurt him. But I need – something else now.' Her cool fingers touched his neck, warming as they picked up body heat. Her touch was very delicate and she knew where to put her fingers.

Abruptly, it did not seem absurd to him or even wrong but merely the most natural thing to do. He wanted it too. 'Over there,' he said thickly and led her by the hand into the high grass.

She sank with him onto the earth.

'I'm so lonely,' she said, her lips against his so that he felt as well as heard her words.

Slowly he stripped off her gown and her skin glowed in the night, a beacon lighting the way towards what? Solace? Salvation? Perhaps nothing so complex. Pleasure only, perhaps.

Her skin was softer than any he had ever known and so moist that he could believe she was a nocturnal flower covered in dew.

He spent a long, long time with her. A lifetime, perhaps. And all the while she whispered to him, soft words and endearments, cried questions and languorous replies and these soul-torn communications he remembered more clearly than the feel of flesh against flesh, the sensual contacts which were, in a way, incidental, though as part of the whole, important.

When it was all over, her cheeks were streaked with tears for what he had given her, the chasm he had filled, what she now possessed. It was the intimacy of the listening amongst the most basic and beautiful of acts. In concert.

It was a very special gift.

He stayed on in the chirruping night after she had returned indoors. After she had kissed with her lips and her artful tongue his mouth and cheeks and eyes. Thinking. It had given him great pleasure and a release from a building tension. This had been the beginning: to know that he was doing it with *her*, knowing whom he was cuckolding. But it was because of her, what she was, that this action was soon trivialized into a childish fantasy. For there was an honesty about her, a genuineness that had touched him, transcending circumstance. She had approached him without guile, made no bones about what she needed. *Can you give this to me?* she had asked him silently with her fingers and her lips. *And this? And this? And I, in return, shall give you . . .*

More than he could ever have anticipated.

He became aware of something settling over him and he rose and went out into the grass, naked still, clothes forgotten, as he had when he was a little boy and his father would call to him to put something on and his mother, laughing, would just shake her head from side to side and let him go, until the house was but a black silhouette punctured by smeared yellow light. He turned for a moment and the blaze from the kitchen windows seemed quite remote, as if on the other side of a vast gulf.

He felt now as he had always felt in his father's room – a warmth, an ancient protectiveness cloaking him. And, at last, he knew what this feeling was, the long violent history of the Iskamen, as palpable and as potent as a living entity. Truly he belonged to them and they to him.

He faced outwards, towards the distant but invisible mountains where the Hand of God had fashioned the tallest peak to guide the Iskamen to this, their home.

The night beat on around him. He was aware of the tall grass brushing his calves, the cicadas' wail, the stands of aromatic cedars and, further away, the luminescent birch, scattered among the grazing land, rising like signposts. Above all, the mountains made their presence felt. He felt himself brushed by –

'Hello,' he whispered.

'So you have come back.'

'The wind brought me. It told me of your dying.'

'The wind,' the voice was scoffing. 'It was God. God told you.'

'The wind. God. Does it matter?'

'You speak as a foreigner.' The tone turned bitter. 'But you did not have to leave home to speak thus. Your brother –'

'Would you have me as Jesah is?'

'He is faithful to Iskael.'

'He is unhappy.'

'He is faithful.'

'As am I.'

'You are faithful to yourself only.'

'That is the difference between us. I see that as good. You do not.'

'You turned your back on me a long time ago.'

'No. Never on you. Only on what you tried to make me.'

'I knew what was best for you.'

'No, you didn't. The sea is where I belong. I am happy there.'

'You have always defied me!'

'I defied only the reins by which you meant to hold me to yourself. People are not animals. You cannot harness them in order to make them do as you wish. This is the message of Iskamen history –'

'Do not blaspheme!'

'Is that what I'm really doing? Listen to what I say for once, for once.'

'A child has a duty to his father. He must respect him. Obedience is a sign of that respect.'

'But you never understood that that respect must be earned. If you had listened to me, heard what I was saying, you would have understood that I was a *person* and not an extension of you. The Iskamen broke free of their bondage in Aden. This you can accept. Can't you see that this is the same. I had to be free to choose my own destiny.'

There was silence for a time. Even the cicadas had fallen still.

'I was always a stubborn man. I did not want you to leave my side.'

'I never saw that,'

'I could never express it.'

'Some day, I will return to Iskael again, perhaps to stay.'

'You will never stay for long. But now I know your heart, just coming back, that is enough, now – my son.'

And he was alone in the night, tears distorting his vision, thinking, Gone, gone, gone. He's gone.

Sardonyx

They gained the far shore of the Deathsea at dusk. Nearing Mistral, they passed through a vast undulating field of daffodils and buttercups, their heavy bells swooshing in the breeze heralding the beginnings of night. In the sudden darkness, their lush saffron was chilled in the ruddy moonlight. Fireflies zoomed and swooped about them.

When they broke, without warning, from the lush field, they found themselves upon a jutting rock promontory below which was a drop of perhaps six metres to a rushing, foam-filled river beyond which Mistral stood.

It was set on the peak of the high ground, though beyond it lay land that was higher still as the topography gradated towards the steppes and mountain range in the northwest.

Mistral might easily have been mistaken for a crag itself, for its foundations were composed of rhyolite, a kind of greenish granite that, nevertheless, was once more volatile as volcanic magma. At its base, the castle was four-sided but, above, the battlements, towers and crenellated ramparts branched off into so many angles that it hurt the eye just to stare at it too long.

The portcullis stood open and, as they went through, they felt vulnerable indeed. Inside, the courtyard was deserted but they were startled to hear music, as if on the very air. Looking up, Moichi saw that as the wind passed through the turrets and fenestrated needle-like towers, it set up resonances and harmonies within the complexities of the architecture so that it was the castle itself which sang this mournful tune.

Before them, the stone doors to the main hall stood open as if awaiting their arrival.

They dismounted and went up the wide steps. Above him, Moichi saw an enormous atrium towering the height of the structure and this, he realized, was what relieved much of the heaviness of the stone.

He saw the narrow staircase, made all of shiny obsidian, arching like the tendril of some mammoth spider's web and he turned to Chiisai to tell her –

'You have been expected,' Mistral said.

He sprinted for the double doors but it seemed a terribly long way now, saw them swinging shut even as he thought this, clanging home with funereal finality. He stopped. There were no handholds on their inner side.

Chiisai was gone. But how? He was certain she had entered with him.

'There is no escape there,' said the voice. 'Nor anywhere – unless I grant it.'

He whirled around, 'Where are you?' he cried. 'Show yourself!'

'Here I am.'

He turned. Indeed the voice had seemed to coalesce and he looked up, saw a shape at the first landing on the staircase. He crossed the hallway and climbed the stairs.

He confronted a girl of perhaps ten, slender, light-eyed with a compassionately beautiful face without a single hard edge. It was the face of innocence.

'Where is Chiisai?' he demanded of her.

'In another place,' she said, smiling sweetly. 'Quite unharmed but also unable to interfere.'

'Interfere with what?'

The girl ignored this, reached out one hand. 'Come,' she said. 'Come with me.'

'I want to see Aufeya.'

'I will take you to her.'

Her eyes were soft and full of life as she stared at him, daring him to take her proffered hand.

At length he did, and she took him up the spiralling staircase.

Her long hair shone, swaying with her motion. 'You shall

see your Aufeya. In time. But there are other things you must view first, after which' – she shrugged – 'who knows, you may not even wish to see her.'

They were at another landing now and the girl led him to a door banded with iron. It appeared firmly locked but, at a sweep of her thin arm, it opened outwards silently. 'Behold!'

It was a room dimly illuminated by one squat oil lamp sitting high up on a ledge like a giant insect. The cubicle was filled with gems, cut and uncut, of every description. Great glowing emeralds and fat bloody rubies, flawless diamonds of untold carats and sapphires as blue as the noonday sky. Interspersed among these were the lesser gemstones, enormous dusky topazes, smouldering amethysts, fiery opals and glowing pearls and, in one section, the deep translucent green of royal Fa'sui jade, the rarest in the world.

'What say you to this, Moichi?' the girl said. 'What care you for one woman when this wealth is here for you to use as you wish. Why, with this treasure you could buy the city of Ala'arat!'

'Ala'arat?' He swung on her. 'What know you of Iskael?'

But the girl was gone. In her stead was a woman with the head of an ibis. Her lush body was clothed in a gown of iridescent multi-coloured feathers. Her head was as white as snow.

'Come,' she said, taking his hand again, leading him upwards.

On the next landing was another door behind which he saw his house in Iskael. It was the rear, just outside the kitchen. He saw Sanda and Jesah obviously arguing but he could not hear their words. Jesah struck her and Sanda whirled, running off into the night.

'What know you of my home?' Moichi asked. 'How can you conjure such a thing?'

The ibis ducked its head and smiled, not an easy gesture for an avian face. 'Such images come quite easily after a time, you'd be surprised.'

I'm already quite surprised.' He eyed her. 'I had a dream last night.'

'Of home.'

'Yes. Of home. Was that your doing?'

'How could it be? That's quite impossible.'

'Yet you know of my brother, my sister Sanda, my house.'

'I know these things, yes.'

'How?'

'As I said, it is not so difficult, in time.' She turned and gestured. The door swung to. 'Come.'

They went up to the head of the stairs. They were close to the top of the atrium and the strange music was louder here, differently pitched.

'What –'

He stood next to a tall woman with skin of gold leaf. Her hair was platinum flex and her eyes were great faceted rubies. Her nails were translucent sapphires and her half-covered breasts were opals. Her robe was cloth-of-platinum, a material no ordinary seamstress could work, and her low sandals were crafted from the pelts of snow-ermine. She wore a platinum helm, high and conical and horned.

'I have been to many places.' The voice had changed now so that it had a hard almost metallic edge. Was this her real voice? He had no way of knowing.

They went along the narrow balcony; a low stone barrier, coming to just above his knees, protected them from the sheer drop to the floor of the main hall. Through a sculpted archway, they entered a sort of sitting room. The stone floor was strewn with ermine pelts before a large plush sofa and several high-backed chairs. Behind the sofa was a wall which jutted out three-quarters of the way into the room. To the left were a series of severely narrow windows; the room was dark beyond them and he had no idea of what might lie there or even how far back it went.

Upon entering, she threw herself down, lounging at full-length upon the long sofa. 'I would offer you something to eat or drink,' she said with no trace of regret in her voice, 'but, as you can see, there is nothing of that nature here.'

'Why don't you conjure it up?' His left hand was on the hilt of his sword.

She smiled disconcertingly, her face glittering. 'An amusing notion.' She put a forefinger to her lips. It looked like a slender jewel. 'You are an intriguing fellow. I would like to know you better.'

He laughed humourlessly. 'I hardly think that likely.' He came across the room to her, sat on the edge of the sofa and reached out one hand.

'What are you doing?'

'Is this all real?' He indicated the room, everything about them.

'As real as is anything,' she answered gravely. But a soft smile still played on her lips.

'But you are not.'

She evinced surprise. 'I? I'm as real as you are. Come, touch me if you do not believe me.'

His hand hesitated in mid-air.

She threw her head back, laughing. 'Do you expect deceit, then?'

He glanced around. 'There seems to be nothing here but illusion.'

'Ah, no,' she said, her head against the back of the couch. 'Now you do me an injustice.' She took his hand, brought it to her. She pressed his fingers against one breast. He was surprised to find it warm and resilient; she was flesh and blood, after all. He felt her heart beating. 'Now what do you say?' Her voice was almost a whisper. Slowly, she contrived to move his hand. Around and around. He could feel her nipple now.

He took his hand away and stood. From this position, her eyes seemed heavy-lidded as she gazed languidly up at him. 'Why are you afraid to show me what you really look like?'

'Afraid,' she said, 'I am not afraid of anything.'

'You're afraid of the truth, Sardonyx.'

'I like the way you say it, my name.' She rose, stood next to him. 'I shall prove to you that I am not afraid of the truth. Ask me anything.'

'Where is Aufeya?'

'Here. Above us.'

'Is she alive?'

'Why, of course.'

'Have you tortured her?'

'My dear sir, what do you take me for?'

'I'd rather not answer that.'

She smiled wryly. 'Yes,' she said. 'I do like you rather.'

'What was your business in Iskael?'

'Why, my *business*, as you put it, was the same there as it was wherever I journeyed. I bartered, traded –'

'Pirated,' he finished for her.

She nodded. 'True, I am a freebooter. A time-honoured profession.'

'And a sorceress.'

She laughed. 'Who told you that?'

'I learned it – from a friend.'

Her face turned hard and there was a brittle edge to her voice now. 'A friend from Corruña, perhaps?'

'Perhaps.'

'What lies has that bitch told you about me?'

'Tsuki only wants to be left alone,' he said evenly.

'She should have thought of that a long time ago, my friend. Too late now. Far too late.'

'There's no need for –'

'Don't be a fool,' she snapped. 'It ill becomes you.' She lay back down on the couch. 'Yet I am what I am,' she said seriously. Her thighs moved slightly and the slit of her gown widened, exposing her legs to the hip.

He turned away, crossed to one of the slit-like windows and peered out but there was nothing really to see. He turned back to her. She had not altered her position.

'Where are you from?' he said.

She made a sound like a snort. 'What's the difference?'

'I asked therefore I'm interested.'

'I hardly think you would believe me.'

'You've given your word, Sardonyx, to tell me the truth. Even sorceresses must have ethics.'

'Yes.' She nodded. 'I am not so different from you as you would believe.' She took a deep breath and he watched her heavy breasts rise against the platinum material of her gown. 'I was born in the land of Aden.'

'Aden,' he said wonderingly. 'South of Iskael. Our ancient enemies.'

'The two countries border,' was all she would acknowledge. 'I was born in the mountains, however. Nowhere near the border. At a very early age, my parents, being poor and my mother, crippled and unable to work, sold me into slavery.' She shrugged. 'Not so very uncommon among those people.' He noted the lack of her use of 'my'.

'I was sold to a man. A merchant so wealthy that he had no need of work for many seasons. Others saw to that. The vast amounts of free time left him bored and filled with ennui. Thus he turned to buying women – girls, to be scrupulously accurate. I really think *women* would have intimidated him too soundly.' She stretched, her arms behind her head. This was most distracting for it pushed her already straining breasts even further towards him. 'He enjoyed tying me up. Then he would beat me for a long time until – well, I need not go into details. Surely you can figure out for yourself what would happen next. Suffice it to say that it was most – unpleasant.' She smiled. 'At first, of course, I did not resist. As I said, slavery is well-known in that land –'

'How well the Iskamen know that, Sardonyx.'

'Yes. Of course, you're quite right. The Iskamen rose up and broke their chains of bondage and went out of Aden.'

'With the aid of God.'

'The God of the Iskamen.' She gave him a peculiar penetrating look. 'How I envy you that.' But he did not know whether she meant the freedom or the faith. Perhaps it was both. 'After a while, though,' she continued, 'I found I had far too much respect for myself to allow this to go on. And during the days, while he played with others of his toys, I sought out the things I needed. One night, after he had had his way and lay snoring contentedly, I drew out four lengths of stout hemp which I had scavenged and carefully bound his wrists and ankles to the brass posts of the bed. He was a sound sleeper and I knew if I was most careful, he would not awaken. When that was done to my complete satisfaction, I removed the bottom half of his silken pyjamas and I – bent to my task.' She paused, eyeing him. 'This isn't getting too graphic for you, is it?'

'Go on,' was all he said.

'He awoke, of course, just as the pleasure was filling him. He opened his eyes and stared down at me. "Go on," he said imperiously. "Go on, go on. I had no idea you had such a taste for it."' She smiled. 'He didn't know how right he was. I used my teeth.' She flicked an invisible bit of dust from the golden flesh of her thigh. 'I think, in the end, he drowned in his own blood.'

Moichi watched her face as if those faceted ruby eyes could tell him something that her voice did not.

'I fled into the mountains,' she said. 'They had been my home and, I suppose, I felt safe there.'

'And then,' Moichi said, his tone ironic, 'you came upon an old woman, living far from civilization, who taught you how to be a sorceress.'

She laughed. 'You've got some sense of humour, you know that. But that's all part of a children's story. Nothing of the sort really happened, of course. They came after me and eventually caught me.' She shrugged. 'It was a blessing, perhaps; I was half-dead of hunger and exposure when they found me. Not very much left.' She sat up, hands in her lap as if she were some demure virgin. The slit in her gown had somehow disappeared under her. 'They threw me in a cell and left me there to rot.' She laughed again. 'Which was not, I suppose, very far away at that point. But I couldn't complain too much. I got food and water every day and no one bothered me. It was all right until I got my strength back. Then I wanted to get out.'

'And you did get out.'

'Naturally,' she said. 'Here I am.'

'And how did you escape?'

'I bribed my way out.' She smiled. 'With my body.'

'That hardly explains all of it,' Moichi said.

'Of course not. You surely can't expect a girl to give you all her secrets. At least not right away.' Her eyes glittered. 'And we've only just met.' She rose. 'Now excuse me but I must leave you for just a moment.' She touched the back of his hand. 'Now do be a good boy and don't wander away. This place can be dangerous.' She turned away from him and went around the end of the wall to the left, disappearing into the darkness.

For a time, he stayed where he was, listening to the song of Mistral. Then, as if abruptly making up his mind, he whirled and followed her.

He turned the corner.

There was no light. It was as if he had unexpectedly stepped off a shelf of rock in the shallows and plunged to the bottom of the sea. He turned around the way he had come but he could see nothing. No wall, no windows. He put his hand out, questing. Nothing.

He heard laughter from behind him and swivelled to meet it. It was Hellsturm, one hand on his out-thrust hip, insouciantly glaring at him. He lifted his other hand, beckoning Moichi on.

What is this, Moichi thought. Another illusion? Or – and now he felt a premonitory chill go through him – did I do battle with and kill an illusion in the forest?

He ran at Hellsturm and the tall man fled before him, his peculiar bestial laughter echoing behind him like a stream of bubbles.

Moichi drew his sword, slashed at the figure, cutting it in two. But when he looked at the corpse, it was Aufeya's and, as he stared, horrified, the things slithered away like a serpent into the blackness.

Then he understood and, sheathing his blade, stood quietly, waiting. After a short time, he could discern the slap of her sandals and then felt her hand, firm and cool, taking his, leading him out.

He was back in the sitting room.

'I told you to wait here.'

'What is that place?'

'A room. It is a room, only.'

'A room to conjure images.'

'Dreams, perhaps.' She shrugged.

'He's not alive, then.'

'Hellsturm?' She laughed. 'My god, I hope not. Not after what you did to him. No, he's quite dead.' She smiled. 'I thank you for that.'

He looked at her sceptically. 'Pardon me if I am wrong, madam, but that devil was in your own employ, I believe.'

'Was, I think, is the operative word,' she said evenly. 'He served his purpose. His effectiveness was being destroyed by his growing attachment to that bitch in Corruña and he was becoming more trouble than he was worth. No, he had quite outlived his usefulness and would have died the moment he crossed the threshold at Mistral. Fortuitously, he never got that far.'

'I'll take Aufeya now, as my reward.'

She laughed and the golden goddess was gone. He saw instead a woman with a flat face and high cheekbones. She had copper-coloured hair down to the small of her back and eyes like chips of cobalt. Her skin was soft and dusky like the women of Iskael and Aden. She wore a mirrored corselet over which was drawn an old leather waist jacket. Below that she was clad in butter-soft black fawn-skin pants tucked into hunting boots reaching up over her knees. A narrow black leather belt was slung low on her hips from which hung a long scabbarded hunting knife. She was surprisingly small.

'Is this the real Sardonyx at last?'

'If you wish it so.'

'You are so full of surprises.'

'No more than any other woman.'

'Can we end this now?' he said somewhat harshly. He stepped closer to her and her eyes turned wary.

'End what?'

'Impressing the country bumpkin.'

Her face darkened for a moment as if he had hit a nerve but when she spoke her voice was very soft. 'That was certainly not what I intended.'

'It's the impression you gave.'

'I'm sorry about that. Really I am.'

He said nothing though he suspected she wanted some kind of confirmation from him, needed it even. But perhaps that was mere fancy on his part. Why on earth should she care what he thought?' 'I want Aufeya.'

'And me?' she inquired. 'Do you not desire me?'

'That would be far too easy. Is this you?'

'It doesn't matter,' she said softly, touching his arm. 'I can be anyone you wish.'

'Sanda?'

She became Sanda. 'Yes.'

'Elena.'

She became Elena. 'Yes.'

'Tsuki?'

There was a moment's hesitation, then Tsuki stood before him. 'Even her.'

'It's too much,' he said. 'Or too little.'

She returned to the woman with the copper-coloured hair.

'I was afraid you would say something like that.' She looked disappointed. 'Too rich for your blood.'

'Perhaps another time –'

'Another place.'

'Who can say?'

She smiled. 'Go out through the way you came. There is only one staircase to the floor above this one. Aufeya is there. The Bujun woman also.'

'Then we are finished here,' he said, his hand upon his sword-hilt. 'You will not prevent us from leaving?'

The copper-coloured hair shivered as she shook her head. 'No. Not now. You may leave any time you wish.' She had been standing near the windows and now she moved back into the darkness beyond, fading. 'Farewell, Moichi Annai-Nin of Iskael.'

He went out almost immediately. There was no point, he knew in going after her. Only she had the key to controlling what lay in the blackness. It was a waste of time for him.

Upstairs, he saw Chiisai first. She was bending over a supine figure but she straightened up when she saw him.

'Moichi!' Relief flooded her face. 'Thank the gods you're safe. I had no idea what happened to you. As I crossed the threshold I – well, I found myself stumbling around in utter darkness. Then, just as suddenly, I found myself here. Where –'

'I've been with Sardonyx,' he said, anticipating her query.

'Then you've defeated her,' she said delightedly. 'Then we have no worries about the Firemask.'

'The Firemask?' Moichi frowned. 'I had forgotten about that.' How could he have forgotten something so important?

Chiisai grabbed at him. 'Moichi, where is she? What happened to Sardonyx?'

He brushed past her, kneeling. 'Right now I'm more concerned with Aufeya's condition.' Her face looked pale and drawn and dark blue circles under her eyes looked like massive bruises. He put one hand under her head, lifting it up somewhat.

'Aufeya,' he said softly but urgently. 'Aufeya.'

Chiisai was close beside him. 'Moichi, where is Sardonyx?'

'Gone,' he said, concentrating on Aufeya. 'I know not where. What's the difference, anyway?'

Aufeya opened her eyes. At first they were glazed but they soon focused and she started when she recognized him.

'Moichi.' It was but a fragile breeze.

'I'm here, Aufeya.'

'She told me you were dead. She said that Hellsturm had – had –' Her eyes welled with tears.

'It's all right,' Moichi comforted her. 'I'm here now. Everything's going to be all right.'

But Aufeya continued to weep, saying, 'No, you don't understand. It's not all right. When she came to me now and told me – told me you were dead, I gave up all hope.' Her eyes looked at him, pleasind forgiveness. 'Moichi, I told her – told her my half. She knows – she knows –'

So that's where she went, Moichi thought.

'Now she's got the Firemask,' Chiisai said, her voice like the tolling of heavy bells. 'And she means to use it.'

He reined in at the foot of the steppes, cursing himself for being taken in by Sardonyx. But, oddly, he felt no anger towards her. She had not deceived him. Her plan was plain enough and he had had ample opportunity to discern it but his brain had been somewhere else.

Beside him, Chiisai looked upwards. There was little either of them could do for Aufeya at the moment and, though Moichi had wanted her to stay with the Daluzan woman, he had respected Chiisai's request to accompany him.

'Look,' she said, pointing upwards. 'I was right.'

Moichi lifted his eyes as they rode on, into the steppes. The moon was riding high and full – impossible since it had been but a sliver just last night – and it no longer appeared flat. It was round as a ball, resembling more than anything else a giant, fireflashes of silver pink emerald blue, winking down at him. He lowered his gaze and stared at Chiisai. Her face was grim as she nodded. 'The legend lives, Moichi. There is little time now.'

Only the bleak stars, dwarfed by the awful opalescent light to guide them through the hazardous steppes and ever the great mountains loomed before them, black as onyx in silhouette against the sea of stars ribboning the heavens.

Once they heard a howling, shivering the night and their luma, normally fearless animals, snorted and reared in terror. But it did not come again and they galloped on, flying through the steppes until, at length, they came to the steep shaled side of the mountain and, gazing upwards, they saw a spark of light, illuminating for a moment a sharply-defined ledge perhaps forty metres up. It came again, then went out.

'Quickly,' Chiisai said, dismounting.

They found the semblance of a path to their left and made all possible speed ascending the rock-strewn face.

Just before they reached the ledge, Moichi stopped them, whispered in Chiisai's ear. 'Let me go first. She will be expecting me. If I can distract her –' Chiisai nodded and they crept on.

The moment he reached the ledge the spark came again and he called out, frightened now that it was already too late. If she had gone through, there was nothing he or anybody else could do.

'Sardonyx!' he called again, his voice echoing off the mountainside hollowly, seeming to mock him. 'We have a bargain to complete! I have reconsidered!' He would say anything now to delay her even a moment.

He came along the ledge and, abruptly, the flash of light came again and this time he saw her, a figure blacker than the night and he came on, crossing her sharp shadow, calling again and now she heard him.

'Too late, Iskamen. Regrettably, it is too late.'

Something odd in her voice and as he came closer she turned and he gasped in spite of himself. He felt his mind screaming. Get away from here! Get away now while you still can!

She wore the Firemask.

It was hideous, unholy, the depiction of the ultimate monstrosity. It was beyond the aspect of a gargoyle, beyond any human conception; so alien, in fact, that his brain had a hard time orienting on the information his eyes were relaying back to it. Its surface seemed to be composed of some substance with a mirror-like finish and it was this which sparked now and then in the moonlight. However, here she was still on the ledge. Beyond her he saw the forbidding blank entrance to the cave, a great gaping maw down which, he felt certain, was the eye of time. Why had she hesitated out here? Surely she knew that no mortal would follow her inside the cave once she had donned the Firemask.

'I had hoped that we would not meet like this,' she said calmly, her voice somewhat distorted by the thing she wore. 'Not like this, Moichi. I have no desire to oppose you. Quite the opposite, in fact.'

'I wonder why I don't find that in the least flattering,' he said, edging closer to her. His sword was already half out of its scabbard. Still, he was reluctant to draw it fully.

'Now you mock me,' she said sadly. 'I do not deserve your contempt.'

'Are you not content with wealth? With your – gifts?'

She laughed harshly. 'What is wealth but the ultimate illusion. I, better than anyone, know that as truth. What has my wealth brought me but sorrow.'

'What could you expect, sealed away in Mistral? There is all the world out there – waiting for you.'

'The world,' she scoffed, 'wants nothing to do with me. It was people who drove me to my asylum of Mistral, Moichi, or didn't you know? Didn't your friend, the bitch of Corruña tell you that about me?'

'I know nothing of this.'

'And now's not the time to tell you.' She took one step along the ledge towards the cave's waiting mouth.

The whisper of metal in the night as he withdrew his sword.

'Do not oppose me, Moichi. Please.'

'I cannot allow you to enter, Sardonyx.' He raised his weapon.

'Ah,' she said softly. 'The final solution.'

'You have your way and I have mine.'

'How true,' she said sadly. And raised her arms.

Then he did jump back, his heart pounding mightily in his chest for before him crouched not Sardonyx but a creature out of the fevered nightmare of man.

It flapped its leathery wings and opened its all too human mouth and he saw the rows of jade teeth as sharp as two-edged sword blades. It called out, giving off a chilling inhuman cry and he felt cold sweat break out on his face. The short hairs at the back of his neck raised.

He faced the giant man-bat out of Daluzan mythology and religion. From what deep hell had Sardonyx called it?

Diablura, emperor of the underworld.

Now Chiisai was beside him.

Her sword was drawn but she said to him, 'This thing is but an illusion, Moichi. Surely it cannot exist.'

He shook his head. 'Illusion or no, Chiisai. It is solid enough and –'

'I don't believe it,' she said and launched herself past him along the shelf of shale, directly at the diablura.

'Wait!' he cried but she paid him no heed.

The thing screamed and rose a metre into the air, its wings beating carefully so that it would not hit the projections of the mountainside. It was an eerie slithering sound that the pocked rock face picked up, echoing and magnifying, until it filled the night like a howl of a demon. It raised its lower extremities, two horny four-toed feet ending in long curved talons.

It rushed at Chiisai, claws clicking and the dai-katana slashed into the thinly-furred lower body. It screamed again, its jade teeth blanched in the opal moonlight, and the talons raked at her. She swung the dai-katana again but the thing was far too powerful and the talons lashed out in a blur, ripped into her left shoulder. She tried to roll away but the thing had hooked her flesh and she was impaled. Still she fought on with one free arm, the edge of her blade biting into the furred flesh again and again.

She saw what she had to do but she lacked the position, caught as she was. And now he saw it, too. He ran at the flapping thing and, lifting his sword high over his head, he slashed downwards, through the dusty cartilage of its right wing. It tore like a sail and he was hurled backwards against the mountain's face as the diablura lost its balance for a moment and, screaming, flew inwards and down.

He coughed in the dust and, swinging again, severed the major cartilage along the upper part of the wing-frame. The diablura's body shuddered as it flailed to regain purchase in the air and Chiisai was swung into an outcropping of rock. Her sword fell from her hand and Moichi rushed towards her. He threw the sword point-first at the thing, saw it bounce off the bony chest and clatter to the floor of the ledge. Stupid. But his only concern now was Chiisai. He grasped her in one arm, cradling her while he worked at the embedded talons with the other.

Freeing her, he laid her down on the rocks and turned to face the diablura. The thing was still flapping its loose and useless appendage, trying to fly, dipping and rising.

He timed it well and, as the diablura neared him, he leapt upon its back. Drawing out one of his dirks, he slit the thing's throat. It wailed and rose upwards. Up and up and up, ascending towards the stars, a thin stream of dust, glittery and dry, ribboning the air about it. He seemed high enough now to reach up and grab hold of the opal moon, bring it spinning downwards to the earth.

Then the diablura canted over at an acute angle and began to fall. It plummeted out of the sky with appalling swiftness. It crashed once, twice against the mountainside. On the third time, Moichi was thrown loose, tumbling head over heels.

He flung himself outwards, using the length of his body and reached for the lip of the ledge. He hung there, swinging with heavy momentum, back and forth, his nails digging in as he began to slip, feeling behind him, his back crawling with sensation, the night air reverberating with the frantic death throes of the diablura, still moving, juddering galvanically, spastically fluttering like an impaled butterfly as it careened away, down and down the mountainside, spiralling lower and lower as if, even in death, it was reluctant to relinquish its reign over the air.

He took a deep breath and swung himself upwards, his right leg lifting to catch the upper edge of rock. Missed. Tried it again and made it this time, levered himself up onto the ledge.

Stayed there for a long moment, gasping, until he remembered Sardonyx and the Firemask. He had to roll onto his left side to get up, his wounded shoulder aggravated by the enormous strain. He saw Sardonyx standing before the mouth of the cave. Why had she not gone in? He went towards her.

There was the sound of hammers clashing onto ten thousand anvils, the chittering of a cloud of locusts, the trumpeting of great rams' horns, the sizzle of flames against bloody meat, the dancing of dust motes, the trumpeting of elephants, the crackle and rumble of an electrical storm, echoes upon echoes upon echoes.

And a heat fiercer than the sun.

He reeled. Someone grasped him, pulling insistently until he moved, his feet like lead and then he was away from the cave's mouth, gasping for breath, his lungs on fire, his eyes water, his brain besieged by crawling insects.

Sardonyx, face covered by the mirrored monstrosity of the Firemask, held onto him. 'How could you be so stupid,' she said softly. 'Another moment and you would have been killed.'

He stared at her, fighting to regain his breath. After a time, he said, 'I do not understand you.'

She patted his arm. 'What's to understand. I told you I liked you.'

'I must be going mad.'

'That won't solve anything.'

'Take off that thing.'

She reached up and unsealed it. 'I might as well, I cannot get it to work.'

He saw the woman with the dusky skin and copper-coloured hair.

He stood between her and the cave's mouth.

'I don't know what's wrong with it,' she said, looking down at the thing, turning it over and over. On its reverse face, he saw, it was a matt black, deeper than the night. 'It offers no protection now.'

'Too old, perhaps,' he said. 'All the magic's gone.' He looked at her. 'But if that is all –'

'It's not all, of course.' She was still trying to find the key. The opal moonlight flashed against its outward face for an instant, turning it into the beacon he had seen from below. 'It's supposed to allow it's wearer to either open the eye of time or close it for ever.'

And he knew. It had been right before his eyes from the very beginning – the dazzling key. He reconsidered. In fact, he didn't know. He suspected – and one, he told himself, was quite different from the other. If this were some story, there would be no indecision. But this was life. His life. And he valued that highly. He had places to go yet, many far lands to see, and many people to meet. He was not yet prepared to die.

'Since it's no good at all now,' he said, his voice thick, 'you won't mind if I take a look at it.'

She eyed him suspiciously. 'Over my dead body.'

He shrugged, began to move away. 'All right. I'm going to look after Chiisai.'

'What are you up to?'

He stopped and turned. 'My dear Sardonyx, I know far less about that thing you hold and call the Firemask than do you. What could I possibly be up to?'

'I don't know but –'

He hit her a short chopping blow to the side of her head just under her right ear and she went down without a sound. He caught her as she fell, murmured, 'Now we're even.' He laid her out on the shale ledge, took the Firemask from her acquiescent fingers.

'I'm happy we didn't have to fight, Sardonyx,' he said to her sleeping face.

He turned the mask over, grimacing at the hideous formation, seeing his own face grotesquely replicated over its mirrored hills and dells, as if he were viewing from a great height, the topography of the world.

There seemed no way of fastening the thing to his face but still he lifted it up, feeling again the pangs of disquiet, the organism screaming for self-preservation. But that was its job and the only thing to do now was to ignore it.

As the Firemask drew closer to his flesh, he felt a certain sensation, as if his face was made of metal and it was an extremely powerful magnet. It drew itself to his face, adhering to it like a second skin. For a moment, he felt that he could not breathe, then, as if he had found the way, it was all right.

He looked about him; nothing had changed. Naturally.

The moonlight seemed even stronger now and he took one last deep breath knowing that this was, perhaps, the last moment when he would be able to reach up and rip the unholy thing off his flesh.

Instead, he turned his face upwards, towards the opel moonlight.

As the moonlight struck the Firemask full on, he felt a tremendous jolt just as if he had been struck by lightning. He staggered, put an outstretched hand against the rock face behind him to steady himself.

Now he felt a glowing heat upon his face, seeping through the Firemask, into his skin, his flesh, his bones. It spread through his entire body. Vibrations began and, for a brief time, he believed that an earthquake had begun. Then he realized with a start that the sensation was entirely internal.

The strange opal moonlight had been the key and he knew now that the Firemask had been activated. But like some sort of alien sponge, the Firemask continued to soak up the lunar energy, charging itself until he thought he would shake apart with power.

He turned completely round, saw the supine form of Chiisai, closer to where he stood, Sardonyx, then behind him, and stared into the cave's mouth. He knew something of what lay within, having experienced the briefest of exposures without any protection.

He moved to the mouth of the cave.

It was no longer dark in there. The blackness was dissolving, irising open to form textures; textures in lieu of colour.

He entered and was immediately inundated with the sounds of the eye of time. The clash of burnished insects, the flapping of birds' wings, the swirling of underwater currents, the skirling of inhuman instruments, on and on and on.

He paused for a moment, confused. He had been certain that with the Firemask on he would hear nothing. He had been wrong. The sounds were there – all of them – and more. But they no longer sounded like a maddening cacophony bursting concussively on the eardrums and the mind. They were filtered now through the Firemask.

And as he moved cautiously forward, he came to understand this. For there was no light; and in the absence of colour, sound became all-important, for both volume and pitch would guide him to the eye of time.

There was no solid floor, no left, no right, no up or down, his legs moving through the brambles now. It was hot and he took off his shirt, feeling the warm sun drying the sweat. The fence was down in this section and he found the spot without difficulty and set about repairing it. Some large predator had burst through, uprooting several stanchions. It was hard work but he continued to move forward, step by step with the bellowing all about him, filling the colourless world with the rushing as of torrents and the buzzing of flies and he was at his desk in the large rural school with its smell of pine tar and beeswax and cherry wood. He was too young yet to ride the family's land, as his father would one day decree, uprooting him from school and substituting a tutor. Heard the instructor's voice droning away as if from a great distance, his voice, too, like the buzzing of drowsy insects All-in-a-mist now like the pearled dawn, the silver night, the golden noon, the amethyst dusk, one foot in front of the other, hearing the moaning of the tides, the gnashing of langoustes' claws along the sea bed, the stiff rustle of dragonfly wings, the soft sibilance of a forest breathing, standing on a hillock with the sky hanging over him marbled in white and blue and grey streaks, turning northeast from his vantage point, the highest on his land, shading his eyes against the sun, searching for the low sprawl of Ala'arat and, beyond, the silver splash of the beckoning sea, green in the troughs where the sun didn't dance like diamonds off its surface Oh, my sea, my sea! Walking forward, ascending now into the mountains with the fear of God within him, his limbs trembling, his body shaking, his bladder about to burst, falling down upon his knees as he beheld a peace filling him at last as the ship set sail from the port of Ala'arat, taking him from Iskael. The figure of his father as tiny as an insect, standing on the pier. Are you crying, father? On the sea, at last; the sea which had sustained him through all the long arduous days and nights. Not all of them, for he thought of the times, running triumphant and laughing through the apple orchards with Sanda on his shoulders, rolling upon the soft ground, shinning up the trunks, shaking the branches so that the ripe fruit fell upon their heads, all about them in a shower; or, in another season, walking with her amidst the trees filled with clouds of white and pale pink blossoms slowly drifting through the air, dusting their hair and clothes, coating the grass and the earth like a mattress from heaven. Turning away from the land, turning away from Sanda and the lush orchards which would never see him now, not this year, nor the next, nor . . . He steps downwards and finds himself on solid ground at last, a kind of promontory in the mist that is no mist at all. Echoes still crashing like surf upon his mind, the images out of time, eddies from, he is quite certain now, the eye of time, lapping at him, increasing in intensity as he approaches.

He sees before him a swirling vortex, coalescing, dividing, reproducing, fissioning. A great iris. Neither open nor closed. Crouched. Waiting.

The eye of time.

The portal into endless yesterdays and unlimited tomorrows.

Now he is inescapably drawn towards it, volition draining out of him. Hypnotized by the incipient openings and closing, almost, not quite, stopping frustratingly short of completion.

Shapes changing forming twisting spiralling sucking lapping churned by a force so elemental that it could have no name for the concept of language superseded it, could only be expressed in the complex symbology of the mind. Directly.

The sounds changed subtly, suddenly so that they beat upon his eardrums most painfully even through the protection of the Firemask. He claps his fists to his ears but there is no change only now the sounds cease to be painful and an ecstasy such as he has never known permeates him, a heat, a fusion, an excitement he can only relate to sexual though even that seems a pitifully inadequate comparison. His hands reach out as he closes in on the vortex, drugged and exhilarated and as he approaches, another sound cuts through the others, a tone. Trembling fingers almost at the tensile barrier about to caress it as a lover might and the eye of time begins to iris open, revealing –

No!

From somewhere deep inside him, so deep that the sounds of the vortex have not penetrated, a voice of reason cries out. Use it! It cried. Use the Firemask!

At first he does not comprehend and he is so close to the

kinetic framework that perhaps it has become impossible to understand.

He halts his motion, pushed onward by some unseen but heard tide of immeasurable force and it feels to him as if he is attempting to hold back the spin of the world.

Think!

Use it! Now!

He concentrates. It starts in the brain, aflame with the true music of the spheres, pushed outward through his eyes.

And now it comes.

The stored energy of the opal moonlight, directed by him. Through the skin of the Firemask it rumbles and flashes like spot lightning. The heat builds just as it did outside on the shale ledge so far away.

Crackle boom of thunder.

His face is on fire.

Light of a cosmic beacon.

Energy pouring forth and for the first time he sees the truth of the vortex, its ultimate sinister nature and like a surgeon, he carefully sutures up the rent in time. Slowly, slowly, with infinite deliberation, sweating with the whole outpouring of sizzling energy, concentrated and focused until, at length it is done.

He relaxes and the vibrations begin explosions building and he knows that the moonlight energy has built up too far and threatens to run amok. He bears down, his entire body trembling with the effort and he damps down on the field. Slowly, ever so slowly, the heat recedes from the Firemask, from his face and, stumbling, he turns away from the dense intense quietude.

Running, running now out of the cave, out of the silence and into the spangled night.

FOUR:
Lion in the Dusk

Idyll

The first thing he saw was that she was gone.

He reached up convulsively to pull the Firemask away from his flesh but his fingers came away coated in a dull grey powder. All that was left.

He went quickly along the ledge but there was no trace of Sardonyx. Chiisai sat, her back propped up against the mountainside. She had managed to shred the lower half of her shirt into strips, wound them around her wounded shoulder.

She stood up when she saw him, smiling as he came wearily towards her.

'It's over,' he said, his voice sounding odd to his ears.

She handed him his sword and they went down off the ledge, winding down the mountain.

He told her briefly and as best he could what had happened.

'Did you see Sardonyx?' he asked her.

Chiisai shook her head. 'She must have been gone before I awakened. I did not see her.'

The luma were waiting patiently for them at the foot of the mountain, contentedly cropping grass. They mounted and, as they prepared to go, he took one look back, wondering what seemed to be missing. The carcass of the diablura was nowhere to be seen. Surely he had seen it tumble over the side of the ledge.

Mistral loomed ahead of them and now he was anxious to get Aufeya and leave this land far behind him.

All was quiet as they reined in in the courtyard but as he dismounted they heard a rumble from high above them and peering upwards saw a section of the wall of a high turret shattered, stone and masonry gouting outward, hailing down.

Moichi ducked through the falling rubble, ran through the doorway into the main hall. He took the spider's web staircase three steps at a time, calling, 'Aufeya!'

Another quake shook the castle and he thought, God, the whole place is breaking up. Dust filled the vault of the immense atrium and walls were trembling.

He raced upwards, at last gaining the top and found Aufeya where they had left her. Still pale she looked somewhat recovered from her ordeal.

He bent and scooped her up, sprinting for the stairs just as the chamber next to where she had been imploded. Choking dust billowed out with a scream of demons.

The chill north wind now howled dissonantly through the splintering architecture. On the second landing, part of the outside wall ballooned outwards and the door to the jewel room ripped open. The chamber was empty save for the squat lamp.

Into the main hall and he felt the structure itself shudder and he leapt through the doorway. Outside, Chiisai had his luma ready. He thrust Aufeya up onto the saddle. The entire front wall of Mistral began to cave inwards. Stones flashed by them with the buzz of angry bees.

Moichi leapt up behind Aufeya and they were off, speeding through the shattered portcullis, jumping over the strewn rubble.

Behind them, Mistral rent itself, a funeral pyre rising into the night sky, obscuring for a time the bloody horned moon.

On the way south, she whispered it all in his ear, ridding herself of the terror she had lived with for so long a time. 'I became other people. At first, they were people I knew or had known then they turned unfamiliar, becoming stranger and stranger, distant and – hostile. That was bad enough and, foolishly, I thought, I could endure anything but that.

But it was worse when it stopped because I became all manner of animals with minds as dull and syrupy as mud. I tried to think and could not. Then reptiles, by turns lethargic and energetic like some monstrous manic-depressive, for when my reptile mind could function all it thought of was food to fill the vast stomach, a killing urge that was impossible to ignore. Then the insects, brain buzzing with a thousand sights and scents, making up for deficiencies in other senses. I tried to think but there was too much interference. And then I was a fish, placidly swimming with nothing on my mind. Who was I? There seemed to be nothing left. Was I truly a fish? Or perhaps a bird, or another animal or – the human me was gone and I felt the loss all the more terrifying because I could not remember what it was I had been. I was not even a serpent dreaming of being human. Even that small thing was now denied me.

'I screamed then and went on screaming until Sardonyx came for me, scooping me out of the water. That is when I told her what she wanted to know,' she said against his ear. 'And you know the really odd thing? I'm not sorry. I wanted my humanity back. Whatever the price had been, I would have paid it. Gladly.'

Moichi understood her all too well and could not find it in himself to blame her.

'Tell me,' she said, 'what happened beneath the opal moon.'

So he told her all that had transpired. She seemed the most fascinated by what had taken place in the cave of time and he was happy to elaborate, feeling that it was taking her out of her own memories for a while.

He felt her lips open against the soft flesh of his neck as he spoke, the licking of her tongue, inquisitive and naive as a child's licking the salty sweat and, with that, all his fear and anxiety for her safety dissipated, as if with this simple gesture, she had freed him as well as herself from the enslavement of pity.

* * *

He made certain that they took their time on the way back. Not that he did not have a desire to return to Corruña and, thence, to Sha'angh'sei but they were, all three, like the walking wounded and he deemed it more prudent that they did not expend their last reserves of energy on a hard ride but rather gain strength through a leisurely journey. He did not, perhaps, think consciously of the fact that he wished to be with Aufeya, knowing, instinctively, that when they arrived in Corruña, they would have to say goodbye.

But Chiisai knew and, during the endless afternoons – they travelled only in the coolness of the mornings and the slanting, diffuse sunlight at the end of the day – while they rested, would wander off under one pretext or another, leaving them alone. Most often, she would explore the ruins of past civilizations which dotted the countryside.

For her part, Aufeya understood the chemistry and relaxed into it, grateful that Chiisai was so intuitive and understanding and not at all jealous, delighted to be alone with him each day. So that it was, ironically, only Moichi himself who did not clearly understand the vectors of human emotion within which he found himself.

In the dappled sunlight sweeping over them like honey, they held hands and spoke of their pasts. Aufeya recalled her father with great fondness, remembering most clearly the times when he had taken her aboard one of his ships. There was one day, she told him, when he took her up the Daluzan coast to the town of Puerto Chicama, from whence, she later discovered, he ran illegal ruuma into the interior. 'Why, there's nothing wrong with the drink,' he had told her later. 'Only the sanction of the Palliate causes it to be outlawed. Do you think, though, that this makes it unavailable? No. Only more expensive for more hands must be greased' – he winked at her – 'including a number of curas I could name.' Later on, she told him, she had taken a trip into the interior and there saw that what her father said was true. Ruuma was drunk almost universally with no appreciably harmful effects save for a short doze in the heat of the afternoon.

'And your mother?' he asked her one day.

She let off a stream of idiomatic invective that left no room for debate.

He knew better than to argue with her and he quickly changed the subject. And, indeed, this was the only sour note in all the time they spent together. The days and nights ribboned together as their flesh, and Chiisai's, too, mended and healed until only red scars remained and the pain came in infrequent remonstrating twitches now and again, perhaps at the end of a day more strenuous than most or when they came upon heavy rain clouds rolling darkly on the horizon and the air turned humid and the pressure dropped.

At night they all slept separately, peacefully near one another, around the cheerful, crackling fire. But during the afternoons when Chiisai was away on her archaeological sojourns, they would make love passionately and then languorously, revelling in the hot sunlight on their naked flesh. Then they would splash and paddle about in the rushing streams that became more numerous as they travelled further south, making love once more. It seemed to him that he could never get enough of her but perhaps this was because he understood that their time together was finite. Certainly he found that all his senses were heightened because there would be an ending.

Chiisai invariably returned just before they were preparing to move out, giving them as much time together as possible. But one day, when they were already packed, she still had not returned. The sun slipped from the sky and in the rather awkward silence of the waiting, he realized how unfair they were being to her.

Dusk was already giving grudging way to night when she appeared over a low hillock embroidered with a copse of plane trees. Over her left shoulder was slung the carcass of a small hairy boar. They had not eaten fresh meat for some time, having grown used to foraging for nuts and fruit and, when the opportunity presented itself, spearing freshwater fish.

Thus it was cause for no little celebration and they set about searing the skin of hair, slicing open its belly and gutting it. They let Chiisai build up the fire as they went about their bloody, stinking but joyous work. They braised the outside, crisping the skin then began the roasting and the rich scent was so fragrant and delicious that they all wondered if they could wait until it was fully cooked. While Aufeya washed the intestines in the nearby stream and went to find nuts and berries to stuff them with, Moichi contented himself with watching the stars, cold and glittery and remote. They were far out of the land of the bloody moon and the one that reigned in the sky these nights, he was happy to see, was his old friend, silver and flat as a coin. It was three-quarters full.

Across from him, Chiisai sat near the fire, sharpening her dai-katana. He came and stood next to her, watching the quiet expertise of her hands as they went about their work. He cleared his throat and she looked up. Her hands poised over the blade of the sword. The firelight flicked off it, illuminating its long precision-honed edges. It was indeed a most magnificent instrument.

'I'm afraid that Aufeya and I have both been rather selfish.'

'Whatever makes you say that?' She wiped the long blade, took it off her thighs and sheathed it. 'I've been quite content to explore this land as we go.' She laughed. 'You would have known if I was unhappy with the arrangement.'

'Still –'

'Besides, Moichi. to tell you the truth I needed this time by myself. There are a number of important decisions I've got to make when we return to Sha'angh'sei. I want to make certain I'm prepared.'

'You're sure?'

She stood up and, standing on the tips of her toes, gave him a long kiss.

That night with the moon riding high in the sky they commenced an orgy of eating. Yet, rationed after that, the rest of the meat lasted them all the way back to Corruña.

During the last days of the journey, they spent more and more time on the move, as if the closer they came to the city, the stronger the magnetism of its heart. They spoke little during the days but at night, under the moon and the stars, Chiisai told them stories of Ama-no-mori and the Bujun.

Neither Moichi nor Aufeya seemed much inclined to talk and this Chiisai put down to the simple fact that, quite soon, they would be parting perhaps for ever. And she found herself, unknowingly, feeling sorry for Moichi.

She knew she loved him but it was in the manner of the Bujun and thus was not an easy thing to express to outsiders. It was the love of one warrior for another, growing together through adventure and peril; when the two became closer than family or lovers. She knew, for instance, without having him tell her, that Moichi hardly considered himself a hero. Yet, she knew that he was. For it was some singular inner vision that powered him, moved him onward. He was his own morality, his own strength, his own glory, his own world. She had supposed that she would envy him this heroism but she found that she did not, only loved him all the more for it.

In that sense, she was content now, for she believed that, at last, she knew why the Dai-San had suggested she journey to Sha'angh'sei, and to Moichi. Perhaps he had not actually known of this – of the Firemask or Sardonyx or even the eye of time but, surely, he knew the karma of his friend. She was grateful to have been part of this adventure. Yet again and again during those long drowsy afternoons amidst the crumbling, fabulous ruins on the outskirts of Dalucia, as she strolled with the darting butterflies, feeling the weight of the hot slanting sunlight like bars of dusty honey illuminating these markers of an enigmatic past civilization, she found herself wondering whether for her that was the end of it.

And then, like every Bujun before her who had thought much the same thoughts about an uncertain future, she shrugged to herself. She would accept whatever would befall her.

Karma, she thought.

They passed through the western gate of Corruña just past mid-day, riding swiftly through the vast warehouse district, scattering the cambujo workers as merchants with dark shining faces and thick curling beards shook their fists at them for the interruption, their shouts echoing off the flat and featureless warehouse walls.

The Plaza dell' Pesquisa was placid when they arrived, their lumas' hoofs loud upon the tiles of the plaza. The two old men, dressed in their immaculate white Daluzan suits, were in their accustomed place on the bench in the shade of the olive trees. The fountain was hidden from them by the verdant foliage but as they dismounted they could hear the almost musical tones of the water splashing.

Now that they were actually here, Moichi was troubled by what Aufeya's reaction would be to coming home. He knew that he had an obligation to return her here and for many days he had fought to keep the consequences of this moment from his mind. Tsuki, he knew, wanted her daughter back home. But what of Aufeya herself?

He took her by the hand and led her up the winding stairs to the front door. This was thrown open before he had a chance to knock and Chimmoku loomed at the threshold. His face was split by a grin and he said, 'Welcome home, Aufeya!' with such obvious love that Moichi's mind was put at ease. Perhaps it would be far less difficult than he had imagined. The mind had an uncanny ability, at times, to throw things out of proportion.

'Come in! Come in, all of you!' Chimmoku was saying, stepping back. 'We have prayed for your safe return.'

Moichi took Aufeya down the hall until they stood at the

foot of the ship's figurehead staircase. He gazed upwards.

Tsuki stood immobile at the top, one hand clutched at her throat. She looked tall and regal as ever but her eyes darted from one to the other.

'Aufeya,' she breathed.

Aufeya said nothing.

Tsuki's gaze alighted on Moichi. 'And Sardonyx?'

'Gone,' he said. 'Defeated.'

'Thank you for returning my daughter to me. Both of you.'

'It was nothing, madam.' He made a mock-formal bow.

She lifted her arm, fingers outstretched. 'I'm sorry, Aufeya, for everything. Welcome home, darling.'

'Go on,' Moichi whispered in Aufeya's ear. He gave her a small pat on her backside. She turned to him, gave him a tight smile.

'Wait for me,' she whispered. 'I'll be right down.' Then she slowly ascended the stairs, one hand sliding along the polished banister.

Tsuki put her arm about her daughter's shoulders and together they disappeared down the hall. A moment later, he could hear the door to Tsuki's bedroom closing softly.

'There are no adequate means to thank you,' Chimmoku said to them when they were alone in the hall. 'The Senhora has been beside herself ever since you left. She was guilty for not having gone, but she felt she would be more of a hindrance.' He pulled abstractedly at his long drooping moustache. 'In many ways Aufeya takes after the Senhor but in this she is exactly like the Senhora.'

Moichi laughed. 'You've forgotten about the time the Senhor took her up the coast to Puerto Chicama.'

Chimmoku looked at him blankly. 'I beg your pardon.'

'When he went to sell the ruuma.'

Chimmoku pulled himself erect and his voice took on a steely edge. 'Senhor, Milhos Seguillas y Oriwara would have no more to do with that illegal and highly toxic drug than would I. He would not lower himself to do such a thing and certainly not with his beloved daughter.'

Moichi felt a sudden tightening of his stomach as if all the air had suddenly gone out of his lungs. Still, he persisted. 'Surely you must be mistaken. I –'

'Senhor, I assure you that Aufeya has never been to Puerto Chicama with her father. Perhaps during the time she was away –'

But Moichi had already brushed past him, leaping for the stairs. He felt chilled, thinking, When had it happened?

'Senhor, I do not think that you should disturb – !'

'Chiisai!' Moichi called over his shoulder, ignoring the other. 'Outside! The Senhora's bedroom window.'

Chiisai turned and ran down the hall, opening the front door and disappearing down the steps.

Meanwhile Moichi had gained the second floor and was pounding down the upper hallway. The door at the head was closed. There seemed to be no sound from inside.

He tried the doorknob but it was locked. He stepped back and, using one booted foot, smashed at the lock. It gave somewhat but still held. He kicked again, putting all his strength into it and the lock shattered, the door flying inwards. He rushed into the room.

The room was dark, the curtains drawn. At first it appeared empty. Then, as his eyes adjusted to the low light, he saw a form upon the bed. He ran to it.

Tsuki lay sprawled on her huge bed. Blood drooled from one corner of her mouth. Her dress was ripped and she clutched a pillow to her breast as if she were a child who had just awakened from a nightmare.

But he knew now that she had awakened *to* a nightmare.

The hilt of the saw-bladed dagger protruded from a spot on the pillow below which her heart would be.

But it was her eyes which haunted him and would continue to do so for a long long time. They held an immeasurable portion of disbelief.

He went up onto the bed, scooping her up and cradling her body. The room, he knew, was empty and the window was the only other exit. He did not even bother to cross to it to make certain. Let Chiisai take care of the murderess for now.

The first thing he did was carefully close her eyes, even before he withdrew the dagger from her chest. He was crying now. She had not deserved this. Not this. Such a terrible way to die. Thinking you had been murdered by your own daughter. And the very worst of it was that it was a lie. Tsuki had not been killed by Aufeya. Yes, it was her body but, he was certain now, Sardonyx had been animating it. How long, he wondered, was I making love to her?

He had failed in the end. Tsuki was his friend's first love. He had had an obligation to protect her. As he had allowed Kossori to be killed, so had he allowed Tsuki to go to her death. He knew, in his innermost being, that he was being far too harsh with himself. He did not care.

He heard, as if from far away, raised voices, recognized among those Chiisai's calling him.

He ignored it, staring down at Tsuki's now placid face, the fallen moon, set at last.

They stood far apart at the graveside, Moichi and Aufeya. Observing this, Chiisai sighed inwardly, composing herself as the coffin, smooth as glass, was lowered into the newly-dug grave beside the headstone of Milhos Seguillas y Oriwara. She paid little attention to the words of Don Hispete as he intoned the liturgy of the dead.

She had had no trouble subduing Aufeya as she scrambled down from the second-storey window in the garden of the house. But by that time it had been too late. She was, again, Aufeya, bewildered at being in Corruña, let alone outside her own house. It was some time before they could tell her what happened. She was stoic throughout. Which was more than Chiisai could say for Moichi. He had walked out mid-way through the telling and now Aufeya knew that there had been something between Moichi and her mother. Consequently, they had not spoken in two days.

Don Hispete made the sign of the Palliate over the lowered coffin. Chiisai was grateful that the ceremony was at last over. With the swirling of emotions, tension had been at a peak and it seemed as if they had all stood here under the shade of the huge olive tree for half a day though she knew that it had been far less. She was grateful, too, that Moichi had told her that they would embark for Sha'angh'sei this afternoon, directly following the service. She had had enough of that dark dispirited house with its gloomy self-flagellatory paintings and its almost relentless aura of doom. Too, her own decision had been made and she was anxious to return to Sha'angh-sei. She looked at Moichi's glum face and smiled secretly to herself. His attitude would soon change when he got a look at what was waiting for him in Sha'angh'sei.

Everyone had gone, now, save the three and now Chiisai turned away without looking at either of them; she no longer belonged here. She heard the sound of someone running towards her. She stopped and turned.

'Are you going back to the house?' Aufeya asked.

'No, I'm going to the mercado. I want to say goodbye to Martyne before we leave.'

'You – When are you – leaving?'

'This afternoon. Almost immediately.'

Aufeya shook her head, dismayed. 'I didn't know. I –'

'If you two were talking to each other –' Chiisai was abruptly fed up. She had done as much talking in the last couple of days as she cared to do. 'Excuse me.' She walked off.

Moichi stayed on, alone, as the attendant shovelled the dirt into the grave. It had a hollow sound as it hit the coffin's top but that soon changed as the soil built itself higher.

Then the man was gone and Moichi was alone with her.

The place was very still.

'I am sorry, Tsuki.' But, as he said the words, he knew just how inadequate they were. Hiş shame was so great that, had he been of another folk, he would have killed himself there. But he was Iskamen and that was not his way. He would have to live with his shame. That would be his atonement. He smiled inwardly, sadly, recognizing the voice of his father and his father before him. On and on. The history of the Iskamen inescapable. He might just as well stop breathing for it flowed through every molecule of his body, through blood and bone, through muscle and sinew, through brain and heart.

Through his mind, then, flashed a scene. The moment just after he had met Chiisai on the dock at Sha'angh'sei. What an odd thing to think of at this time. Then he realized what had jarred the memory. The shindal and her prophecy. What had it been?

The Sun: significator of great change.

The Past: this is what aids you. It had been a corpse on a bier. Tsuki, from the past, now dead.

Everyone: this is what crosses you. Sardonyx.

And what was he to make of all that? Nothing. Nothing at all.

He became aware of a presence behind him.

'There is nothing –' The words caught in her throat and she swallowed convulsively. Aufeya's mouth was dry because of the fear. She recognized this as the most difficult thing she had had to do in her life. Part of her screamed against it, vexed, a child railing but she gritted her teeth and plunged onward because deep down she knew that it was her only chance, that without this, she was doomed, chained and bound here for ever. 'There is nothing she has to forgive you for.'

Moichi stared at her, watched her face, seeing the wild animal in her receding further back with every passing moment. And, abruptly, he understood the depths of his own self-pity.

'I see that, I think.'

She glanced down at the new grave then back up at him. He stood silently, watching her still.

'About the other thing,' she said softly.

'What other thing?' He knew very well what she meant. He just wanted her to say it.

'About you and mother –'

'It wasn't what you imagine, Aufeya. She wasn't that kind of person.'

'Don't tell me about it,' she said. 'That's all I ask, I just felt –' She broke off and her eyes filled with tears. 'She was always so beautiful, so very very beautiful.'

He put his arm around her and they walked away from there. In the spring, the grass would begin to grow over the dark brown earth that no one had bothered to pat down. It would not matter to Tsuki Seguillas y Oriwara, only to those who would come to visit her.

And All the Stars to Guide Me

Sha'angh'sei, eternal Sha'angh'sei, *Moichi thought as they entered the harbour, manoeuvring around the myriad larger merchant vessels, keeping well clear of the bobbing tasstans close to the bund. How it swells my heart to see your shoreline once again. Yet still, Iskael for me now. Home again.*

Chiisai stood on one side of him, unaccountably nervous. Aufeya was on the other side.

'I would come with you to Sha'angh'sei,' she had said to him.

'But what of the family? The house?'

'There *is* no family, really. Not any more. Just me. The last of the Seguillas y Oriwara. With mother gone, Chimmoku no longer wishes to remain. And I no longer belong here.'

'I will not stay in Sha'angh'sei for long, Aufeya.'

She smiled. 'Is that a warning?'

'I just want you to know.' He looked at her seriously. 'What will you do then?'

'One decision at a time, Moichi. All right?'

He sent a kubaru runner to notify Aerent as soon as they had docked and Chiisai went with him.

It was near to dusk. The vast sprawling city lay entangled in its smoky matrix. The sky was hazed a deep amethyst, punctured by the flickering lemon lights already coming on along the streets. High up on the hill, the rooftops of the lavish homes of the city's hongs in the walled city were already partially obscured by the mist, as if they belonged to some other far more ethereal world.

Along the jumble of the bund they went until Moichi

hailed a passing rickshaw and they were immediately engulfed in the maelstrom of Sha'angh'sei.

They had taken over the long balcony of a restaurant high up in the city yet with a spectacular view of the harbour. Below them, the brown waves washed against the ancient pilings and the bobbing tasstan community was a swarm of light as the kubaru began to clean up after their evening meal.

Aerent sighed expansively and leaned back in his chair. He clapped Moichi on the shoulder. 'It is good to have you back, my friend. You were sorely missed.'

'I am sure not,' Moichi said, wiping his lips.

'Oh, gods, he is right, Moichi,' Llowan said from across the table and litter of platters and plates and empty decanters. 'The business is a mess without you.'

Moichi laughed. 'Now I know you have both gone mad.'

'What will you do now, Chiisai?' Aerent asked. 'Return to Ama-no-mori?'

There was a gleam in her eye. 'No, Regent. I've not yet had my fill of the continent of man. Besides, I've never really got to see Sha'angh'sei.'

'Very good, lady!' Llowan said, raising his goblet. 'Well said! I salute your resolve' – he laughed heartily – 'and your nerve. You may, if you wish, reside in Moichi's old quarters.'

'Now wait a minute,' Moichi said. 'I did tell you all that I was bound for Ala'arat but, as you all know full well, it won't be as easy as all that. There still are no ships available.'

'Oh,' Aerent said smiling, 'we'll get you off, one way or another.'

'As long as it's a proper ship,' Moichi said. 'Iskael's a long way south and I do not propose to paddle all the way.'

'Well, if we are all finished,' Chiisai said, standing up, 'Why don't we all take me for a walk. I haven't had a chance to see Sha'angh'sei by night. Moichi spirited me away far too quickly for that.'

And that was how Chiisai came to give Moichi his second gift from the Dai-San. It was there, as it had been, since the morning she arrived.

'The *Tsubasa,*' she said, smiling. 'It's your ship.'

'Mine?' He could scarcely believe it.

'Yes. Now you can go home.'

'Home to Iskael,' he breathed. 'And what about you, Aufeya?'

She stood close beside him. 'I wish to come with you to Iskael.'

'What? I do not think you have given this much thought. It is not the kind of decision you –'

'On the contrary,' she flared, 'I have thought of little else for some time.'

'But, Aufeya –'

Then he saw the hurt in her eyes and he knew the mistake he had made.

'All right!' she exploded. 'You're right. It was a childish idea. I don't know where I got the notion you would want me to come!' He reached out for her but she whirled away. She wanted only one thing now. To hurt him as deeply as he had hurt her. 'Say it! Say it in front of all your friends. I'm sure they'll understand. You don't want me. You never wanted me. It was my mother! You're like all the rest of them who came into the house. They came in and they saw her. It was always my mother! Why didn't anyone pay attention to *me*?' She flung herself away from the group, running out onto Three Kegs Pier.

Behind her a heavy silence fell like an opaque carpet of snow damping all sound. Moichi stared at Chiisai for a moment, feeling helpless and alone but she was studiously staring at the whorls in the wood grain of the pier plankings.

He cleared his throat and went after her.

The world was now a forest of black masts and, beyond it, the vastness of the rolling sea.

He came up to her, stood beside her without touching her, knowing, instinctively, that she would not tolerate that now. The wind, coming in off the sea, whipped her hair back from her face and at that moment, with the moonlight gilding her face, she never looked more beautiful nor more her mother's child.

'I'm sorry,' he said softly. 'You took me completely by surprise and I –'

'Yes, and I'll always be just my mother's daughter to you,' she said acidly. 'Why don't you just get away from me.'

'I want you to come with me.'

She said nothing. To their right, past the *Tsubasa*, on Four Winds Pier, a kubaru song started up, bitter-sweet in the night. He could not see any of them but their voices rose clear and strong in their indomitable hymn.

'Your mother loved you very much, Aufeya. More than anyone or anything else in the world.'

'So she was fond of telling me,' she spat. 'Words don't mean anything after a while.'

'Her life had little meaning without you.'

'Do you expect me to believe you?'

'Aufeya, listen to me. She was going back to Hellsturm in order to ensure your safety.' He had not wanted to tell her this but what choice did he have now?

He saw the shock register on her face. 'Dihos, no!' she cried. 'She wouldn't have!'

'On the contrary, it had already been arranged. And it would have happened save that Sardonyx crossed Hellsturm.' He reached out for her now. 'Aufeya, there is no one your mother could have hated more than Hellsturm.'

'Yes. I learned that, at least, at Mistral.'

'She loved you dearly.' As he said it, he became aware that what he was saying about Tsuki was just as true for his father and himself.

They held each other, as if for the first time while, beside them, the crew of the *Tsubasa* made ready to get under way.

Dawn.

Aerent and Llowan were already dockside, having said their farewells. He turned to Chiisai.

'Not the end, as I once told the Dai-San.'

'No,' she said. 'I understand.'

They embraced.

'I wish you fortune, Moichi.'

'And I, you. In all you do.'

Chiisai kissed Aufeya and then she, too, was gone from the ship.

The gangplank was hauled in and he gave the signal. Men scrambled to release the lines, fore and aft and the anchor was weighed.

'All away, pilot!' came the call from his first mate at midships.

'Aye,' he called back, climbing the aft companionway to the high poop-deck. 'As soon as we are clear of the harbour, set all sail.'

'Very good, sir!' He turned and gave a series of sharp barking orders and men scrambled up the ratlines into the shrouds.

He spent the next moments guiding the *Tsubasa* through the difficult and absorbing maze of Sha'angh'sei's harbour. Aufeya went below to change into her sea clothes.

Presently, they were well clear of all ships and he heard the first mate's strong command, then the bright quick snapping as the men broke out all canvas. He's a good one, Moichi thought as he turned to the helmsman and gave him the course, 'South by southeast.'

'Aye, sir!'

The ship leapt forward, her bow waves high, her wake rich and creamy.

The sun was rising in the sky ahead of them, turning the

deep blue to white near its position. Not a cloud could be seen in any direction but, far off, near the western horizon, the pale moon, full now, could just be discerned over the rooftops of fast disappearing Sha'angh'sei.

He left the helmsman's side and, leaning against the starboard taffrail, luxuriated in the feel of the ship, the roll and scent of the sea, and exulting in his mastery over them both.

'Isn't it strange that the moon should be visible at this time of day?' The female voice came from behind him, rich and melodious and almost half-mocking.

He turned quickly but he saw only Aufeya, clad in high shining sea boots and sailor's loose shirt and pants, coming across the poop deck, the sun in her eyes, smiling at him.